Wicked Haunted

Wicked Haunted

An Anthology of the
New England Horror Writers

Edited by

Scott T. Goudsward
Daniel G. Keohane
David Price

Knock Knock by Kali Moulton

"The Thing With No Face" © 2017 by Peter N. Dudar
"Lost Boy" © 2017 by Bracken MacLeod
"Scrying Through Torn Screens" © 2017 by Patricia Gomes
"They, Too, Want To Be Remembered" © 2017 by KH Vaughan
"Everything Smells Like Smoke Again" © 2017 by Curtis M. Lawson
"The Boy on the Red Tricycle" © 2017 by Daniel Szczesny
"East Boston Relief Station" © 2017 by Paul R. McNamee
"Mouse" © 2017 by Larissa Glasser
"The Walking Man" © 2017 by Matt Bechtel
"My Work is Not Yet Complete" © 2017 by Nick Manzolillo
"Ghosts In Their Eyes" © 2017 by Trisha J. Wooldridge
"They Come With The Storm" © 2017 by Dan Foley
"Turn Up The Old Victrola" © 2017 by Tom Deady
"Ghost Maker" © 2017 by Emma J. Gibbon
"The Pick Apart" © 2017 by Paul McMahon
"The Stranding Off Schoodic Point" © 2017 by R.C. Mulhare
"Triumph of the Spirit" © 2017 by GD Dearborn
"The Road to Gallway" © 2017 by Rob Smales
"The Thin Place" © 2017 by Morgan Sylvia
"Tripping the Ghost" © 2017 by Barry Lee Dejasu
"we're all haunted here" © 2017 by doungai gam
"Murmur" © 2017 by Jeremy Flagg
"Pulped" © 2017 by James A. Moore

Cover Art © 2017 by Mikio Murakami, Interior Art © 2017 by Kali Moulton, Ogmios, and Judi Calhoun
Published in October 2017 by NEHW Press
ISBN 0-9981854-1-8 / 978-0-9981854-1-5
www.newenglandhorror.org
Printed in the United States of America

Other Anthologies of the
New England Horror Writers

Epitaphs
Edited by Tracy L. Carbone

Wicked Seasons
Edited by Stacey Longo

Wicked Tales
Edited by Scott T. Goudsward,
Daniel G. Keohane and David Price

Wicked Witches
Edited by Scott T. Goudsward,
David Price and Daniel G. Keohane

*In Appreciation for the stories of Shirley Jackson,
one of the Greatest New England Ghost Writers…*

Table of Contents

The Thing With No Face
Peter N. Dudar

I don't want to remember…Please don't make me remember!

Kevin Ellis woke up just after three a.m., his heart jack-hammering in his chest, his skin cold and clammy from the skein of midsummer sweat. He'd only been home (his childhood home in Latham) for two days, and the nightmares had returned. Kevin's bedroom had remained unchanged for the last three decades; a shrine to the life of an introverted teenager of the eighties that Kevin had, over the years, sloughed off like the dead scales of a snake. Faye Ellis had sworn as far back as Kevin's wedding day that she was going to box up all his belongings and he either could take them home with him or she would have them hauled off to the town landfill. His mother had intended to turn the bedroom into a guestroom, with enough space for a crib for when he and Carrie finally presented her with a grandchild. The divorce two years later put the final nail in that fantasy. There, in the darkness, Kevin found himself wishing things might have been different.

In the dark, the sameness of his childhood bedroom made it feel like no time had passed. In his heart and his mind he was twelve again, and the sameness meant the past still existed.

Kevin pushed the switch on the bedside lamp and shielded his eyes as the light singed away the image still lingering from the dream. He sat up and let his legs slip off the mattress until his feet touched the floor. The air conditioner in his window kept the humidity at bay, but the air in the room still felt warm and uncomfortable. He found himself wishing he'd just checked into the Econo Lodge Motel over on Route 7. He'd have had his privacy, and would probably have been able to escape the nightmares that invariably returned every time he came home to visit his mother. But after his father's passing seven years ago, there was no way to escape Faye Ellis's guilt trips about how his visits were growing less in frequency and duration.

The room felt warmer than usual. Kevin stood, scratched himself for a moment, and then wandered over to the air conditioner to see if it might be dialed down to a lower setting. The green digital number read sixty-six degrees (the temperature his mom had pre-programmed before he arrived, and would complain about if he forgot to set it back when he started his day), but he was sure it could go down to at least sixty-two. He smiled as he pressed the button, and just like in his childhood he felt the supreme joy of secretly going against his mother's wishes. The green digits dropped to 62, and the extra blast of cold air made his sweaty skin prickle with goose bumps. Kevin crossed his arms against his chest and turned to climb back into bed when he heard the dog barking from the yard behind the fence. Kevin froze in place as the yelps pierced the darkness and echoed off the window pane. His heartbeat pounded in his chest and temples as his mind slipped back to childhood again.

Old man Grady's dog.

Of course, that was impossible. They put Butch down over two decades ago, back when…

He crept up to the window and peeked out from the slits in the blinds.

The thing outside was watching him.

He froze in place, and let his eyes penetrate the darkness of the backyard. Seeing it now under the hazy summer starlight, the land beneath his window looked like a long-forgotten realm of sinister shadows and unnatural contours. In the darkness, lawn furniture resembled hunched dwarves offering dreadful devotions to the night. The tool shed was an ancient castle, with dragon eyes peering out whenever the headlights of the neighbor's car threw reflections on the glass. The flowerbed along the back fence was a row of tombstones whenever the full moon rose above them. These things Kevin knew by heart from childhood and he'd long since learned to see them for what they really were. But the thing standing directly in the center of the lawn was loathsome; a silhouette of spindly white arms and legs that fluttered in the hot pre-dawn breeze like a frayed flag. The apparition floated in defiance of the tangible things surrounding it, as if it somehow wanted to find the same permanence but could not. Kevin struggled to make his eyes focus harder, trying to see what was looking up into his bedroom, but the thing seemed to have no face. No eyes or nose or jaw line to give it the missing touch of humanity. Whatever it was simply *was*, an ethereal reflection of something long dead.

He leaned closer to the glass and cupped his hands around his eyes to lower the glare from the lamp. Holding his breath to keep the window from fogging, he glared at the phantasm. The thing with no face tried to glare back, to make eye contact, and when it decided it could not, its head split apart where the mouth should have been and the screech from lifeless vocal chords pierced the darkness. Kevin fell away from the window just as the electricity went out and the noise of the air conditioner died away.

It was when he realized the dog had stopped barking and the night was deathly silent again, and that his nightmare had passed from the dreamtime into reality.

*　　*　　*

"You've hardly touched your breakfast," his mother commented as she sat down at the table and unfolded the morning newspaper. Faye Ellis had already eaten her slice of toast with cottage cheese and her cup of diced peaches, and had already cleaned her dishes. Judging by how little coffee was left in the urn, she'd also finished at least two cups, although he couldn't be sure she'd actually made a full pot. At least she was still in her pajamas and bathrobe, and to his estimation Kevin couldn't understand how she didn't melt under all those layers. The morning was already pushing 80 degrees.

"I didn't sleep well, Ma."

"Well, I can't say I'm surprised. The neighborhood must have had a blackout last night. Too many air conditioners draining all that electricity away. It happens every now and then, when the summer gets too hot."

"Mom, did you hear something outside this morning? Just after three a.m.?"

Faye picked up her coffee mug and took a long sip, then flipped through the newspaper to find the obituary page. Kevin couldn't help but flinch as she spread the paper out on the table, revealing rows of names and photographs of those once living the day before. From where he was sitting, the newspaper could have been the map to a graveyard. This was her daily routine; one that hadn't changed since he moved out of the house to start his own life.

"Like what?" she said. "Maybe you heard one of the transformers shorting out. That's usually what happens when we lose power. Sometimes they even sound like a small explosion."

"No, Ma, not like that. I just...I don't know." Kevin pushed his fork into the fried egg on his plate and cut it apart. Seeing the slit he'd made oozing yellow yolk made him think of the thing outside his window again, just before it screamed. He placed the fork on the plate and pushed it away from him. "Never mind, Mom. I'm sorry, but I'm just not very hungry right now."

Faye looked up from the paper. "Honey, you get this way every single time you come here. Why won't you just talk to me about what happened? You'll feel a lot better if you'd just talk to me. I want for you to not carry things around inside anymore. It's not healthy for you, sweetheart."

Kevin glanced at the rows of obituaries in the paper and sighed. It was painfully obvious that *she* was still carrying things inside as well, that she was just as obsessed as he was with the past but in her own quiet, accusatory way. Perhaps this was her way of trying to get him to surrender and say something first, but that would require making himself remember and that was the last thing he wanted to do.

"I said *never mind*."

"Okay, fine. I'm not going to press it." Faye leaned over and resumed ogling the names of the departed. "If you aren't going to eat your breakfast, please scrape your plate into the trash and wash it. Maybe you'll feel hungry enough to eat later on."

Kevin stood up and walked his plate over to the trashcan. He was just beginning to scrape when his mother broke the awkward silence that had risen between them.

"Oh, my! Charles Grady passed away yesterday."

Goose bumps prickled up Kevin's arms and neck. He glanced out the kitchen window at the fence behind the house, toward the house sitting on the opposite side. The Grady house was a derelict gambrel with brown clapboard siding and filthy white shutters weather-worn and rusted until they resembled scabs. From his bedroom window Kevin could see most of the backside of the Grady house, but preferred not to.

"I didn't think that guy was even still alive," he said as he turned on the faucet and squirted detergent on the plate. "I'd just assumed he died ages ago. God, he was an old man even when I was in high school."

"Charles wasn't *that* old back then. But the column said he was eighty-one, so he lived a full life. I suppose it's been ages since I've seen him at the grocery store or walking into town. It doesn't say in the newspaper how they found him or what he died from."

Kevin walked to the window (the wet plate in his hands spattering droplets onto the floor) and looked at the house behind the fence. From the angle he was looking, he couldn't see the doghouse that he knew was in old man Grady's back yard. He'd have been able to if he looked from his bedroom window, but he...

"Mom, how long has Butch been dead?" The question escaped before he even had time to consider what roads the discussion might lead down once asked. Butch had been one of those things he was fighting to not remember. But now that his mind was rolling, the image of the mangy, always-vicious pitbull was at the forefront. He could see the leather collar that looked as if it was too tight, always gouging into the dog's neck until the fur beneath rubbed clean off. And the hate in its eyes, or the way its fangs protruded like white daggers when it snarled.

Faye pushed the newspaper aside and looked at him, sizing him up with those judgmental hazel eyes.

"Oh, gosh…well, you know they put him down after what happened. Does this mean you're finally ready to talk about it?"

Kevin felt his cheeks flush.

"No. No, I was only wondering. Did old man Grady ever get a new dog? After Butch died?"

Faye frowned. "Yes, he bought another dog long after you moved away. That one was a Rottweiler named Champ. That thing was a lot more timid than Butch was. Charles was not a good pet owner. He used to put the fear of God into them until they did whatever he commanded."

"Does he have a dog now? Because I heard it barking last night, and if they took his body away without knowing there's a dog in the backyard, someone needs to call the police and tell them."

"No, it's been a few years since Champ died. He never got a new one after that. Sweetheart, you know there are no bad dogs, only bad owners. And Charles Grady was a terrible owner. Whatever happened to Reggie that day…"

"Mom, I *don't* want to talk about it."

He turned to storm out of the room but realized he was still holding his plate. He tossed it onto the counter where it clanged and vibrated for a moment before falling still. He was already out of the room by the time it finished its vibrato dance on the countertop.

*   *   *

The bedroom had cooled considerably, and Kevin found himself glad he hadn't raised the temperature back up to the Faye Ellis setting. Sunlight streamed in from the slats in the blinds, but even with the windows partially obstructed he could detect the storm clouds moving in over town. A thunderstorm was definitely on the horizon, probably hitting sometime before sundown but destined to linger throughout the night. *The angels are bowling*, his father used to tell him when he was young and the crash of thunderclaps shook the house until he couldn't sleep. *They'll tire out eventually and go to bed, just like you need to do.*

Parents say a lot of things to their children to pacify them.

What would dad have said about hearing the dog this morning?

Kevin moved over to the window, turned the rod until the slits on the Venetian blinds were fully open, and looked over the fence into old man Grady's yard.

The old, red doghouse was still there, only there was no dog in sight.

"It looks like Snoopy's doghouse," Reggie Acton used to say. "You know the one he flies around on like an airplane when he's chasing the Red Baron?"

The voice was in his head, but it sounded so real that Kevin gasped and stepped back away from the window. He was almost certain the voice came from somewhere behind him, but that would have been as impossible as hearing a dog barking that wasn't there…or seeing a faceless ghost standing in the backyard.

Please…I don't want to remember any of this!

Kevin gritted his eyes tight, turned around, and then opened them slowly.

There was nothing in the room with him.

He released the breath he'd been holding (he hadn't even been aware his breathing stopped), and turned back to the window. The sky was growing dark rapidly as the clouds passed like a razor's edge across the last vestiges of blue sky. He was certain the temperature outside was going to fall fast, could feel the change in the air and on his skin…

Just like Carrie…she turned cold fast and without warning as well. How much time has passed since she demanded the divorce?

…and switched off the air conditioner. Kevin glanced down into the backyard one last time to see if the faceless thing had returned, and when he was satisfied that it hadn't, he twisted the rod until the slits were closed tight. Coming home felt like an enormous mistake, just like it had with every previous trip. The only thing left to do was start inventing a new excuse to pack up and hit the road early. Kevin lay down on the bed, closed his eyes, and tried to concoct some new fabrication to spring on Faye Ellis. In his mind, guilt was a thing with no face—only an incessant weight that tried to squeeze his heart until it stopped beating. Maybe then he would finally find peace.

*   *   *

He'd fallen asleep.

The nightmare resumed, just as he'd been certain it would. In the dream he was twelve years old again and Reginald Acton was still eleven and still living in the house next door. All the houses on Sparrow Drive were identical Cape Cods, as if the contractors responsible for developing the cul-de-sac followed the same blueprints and merely changed paints to create any sense of individuality. Kevin's home was green. Reggie's was canary-yellow. But dreams never follow rules, and in the movie in his head—the memory he was trying so desperately to not remember—Reggie's house was the same red as Butch's doghouse. When Kevin squinted his eyes to look at it, the red bled into a deep crimson that clung to the back of his eyelids. In the dream, they were playing in Kevin's backyard.

"It looks just like Snoopy's doghouse," Reggie said as they peered through the slats in the fence at the sleeping dog. "You know the one he flies around on like an airplane when he's chasing the Red Baron?"

Butch's left ear twitched, almost as if the beast was eavesdropping rather than snoozing in the shade of the maple tree. Kevin could see the leather collar curling tight into the dog's neck, and the ratty piece of clothesline rope that cinched from the collar to the big iron spike in the middle of the lawn. The rope was long enough to chase intruders to the fence and nab them down before they could get away. It occurred to him even back then that the only way to escape that damn dog was to get it to chase you around his doghouse a lap or two before trying to jump the fence again, and even that was a snowball's chance in hell. The years of having Grady for a neighbor meant any Frisbees or softballs or toys that accidentally sailed over the fence were lost treasures...unless old man Grady felt generous enough to toss them back over again while out feeding Butch and cleaning up the festering piles of dog turds.

"You never did get your glider plane back, did you?" Reggie suddenly asks—a question that has haunted him for more than three decades. The plane was a Styrofoam jet nearly two feet long, with wings and tailfins you could adjust to suit your flight plan. The glider had been a birthday gift from Kevin's father; one which accidentally passed over the Bermuda Triangle of their creepy neighbor's back yard. "Grady never threw it over the fence so you could have it back."

"Nope." He nodded to the dying hydrangea bush, with the foam jet's tailfins protruding toward the rear.

In the dream the thunderclouds roll in, and in the dying daylight Kevin turns to Reggie and says, "But I think I know how we can get it back."

"How?"

Kevin smiles as he espies the sleeping dog through the slats in the fence. He's amazed at himself for never realizing just how simple it would be. "I'll go over the fence and get Butch to chase me. If I can get a lap or two around the doghouse, that will take up enough slack on his line to keep him tied up. Then *you* jump the fence, grab the glider plane, and jump back over. Once you're safe, I'll come back over, too."

In the dream, Reggie flashes a grin that is both innocent and mischievous at the same time. It makes his freckled nose crinkle and his eyebrows float up his forehead until they almost touch the bushy locks of his bright red hair. It's the same Reggie Acton that haunts Kevin every day of his life; the image of the boy while he still has his face. The sleeping Kevin Ellis is already turning and struggling in the twin-size bed, desperately wishing he could stop the dream from progressing until both children are in old man Grady's backyard and Butch's clothesline rope leash snaps, and...

*   *   *

The roar of thunder echoed off the walls around him, and Kevin opened his eyes. The ghost was hovering above him, its face still marred where the pitbull mauled away the flesh and cartilage. The freckles and the bright red hair were now thin white vapors of cold eternity. The ghost lifted a wavering hand into the air and placed it in front of its mouth as if to say, "Shhhhh." Before Kevin could protest, the thing with no face waved its arm slowly, as if beckoning for him to follow.

"Go away," Kevin whispered. "Please, just go away!"

The ghost peered silently for a moment, lowered its head as if in defeat, and floated out the bedroom door.

Kevin gripped his blankets tight around his body and cried himself back to sleep. Outside the window, raindrops pelted the aluminum siding and lightning flashes turned his bedroom into unbearable moments of daylight until the thunderclaps snuffed them back out again.

*   *   *

When he awoke, the room was freezing. He'd left the air conditioner shut off before falling asleep but now it was on again, thrumming strong at sixty degrees. Kevin sat up slowly, pulled the comforter tight around his body, and walked across the room to turn it off again. He lifted his finger to press the off switch, but before he could touch it he heard the dog barking from old man Grady's yard. He jabbed the switch, and then twisted the rod and opened the slits in the blinds.

It was just before dawn, and the air was saturated with a wall of fog that made it nearly impossible to see. The dog continued barking, agitated at first and then falling into a slow, steady howl that resembled fear or injury. Kevin leaned closer to the glass, held his breath, and gazed harder into old man Grady's backyard. The doghouse came into focus, like a blood-red heart just off center of the decrepit lawn. And just outside its front was the ghost of a little boy that had once been his next door neighbor. Reggie Acton was hunched over, gazing into the open front of Butch's doorway, as if trying to call to whatever was inside. Whatever *was* inside whimpered and yelped in despair. Watching the scene from his window made his blood run colder than the temperature in his bedroom.

"There *is* a goddamn dog in there," he said to himself.

He picked up his jeans off the floor and threw them on, then slipped his feet into his sneakers. The world around him felt like a dream. He crept down the stairs and slipped through the house quietly, hoping that his mother was still asleep; dreaming her own dreams in her guilt-free world where husbands didn't suffer heart attacks from too much fatty foods and where there were no bad dogs, only bad dog-owners. The world of Faye Ellis meant making justifications and excuses while neighbors moved away after losing their child to an angry pitbull. Even after Reggie's body was recovered and taken away, and after the police questioned Kevin over and over again about what happened, his mother never once insinuated that what happened was her son's fault. But it was.

It was *his fault.* Guilt *did* have a face if he was brave enough to look in the mirror and accept that what happened was because he'd convinced Reggie to jump the fence and help him get his glider plane back.

Kevin wrapped his hand around the door handle and threw it open. The cool morning fog draped his flesh, wetting it to the touch with glistening beads. He steeled himself and marched across the back lawn until he reached the white picket fence that separated the two yards. It was time to tell Reggie Acton that he was sorry, time to finally accept responsibility for what happened. He gazed over the fence at the doghouse.

The thing with no face was gone.

He could feel the tears welling in the corners of his eyes. His heart pounded in his chest, and butterflies flitted and scratched at the pit of his belly.

"I'm going crazy," he whispered.

From somewhere inside the doghouse, an unearthly howl responded as if to confirm the sentiment. Hearing it filled him with dread deeper than he'd ever felt, deeper even than the day Reginald Acton was buried in Shady Acres Cemetery. For one brutal moment he felt absolutely paralyzed, and he could almost see the puddle of blood that had collected where Butch had knocked his eleven-year-old friend over and ravaged his face completely off. He could almost see the weathered clothesline leash, could picture where the rope had broken away from the stake and how it slithered in the mud like a snake as Butch attacked and shook his head back and forth with Reggie's cheeks and nose planted in its maw.

The moment passed, and then Kevin jumped over the fence and crept up to the door of the doghouse. He drew a deep breath, held it in, and then swung around so that his face could look in to see what was hiding inside.

The doghouse was empty, except for his Styrofoam glider plane leaning toward the back wall. The fuselage wings were bent into a crooked angle, but for the most part the toy looked unharmed.

Kevin exhaled slowly and waited for his heart rate to slow down before falling onto all fours and pushing his way inside the doghouse. He crawled to the back, sat with his legs crossed beneath him, picked up the airplane and wept. He clutched it tight against his chest and sobbed as all the years of guilt overtook him at once. Kevin hitched and gasped for breath as he thought of his friend's lifeless body on the ground, and the way he'd jumped the fence and ran back to his own house screaming for help, waiting to feel Butch's fangs sink into the back of his legs and then rip him apart as well. He remembered the penetrating anger in old man Grady's face when they removed Reggie's body from his backyard, and the absolute hatred in his eyes when they took Butch away to put him down. Kevin remembered everything.

"I'm sorry, Reggie," he whispered, gazing down at the foam glider through tear-blurred eyes. "It was all *my* fault. I didn't know the rope was going to break. I don't care about the goddamn plane. I wish I could have you back again. I'm sorry I let this happen."

He wrapped his left arm tighter around the plane, and with his right arm he tried to scoot back to the entrance of the doghouse, and then stopped when he saw the ghost blocking the doorway. The thing with no face had trapped him, and beside it was the ghost of Butch, who had planted his haunches hard onto the ground as if ready to attack. Reggie's face was missing, but the expression on the mauled and mottled specter still managed to exude terrible satisfaction. The slit where its mouth had once been slit open and the thing with no face shrieked in vengeance.

Kevin closed his eyes and waited for Butch to unite them forever.

Lost Boy
Bracken MacLeod

Out on the wastes of the Never Never—
  That's where the dead men lie!
There where the heat-waves dance for ever—
  That's where the dead men lie!
That's where the Earth's loved sons are keeping
Endless tryst: not the west wind sweeping
Feverish pinions can wake their sleeping—
  Out where the dead men lie!
—Barcroft Boake, WHERE THE DEAD MEN LIE

Sam tried to pay attention to his date, but the child at the other end of the restaurant wouldn't stop staring at him. He looked at his plate, at his hands, at the tables to his left and right—anywhere but at the woman sitting across from him, because the gaze of the boy over her shoulder was relentless and unnerving.

She furrowed her brow and said, "You haven't heard a word I've said."

He held up his hands in protest. "I have. Really. You were telling me about your co-worker who strapped their 'Fatbit' to a ceiling fan to win a step challenge. It's funny." He *was* listening. Joye was interesting. She was smart and witty, told good stories, liked jazz and thrillers, and looked absolutely nothing like his wife.

"What then? What is it?"

He looked up from his hands, leaning slightly to the right to angle her head in between him and the inerrant gaze of the child. "It's… nothing. I'm just… It's…" He shook his head. "It's me. I'm sorry. This is my first date in a really long time—like a decade. I'm rusty, I guess."

He could almost see the red flag snake up the pole in her mind and flutter in the breeze of her building judgments. Her eyes darted to his left hand resting on the tabletop. He resisted the urge to pull it back and set it in his lap. He didn't have a tan line, but when he looked, there was still a slight indentation where he used to wear his ring.

"Your profile doesn't say you're divorced."

"I'm not."

"But you're not married, right? *Right?*" She smiled, but it was unconvincing. Behind her eyes, he could see she was thinking of ways to end things early. She took a big drink of her wine, and set the glass on the table a little too forcefully. The stem didn't break, but a little of her pinot gris splashed up over the side of her glass and slipped down the side. In a few seconds, she'd polish the rest of it off, and that would be the end of their date.

"Not anymore," he said.

She wiped at her mouth and folded her napkin, getting ready to push back her seat. "My profile very clearly says, no divorcées. I'm not interested in someone with—"

"I'm not. Divorced. My wife... she died a year ago." He looked around at the tables nearest them. No one was looking at them, but it felt like the words he spoke had resonated through the restaurant, echoing off the walls and wine glasses. Saying those words always seemed louder than anything else he ever uttered, even when he whispered them. He felt like he was sitting at the epicenter of a sonic boom and everyone was staring. But no one was. No one but the kid in the back. Still staring.

He wanted to hold up a hand to encourage her not to leave, but instead kept them flat on the table so she wouldn't see them shaking. He explained, "There wasn't a box to check for 'widower'. It seems like it should be a thing, you know, but I guess there aren't too many of us on *30 and Flirty dot com*. I'm sorry."

He raised his arm to signal for the check. She reached out and pushed it back down to the tabletop, leaving her hand on the back of his. Her skin was dry and cool. She had thin fingers that didn't get enough circulation, no matter what she did. He didn't know that for sure about Joye. That was his wife, Liv's explanation. But, making the association felt good. Joye looked nothing like Liv, but deep down, he kind of wished she did. When he'd filled out the online questionnaire, he'd put in preferences that were opposite of the ones belonging to the person he'd married so long ago. As it turned out, a complete opposite was as much a reminder of her as someone with a resemblance.

He enjoyed the familiar sensation of her touch. It had been a while since anyone touched him and let it linger. Still, as welcome as her touch was, it made him feel that ever familiar tinge of loss that had been in him since Liv's last days.

Maybe he wasn't ready yet.

"I'm sorry," she said. Her face softened. He still didn't know what to say. *It's okay?* It wasn't okay; it was killing him. He had opted for "Thank you" for the longest time, though that still felt wrong somehow.

"Thank you."

Joye stared in his eyes with a look that was part sympathy and part fear. Though she was visibly relieved he wasn't a philanderer, she didn't seem to be fully committed to riding the night through either.

He slipped out from under her fingers and patted the back of her wrist softly before placing his hands in his lap. He smiled, but knew it looked strange. He was still getting reacquainted with the expression. In that moment, it felt false. Like he was wearing a mask that didn't fit quite right. A clown face drawn over a frown. He tried again, letting his mouth relax and the smile shrink a little. He tried to think of something that made him feel good. Surprisingly, the night with Joye up to this point was it. He got the expression right the second time.

"I am not a project. I promise." He held up his hands in defense. "And I know everyone who says, 'I promise' is lying, but I swear I'm not. I am *not* a project, and I'm not looking for someone to fix me. Soooo, you know. That."

She grinned, raising an eyebrow. "Well, that's good for you, because I am shit at projects. I have a whole apartment full of half-built Ikea furniture."

"I can't read their instructions. You have to have a degree in Egyptology to assemble their bookshelves."

Her smile grew. "I don't take the fake families out of the frames I buy. I just prop my pictures up in front of them."

"I never even print out the pictures I take of my friends. That way no one can complain about how they look in them." They laughed. He put his hand back on top of hers. She didn't pull it away. There was a pause while they both searched for another witticism to share about their mutual inability to complete simple tasks. They laughed at the same time as if the growing silence itself was evidence of their lack of follow through.

"See?" she said.

It felt good to share a real joke. Not one that was forced through the filter of grief, but honest playfulness. He wanted more of it. Searching for a way to get the conversation going again, he fished for something to say, and alit upon the worst possible idea. "Seriously, though. I'm not looking for anyone to fix me."

"Say it again, and maybe you'll believe it." She winked, but he was wounded nonetheless. Her expression changed as he felt his own darken. The ghost of his wife felt like someone sitting in the next chair at their table. Joye placed her other hand over top his before he could pull it away. "It's okay. I'm not interested in fixing you. But I am interested in *you* right now. Is that good enough?"

"That's perfect."

Their server approached the table and asked how they were. Joye looked at her plate. Her jambalaya was almost all gone. Sam's salmon, by contrast, looked like it had barely been touched. He said, "Everything's fine. Can we get—" He meant to ask for another couple of glasses of wine. Instead, Joye broke in.

"The check, please. And a to-go box for Mr. Follow-Through's fish."

"It never reheats well," he said.

"Like you'd even try."

The waiter frowned with confusion, while they laughed at the private joke. He pulled the bill folder from his apron pocket and set it on the table, saying, "Whenever you're ready," walking off before Sam could get his credit card out of his wallet.

Joye said, "I know a place around the corner that serves the best cocktails. Before we go, I need to use the powder room. I'll be right back."

"Take your time. I'm sure our waiter will." He stuck his card in the folder and set it on the edge of the table.

She smiled and walked off, looking over her shoulder once before disappearing into the ladies' room.

He turned back in his seat, to face the child still staring at him. Without Joye sitting across from him, Sam had no one to hide behind. Sam pulled his phone out of his pocket, turned sideways in his seat and opened Facebook, even though he didn't care what anyone on the app had to say. He scrolled past all the people who hadn't called him in months looking for something to distract him while he waited.

Still, he felt the kid's gaze burning through him.

When Joye came back from the bathroom, the waiter still hadn't been by to take the folder. Sam pulled cash out of his wallet and substituted it for his card. The tip was less than he intended to leave, and it left him with nothing to take to their next stop, but that was the price of wanting to leave in a hurry.

"Let's grab that cocktail!"

"What about your fish."

"You're right. I'll never reheat it." He probably would have eaten it eventually, but he just wanted to get out of the restaurant. And away from the kid.

*   *   *

There was a line to get into the bar, but the night air was nice and Sam didn't mind a little wait under the stars—all three of them that could be seen from the city. The temperature had dropped a little since the start of the evening, but Sam felt a hot flush rise in his cheeks as Joye slipped her hand into his. Despite the evening chill, he felt the urge to take off his sport coat before she could see him sweating through it. But that would mean letting go of her hand to slip it off. What if she didn't reach for him again? What if he tried to take her hand and she pulled away? He told himself he was being ridiculous—she'd reached out for him, after all—self-doubt got the better of him and he decided he'd rather sweat than break the contact.

She asked about his job while they waited. He told her as much about being a copyeditor for a textbook publisher as he could without utterly boring her. That conversation lasted less than five minutes, and didn't get them any closer to the door. "I am writing a novel, though."

"Ooh," she said, with apparent sincerity. "About what?"

He shrugged and waived his free hand dismissively. "It's nothing serious."

"Oh, you don't get to tease me. Spill it."

"It's about a person who finds a thumb-drive in a bathroom with a video of what looks like a murder on it. The police tell him it's just a prank when he takes it to them. He spends the rest of the book trying to get away from the killer who's tracked him using a Trojan on the same memory stick. I told you, it's just a genre novel."

"I love thrillers. Have you read Neil Hunter's 'Missing Autumn'? It sounds kind of like that."

His eyes went wide. He'd never met anyone else who'd read Neil Hunter.

The line moved forward and they inched closer to the door talking about their favorite books and Sam felt less and less like he needed that drink after all to help him relax into the conversation. Eventually, the bouncer waived them in when space opened up. They descended into the basement establishment, and found a pair of empty stools on the far side of the square bar. The bartender wiped his hands on a towel, leaned over, and asked what they'd like. With his vest, sleeve garters and handlebar mustache, he looked like a time traveler, or a ghost. Joye told him she wanted something "tart, with whiskey." The bartender nodded, said, "Gotcha covered," and went to work. A minute later, the man set a drink in front of her and waited. She took a sip and said, "Perfect." He nodded, turned to Sam, and asked what he wanted.

Sam opened his mouth to ask for a Manhattan, when a flash of movement in the window behind the bartender caught his eye. He glanced up in time to see a child's legs walking past the window. Sam waited a moment for a pair of adult feet to come chasing after them. But none did. A knot in his throat choked him as the bartender asked him again what he'd like.

"Um, a… Manhattan, I guess."

The man furrowed his brow, and said, "You can get that anywhere. Let me make you something worth coming in for." Sam nodded his head and the man went to work. This time, however, Sam wasn't interested in watching him pour intuitive volumes of ingredients into a shaker and chip ice off of a block with a pick. He kept staring out the window.

"Are you all right?" Joye asked.

He nodded, though he felt certain his face was as white as the bartender's shirt. "I'm okay. I think I just need to duck into the bathroom real quick. It must be the fish I didn't eat." He winked at Joye, but she still looked worried.

Sam blushed again. He wanted so badly to sit back down and grab ahold of her hand. Instead, he leaned over to give her a small peck on the cheek. She turned into it and he ended up kissing the side of her mouth. Her lips tasted like rye and lemon and he wanted to kiss her again. Taste more. Instead, he straightened up, shrugged off his sport coat, and draped it over his stool. "Save my seat," he said, patting his jacket. "I'll be back in two shakes."

"Any more and you're playing with it," the bartender said as he mixed the ingredients for Sam's drink in a Boston Shaker.

"You should leave that to me," Joye purred. The bartender let out a wolf whistle and started stabbing at the block of ice in front of him with a long metal pick.

A lump grew in Sam's throat and he tried to think of something witty to say in reply. Nothing came out but a hoarse whisper that was lost in the din of the bar. He turned and headed for the door.

The bouncer sitting at the door said, "No reentry," as Sam stepped past him.

Sam stopped and looked at the man perched on the tall stool. "I just want to get some air," he said. "It's, uh, stuffy in here." The air conditioning was cranked, but needing some air sounded more reasonable than that he thought he'd just seen a child walking all alone up a city sidewalk at ten at night and if he didn't make sure he was all right, he was going to have a panic attack.

The doorman seemed unsympathetic. "Whatever, bro. Your call. In or out. You can't be both."

An anxious woman standing on the other side of the glass door opened up her palms as if to say, come on—just leave already. Sam held up a hand and mouthed, "Sorry," to her. She rolled her eyes and began talking to her friend in line. Her raised voice filtered softly through the door. "Will you look at this asshole?"

Sam turned and nodded at the doorman who didn't nod back, and went to the bathroom instead.

At the sink, he splashed some water on his face and stared at himself in the mirror for a moment trying to push his anxiety down. The man who stared back wasn't a stranger; he had the same haunted look Sam was very familiar with. He'd been wearing that look for over a year now.

In the reflection behind him, he saw a pair of feet dangling under the first stall door. Small feet in bright colored sneakers that couldn't quite reach the ground. Sam's breath caught. He squinted his eyes shut and held his breath while he counted to ten. He opened his eyes when a man shoved his way into the bathroom took a place at a urinal, sighing loudly. Sam turned and looked at the stall. The door was open. No feet. No child.

He turned off the water and plucked a handful of paper towels off the counter beside the faucet handle, refusing to look at his reflection— or what might be behind it—again.

When he returned to his seat he found his drink waiting for him. Joye's glass was full as well. Either she hadn't drunk any of it during his absence, or she'd ordered a second already. He apologized for being gone so long. Joye said, "I was starting to worry." He smiled and told her that everything was just fine. He took a sip of his drink and murmured his approval. Joye reached out and put her hand on his. "You sure everything is all right?"

"Right as rain," he lied. He tapped his glass to hers and smiled before taking another sip. Joye lifted hers, and took a big swallow. She pulled her nearly empty glass away from her mouth and smiled. Her lips glistened with whiskey and his stomach knotted at the memory of kissing her a moment earlier. He wanted to shoot his cocktail and order them both another. He wanted to look like he had his shit together more, and kept sipping instead. Joye finished, and slung the strap of her purse over her shoulder.

"I'm sorry, did I say something?" he asked.

Joye leaned forward and kissed him squarely on the mouth. "You better finish that. Unlike the fish, I hate to see good whiskey go to waste."

"I... are you..."

"She left a twenty and a ten on the bar and stood. "Are you coming?"

He slammed the rest of his drink, not regretting for a moment not taking the time to savor it.

*   *   *

Sam opened his eyes in the dark and felt a moment of panic overwhelm him. He was disoriented with sleep and the dark room felt cavernous, less like a deep hole than a void. He lay there for a long moment, breathing deeply and letting the darker shadows in the room deepen into the silhouettes of his familiar things and ground him. His dresser, the bookshelf, the open door to the hallway came into focus as his eyes adjusted and revealed to him the things returned from nothingness. He turned his head toward the unfamiliar shape in bed next to him.

Another person. It had been so long since there was another person in his bed. He recalled Joye's enthusiasm as he unlocked the door to his condo and let it swing open. Without waiting to be shown in, she'd stepped through first and reached back to pull him in after her. Liv hadn't been assertive like that. She'd liked the dance they did when she dropped a subtle hint here or there, and Sam would wrap his arms around her and place a soft kiss on her neck, waiting a moment for silent permission to kiss her again. She'd lean her head back into his shoulder and he'd kiss her and nudge her toward the bedroom, and she'd say something like, "Oh you think so, do you?" reminding him who was in control.

Once again, Joye was her opposite and wasn't.

He watched the shadow outline of her shoulder against the deeper black of the room beyond her body. He watched until he saw the subtle rise and fall of her shoulder with her breath. Then he let his out.

He touched her hip with a timorous hand. Her bare skin was warm and soft and felt like electricity under his fingers. He let his hand slid down the arc of her hip, to thigh, to bent knee. She didn't stir, but let out a contended sounding sigh. In the dark, he had only hints of the features of her face. A small chin, a long thin nose, and hair that seemed like a burst of darkness. A dark stain that made his stomach tighten and his heart beat a little faster.

Everything's fine, he told himself. He pulled back the sheets gently and slipped out of bed. He found his boxer briefs on the floor and stepped into them, though he thought he might slip them off again when he came back to bed. Even though he lived alone, it felt strange walking around the house without anything on. As if he might have to run out into the hallway in a hurry and beg a neighbor to use the phone because *oh god she isn't breathing and my battery is dead and please just call 9-1-1 and tell them to send someone right away because she's not breathing and cold and I don't know what to do because I can't find her phone and mine is dead and please help me*, and he didn't want to ever feel as vulnerable as that again, and wearing clothes felt a little like being in control. He was in control of his body, if nothing else.

He stepped into the bathroom and lifted the lid, careful not to let it bang against the tank behind. He tried to pee into the bowl at the edge of the water so the splash of his urine wouldn't wake Joye. He felt a little splash against his shin and re-aimed, frustrated that he'd missed. But he was still groggy from wine and whiskey and sleep and hadn't turned on any lights.

So not to wake Joye.

Because when she woke up it would all be over. She would get dressed, maybe kiss him a little, and then she would collect her things and go home, because, even though she'd slept with him, this was still a first date and she wouldn't want to stay the whole weekend. It was too early for a weekend together. Slowly. One day at a time.

Just like surviving.

He finished, closed the lid quietly and debated whether or not to flush. He decided the noise was a better risk than leaving that for Joye to find if she woke up before he did. He waited until the loudest part of the process was finished before opening the door and returning to the bedroom.

He padded down the hall, and stopped in the doorway. It took him a minute to make sense of what he saw. She was sitting up in bed.

"I'm sorry. I didn't mean to wake you," he whispered. She said nothing. "Joye?" He turned on the hallway light, thinking that she might have to use the bathroom too, but didn't know where to go in the unfamiliar dark. Light will cast out the darkness.

The child sitting on Joye's chest looked at him with black eyes that reflected back the hallway light. It stared at him the same way it had in the restaurant.

He wanted to scream at it to get away from her, but he lost his breath. His throat felt constricted like strong little fingers had wrapped around it. The child leaned forward, closer to Joye's face, but didn't turn its gaze away from him.

"Stop," Sam choked out. He took a rasping breath and tried to say it again. "Stop, please. Don't."

The child's eyebrows knitted and it titled its head a little to the side. "Why?" it asked.

Same didn't know what to say. Why? *Why?*

"Because, I like her. Please, stop. I need this. I need her."

The child's face shifted, upturned eyebrows knitting together, making its expression as dark as any moonless night or bad intention. "I needed you."

"I…"

Gooseflesh rose on Sam's body and his breath billowed out of his mouth in a humid cloud that fell apart as fast as his courage. He felt a sheen of filth in him that couldn't ever wash away. No matter what he put in the past, walked away from, it was there coating his mind, his heart, his entire essence. It was as black as the boy's eyes and shiny like them too. And nothing he could ever think of to say would wash him clean. Not after what he did.

"I'm sorry."

He knew saying I'm sorry never stopped a hand already swinging. It never took away the sting of a struck cheek or the feeling in a child's stomach after the threats were made. Sorry did nothing. The child looked away from him toward Joye, still sleeping, a look on her face that mirrored the child's own frown. It leaned forward and put its hands on her throat.

"Please. No. PLEASE! STOP!"

"Make me," it said.

A child's dare. *Make me*. Said in the full realization that he absolutely could not make it do anything. Not without touching it. And he knew that touching it was something he absolutely could not do. Not ever.

Not even to save Joye?

Make me.

He took a single step forward, and stopped. A hollow threat. The child knew it, and its fingers tightened. The image of Joye and the boy astride her blurred as tears flooded his eyes. His knees felt week, but he stayed upright and attempted another step.

Make me.

He reached out. His hand not held up to push or slap, or even to signal for the boy to stop. He reached out to merely lay his hand on the child's back. To let it know he was sorry. For not being the person he needed to be, for not being strong enough to stay, for everything he had been too weak his entire life to face.

He was sorry for burying the boy without ever saying a word of regret for what that loss meant.

But sorry was not enough to heal a single scar.

It couldn't bring back a lost boy.

It was worthless.

Forever.

He touched the child. A chill spread through his body, raising gooseflesh on his skin. His breath billowed out again in a cloud of condensation like his spirit escaping. The boy shimmered and Sam's hand passed through him and settled on Joye's chest. Her eyes fluttered open, and her frown became a smile. "Hey, you. You're freezing."

"Hey," he said, trying not to sob out loud and failing.

"Are you okay?"

Sam shook his head. She took his hand from her chest and held it up to her mouth. She kissed the palm with which he'd tried to comfort a lost boy, and felt only hurt and hate. When he moaned, his breath hitching at the pain of her kiss, she pulled him down to her and held him against her warm, bare skin, and smoothed his hair, whispering "Shhh," and "It's okay. You're okay."

Eventually, he fell asleep on her chest, listening to her breathing—to her heart beat.

* * *

In the morning, Sam awoke alone. He felt the emptiness of his bed gnaw at him and he placed his hand flat on the mattress, trying to feel the heat of a woman who wasn't there. Another woman, who wasn't there. But it was cold. He'd told her he wasn't a project, but of course he was. He was a terrible, ruined project that had been started and abandoned and restarted and broken a little worse until he was a collection of pieces barely held together by a bond that was wearing away. He didn't blame her for leaving. She'd said she was shit at projects. And he was an unfixable one.

He heard the clink of the coffee pot and sat up straight. He jumped out of bed, still in his underwear, and ran into the kitchen where Joye stood pouring herself a cup of coffee, wearing one of his t-shirts and a pair of his boxer briefs. Her hair was a mess and she'd scrubbed her face clean and was radiant. She smiled at him and he let out a long sigh.

"Good morning," she said.

"I'm so sorry about last—"

Joye held up a finger to silence him. It worked. She took a sip of her coffee before asking if he wanted a cup. He nodded, still unsure whether he was allowed to speak. She grabbed down a mug that read, "Shhh," at the top, "Almost," in the middle, and "Now talk," at the bottom. Liv's favorite. She filled it to Shhh and handed it to him.

Leading him by his elbow over to the breakfast table, she pulled out his chair and waited for him to sit before pulling a chair over next to him. She sat and leaned against him while he drank, and didn't say anything for a long time. She just touched him and was there.

Eventually, she broke the silence and said, "I was looking at your pictures." She nodded toward the collection of framed photos hanging on the wall. Liv had said she always wanted them to be together for meals, even if they were apart, so she'd gone on the hunt for photos in shoeboxes and albums and thumb drives. She framed them and hung them in a cluttered collage on the wall beside the table. They clashed with the rest of their décor, but somehow she made it work. "Is that her?" Joye asked, pointing to a shot off to the side of the array of a woman smiling devilishly behind an ice cream cone.

"That's her. She had a thing for ice cream." He directed her gaze to another picture of a child holding a cone. Same smile. Same pose. "That's her when she was a kid."

"And who's that?" Joye pointed to one next to it. The boy from the restaurant, from the street, and the stall... and the night stared at them from the frame. The boy's face was solemn and drawn. He'd been told to stand there and smile, but he hadn't wanted to have his picture taken. He didn't want to smile. A woman's hands gripped his shoulders, holding him in place. They could make him do that much.

"That's me when I was a kid."

"He's cute."

He swallowed hard. "I don't like it. I asked Liv not to hang that one up."

Sam hated being that boy, and as soon as he could manage, had made himself into someone else. Someone who couldn't be told what to do, or how to feel. Who couldn't be forced to endure things he didn't agree to. He'd hated that boy for being weak. Hated him so much that he killed the thought of him and buried it deep in the desert of memory, certain there was no way back.

Joye snuggled up closer, leaning her head on his shoulder. "Aw. *I* like it," she said. "He looks sweet. I want to know who he grew up to be."

Sam snorted a short laugh. "He's been lost for a long time."

"I found him, didn't I?"

He nodded. But he'd found his own way back. The ghost of a boy back from the Never Never.

Scrying Through Torn Screens
Patricia Gomes

In an old house on Court Street, brown craft paper covers the windows of the sun porch. The paper is folk art hearts, laurel wreaths, and doves cut to disguise neglect.

I see spectral women quilting on the other side. Cloaked in tan light, they're whip-stitching jagged teeth and baby hair to bamboo mats. My father-in-law, four years in his grave, visits here; they treat him well.

Uncomfortable and tense, I sit cross-legged on the drafty floor reading wills and final testaments. The sun porch is unheated, but there you are in just an undershirt thirty years before my baptism. I would bring you sweet cold wine if I'd be allowed to kiss
the stain from your lips.

The stingy light coming through the Amish hearts is barely sufficient for a game of anagrams. Home is better   far better   than this.

They, Too, Want to be Remembered
KH Vaughan

The horses are screaming. They struggle to stand, but the more they twist and thrash, the worse it gets. Their noses and throats clog with something thick and viscous. Suffocating. It's forcing its way into their lungs. It bubbles from their noses until it gets too thick and they grow still, eyes rolled back, moving only with the sluggish, spreading tide. I wake up in a cold sweat, hyperventilating, a cloying taste in my mouth.

The nightmares have been coming more frequently. Night-*mares*. It would be funny if it wasn't terrifying. I need an Ativan to calm down enough to get ready for work, and I'll need an extra-large Dunkin to make sure I don't fall asleep on the T.

I change for work: jeans, thermal-shirt and flannel, and a heavy Carhartt jacket. The ground is usually frozen solid in January, but this year hasn't been so bad, at least until this weekend. Today will be frigging freezing. I stuff cigarettes and leather gloves in my pocket on the way out the door. It is dark as I walk to the Red Line and the footing is treacherous after the snow over the weekend. People in Boston will fight over the parking spaces they cleared, but their sidewalks? Screw you, buddy. Grow a pair or move to Florida. My breath trails away in the light wind and I turn my collar up. The tips of the corners cover my peripheral vision. A gust catches me as I enter the Porter Square Station. It will be more comfortable below ground.

Even at this hour, the station is busy. Working people, suits, and all the service people that have to be there for them. They say construction is a rough gig, but I couldn't do restaurant or delivery. Those people work hard and don't get much back. I guess we're all invisible to the investment bankers and brokers up in their office towers. I hear an incoming train. The squeal of brakes and the rattle of the wheels on the rails echo down the tunnel and against the high tiled ceiling of the station, and it reminds me of my dreams again. Fuck. I focus on my coffee and the chill and the battered sneakers of the woman in the skirt and jacket across the aisle. No doubt she will trade them for heels when she gets to work, unless she's in one of those offices where they won't allow her to walk in without proper dress. They slip on shoes at the top of the escalator or hop awkwardly on the sidewalk around the corner from their work so their manager doesn't see.

By North Station the train is crowded. I could have gotten a ride with one of the other guys, but I'd rather take the subway. Trapped in the cab of someone's truck you have to make small talk. On the train, people leave you alone. It's short walk down Causeway to Commercial and the park. Light flakes of snow drift in the air. Langone Park is right on the water at the mouth of the Charles between Puopoulo field and the skating rink. A ball field, playground, and some benches. All of it has about six inches of heavy packed snow. There's tons of history around this place. Across the water is Bunker Hill, and behind us, just a little over, is the church where they hung the lanterns for Paul Revere, and the old Copp's Hill Cemetery. When we dig, we find debris from the last dig. Some places, you find old, old stuff, but we aren't going to here. This land is fill, like a lot of the city. They built out between the piers with salt mud, coal ash, gravel, and garbage. No history like there is across the street. When the next crew has to do a job here, they'll find the same shit we did, plus whatever new trash we leave behind in the trench.

*   *   *

I'm early on the site. The foreman, O'Brien, is already there. He's Irish from Southie. Likes to throw in Matt Damon quotes in an exaggerated accent. He nods his chin at me and throws me an orange safety vest.

"Hey, Gomes. You want to start on the backhoe or down in the trench?" he says.

"You giving me a choice?" I say.

"Well, I'm feeling generous today and that little shit Parker ain't here yet, so you get to choose."

"I'll start on the backhoe then."

"All right, then. You watch the games this weekend?"

"A little. Wildcards are usually uneven, you know? It's the divisional games where it starts to get competitive. Besides, the Pats... I don't know. They're playing with a grudge this year, but that defense..."

"They're gonna jam that Lombardi right up Goodell's ass."

31

"Maybe. Pittsburgh's tough and I don't think we can hang with Atlanta."

We go back and forth and in a few minutes Parker pulls up in his pickup with Reeve and Biggs. O'Brien waits for them to get out of the cab and stamps out his cigarette.

"Hey, Pahkah!" he yells. "You're in the hole. *How d'ya like dem apples!*"

* * *

We tear up the asphalt in the rectangle we'd cut with a concrete saw last week, careful to avoid the communication lines underneath. Com is marked in orange spray paint, gas in yellow, electric in red. You don't want to dig up the wrong shit or you *will* pay for it. I'm glad for the backhoe's cab. It's not even twenty degrees outside. I get about an hour out of the cold before O'Brien switches me out so Reeve can warm up and Parker can go for coffee. Weather like this, we'll rotate a lot. I climb down and pick up a shovel. The North End project has been going on for a few years now. Gas, sewer, water mains, storm drains. A lot of crews working, trying to keep it all coordinated. There's pipe a hundred years old down here and a lot of houses still have lead hookups.

It's a clean trench. We're through the gravel backfill, and I scrape around the bottom to get at the flange from the catch basin to the old iron pipe to the storm drain. Getting into old dirt.

The hole is out of the wind so it's not too bad down here. Parker comes back from picking up coffee and is handing out the cups from a cardboard tray. Biggs is laughing at something Reeve said when my shovel hits something hard in the dirt. My hands sting and I drop the handle.

"Ah, son of a..." I say, and bite my lip.

"You got a stinger there, Joachim?" O'Brien says. Everyone calls me Jack, even my pop, but O'Brien likes to call me by my Portuguese name when he's in a good mood.

"Yeah," I say through gritted teeth and try to shake the mix of numbness and needles out of my hands. "Got me good."

"Oh, man," Reeve says, laughing. "That softball game against the Boston Gas guys last year I caught a good one, yo. You remember that?" He's hopping up and down at the edge of the hole, trying to stay warm. I don't, especially, but I nod anyway. I bend down to dig through the packed dirt to get the old paver or chunk of concrete I hit. I pull up a piece of metal. Confused, I knock the dirt off of it.

"The fuck?" I hold it up so they can see up top. "It's a horseshoe."

"So? You want a cookie?" O'Brien says. "Throw it on the pile and let's go." He takes a sip from the Styrofoam cup and spits. "Jesus Christ, Parker! How much sugar did you put in this?"

"I told them two like you like," Parker says. "They marked it right on the cup."

"Well, I can feel my fucking fillings falling out," O'Brien says. "Jack, what the hell are you waiting for down there?"

"What's a horseshoe doing under the street?" I say.

"Came over on the Mayflower. Fuck should I know? Jesus. All right, climb out of there and get your coffee."

"They got horses on the Mayflower?" Parker says. "I didn't know that."

Biggs snorts and almost chokes on her coffee laughing. Never used to have women on the crews, but Biggs did a couple of tours in Iraq and Afghanistan, so she's plenty rugged enough for this and doesn't take any shit from the guys.

We huddle in a small circle with our cups. I look down toward the water across the untouched snow crust of the ball field. The water is gray. Even the gulls have sheltered somewhere. I can see the masts of the Constitution across the inner harbor and if I walked to the water's edge I could see the Cassin Young too. I like those old ships. There is a break in the wind and more of those light feathery snowflakes drift lazily around us. I'm finally settled from the morning. Just enough coffee to keep me awake without feeling like I'm vibrating. Looking at the rest of the crew, they all look tired. There is a scream nearby and I start, but it is a gull, not a horse. Biggs tenses up at well, but her face goes hard fast. Coffee finished, we go back to work. No one is talking much now. I take over flagging, wave the traffic by. It's a little light. Only the people who have no choice are out today. Cabs. Delivery drivers with their trucks full of whatever. I stifle a yawn.

On the way home, the subway is filled with exhausted people lost inside themselves and, on the turns, the metal groans from strain. And somewhere in the background beneath the clatter and squeal of the steel wheels I can almost hear the horses again.

*　　*　　*

I'm on the second floor of an old three-decker with faded vinyl siding and an absentee landlord who lives in Jamaica Plain. I nearly fall on the ice on the stairs. The plastic bucket of ice melt in the front hall is empty, so the neighbors dumped it out and then didn't bother to refill it. The landlord keeps the extra salt in the basement because, I guess, someone might break in and take it out of the hallway. I unlock the door and find the light switch. There's no cover on the switch, and I can feel the edges of the metal electric box. The stairs down are narrow. I have to crouch because the hall stairs are right above these, a low slanted ceiling.

The building is old. The stone is settling because the old wooden pilings beneath the streets are beginning to rot. Cracks in the plaster, with crumbling brown undercoat falling away down to the lathing. Cracks in the stone foundation. A hard turn at the bottom of the stairs by the fuse box. Half the breakers are double-tapped and there are old-school fuses in small cardboard boxes on the wooden shelf next to it, all covered in thick grey dust. There's no way this is up to code.

The basement is low with an old dragon of a boiler and pipes wrapped in thick asbestos. There are three stalls along the wall, wooden pens with chicken wire door frames, maybe seven by ten. Storage for each floor. I don't keep much in mine.

The salt is under the stairs in a heavy wooden shipping crate stenciled with "The Murray Company" on State Street. A yellowed sticker reads "grapeade soda." Full of salt, it weighs a ton. I can't imagine having to haul freight back in the day. I reach for the coffee can that I use to carry salt upstairs and I hear the thumping of the first-floor tenants. The Milsons are usually quiet, but they are sure loud tonight, running heavily back and forth the length of the floor, knocking dust from the unfinished subflooring overhead. The motes swim in the florescent light. I grab the can and turn. The hanging lights are swaying slightly.

The boards flex so much that they pull the nails from the wood. There is a terrible creaking and a sound, rat-tat-tat, like a machine gun. A dark tide begins to seep in through the windows and foundation cracks in the basement, at once both horrifyingly fast and languid. It rises up and I struggle to swim. It presses on me, thick and sticky. I cannot move in it. The fluorescents flicker as I lose my footing and begin to sink. I gasp for air but the muddy water clings to my face like a caul. I inhale it deeply, pull it into my lungs like mucus. My ribs ache from pulling against the thickness filling my throat. I cannot get any air.

Dark forms move in the flood, kicking and thrashing beside me. I can't make out their shapes, but they, too, are dying. Then I cannot see, except for red flashes behind my eyes, and then nothing. Eventually, I wake on the floor beside the crate. The basement is dry and I am alone. Inches from my nose, in a glue trap by the wall beneath the stairs, a mouse lies dying. It cannot move at all, and takes rapid shallow breaths. As I watch, helpless, its breathing becomes sporadic and stops.

It's all the sleep I get.

*   *   *

By Wednesday, time seems to be stopping for me, days bleeding into each other. I'm pounding Red Bull to keep my eyes open. It warmed up so fast, from the twenties to the fifties in two days. Joggers and walkers are out in force, on the sidewalks and along the seawall. I'm wearing a t-shirt under my vest, waving traffic past the site with a flag. It's been spitting a little rain on and off, but not too bad.

I think I bruised a rib trying to suck in air during a dream, and I'm trying to keep out of shoveling. The remaining snow along the edges of the road is shrunken and packed and blackened with exhaust. The snow at the park is trampled and brown. The turf beneath is all chopped up as if someone spent the night tearing at it with a post digger. I'm so exhausted from the nightmares I can't pay attention to anything. I swear I saw the horses in the subway tunnel, running along the side of the car outside the window where I was leaning. Chasing along with me, keeping pace.

I don't know what's happening.

The other guys, Biggs included, all look exhausted, but no one will talk about it. I think I hear hooves on cobbles, but when I look up it's just the click of skateboard wheels. Parker is saying something from down in the trench, but I don't know what.

"So, we went there, did the thing, and then we came back," Parker says.

"Great story, Parker," Biggs says. "You got me on the edge of my seat with that one."

Reeve nods in agreement. If he hears the sarcasm in her voice he doesn't let on.

O'Brien, across the trench on the sidewalk side, looks like he's worse than any of us. He's past fifty, and his face is drawn and paler than usual. He's also in a foul mood, scowling down at Parker in the trench.

"No, you idiot," O'Brien yells. "You can't do it that way, you gotta take that one out first and *then* the other thing. I don't have time for this shit. Jesus. Reeve, get down in there with him. We gotta fill this section today and keep moving."

Three kids who should be in school zoom past us on their bikes in the small gap between the traffic barrels and a bright yellow chicken salad delivery truck.

"Damn fools are gonna get themselves killed doing that," Biggs says. The cartoon chicken with a bowtie and paper deli hat smiles at us and gives a big thumbs up.

"Hey, Biggs. Can I ask you something?"

"Yeah."

"It's like, ever since we turned the corner by the rink and started digging down here by the park, I'm getting these bad dreams."

"Oh, hell, no," Biggs says. "I don't know anything about it. Don't ask me."

"But, before I heard the horses and it looked like you—"

"Uh-uh. I ain't about any of that weird shit, you understand me? You get your own answers for whatever you think you're seeing. I don't know nothing about it. When I get off shift I am going home, have a glass of wine, and read a book while my baby rubs my feet. Why are you even asking me, anyway?"

There is a squeal across the street. An Asian woman in a jacket and skirt has stumbled. Bystanders help her up. She is tall and thin with long legs, almost gangly in her professional attire. She snapped off a heel, and is laughing with the people who helped her stand, so she must not be hurt badly. Tall heels. I'm surprised she didn't break a leg. She hobbles off, lame but moving.

"Glass of wine sounds good," I say. "My pop makes his own by the barrel."

"Yeah? Well, you carry some down here I'll bring it home and try it."

"Portuguese wine is pretty sweet."

"That's all right. I'm pretty sweet too."

We laugh. Behind us, O'Brien's yelling sounds more complimentary and encouraging now, so I figure we can fill this part of the trench and be done with it. Maybe once we do, the nightmares will stop and I can get some sleep. The afternoon is quiet and we use the backhoe to pack the pile of excavated fill back into the hole on top of the new pipe section with the litter of coffee cups and cigarette packs. We're not supposed to dump that stuff in, but no one will know what's down there until someone digs it up again. Hell, the whole airport is built on trash fill, so what difference can it make?

I do not see or hear any horses on the way home, and I believe that, whatever that was, it is over now. I am happy to forget it and get on with my life.

*　　*　　*

But I am not so fortunate. I wake with a start to the sound of destruction and mayhem. There are horses in my apartment, crashing through the windows and rearing high enough to scrape the ceiling with their hooves. My coffee table and flat-screen are toppled and smashed beneath sharp hooves. Their eyes are wild and rolling.

This time I am not dreaming.

I manage to grab my coat and boots from the hall outside my door and flee the apartment into the night. They drive me, their roars echoing in the streets. They call to each other, herd me toward the subway station with snorts and gnashed teeth. I barely make the last inbound train, and sit alone in a car in my boots, sweatpants, and a t-shirt. Outside, they gallop and lunge, thudding against the windows. A shod hoof smashes at my face and cracks the Lexan. I change to the Green Line and emerge again at North Station. No one sees the horses but me. If I try to move in any direction but toward the park they rear and block my path. I hurry down Causeway toward the water.

*   *   *

I am back on Commercial Street, but not the one I know. It takes me a minute to get oriented. The park is gone, replaced by the elevated train, the city paving yard, and piers. The street is covered with rail tracks. Stevedores and carters load horse carts with heavy barrels and crates. The air is heavy with the smell of coal smoke, manure, and the metallic tang of blood from the slaughterhouse. Underneath it all is a deep and permeating scent that is overwhelmingly cloying. The neighborhood is busy with activity. Italian women hang their laundry from tenement windows in the hazy air. A group of children walk home from school on the sidewalk.

Ahead stands the brick facade of the Purity Distilling Company. It is dwarfed by an enormous brown steel tank, taller even than the elevated tracks of the Atlantic Avenue line. It must be nearly fifty feet tall and a hundred across. There is a rumble and I look for the train that must be coming down the track but there isn't one. People pause in the street, unsure of where the sound is coming from. The rumble becomes the groan of straining metal, the machine-gun popping of steel rivets. With a thunderous explosion, the steel plates of the tank give way and a massive, ponderous wave of dark brown syrup courses from the ruptured vessel. It expands outward, tearing down the buildings of the paving yard and twisting the steel uprights supporting the train tracks. The wave washes across Commercial Street, eight feet high, impossibly fast yet languid at the same time and breaks against the tenements at the base of Copp's Hill. Within minutes the whole area is a thickening pool of dark brown liquid filled with debris and bodies. It is over my knees. I wipe it from my face and taste molasses. It is everywhere. In every direction, it looks like the aftermath of a storm surge from a hurricane. Buildings lie in sticky ruin, or in half collapse, torn from their foundation. I cannot see the children in their school clothes.

Forms struggle in the congealing mass, impossible to tell if they are men or women, or even human beneath the surface. And, above it all, I hear the horses screaming. They have been torn from their harnesses and ripped from their carts. They flail and thrash, struggle to regain their footing on broken legs, but they cannot. It is a swamp and it pulls them under. I try to help, to grab one by its bridle and pull it up but it is too heavy and the molasses too thick. I can do nothing. Across the yard, dark figures roll and reach up, a hand or hoof breaks the surface and then submerges again. The horse before me snorts and tries to blow thick brown foam from its nostrils but it is filling up. The weight of the molasses presses on its ribs. I can see the scars of lash marks on its back beneath the sweetness. It chokes. Its lungs fill. Its eyes are deep and brown and filled with terror that it cannot voice. I tell it that it will be o.k. and tears run down my face. I slouch down in the mire and stroke its sticky head while it dies. Around me, I can hear more horses crying out for help, but I cannot reach them. My hand is covered with a mass of hair and syrup. Chicken feathers from a crushed slaughterhouse float gently in the air like snowflakes.

People come. Firemen, locals. They try to pull the people from the swamp, but the horses remain glued in place. The last one moving is a powerful draft horse, perhaps a bay beneath the treacle but impossible to say. It turns laboriously, hitched to the Catherine Wheel of its dead harness-mate in a tangle of reins and straps, with a splintered yoke between them. It circles the corpse of the other horse in a sluggish orbit until it can no longer move and, finally, settles slowly into the mire. By the time the sun begins to set, men start to shoot the horses that remain alive until the screaming stops.

They are all dead. Dozens of them.

They are all dead, now.

*   *   *

The vision of the flood recedes through the sepia of old photos and then I am back at the jobsite. The crowded tenements, the elevated train, and the ruins are all gone. The park, quiet and beautiful against the water in the night, remains.

The horses remain as well. Vaporous forms in the streetlights, their breath steams, and steam rises from their lathered backs. They stand in a loose semicircle, eyes rolling. I try to move to the side but they snort and rear, and press me back. I scuttle along the sidewalk in shaking hesitant steps, afraid of what revenge they intend to take upon me. They pin me up against a low stone wall by the entrance to the bocce courts, standing over me, hooves stomping against the concrete, echoing into the night. It is strangely quiet for the city, other than the sounds of the horses. They part, and another human is backed against the wall with me. It is O'Brien. He is wearing pajamas and his face is ashen. He mumbles prayers to Saint

Mary and doesn't respond to me. I see, behind him, a green plaque against the wall, and press against his shoulder until he slides over. I read it and then gesture for him to read it too.

Boston Molasses Flood

On January 15, 1919, a molasses tank at 529
Commercial Street exploded under press-
sure, killing 21 people. A 40-foot wave of
molasses buckled the elevated railroad tracks,
crushed buildings and inundated the neigh-
borhood. Structural defects in the tank com-
bined with unseasonably warm temperatures
contributed to the disaster.

-The Bostonian Society

These are the other victims of the flood. In their lives, they were harnessed and bound. Whipped, cursed and misused. They were not buried or mourned. They were sold for glue or dogmeat. Shot, rendered, and consigned to nothingness, nearly a hundred years ago.

They are not seeking revenge for our disturbing this place.

They, too, want to be remembered.

"The horseshoe," I say.

O'Brien nods.

*   *   *

Under their watchful eyes, we move back to the hole we filled in the day before. We don't have the keys to the backhoe, so we dig with our shaking hands in the muddy fill. Some stand in a ring around us while others tramp restlessly in field and the street, sighing and groaning.

"We find that goddamned thing, I'm gonna weld it to the cab of the backhoe, right on front there," O'Brien says. I can only nod numbly.

We are fortunate that it is not buried deeply. I find it packed beneath crushed coffee cups and cigarette packages.

"I got it. I got it," I say. I stand up and hold it high over my head so they can see. "See? We won't throw it away again. I promise."

A fog has come in from the ocean, softening the noises and edges of the city. The horses move again. They whinny and nicker across the fields, rearing and cantering freely. I can hear their voices as they echo away into the streets of the North End and disappear. They are gone now, and me and O'Brien shiver at the edge of the dirt pile in the dark, the horseshoe on the ground between us.

"Hey, Boss?" I say. "We got, what, four hours before work? You think maybe it'd be all right if I called in sick and got some sleep?"

"Yeah," he says. "That's a good idea. Think I will too. Biggs can run the site."

"I never seen anything like that before," I say. O'Brien shakes his head absently and stares across the street. He feels his pockets for a cigarette and comes up empty. I fish a pack from my coat, light up two and pass him one. A Boston PD cruiser passes slowly by and I give an easy wave. He drives on as if two guys smoking on a dirt pile by a hole on Commercial Street in the rain is perfectly normal. Maybe it is. It's more normal that what I've been doing since we first broke ground down here.

"Ghost horses. Fuck," O'Brien says finally. "How do you like *them* apples?"

Everything Smells Like Smoke Again
Curtis M. Lawson

December 12th

He's dead. Eric's worried because I didn't cry. I overheard him talking to the boys, telling them that I'm keeping a stiff upper lip. That's not it, though. Truthfully, this has been a long time coming, and he doesn't deserve my tears. That well ran dry long ago, and mostly because of him.

Do I feel a tad abnormal about my callousness? It's fucked up I suppose, but not as much as Eric must think. He can't really comprehend what it was like for me, growing up the daughter of addicts. His childhood wasn't perfect, but it was normal; vacations, family game nights, never finding suicide notes and empty pill bottles.

Eric and I are from different worlds. My in-laws, the people he grew up with, are wonderful, and I love them, but their stability has always left me feeling out of place. The way they have their shit together — it feels alien and untrustworthy.

Still, after fifteen years of holidays with them, anxiety swells inside me as I wait for things to go sideways at every get-together. I look at Eric's dad and wonder how many beers he's had and if this will be the one that pushes him over the line from buzzed to monstrous. I wait for my mother-in-law to take some off-the-cuff comment the wrong way and send Christmas dinner whizzing past my head. It never happens. I know it will never happen. Still, that fear persists.

It's the same with Eric, himself. My husband is a caring and hardworking man. He's not a drinker, or a party guy, or a skirt chaser. Despite him proving his worth over fifteen years of marriage, I get a knot in my stomach if he's late from work. I feel sick when he catches the occasional buzz. Jealousy and insecurity overcome my heart if he mentions some female colleague too many times. Not once has the man ever given me cause to doubt him, but when the floor falls out from under you for eighteen years straight you learn to tread lightly.

It's over now. Dad's dead. To be fair he'd had one foot in the grave since Mom passed. After her death he quit partying and abandoned street narcotics, more fully embracing his pedestrian, solitary addictions. Cigarettes, pain pills, and nostalgia mostly. I can think of maybe two times in the decade-plus since Mom died that he'd left his depressing little subsidized apartment for anything other than a trip to the dollar store or the packie.

I suppose I could have been a better daughter. Yes, I could have reached out and been a shoulder to cry on. The kids were young though, and Eric and I were building our own life — a healthy life for the family I had chosen, rather than the one which fate had burdened me with. My father wasn't going to ruin that with his depression and addictions. Enough of my life had been compromised for him. I wouldn't allow him to take what I'd built for myself.

When he started getting sick last year, really sick as opposed to his normal state of perpetual unhealth, Eric suggested he come to live with us. I shot the idea down straightaway. Sure, I dreaded the thought of being around him, but that wasn't it. There were also the kids to consider. I didn't want them to see him sitting there day after day, popping pills and smoking butts, waiting for the reaper.

In addition to his habits and addictions there was also just... him. His backward, victim mentality and that acidic anger born of insecurity. How could I let his noxious, *woe is me* world-view infect their minds? To Dad, nothing was ever his fault. He was destitute because he had "been dealt a losing hand," not because he burned every dollar he could have saved. His poor health was part of that same unlucky draw, and certainly had nothing to do with the abuse he'd put his body through. Even when Mom died, he blamed everything from God, to fate, to poor health insurance; but never the shitty life decisions the two of them made. I couldn't let my kids grow up around that, thinking it was *normal*.

Is there a level of guilt for letting him wallow in the purgatory he'd built around himself? I suppose. We all make our own beds.

December 13

I couldn't sleep last night. After the kids had gone to bed, and Eric turned in for the night, I lay awake thinking about my father's lifeless face, framed by the funerary upholstery of his casket.

There is a level of surrealness at any funeral, staring down at a corpse that looks like an amateur wax museum replica of a loved one. The subtleties of their complexion are off just enough to make you doubt the legitimacy of the body. That one-size-fits-all expression of peace. The whole thing conjures thoughts of body snatchers and doppelgängers.

It was with such ideas in my head that I smelled smoke drift into my bedroom. Not the smoke from a stove left on, or an electrical fire in the walls, but the distinct smell of burning tobacco.

I didn't smoke and neither did Eric. We never had. I wondered if one of the kids might be dumb enough to take up such a filthy habit, and in the house nonetheless. My nose crinkled as I rose from bed to investigate.

Our room was next to the boys'. I poked my head in to check on them and sniffed at the air. I could still smell the smoke, but not any stronger than I had from my own bed. Both Kyle and Georgie lay fast asleep, the funeral having been emotionally exhausting for them as well.

I turned and followed the smell down the hall, across the checkerboard tiles of our kitchen. It was dark and still. Neither the stove nor the oven were alight. Visible in the darkness, a trail of pale smoke snaked across the threshold, beckoning me into the living room.

Moonlight from the December sky poured through the open curtains, lending an otherworldly glow to the smoke, which terminated a few feet above the couch. Marla, our dog, growled low and glared at the wispy cloud. Her tail was tucked between her legs, and hackles stood up like a porcupine's quills.

I searched between the cushions, looking for a burning ember of...something. Nothing was there. I placed my hands over the outlets, feeling for heat. More nothing.

A glowing dot of orange formed in the air — an angry little pixie — then faded away. A fresh puff of smoke followed the disappearance of the glow. Ashes from the burning nothing floated to the hardwood floor.

Not believing what I was seeing, I knelt down and pressed my finger into the gray soot. It was warm to the touch, and left a charcoal smear across my fingertip.

Eric called from the other room, concerned that I had wandered from bed. I looked up from the floor to find that the smoke had vanished and no angry, burning dot floated above me. Still, my finger was stained with ash. Confused and afraid I pressed my finger to my tongue. The bitter taste confirmed the ash as real.

December 18

I wished I were sleepwalking, experiencing some somnambulant night terror, but everyone could smell the smoke now. Eric grilled the boys, sure it was them secretly lighting up in the house or carrying the smell in on their clothes.

It wasn't Kyle or Georgie, of course. Eric doesn't listen when I tell him that, and I can't quite be truthful — that each night I'm awoken by the smell of phantom cigarettes. What kind of nut house would they lock me up in if I told him how it mocks me through the night — the floating ember, burning to life then vanishing, followed by the puff of smoke exhaled from an invisible man.

Yesterday I cleaned the house while Eric and the boys went shopping. I sprayed the couch and the curtains with Febreze. Ignoring the cold, I opened the living room windows, and let the crisp winter air fight the acrid odor. It was then I noticed the stains on the wall. Yellow smears of tobacco, like the ones in the house I grew up in.

Scrubbing didn't help much. Neither did the Febreze. Nothing really gets smoke out, except for time.

December 21

Things were getting stranger. Things were getting worse. I hadn't slept in days. Last night I was determined to ignore the smell. At ten o'clock I snuck a few Tylenol PM capsules and rested my head. This is my new bedtime ritual, though it didn't keep me asleep in this particular circumstance.

Just after midnight, a sound came from the living room and drew me from slumber —audial accompaniment for the smell of tobacco. Laugh tracks and pleasant, inoffensive music called out.

My eyes were heavy from the pills as I shuffled into the hall and through the kitchen. A blue glow, shifting in intensity, poured across the threshold. The ghosts of tar and nicotine were afire in the cold radiance.

Crossing into the living room, I could see the now-familiar burning dot floating above the couch. It pulsed in and out of existence, clouds of cancer billowing from the nothingness in between the moments of fiery glow.

The TV was on. This was a new phenomenon. A young Ron Howard looked up at Don Knotts, taking poor advice with earnest. Everyone laughed. Everyone except for me.

I clicked off the TV and went back to bed.

December 28

For the past week the TV wouldn't stay off at night, and the smoke had become ever present. I couldn't sleep anymore, not without chemical assistance, and the recommended dosage wasn't cutting it.

Eric and I got in a fight. He thinks I have a problem — that I'm abusing the Tylenol PM. Listen to how stupid that statement sounds. It's an over the counter pain killer, not OxyContin. Also, I would fucking know if a I had a problem. I grew up with addiction. I watched it every day of my childhood. What the fuck does he know about it? He watched an after-school special once? Or maybe a piece on Dr. Phil?

So I overslept and missed a few days of work. Who cares? It's not like I'm the bread winner. I only work so we can have play money.

The actual reason he's pissed, if I were to guess, is because of Christmas morning. He and the kids couldn't wake me and had to go about the morning ritual sans mommy.

I get it. He had a perfect fucking family, and Christmas was magical. Well, the kids are almost teenagers. They don't need mommy to get up and watch them open their presents. If I want to sleep in a little on a day off, then who the hell is Eric to judge?

He says I have a problem, and that I should talk to someone about losing my dad. I do have a problem, but it's not the death of my loser father. It's finding him in my house, breathing his poisonous tobacco, dragon smoke all over my life.

December 30

Everyone's avoiding the living room. They don't consciously realize he's there, haunting our house, but they all feel it on some level. The TV only plays old, black and white shows and movies. Every channel is monopolized by the monochromatic dead. Kyle and Georgie don't even bother with it.

Marla won't step in there. She's abandoned her dog bed and sleeps on the cold tile beneath the kitchen table. Even passing through the living room on our way out for walks makes her fur stand on end. She growls and yips in the direction of the couch, at that taunting, invisible specter.

Eric keeps complaining about drafts and insulation. He goes on and on about getting new windows, not realizing that the chill is emanating from my father's rotten ghost.

January 2

New Year's was a shit show. It started off well enough. We stayed in the kitchen, playing board games and listening to music. We ate cheese and crackers, and drank Pepsi and champagne. There was even an unspoken agreement to pretend that the living room didn't exist. I was perfectly happy with that.

Around midnight Eric decided he wanted to watch the ball drop on the big TV. Georgie and Kyle seconded him. I nervously assented and we adjourned to the living room.

It was cold, and wreaked of smoke. Kyle's nose crinkled in disgust, and everyone's mood dropped three notches after crossing the threshold.

Eric turned on the TV. It went straight to a twilight zone rerun, the one where the last guy on earth loses his glasses and can't read all the books. Dad's favorite.

Eric fought with the remote and the cable box for two minutes before finally bringing up the New Year's countdown. When the camera moved away from the gathered crowd and came to focus on Ryan Seacrest, in lieu of the late Dick Clark, the signal wavered sending ripples of static down the screen.

I turned to look at the couch. As I expected, an angry puff of smoke manifested in the air. My dead father was throwing a temper tantrum because he wanted The New Year's host he was used to.

Eric grumbled about the cable company and the reception, but my eyes were focused on the pulsing ember that floated in mid-air. On the TV, all of Times Square counted down from ten, as did my boys, but all of that was background noise behind the labored moans of my paternal ghost.

Eric joined in with the counting, abandoning his grumbles about the wavy lines obscuring the broadcast.

Five. Four.

The smoke in the air took on familiar features. My father's miserable, ethereal face stared through me and at the television. He looked the same as he had in life, greedy for misery and pissed at the world.

Three. Two.

The line of smoke that made his mouth twisted into a hateful smirk. A second before midnight the image collapsed into a formless cloud and the lights cut out. Sparks erupted from the power strip, the fixtures, and the sockets.

Georgie let out a cuss word that we ignored, then all was silence. After a few moments Eric chimed in with a sarcastic, "Happy new year?"

I disregarded my husband's satire. My back was turned to my family. I stared intently at the couch, waiting for the orange dot of my father's cigarette to appear. When it did I lost my mind.

"Get the hell out!" I screamed. "Get the hell out of my house!"

I can only imagine that Eric and the boys stared at me with slack jawed horror. A hand touched my shoulder, presumably Eric's. I shrugged it off and continued my verbal assault,

"You can't have this! You're dead and this is mine! My house! My family!"

The phantom cigarette vanished and a puff of white smoke hit me in the face. I collapsed to the floor screaming, not words but raw emotion. I kicked and thrashed on the ground, until Eric eventually restrained and calmed me.

He got me into bed, then took the kids aside. He probably gave them some feel good psychobabble about how their mom wasn't crazy, just emotionally strained.

Soon after that he came to bed. We didn't speak. He just held me as I cried. The smell of smoke wafted in, but I ignored it and gave myself to my husband's embrace and to sleep.

January 7

They're gone. Eric. Kyle and Georgie. Marla. Gone.

Eric kept begging me to get help, especially after New Year's. I refused. What help was there to be had? Maybe if he meant an exorcist, but no, he wanted me to see a damn shrink, as if talking about my feelings would send the ghost in our living room packing.

It was becoming unbearable. The smoke, the blue flickering light of the TV, the bullshit happy facade of classic television.

I upgraded from Tylenol PM to Ambien. When Eric found out, he lost it. He threatened to leave me and take the kids. I knew he was bullshitting at that point, trying to scare me, but then my fucking father ruined everything. Just like he'd always done.

I know I put the cover on the pills. I know I put them away, but somehow they spilled. Poor Marla gobbled them all up. She died painlessly, but that didn't make things easier for any of us.

Eric didn't believe me when I said my father dumped out the pills and killed our dog. He didn't believe that the dead bastard wanted to take everything from me.

We screamed and fought. Eric made terrible, unfair accusations. He said I was just like my parents, letting the boys find me passed out with pills strewn across the floor. He cried and hit the walls, blaming me for Marla's death.

I fought back. I hit and screamed and told him it wasn't my fault, but he wouldn't listen. All the while my father sat there on my couch, puffing away, watching Wally and Beaver as my life crumbled around me.

That was yesterday. I called Eric today, but he wouldn't answer no matter how many times I tried. At first, I was cordial. I tried to apologize and pretend everything was normal. Each time his voicemail picked up I grew angrier, until my messages were seething with venom and my voice was hoarse from screaming.

January 25

I've stopped avoiding the living room, and I can barely smell the smoke over the gasoline. Andy Griffith is playing on TV. I forgot how much I used to like it. Classic television is really one of the only good memories I shared with dad, so I might as well make the best of it.

It seems Eric and the boys aren't coming back. Eric says he can't let me near our sons until I get some help, but what help is there? This is just the hand I've been dealt.

I light up a cigarette and sit down next to dear old dad. The gasoline soaks through my jeans. The carcinogenic mist burns my lungs, but pain is a familiar place. Falling back into its embrace almost feels good. It's like waking up from a dream of normalcy.

I tell my father that I love and forgive him. He places a cold hand on my knee. We both lay our cigarettes down on the couch and wait for the fire to take us home.

The Boy on the Red Tricycle
Dan Szczesny

Nothing prepares you for a ghost.

Not popular culture. Not funerals of your own loved ones. Walk through a thousand cemeteries at midnight, or fire up the Ouija board at a city morgue. You'd think that first time – that first feeling of electric air or the moment that your skin prickles – you'd be ready for it.

But you won't be. I wasn't.

It was Christmas. No wait, it may have been a couple days after. Two years ago. I'm not from New England, spent most of my life kicking around the Rust Belt because that's where the work was in the '90s. Cleveland and Pittsburgh were cleaning up their waterfront, burying all those heavy metals that came out of the steel plants, turning lakesides into preservation parks.

Did you know that there's a wildlife refuge in Buffalo that is actually a giant dump, with mounds of asbestos, arsenic and mercury buried right under nature trails and concession stands? It's true, look it up. So I moved around. Those outfits were always looking to contract outside guys for cleanup and landscape work, keep the dirty work away from local unions.

You know, not a lot of time for girlfriends or kids. Though yeah, weird how that works when the kid you end up having turns out to be a dead one. But I'm getting ahead of myself.

Tech moved in after the steel mills finally dried up so I had to go someplace where technology hadn't reached and that was New Hampshire, for sure. Don't feel insulted. I like Manchester, really. It reminds me of those days when I was a kid in south Chicago – all alleys and beat cops. And you know, a few years ago they decided instead of tearing those shit-ugly mills down, they would turn them into condos and cafes.

I mean, honest to God, I never thought that would work. This idea that tourists would come to look at hundred-year-old, leaky, broken warehouse buildings just seemed stupid. But you know what, it worked! Well, I don't have to tell you something you already know.

Anyway, that's where I come in. I was hired to do some landscape and cleanup work around Mill No. 5, the one over by the bridge. Pay was shitty, it almost always was, but this time they were putting me up in one of the old brownstones next door, free. So hey, a two-year gig with free rent? That sounded good to me. Trouble was, those brownstones were old and a mess, but I figured as long as the roof didn't leak and the heat worked I could fix up the rest. I can do drywall and I know a little bit about plumbing, so I moved in.

That was the fall of 2014. I had to hustle to get the place up to code before winter set in. You know, this city needs to do something about its code enforcement. No way those residences were ready for occupancy, not even for a lowlife like me, but I figured the developer must have paid a pretty penny to City Hall to keep that quiet. Anyway, I didn't care.

I don't own a lot of stuff. I managed to pick up a couple chairs and some kitchen things like plates and forks from the Salvation Army thrift store. But it wasn't until I got my bed – just a cheap frame and mattress really – that Denny showed up. Maybe he just waited that long because, I don't know, a bed made it real, like I was there to stay. That was maybe two months after I moved in.

There was no warm-up or hints ahead of time, no slamming doors or knocks from the attic. That's all bullshit movie scare tactics.

Here's what happened.

I'd just come home after a late site visit, long day, filthy. The shower head had been clogged for days so I just went to bed, figured I'd wash the sheets the next day, which was Saturday so I was pretty excited to be able to sleep in. My bedroom sits at the end of a long hall, second floor and for whatever reason the light switch is outside the room, that's just how they installed them when the place was upgraded, I guess. It was freezing out, this was March remember, and I had four blankets on me.

You know how you get right to that place before sleep when you're not quite dreaming but not awake either, like you're standing in a doorway? Like you're no place yet?

Right at that moment, way in the background of my head I heard it. At first I thought it was a dream, but then I figured if I'm actually *thinking* it's a dream it must be real, right? It was the sound of little, squeaking tires against a wood floor. Then a little bell, you know like the kind on a kid's bike. I remember turning toward the door, but it was super dark and I don't have a lamp. But a window near my bed faced the street and every so often if a car was coming down off the hill, its headlights would light up the room for a second or two. That's what happened. That bike got closer and closer, the bell pinged one more time, but then it stopped.

Everything was quiet, and I tried squinting into the darkness but nothing. The air was full of static or something; the hairs on my arm were popping up. Then a car outside rounded the turn, a couple seconds of light flooded the window and the kid was there, right next to my bed, sitting stock still on a red tricycle.

Here's another thing you don't realize about ghosts until you actually encounter one. You don't think it's a ghost. My mind just didn't go there. All I could think of at that second was how the hell a little kid got in my house and managed to get upstairs on a tricycle.

"Jesus Christ, kid," I said. "you nearly gave me a heart attack, what the hell are you doing here?"

I rolled to the other side of the bed and felt my way around to the doorway, and clicked on the light switch. When I turned back to look at him, he hadn't moved, meaning his back was facing me.

That's when I started to scream, because the back of the kid's head – well, it was gone, just a mash of blood and bone. I could see his brain. Like someone had taken a sledgehammer to a five-year-old. And as it turned out, that's exactly what had happened.

*   *   *

Why are you looking at me like that? I mean, wouldn't you go straight to the liquor cabinet after seeing something like that? The kid? Well, I guess my screaming like a little girl must have spooked him, pardon the pun. He just faded away, right there in front of my eyes.

I wasn't really sure what to do then. I drank a lot, I mentioned that already. I turned all the lights on in the house, which when you think about ghost sightings seems like a weird reaction. Because as it turned out, Denny didn't care if the lights were on or off, he just wandered around whenever.

Oh yeah, Denny. That was his name. *Is* his name, sorry. I'm talking about him like he's dead – he obviously is dead. Never mind. His name is Denny.

I think I sort of went crazy for a while there, trying to figure out should I move? Should I tell anyone? Go to the police? I went online and there's tons of paranormal groups out there, but nothing really seemed to fit for Denny because he wasn't hurting me, or doing anything, really. But think about it: he was the victim. Somebody bashed his head in with a hammer. This was just one sad ghost.

Anyway, a couple days later he showed up again. That's when he told me his name. I was back in my bedroom, only this time with the lights on, just laying in bed reading. No noise, no tires. I felt that electricity in the air again, and looked up. The kid was sitting cross-legged at the foot of the bed, two feet from me. There was an indent in the bed where he was sitting. He was just staring at me.

"What are you reading?" he finally asked. I was so startled at hearing his voice, just a kid voice, young and wispy, that I just tilted the book cover toward him. Honest to God, he rolled his eyes, just like any kid would. "I can't read that, I'm only five."

"A novel," I croaked. "*Da Vinci Code*."

He shrugged. We sat there looking at each other for a minute. I swallowed hard, then said. "Can I touch you?"

"Why?"

"I – uh, I, just let me, OK?"

"OK."

I didn't know what to expect. I suppose like all the movie ghosts, I figured my hand would just drift right through him. But nope. I cautiously touched first his cheek with a finger, then laid my whole hand on his shoulder. Solid. Flesh and bone. Other than the musty old wool clothes, the kid was an actual solid human. Except of course that he wasn't.

"Well, you're real," I said.

"I'm Denny."

I reached out my hand and he took it and we shook. "Nice to meet you, Denny. I'm Sam."

The kid smiled then, and I felt something burst in my brain or my heart, or wherever something is supposed to burst when you fall in love with your own child. That burst and I began to crumble. I honestly had no idea how badly it would all turn out.

*   *   *

There was the issue of his burst open head of course. Every time Denny would turn his head or I'd come up to him from behind, there it was, blood and brain spilling out all over the place. Of course, he was a ghost, so there wasn't actual blood pouring out or anything. I tried talking to him about it, but every time I brought it up he just winked out of existence. Sometimes he wouldn't come back for days or weeks and I missed him when he was gone so I stopped asking.

That was a mistake, I see it now. I should have pushed harder to figure out what happened – then maybe I would have had some perspective. Or maybe not. Who knows?

Anyway, Denny started popping in pretty much every day. Sometimes he'd be waiting for me in the morning, other times he'd show up when I got home and was sitting around watching TV. Once, I woke up in the morning to discover him sleeping in bed with me. Well, technically not sleeping as I'd never actually seen him sleep, but he was right there, three inches from my face, eyes open but certainly relaxing. I just shut off the alarm that day, called in sick, put my arm around him and went back to sleep. It was nice.

I started taking quite a few days off, actually. Being a private contractor allowed me some freedom, but really it was just about being with Denny. You know, being a good dad.

This is the part of the story where I suppose it won't surprise you to learn that my dad was a violent shit? Nah, I'm messing with you. He was fine, no daddy issues for me. Steady job at a bank, always taking me for ice cream and baseball games. Good advice. The works.

He always did want to be a granddad, though, shame he didn't live long enough.

Anyway, before you think I'm some sort of weirdo, I did do some independent research on the row house and on Denny. And speaking of daddy issues, it only took me about twenty minutes on Google to figure out that Denny was murdered by his dad, a carpenter named Benjamin. It was a big thing in Manchester back at the turn of the last century, the library had a whole folder on it. Thing is, nobody knows why. Seemed like a perfectly normal guy, worked on some of the original mills. Church guy. Denny was an only child and his mom had died of consumption or one of those horrible things we don't have any more.

Then one day, the kid just shows up dead on the front porch, head all bashed up. They trace the weapon back to one of the dad's carpentry hammers. Denny's father killed himself before he could be hanged.

Want to hear about another weird part of the story? Nobody knew Denny even existed before he turned up dead. I mean, obviously he existed but as near as I could tell from the newspaper articles, nobody knew the couple even had a child. Easier to hide back then I suppose, but still, poor kid, right? Basically, Denny lived his whole life inside his house, my house, hidden from the outside world.

Well, I determined to not let that happen.

*   *   *

First, I had to do something about that head wound. You see, Denny was real, by which I mean when he was present, you could touch him, put your arm around him. He wasn't pale or ghostly, his lips weren't blue, he didn't walk through walls or float. He didn't eat but that didn't matter much.

So, one evening, this must have been maybe three months ago, Denny and I were hanging out in the living room playing cards, when I decided to bring up the subject again.

"Denny, I want to talk to you about something, but I need you to promise to stay with me," I said. "It won't be scary. Can you do that?"

"I think so, Sam," he said. I noticed that he slid a bit closer to me. The kid scared easy and didn't like talking about how he died. But that's parenthood, right? Sometimes you have to have the tough conversations.

"I was thinking maybe we get you some new clothes for you, something you'd like." I paused and held my breath waiting for him to pop away. "And a hat."

"You mean to cover my brain up, Sam?"

"Well look, Denny, people wouldn't understand a little boy like you just playing outside or whatever with a, if you are, you know…."

"Dead." The word dropped out of his mouth like a dead weight. "But I'm just me, Sam."

He started to cry, so I just pulled him to me and let him have a good wail on my shoulder. I was careful to not touch the back of his head. As much as I loved the kid, I got queasy by looking at that thing. But I'll tell you, the fact that we were talking about it and he didn't just disappear right then and there gave me some hope.

"It's OK, Denny, I won't let anything happen to you. I love you, kid."

That was the first time I said those words, I surprised even myself. But I really did love him. He really was my son.

"You do?"

I nodded.

"I love you too, Sam," he said between sniffles. "OK, we can get new clothes."

I was elated! I spent an afternoon at the mall picking up some jeans and T-shirts, cool stuff that a little modern boy might like. I was so excited I even just blurted out to the cashier at Sears that I was picking up some clothes for my son.

"That's nice!" she said.

It felt good to say that word. Son.

I admit that by this time I wasn't really working at all. I had some money saved up from past jobs and was putting a lot on my only credit card, but I wasn't worried. Work would still be out there later, after Denny and I really had the time to get to know each other.

Back at the house, Denny was there, just inside the door, waiting for me. I unpacked all the bags and laid out the clothes for him. He selected a regular pair of jeans, Lee because that's what I wear, and a Spiderman T-shirt. For a hundred-plus-year-old kid, he was pretty well-versed in all the latest superheroes and fads. I bought him three different hats: a wool knit pull down with a Boston Bruins logo on it, a wide sun hat that had one of those flaps that hung down to his neck, and a baseball hat with a closed snap in the back. He picked the baseball hat.

"Don't worry," he said, seeing the look on my face, "I'll wear the sweatshirt with the hood over it!"

So that's what he did. There was a long floor mirror in the front hall and after he had dressed we posed in front of it for a picture. That's the picture I showed you, the one with my arm around him. I've looked at that picture often since that day. Turns out that of all the time we spent together, that's the only shot I ever took of Denny. Again, like I said, all that business about ghosts not appearing in pictures, none of that is true.

Anyway, we stood there for a few minutes, father and son. I thought maybe he even had a few of my own features, you know. A long nose, black hair. He was too young for the beard.

And then we went outside for the first time. And for the last time.

*   *   *

That was yesterday, and I have to tell you with no exaggeration, it was the best afternoon of my life. We strolled down Main Street with not a care in the world, like father and son. He held my hand. We smiled a lot.

He had this joke he like to tell. He'd look up at me and say, 'Hey, Sam, what's brown and sticky?"

I'd say, "I don't know, Denny, what's brown and sticky?"

He'd hold up a twig and say, "A stick!" Man, he loved that joke.

We stopped at a pizza joint and he pretended to eat just to humor me, and also because I suppose it would be weird for us to be there and for Denny to just sit there. He said that he could eat, if he wanted, just that he was never hungry.

Honestly, most of the time that I've spent here I've kept to myself, so I didn't exactly have any friends and certainly no family. We did, coincidentally, run into Laura, one of the clerks down at the hardware store where I used to go to pick up seed or tools.

"Hey, Sam," she said. "Haven't seen you around much lately!"

"Been busy, Laura," I said. "Denny, say hi to Laura."

She looked down surprised, like she hadn't seen him. "Oh, my goodness, aren't you adorable!"

"Afternoon ma'am," Denny said.

"And so polite! Who is this, Sam?"

And with pride, I proclaimed, "Denny is my son!"

*   *   *

We stopped at a local park, one of those pocket deals with a slide and swing. Denny loved that.

"I haven't been to a park in a long time, Sam," he said.

Poor kid, more like a hundred years. At one point, on the way down a slide, Denny's hood slipped off and a big blotch of red sparkled for a second in the midday sun, but I managed to get his hood back up before anyone could see.

Later in the afternoon, we had made our way clear to the other side of town, near the arena, when Denny became quiet.

"What's wrong, buddy?" I asked.

"Sam," he said, his eyes begin to tear up. "I'd like to show you where I live."

I didn't know what he meant. "You live with me, Denny."

"No, I mean where I live permanently, over there, in the Valley."

The air suddenly crackled with the familiar electric air as I realized what he was talking about.

"Denny, do you mean Valley Cemetery? Is that where you were buried?"

He nodded.

"I – why go there?"

The kid shrugged and I could see him begin to shimmer, like he was going to fade away.

"OK, OK, Denny," I said. "no problem, just stay with me. We'll go. Can you show me?"

My son once again took me by my hand, and together we walked through the gates of the city's oldest cemetery, one of those garden-variety places, all woods and green paths. I'd never been there before but Denny knew exactly where we were going.

We reached my son's grave just as dust had begun to settle on the city, casting long shadows against the gravestones. And there he was.

Denny's tombstone was tiny, bright white, only about a foot high. He pulled down his hood and stepped up to the rock, ran his fingers against the stone.

There were no other stones around his. It read: Dennis Smith, sweet boy, 1830-1835

I blinked. "Wait ... I thought you died in 1900."

"I did," he said, his back still to me. "And dozens of times before and dozens of times after. So many times."

He sighed and pulled off his cap. He was still the little boy I knew, but suddenly I saw a depth of age and soul in his eyes that I can't believe I missed before.

"And now again today, Sam. Doomed to repeat the cycle."

I wasn't sure what he meant, but I damn well knew it was bad. But I had nothing, no leverage. No friends. No job. "Wait, Denny, I don't understand. You're my son."

"My friend, Sam," Denny said, "of all the dads I've had, of all the friends, you were pure. You really love me, don't you?"

"Yes," I whispered. I fell to my knees.

Denny reached out and brushed my cheek with his fingers. They were warm. "I have to go, Sam, I'm sorry you were caught up in this, I do wish you the best." He smiled and was gone.

***

Well, I suppose you know the rest. I ran home, literally ran, my heart pounding. But when I got to the front stoop of our home, there you were, with him. I'm sorry I caused such a ruckus, I know you and the other police were only doing your jobs. And I imagine finding a little boy on the front porch of my home with his head bashed in was jarring.

It doesn't surprise me that you found one of my shovels in the back shed covered in blood. And I think everybody in this room knows that the blood will match that little boy down in the morgue.

And you can unlock these cuffs, I mean where do I have to go? I lost a son today and he wasn't even my son. He wasn't even real. He was Denny. And he was my ghost.

One Way Dead End by Ogmios

East Boston Relief Station
Paul R. McNamee

If someone stabbed Henry Alvarez in the upper groin with an ice pick, the pain might have matched what he was feeling. He groaned and hissed air through his teeth. Dealing with the discomfort was always difficult, trying to handle the pain while driving a car was worse. Navigating the rainy evening streets of Boston made the drive a complete cluster-fuck.

"*Calculating route.*" The female voice stated from the GPS unit.

"You damn well better!" Henry had missed his turn. Not hard to do, even with a GPS. His business partners had joked about the grid of streets in Boston. What grid? The place had been laid out along cow-paths in the 1600s and no one had bothered to reroute the streets.

Another stab of piercing pain and Henry doubted the intelligence of his decision to drive himself to the ER. He wasn't about to call for an ambulance. Not worth the cost, regardless of what his insurance covered. He didn't know and wasn't going to find out. He could have called a cab. That would have been the smart thing to do but he was already paying for the rental car.

"*Turn right in a quarter mile.*"

Henry glanced at the glowing map on his smart phone. Meridian Street.

The GPS dinged for a turn, he almost missed it. There was no street sign but it must have been the turn. He hoped. Sometimes city streets were so close he wondered if he had turned at the correct ding.

Another stab of deep pain. He cried out. He yanked the steering wheel, pulled alongside the parked cars. Unfamiliar with the rental car controls, he took a moment to find the hazard lights and jabbed the button. He gasped and caught his breath. He grabbed the bottled water from the cup holder and gulped down the last sips, even though his stomach was roiling.

His stomach wasn't the actual problem but the pain nauseated him.

"Fucking kidney stone."

He peered out the streaked windshield. He saw no lit windows, no porch lights or driveway illumination. Only streetlights. Parked cars lined the street. No pedestrians. No luck catching a leaving car.

Where the hell was he going to park?

He drove on, pained and frustrated.

After a few blocks, the GPS chimed again.

"You have arrived at your destination."

He looked at the smart phone in the cradle. The glow lit his pained features. The address stated he was at Boston City Hospital.

Henry craned his neck, looking out the window, past the rain drops on the glass.

"The hell I have."

Across the street, he saw light. A brick building with entrance columns capped with rounded spheres. An old chandelier lit the entranceway. The building matched the age of the light fixture. It looked like a small apartment building, with a row of windows over the entrance doors. Initially, Henry thought the wrought iron fire escape over the door was a balcony, until he realized it was designed for occupants to crawl from their windows.

One window was lit. There were no front steps. A ramp ran from the sidewalk to the entrance. Letters were carved in the stone over the double doors;

BOSTON CITY HOSPITAL
EAST BOSTON RELIEF STATION
EST. 1902

East Boston Relief Station?

What the hell was that?

The place didn't look like a hospital. Henry doubted it had ever looked like a hospital, even in 1902.

Taken with the odd building facade, Henry hadn't noticed the obvious – an open parking space, directly in front of the ramp entrance. He glanced around, looking for signs or meters. Nothing appeared to forbid his using the open street space. Pain stabbed again.

"Jesus fuck!"

Henry whipped the car around and backed into the space. Sweat pouring down his face, he wiped his sleeve across his forehead.

"Ticket. Towed. I don't give a shit."

He grabbed his briefcase from the floor. All his luggage was at the hotel not in the car. He still had two days before his flight home. The business trip would be shot but so long as he passed the damn stone before then and could go home on time.

Henry paused, stood in the drizzling rain and stared at the entranceway. He couldn't possibly be at the right place. No blue light, no red light, no EMERGENCY sign. No ambulance driveway. Wooden doors and brick and stone.

The doors opened. Light from an interior hallway limned a woman. She wore a long white dress, and her hair was tied back. Blue cloth wrapped her head.

A nun.

No, not a nun. A nurse. Or perhaps a nun who was a nurse. Her old-fashioned uniform included a dark blue cloak she had placed over her hair to keep off the rain. A white surgical mask hid the lower half of her face.

She glanced about, looked past Henry and then returned through the doors.

"Wait!"

Henry dashed up the ramp. Dark lines indicated where once there had been tread strips but they had long since worn flat. His dress shoe soles slipped on the wet surface. He almost fell on the hard surface but kept his balance. He let out a gruff growl. Kidney stone – bad. Broken bones plus kidney stone – he didn't want to think about it.

He entered the doors into a hallway of brown and white tile, cold and antiseptic. He saw a flash of dark blue and white turn a corner ahead.

"Nurse!" Henry cried. "Nurse!"

Around the corner, a heavy steel door led to a staircase. Henry took one flight, saw lights through small window on the next door and stepped out. He was in a long hallway, bright fluorescent ballasts leading the way. He saw signs with directional arrows. RADIOLOGY(X-RAY.) BLOOD LAB. 1025-1065. EMERGENCY.

He followed the signs to the emergency room.

A wave of sounds washed over him. Voices. He passed rooms with pinging electronic machinery. Televisions droned quietly. He assumed they'd be shut off shortly. Wasn't it already late?

He hadn't noticed how quiet the night had been outside and in the old entrance. He tried not to consider the entrance too much. He didn't like the idea of anyone being able to walk into the hospital unchallenged – as he had. He thought of patients, vulnerable in their beds. He could be one of them.

Henry lost track of the signs and only realized he'd reached the emergency room when he saw the seats and the usual cast of misfortunate people. Pain etched on some faces. A mother holding her child's crudely bandaged arm aloft. Plenty of hacking, wheezing, and coughing. Old, young, foreign and domestic judging from those who were able to carry on quiet conversations.

A rotund woman behind a desk waved him over.

"Can I help you, sir?"

"Yes, you can. I'm in some pain and would like to see a doctor."

"OK, sir. Have a seat."

Before the woman – Peggy, if her name tag was not borrowed – could ask, Henry pulled out his insurance card and license. He didn't know if she needed the license.

"Thank you." Peggy took the card and license and started typing. "I see you are ambulatory?"

"What?"

"Can you walk?"

"Yes."

"Are you here alone? Did anyone drop you off?"

"Oh, alone. I came in through the old wing."

"The old wing?"

"I'm not from around here. In town on business. I have a rental car. GPS freaked out and turned me all around. Wound up at the old entrance."

"Old?"

Henry paused. He looked back over his shoulder and noticed the emergency room entrance. The proper entrance. Lots of glass, a half-circle drop-off driveway. Even a few parking spaces in a small lot. Well-lit with proper signs. Automatic doors.

"It looked old." Henry shifted back to face Peggy. "The other entrance, anyway."

Peggy stared at him as if he had more information to offer. He didn't.

"Yes, I'm here alone under my own power. Never mind entrances."

Peggy gave him one more overlong glance and then shrugged.

"Do you know why you might be in pain? Injury?"

"Kidney stone."

"Oh. Oh my, you poor thing."

Peggy typed a few more notes.

"All set here." She pointed at the corral of chairs in the waiting room. "Have a seat please. We'll have nurse see you as soon as we can.

"Oh, and Mister Alvarez?"

"Yes?"

"If you need to urinate..."

"Come get a cup and a screen from you."

"You *do* know the routine."

Henry smiled and winced.

He'd been focusing on the pain until Peggy had mentioned urinating. The inside of his pecker burned like venereal disease. He wanted to go but knew he hadn't had enough to drink. His bladder was protesting but not bursting.

A nurse called him into a side room ten minutes later. Her ID badge declared her name as Dora.

"OK, Mister Alvarez. I'm going to ask you some questions." She gave Henry a tiny smile. "What brings you here this evening?"

"Kidney stone."

"Oh." Dora wrinkled a brow. "Already made the doctor's analysis?"

"I've had them before. Save time you some time and a misdiagnosis."

The first time Henry had had a stone, the doctors spent hours on the wrong area, focusing on his intestines because the pain was in his lower abdomen. Only when his kidneys had ached did they get a clue.

All the cartoons and comedians joked about pissing fire and screaming at the urinal. The reality was the pain came when the stone moved through the tiny ureter tube from the kidney to the bladder. That's when the screaming and spinning circles on the floor happened. Once the little fucker reached the bladder, it was home free.

Another stab of pain. Henry winced and clutched the cold steel arm of the chair. He shifted in his seat – a useless gesture. Changing his posture did nothing to alleviate the discomfort.

"I know the drill."

"I'm sure you do."

"Just get me fluids and x-ray me and tell me if I can pass it at home or if you need to go in and get it."

"I'm also sure you understand we have a protocol and a doctor needs to make those decisions."

Henry meant to be knowledgeable and cooperative. He was clipping his words and being curt because he was clenching against the pain. He supposed he sounded like an asshole.

"Sorry. Just annoyed I have another one – away from home, too."

"Certainly."

Dora came around the desk. "Need to take your vitals."

Pulse clip on his finger, thermometer under his tongue, the blood pressure cuff squeezed until Henry thought his arm would fall off. The red-hot ice pick sensation stabbed above his left nut and he thought he'd crack the thermometer, chew glass, taste mercury and spit blood. The moment passed.

"Really shot up there," Dora commented. She undid the cuff and his aching arm was grateful.

"Bad timing. Bad pain right then."

Dora returned to the computer station, typed in the numbers and a note about his pain. She nodded and let a courteous grin cross her face.

"You take a seat back in the waiting room and we'll get you in for an examination soon as we can, Mister Alvarez."

Impatience and pain went hand in hand. Henry tried to be a model emergency room patient. The herd thinned. Two wheezers and one hacker disappeared around the corner. Henry wondered how many beds they had in the curtained bays around the central desk of the emergency room. He hoped some people were being sent home with antibiotics. He knew how long getting a hospital room could take.

Commotion at the entrance dissipated Henry's boredom. Two burly paramedics rushed a gurney through the opening doors. The woman pushed as the man leaned over the body, administering C.P.R. on the run.

"C'mon! C'mon!" The man uttered the phrase as a mantra.

Blood covered the pillow, oozing from a raw wound on the left side of the patient's head. Jacket and shirt open, leather pants – one leg shredded – and heavy boots. A motorcycle accident. Not a surprise with the rain, though Henry was perplexed about the head wound. He thought Massachusetts had a helmet law but he didn't ride motorcycles so it wasn't a point he had checked before embarking on his business trip.

The crew and the accident victim disappeared around the corner where the noise grew louder. The remaining people in the waiting room sat in shocked silence. A few shook their heads in pity. Sick, they were all farther from death at that moment than the man on the stretcher.

Henry felt a lump of empathy, sympathy, and dread settle in his gut. The frailness of mortality crashed against his psyche. Anyone could have their head split open like an egg at any time. You never knew. He briefly pondered what his kidney stone would have done to a person one hundred – two hundred years ago. He thought of his kidneys blocked and filled to bursting and catastrophic failure as they burst. He squirmed in his seat and it had nothing to do with his current pain.

Though, the pain was impressive on its own.

He walked around when he could, clenching teeth when the pain stabbed extra hard. He sipped water from a bubbler. After he'd lost track of how many steps he'd taken, he decided the bubbler wasn't enough. He pulled out his wallet, found some single bills. A sign indicated a vending machine around the corner from the bathrooms.

The slot gobbled his money. He considered, briefly, choosing a soft drink but the best thing for his body was water. He pressed the buttons, the bottled water thumped into the tray.

He groaned as another ice pick stab throttled his guts and groin.

"Jay-SUS!"

Henry closed his eyes and leaned his forehead against the cool glass. He heard footsteps and a swish of clothing. He opened his eyes. In the reflection, he saw the nurse in the old uniform passing behind him.

He turned. She disappeared around a corner.

The kidney stone pain subsided to an aching throb. Henry felt an odd curiosity. He should return to the waiting room. He didn't want to miss his name being called. But she had been at the old entrance. She could explain.

He vowed he would look around the corner and go no further. Just a glance, a moment. Then he'd head back to the waiting room and sit with the rest of the nocturnal invalids.

The blinding white hallway went on forever. A gurney was parked against one wall. Henry saw the soles of boots. The nurse was gone, the stretcher unattended. Henry felt a tug of morbid curiosity. He stepped slowly. He figured it had to be the motorcycle accident victim. No sheet covered the body but the man had to be dead. Henry had spent time in a hospital corridor when an emergency room overflowed but surely someone critically injured wouldn't be shunted into a hallway.

The leather pants were gone. Cloth riding pants were tucked into knee high boots - more suitable for horseback than motorcycle. The boots were wrong. The man who'd come through the emergency doors had worn clunky motorcycle boots with squared toes.

It couldn't be the same man but who else could it be? Henry hadn't had a clear look at the face. The head wound had taken his attention. He looked at the man on the stretcher.

The left side of the man's skull was a bloody ruin. The injury nearly identical to what Henry had seen on the leather clad man.

Henry glanced around, worried. He didn't want to create a commotion. The staff must have known what they were doing. You don't just forget about a cranial injury in an emergency room. No one could neglect their duty so badly.

"Hello?" The hallway swallowed Henry's words.

The nurse couldn't have gotten far.

"Hello?" He spoke louder but his throat squeezed the words to a higher pitch.

The man on the gurney twitched. Henry saw the head loll over onto the wound, blood seeped into the white pillow case. Then the convulsions started, legs kicked wildly, boots thudding haphazardly off the wall

"Jesus!" Henry leapt away from the gurney and ran for the emergency room.

"Nurse! Nurse! Someone! Anyone! Help!"

By the time he reached the waiting room, Dora and Peggy intercepted him.

"What's wrong, Mister Alvarez?" Peggy asked.

"You've got to help!"

"What's wrong, Henry?" Dora chose to use his first name in an effort to calm him. "Are you in pain right now?"

Henry shook his head violently. "Not me!"

"Not you?"

"The motorcycle guy! The one who came through here!" Henry pointed around the corner. "They just left him in the hall! How the hell could they do that?"

The two women rushed off.

Henry staggered into the waiting room, groaned as the adrenalin shock ebbed and the kidney stone stabbed again. Sudden exhaustion battered his body and he collapsed into one of the chairs.

The pain persisted. He felt his hands tingling, skin growing cold. Nausea threatened, his body too stupid to know that even though his guts hurt, you couldn't puke up a kidney stone.

He shut out the world, heard nothing but his own pounding blood vessels and white noise crescendoing in his ears.

"Mr. Alvarez?"

He grunted. He wasn't sure he could open his mouth without vomit coming along for the ride.

"Mister Alvarez, are you alright?" He recognized Peggy's voice.

"Pain has kicked up," Henry said, his mouth clenched hard.

"Do you have a fever?" Dora asked. "Did you self-medicate before you came to us, Henry?"

"Self what?"

"The pain, Henry. Did you take something for the pain?"

Henry shook his head, the motion aching with the pounding and throbbing. His head was getting worse. The kidney stone stabbed furiously. There was nothing but white noise. He wouldn't open his eyes, couldn't. Everything was too bright.

Was he getting a migraine? He'd never had one before. Goddammit. A migraine and a kidney stone.

"Is he okay?"

"Who?"

"The motorcycle driver!"

There was silence. He slitted one eye open against the light. Peggy was gone, returned to the reception desk. Dora gazed at him with a mix of pity and a touch of anger.

"That man was D.O.A. You shouldn't have wandered into the emergency ward, Mister Alvarez." Dora had stopped the informality of using his first name.

"I didn't. I didn't go near the beds."

Dora pressed on, her anger rising, clipping her words. The patients and staff do not need such a disruption."

"I saw him in the hall."

"We don't leave the deceased in the hallways."

Henry held his tongue and didn't mention he had also seen the man spasm on the gurney. He sagged back in the uncomfortable chair and gave up arguing.

"Will I be seen soon?"

"Yes, Mister Alvarez. We're very close to getting a bay open for the doctor to have a look at you."

*   *   *

The circle of round lights glared down. Henry closed his eyes. He shivered. He felt a draft. Why didn't hospitals issue proper pajamas rather than stupid johnnies that never stayed on correctly?

He opened his eyes again. Masked faces of nurses came and went from his view.

"The doctor will be here shortly," a green mask said.

X-rays had shown the kidney stone to be too large to pass. Henry had missed the cut off by a millimeter. At least there would be no incision. He didn't relish the thought of waking up with a sore pecker. Whenever he mentioned his previous experiences with stones, someone always brought up the idea of sound waves and a hot tub. Sit in the bath and get the stone smashed from the outside. Nice idea. No one had ever offered him the option.

Up they would go.

He tried not to squirm.

The doctor arrived - a urologist named Keppler whose bushy salt-and-pepper eyebrows glowered over his surgical mask. He looked over the equipment, traded nods with his staff.

"OK. Mr. Alvarez. We're ready."

A blue mask loomed over his face.

"I'm your anesthesiologist. I'll start you with a little something to take the edge off."

Henry watched the hypodermic needle slip into his I.V. bag.

He didn't feel the next needle prick at all. He hadn't noticed the anesthesiologist leaning over his right arm.

"OK, Mister Alvarez."

A numbing chill crept up his arm.

There was an odor. A strong, sweet smell with a chemical undercurrent. Rum? Almost. Sweet as rum but somehow a thinner, more ethereal scent.

She was there. The nurse with the cape and the old-fashioned hat. White mask over her face. She pressed a wad of cotton against his face and the medicinal smell filled his nostrils, invaded his lungs, moved through his blood.

He tried to scream. His tongue was a lump of useless flesh.

The nurse leaned in closer. Her face pale, her eyes beautiful. An odd brown tone colored her hair. She was a sepia photograph moving through the real world. She heralded salvation and death.

Her heavy, white cotton mask fell away.

Henry screamed and fell into darkness.

*   *   *

The world rushed into Henry's consciousness. He saw light and heard muffled sounds. He was too weak to open his eyes. He focused on his hand, his fingers, down to his pinky. He fought off the returning sleep and put all his will into his little finger. It twitched.

"Mister Alvarez? Henry?"

"Wha...?"

"You're in post-op, Henry. Just take deep breaths. It helps work the anesthesia out of your system."

Breathing was the only activity Henry could manage, so he took the nurse's advice.

Once he felt returned to the real world — albeit tired — he remembered the surgery room. He remembered the smothering. Panic momentarily washed away fatigue. He glanced around.

There were eight beds. Five were empty. Two slumbering patients occupied the others. Two nurses — a man and a woman in proper, modern scrubs, monitored the ward.

Of the caped nurse, there was no sign.

Some hours later, they wheeled Henry into a hospital room. The second bed was empty. No roommate was expected. At least, not that evening. Henry muttered a thanks.

He slept. A real sleep of exhaustion and lack of rest and perhaps a touch of flushing out the last of the anesthetic drug.

A male nurse, square-faced and tan, woke Henry.

"Need to check your vitals."

Henry proffered an arm to the squeezing blood pressure cuff. The room tilted a little.

"Crap. What did they gas me with?"

"We don't use gas anymore." The nurse laughed. "We just give you a shot."

Henry remembered the needle in the I.V. bag, the one he hadn't felt in his arm. Had they injected his arm?

"But that smell." Henry shook his head, the memory strong enough he felt smothered again. He took in a deep breath to dispel the sensation. "The stuff packed a wallop."

"You must be a little disoriented. From what they tell me, you've had a long twenty-four hours."

A memory rose from Henry's past.

"My mother. My mother had her tonsils out when she was a child. On the dining room table. A doctor who made house calls. He gave her ether. She counted from ten backwards and didn't finish before she was out. She never described the odor though. An ether soaked wad of cotton."

"Ether?" The nurse put on a casual smile that didn't hide the growing concern on his face. "Do you think we're savages? Ether went away, long before gas did! Have you been reading historical medical journals?"

Henry forced a casual smile of his own.

"No, no. I guess I'm jumbled up, like you said. I'll get some rest now, if you're finished."

The nurse's expression relaxed.

"I'm all set. You go ahead and get your rest."

Henry slept, drifting between heavy slumber and near wakefulness. A few nightmares bolted him upright, heart racing. He could not remember details of the dreams. He suspected the cause, sepia-haired and white-masked. He dismissed those recollections as soon as they appeared.

He felt the urge to piss and it was real, not a phantom sensation from a kidney stone. For that, he was thankful. No bedpan convenience for him, he was expected to get up and move. The room was quiet, evening settling in. He shifted off the bed, clutched the I.V. stand, and wheeled it along to the bathroom.

He pissed through the mesh and paper colander – a precaution in case they might catch some stone fragments to analyze. Post-op blood colored his urine with a rosy tinge. The stinging wasn't too bad.

He heard someone in the room. Nurses always picked the best times to check in.

"Out in a minute," he said over his shoulder.

He washed his hands, checked that his johnny covered his front and his ass cheeks, and paused at the threshold into the room.

He had a roommate.

"Dammit."

Whoever had brought the patient had disappeared quickly. The patient wasn't hooked to any monitoring equipment and neither were they I.V.ed. The bed had been switched. The buttons, railings, heavy frame absent, it wasn't a bed at all. It was a gurney.

A chill crawled down Henry's spine. No one could have walked out with that bed in the time he had taken to piss. They would have needed to dismantle it.

Half the room had changed. Not Henry's half. Where the separator curtain would have demarcated the territory, the floor tiling changed from uniform beige to alternating brown and white tiles. Tiles he had seen in that lost, mysterious entrance hall where he had first arrived. Only now he recognized the brown was sepia. A three-dimensional photograph overlaid on half his hospital room.

He stepped forward, I.V stand's plastic wheels clacking across the floor.

His head started to ache. The same white noise throb he'd felt in the waiting room. It got worse the closer he approached the room division. It wasn't an evenly distributed headache pain. The left side of his head felt warm and wet, scraped raw. He put his hand there, pulled it back to look, expecting blood but his hand was clean.

The man on the gurney had the same wound. The same man. The one abandoned in the corridor with the out-of-place clothes and boots. Not the man who'd come in through the emergency doors clad in leather and modern motorcycle boots but this phantom.

She entered through the door. Henry knew she would. For some reason her dark cape retained its navy blue color but the rest of her was a sepia portrait walking tall, shoulders back and head high. She stood beside the gurney and stared at the prostrate man.

The scent of ether. A cotton wad in her hand, so soaked it dripped, drops splashing floor where she stood.

Her masked face turned to Henry. He saw her beautiful eyes swelling with tears.

"You knew him. Who was he to you? A husband? A lover? A brother?"

She ignored Henry and pushed cotton wad against the ghostly man's face.

"You." Henry's eyes went wide. "You killed him!"

She raised her hand of sleep and death.

"You euthanized him."

She stepped away from the dead ghost and turned toward Henry.

She let her mask fall.

Henry couldn't understand why he'd screamed in the operating room. She was lovely.

Until she crossed the boundary. Then her face held all the charm of death, a skeletal relief of malice.

Henry broke his trance, gave an inarticulate cry and stepped back. He had forgotten the I.V. stand, and he tripped over it. His ass hit the hard floor. The nurse of death loomed over him.

"It's not me!" He wanted to shout but he clamped down on his hysteria. After the waiting room incident and what he had told the nurse about being gassed, the staff were already eyeing him warily. He didn't want to be carted off to a lunatic asylum. "I wasn't the motorcycle crash! I'm not the one repeating history! He already died!"

He pointed at the bed. "Whoever that man was, whatever year he died, he wasn't me. Isn't me. Leave me alone!"

Her skull face leaned in close. Henry smelled an undercurrent of perfume while the ether stench overwhelmed his nostrils. She held her hand of merciful death to her side, pausing and uncertain.

She nodded then, withdrew across the boundary back into the sepia scene. She approached the bed. An unheard sobbing shook her shoulders.

Henry closed his eyes.

When the ache in his head stopped, he opened his eyes. The room was normal. The second bed, modern and empty. The sepia tones were gone.

He climbed back onto his bed.

There were no further spectral incidents, though they did appear in his nightmares. The following day, hospital couldn't discharge him fast enough.

Henry spent the better part of an hour walking along Meridian Street, searching for his rental car. When he found it—covered in tickets but thankfully not towed—he made it a point not to look at the building facade where it was parked.

The East Boston Relief Station belonged to the past. Henry wanted it to stay there.

The Mouse

Larissa Glasser

1

A year before I was stabbed to death, I saw a mouse in our living room. I was pretty baked at the time, so I hadn't noticed it at first. I'd been watching some old noir film left running on the TV by someone else in the house and I was trying to figure out what it was.

I lived on the top floors of an early-20th century duplex with these two other trans girls Brooke and Debbie who were around the same age as me. The apartment got dusty a lot and was difficult to keep clean. But it was warm and cheap and our landlady was good to us.

I didn't have much to do that afternoon so I'd sat down on the big couch and decided to see if I could gather which film it was. I used to study film as an undergrad but I'd dropped out during my second semester because I went broke. This film didn't ring a bell, but it starred Laurence Tierney. His character killed a lot of people.

My throat got dry, so I reached for my Diet Snapple. When I turned my head, I noticed the mouse resting on the smaller couch at the far end of the wall. It was facing sideways, and when I realized it wasn't afraid, I watched it for a while instead of the movie.

The thing was brownish and very small, no bigger than two inches not counting its tail. The room got darker as evening came. The TV became the only source of light, a cheerless, icy glare. The movie finished, and the closing host commentary was annoying—too chipper—so I muted the sound but kept the TV on so I could keep watching the mouse. I was too invested in this new activity to get up and turn the big light on.

The mouse was breathing rapidly. It never moved from the spot, nor did its tail move.

I knew we'd had a so-called "mouse problem" for a few weeks. We could hear them scuttling in the walls. Brooke, the most industrious member of our household, said she was sick of finding mouse turds in her workshop, so she was going to get some poison before the infestation got worse. I didn't want her to kill anything, but my girlfriend Jennifer had tried to convince me that Brooke was doing the right thing, because mice were all vermin who needed to be killed.

"But mice are cute!" I'd told her when the subject came up.

"They're *vermin!*" she'd said. "They're dirty!"

Some of Jennifer's outer chin hairs, softened from several months of laser treatments, glowed in silhouette in front of my blue lamp. She'd looked angelic. I'd went for a main tuft of the hairs and clutched them. She didn't break away but had stared back at me, trying to maintain her stern expression.

"Mice are cute," I'd told her. "I like animals."

"Come on! Mice are *vermin!* They'll eat all of your groceries and shit everywhere!"

"They're *cute!*"

This game had gone on for a bit, back and forth, and had become increasingly more childish until she just dove at me, wrestled me out of my clothes, called *me* cute, and fucked me high and wild. We usually came at the same time. Sometimes life was nice to us.

Anyway, it looked like the poison was working, because the mouse was breathing at a steadily slower rate. Watching it made me sad, though. I wanted to help it somehow, like with an antidote or something. I could have put it outside to face the city. It was so little. It never meant to hurt anyone. Why hadn't it moved yet? Apart from the debilitating effects of the poison, maybe the mouse hadn't noticed me to begin with.

I turned the TV off, got up from the couch, and flipped the big light on. The mouse was still there and it wasn't moving. I almost went to pick it up and keep it with me for a while, but I didn't. Animals crawl away to die in peace. They know what they know, some sort of resigned meditation. Once I saw a cat stumble behind her owner's couch just to die out of sight.

I went upstairs to my room and tried to read for a while, but it was difficult to concentrate. The words weren't reaching me.

I went downstairs a few hours later to get some water. I hoped the suffering had finally ended for the mouse. I looked in, and it wasn't there anymore.

2

The Christmas before I was stabbed to death, I went to my mom's house just outside the city for the first time after I had finally corrected all my documentation. I didn't dress down nor tie my hair back. I'd had it with her conditional parameters which only enabled her state of denial over who I was—her only child, her daughter. I'd stipulated this before I agreed to go visit. I'd worked too hard at this to just detransition for a 48-

hour visit. My mom said "okay" in a sort of exasperated sigh, as if giving in to a child's tantrum for the sake of blissful silence.

I went in a biz casual, navy-blue, sleeveless A-line dress, and I did my best to look conservative and assimilated. I also wanted to prove to her that I was happier than I had ever been—that I'd done okay despite her throwing me out of the house that past Spring.

I mostly read during the train ride down. The coach was mad-crowded, of course, passengers on their way to gluttony, MVP sports, and capitalist family drama. Many of them also looked tense as fuck, for whatever reasons.

I kept my face down a lot. I was at that embryonic stage of transition where all you can feel are eyes on you, judging you, deriding you, and that everything you're trying to achieve, inside and out, doesn't amount to anything at all.

As we approached the last stop, I put my sunglasses on, and stood up against the window as riders queued for the exit. I caught my reflection and thought I looked very Kim Novak. The trip hadn't been so bad. I just had to keep my shoulders back. A confident posture can sometimes help us pass.

Part of the shopping area by the depot was under construction, which made me think of the poisoned mouse. I didn't know which housemate—Brooke or Debbie—had taken its body off the couch. If it had been Brooke, she'd probably flushed it down the toilet. I would've buried it somewhere leafy and peaceful. I should have done something to help it, to stop the suffering as it held onto life despite the poison.

Had the mouse felt sad? Did it blame itself for all the bad things in life, and for what was happening to it? Did it want to say goodbye to its friends?

My mom wasn't there. I knew I wouldn't look quite as recognizable to her. It wasn't that cold out, so I decided to wait, suddenly wishing I smoked cigarettes again.

A black sedan kept circling, which seemed weird because most of the others were just idling for pickups. On its sixth turn, it pulled up closer to me. Out came my mom, and the trunk popped open for my suitcase. I waved and took off my sunglasses. After a pregnant moment, she smiled at me with closed lips.

We mostly rode in silence. After a few tries at small talk, I finally gave up and watched the dull landscape go by. I missed the city already, and my tuck was coming undone as I sat in the leather car seat. I hated that, most of all.

We got to my mom's house. After the driver took my bags out of the trunk, my mom swiped her card and dashed into the house without saying anything. She didn't look me in the eye ever again.

Not even on Christmas.

3

A month before I was stabbed to death, Jennifer broke up with me.

"What did I do wrong?" I asked her on the phone.

"It isn't you, it's me," she said. "I just need a little space. You know you can be intense."

I told her I'd try to calm down and be less so. I conceded I'd been having a hard time with my mom and being unemployed, and so much of that drama was spilling over. Plus, my estrogen levels felt random and emo.

"Can we at least talk about it in person?"

"I'm not sure what you think that would achieve."

Jennifer had taken me horseback riding the previous summer—I'd never been on a horse before, and the world looked so hopeful and green from up on its back.

Jennifer had kissed me deeply and blown on my neck as we lay together in the shade of a wide oak. She had gotten me into new music. Sleeping with her felt so awesome. Finally, so much had begun to make sense.

And then—it was *over*.

I sat in the TV room a lot, the same place I'd seen the dying mouse. Debbie came in one time, sat down next to me, and smoked me up. We'd been talking about which Drive Like Jehu album was better or something when I suddenly asked her, "Do you remember seeing a dead mouse on the couch last summer?"

"A dead mouse?" She looked down at the cushion and shifted her body out a little. "Gross!"

I told her what I'd seen that one time, and that I'd just left it alone, but that it was gone later.

"Brooke must have gotten rid of it, then," Debbie figured. "D-CON's one hell of a drug, hey?"

Debbie and I had hooked up a few times before I'd met Jennifer, and I was still into her, but she was dating this other trans girl Allison by then, and I didn't want to stir any shit. So, we gossiped about other things. I think Debbie was just being patient with me. After a while, she headed out on her scooter, and I stayed in the living room. I watched the mouse cushion. Everything seemed peculiar there, a whirlpool of energy that pulsed around where the mouse had waited to die.

I wanted me to die instead of the mouse.

Then, in a quick spasm, I *attacked* myself. I tore at my arms with my night-polished nails. I hit my forehead with my balled fists. I kicked the floor. I screamed at the ceiling.

Sorrow convulsed me, so badly I began to hyperventilate. Oh my *god*—

—*I need to die I need to die I need to fucking die...*

I reached the point where I lost all faculty of language and could only scream a single word, rhythmically with each time I hit myself: *DIE! DIE! DIE! DIE!*—

I only stopped because I grew exhausted. I didn't wipe at my tears. I wanted to let them dry.

I tried to take deep breaths. It only helped a little. My throat and lungs felt so constricted.

I felt minus something else, though, like a crucial part of my being had dissipated from me like smoke. My eyes felt sunken. I felt terrified that I reached this new level—how close had I come to finally killing myself?

I wanted Jennifer back. I wanted my mom to love me again. I wanted the mouse to come back so I could try to help it.

Later, up in my room, watching the night sky from a lotus position on my futon, I thought I heard a scuffling in the wall. I perked right up and craned my head. But the sound didn't come again.

4

A week before I was stabbed to death, my mom called me to say she never wanted to speak to me again. She had opened some mail that had come from the library. I had an overdue book. She took one look at the title, and blew up at me.

"There's no way you're one of those *creatures*!" she yelled.

"Mom?"

I stood shaking in the kitchen, listening to her go off.

Wave after wave of doubt and loss crashed through me. I felt like such a failure. I had done everything wrong—there was no other way to explain it.

"Mom, can I at least try to say something?"

"NO! There's nothing you're going to say that is going change my mind about what you're doing to yourself! And you know what? I saw your browser search history at home and I've got your doctor's name! I'm going to sue her for turning you into a *monster*!"

"I haven't been able to afford to see my doctor in months, Mom."

Brooke had stockpiled several months' worth of estradiol and had been generously dosing both me and Debbie for months.

"I'm still going to sue her for malpractice! That way, she'll never be able to ruin another boy the way she ruined you!"

I looked over at the mouse cushion in the adjoining TV room.

There was something going on there in the place where the little rodent had held its death vigil, a tight energy of divining. Then, in keeping with my mom's viciousness, my own desperate screams echoed back at me from the couch—*DIE! DIE! DIE! DIE!*—

NO—I have to just stand up for myself, finally.

"Mom, please stop this," I said quietly, hoping she would reciprocate in tone. "I'm not a boy. I'm your daughter."

I thought I saw the mouse there on the couch again, breathing fast and dying sad. Next to it, I sensed something much larger, a shadow, hitting itself violently. But I turned away and dismissed it as a figment of my imagination, or a latent stress-factor of the conversation taking place.

"You're not my daughter! You're nothing! You're a *freak*!"

I closed my eyes.

"I'm your *child*."

"Not *anymore*! If I'd known what you were going to do to me, I would have *aborted* you!"

Then, I don't know how, everything inverted and I started laughing at my mom.

"Do you think this is funny?"

"I think it's *hilarious*, mom."

Yeah, funniest shit ever.

"Stop laughing, or you just lost a mother!"

I regained my composure after about a minute.

"Mom," I told her, "I really think you need professional help."

"I'm going to make you regret this. And all you will ever know from this will be eternal misery. *Idiot*."

She hung up on me.

I glanced at the mouse cushion again. The energies I'd seen there had dissipated, and all traces of my weeks-old screaming fit had also stopped. Everything was quiet again, and I was alone.

I wonder what my mom did with the library book.

5

The day before I was stabbed to death, I bought my own copy of that book online, along with a couple of others. But they didn't get mailed to me in time for me to be alive to open the box. I hope someone else gets the books and finds them useful.

6

An hour or so before I was stabbed to death, I met Nora for the first and last time.

Debbie had asked me if I'd drive her to this party a little way out of the city. Debbie's scooter wasn't highway-worthy, and I didn't have anything else going on, so I said "sure, let's go!" It would be good to get out of the house for a while and maybe meet new people.

I'm introverted by nature, but I once we got there I felt like I'd been sprung from prison. I'd never seen so many of my people gathered in one place, not even in group. It was like we had our own *nation*. Maybe I'd also felt at ease because Debbie was introducing me around. I'd gotten to talking with Nora because she'd overheard me say something about David Cronenberg.

"Wait, really?" she brightened and swooped in, "I'm from Toronto, he's like royalty there!"

Her face astonished me, very aquiline, and she had green eyes. She had on this sleeveless black dress that made her many arm tattoos stand out in the ochre light. She had thick, black hair that she'd tied up in a bun, and she shamelessly wore a lot of Claire's mall jewelry.

"Which Cronenberg's your favorite?" I asked her.

"Videodrome, of course!"

"No way—that's my favorite, too! Nicki Brand is my spirit mom!"

"I know, right?" she beamed with rose lips. "Long live the new flesh!"

She led me to the living room and the party became this sideways thing that didn't concern us so much anymore. Conversations took place around us about this or that, but we were only us. I even forgot about my mom.

"Yeah," Nora said. "I've lived here for about three months. The commute to work blows, but the job is chill and I can look how I want. Sometimes I even work from home."

"I got fired for looking how I want," I said with my head down.

Nora gestured before me with her gilded hand, and drew me back into her eyes. She looked determined to keep us both charged. She also seemed so confident and comfortable with herself, so I finally asked her.

"How long have you been alive-for-real?"

"Just a few years," she shrugged, not affronted, nor breaking her intent gaze. "I mean, my parents knew something was up, so we all worked it out together. I had a feeling they'd be cool about it."

Damn, if only.

She asked me how I knew Debbie, and I told her how I'd been kicked out of my mom's house and fled to the city where Debbie met me in group, and happened to be looking for another housemate at the time.

"Wait, your mom kicked you *out?*"

"Sorry," I said. "It's really bad with her."

"Don't apologize! She's the one who should be fuckin' sorry."

I asked Nora if she'd like to grab a drink when/if she had a free moment in the city. She said hell yeah and we exchanged info. Turned out she lived in that house.

Later on, I got a text from Debbie saying that she'd decided to stay over at her girlfriend Allison's, and she could catch the train down if I wanted to head back on my own. I texted back "OK COOL I think I will." I didn't want Nora to think I was only interested in a one-night stand. I think about this a lot now—Nora had been practically *dragging* me toward her room. To this day, I don't know why I was so shy about that. It was like I was denying the possibility something good might happen for me. It was like I couldn't fully process her affinity.

She didn't let me get away without a hug, and then an obvious re-invite-kiss.

During my drive back to the city, I realized I totally should have stayed there with Nora.

7

A minute or so before I was stabbed to death, I pulled into this highway rest stop that had a big food court. I got out of my car and looked around. There were some Mack trucks resting in the darkness of the other lot, and beyond them, only the night-full, black woods. The air felt humid, so I was glad I was just wearing my camo tank top and an emerald, knee-length skirt. I looked down. Did my flip-flops make my feet look huge? My hands, shoulders, and neck also? But it was high summer. I hadn't wanted my toenails to smudge, hence the need for open-air feeties.

I wanted to stop thinking about my mom, who would point out every defect in me.

I went inside.

The main area looked mostly deserted, only one dude wearing a crisp, white, collared dress shirt at a far table, calmly eating a cheeseburger. The menu choices up on the displays didn't appeal to me. Pizza Mania, which was closest to me in the hall, had this big, scowling white dude behind the counter. He was staring at me. His face scrunched as I passed by—*not passing.*

I might have made a face right back at him.

Or maybe I just averted my gaze and sped toward the bathrooms.

Whichever it was, I wish I had chosen the *other.*

I went into the ladies' room, and I thought of the mouse again. Had it been a whole year since I'd watched it dying on the cushion? It had been summer then, too.

I think I loved the mouse.

I picked the cleanest stall I could find, sat down, and peed. I thought of Nora. Did she think I was a big dumb jerk? I wondered if I'd ever see her again.

I wanted to.

I flushed with my foot, and went to wash my hands. This place had those pain-in-the-ass, motion-activated towel dispensers, where you have to wave your hand at limited intervals for a little bit of paper. I dried my hands after a few tries.

I opened the exit door, and was immediately shoved back by a *nightmare.*

As soon as my eyes locked with his, my heart started racing. At first, I didn't recognize him as the guy from Pizza Mania. He took that little moment to punch me in the stomach, and then my face. I stumbled back against the sink. It hurt.

The bathroom smelled like decades of wrong in a way it hadn't just seconds earlier.

I realized what was happening, but I couldn't adapt to it. Any semblance of my survival instinct remained passive. My system had given up.

He shoved me with both hands back into the stall I'd used. His eyes narrowed to glistening slits.

"I'm going to *kill* you for coming in here, you *fucking degenerate.*"

He grew so much bigger as he approached. First I tried to get past him, but I was walled in. I fumbled for my phone, then realized I'd left it in the car.

"I'm going to cast each and every one of you freaks into the fire," he promised me as he grabbed a switchblade from his back pocket. "*HE COMMANDS IT.*"

He clicked the weapon open.

Then there was only me, him, the knife, and a suddenly compressed world. I didn't have mace, a panic alarm, a flamethrower, or anything else that might have helped me. Just my ID holder and my keys on a coiled ring. I held the keys sharp-end-out toward him. He smiled and raised the blade. The fluorescent lights hit it just right, and the knife gleamed with divine judgement as it came down at me.

8

A second or so before I was stabbed to death, the Pizza Mania guy looked down at me as I tried to shield myself.

"Please," I begged him. "Please, just let me go home."

He shook his head, and sighed, "It's too late."

"I'll give you my car."

"I take my orders from God," he said. "Not from fags."

I remember thinking I wanted to tell him about the mouse.

The first stab was the loudest as it came in a low arc, right up into the middle of my stomach. I screamed "*NO!*", long and drawn-out. My voice sounded weird.

He grinned wide and twisted the knife in me.

"You're getting what you deserve," he spoke softly into my left ear. "You *made* me do this."

My arms and palms bore the brunt of the assault, until he went for other places on my body, and my screaming and kicks and pleas spiraled into a more exhausted moaning.

"I'll suck your dick if you'd just let me go."

He seemed astonished at my temerity, and said "NO!" in a mocking lilt.

I don't know how many times he stabbed me. It seemed to never be over. The pain got worse every time.

I still feel it now.

When I finally collapsed onto the cold tiles, a mist of simple incredulity enveloped me.

I was twenty years old.

9

A second or so after I was stabbed to death, the air burst with bright energy as I began to rise. I looked down at my body for a second, wondering if I would take long to heal, and would they give me pistachio ice cream in the hospital. My blood pooled beneath me, a creeping oval of darkness. My eyes were wide and still. I looked—*diagonal*.

The pizza guy was washing my blood off his hands when he glared toward the bathroom entrance. The dude wearing the crisp, white collared dress shirt I'd seen eating at the far end of the food court was aiming a handgun at him with two strong arms.

I began to weep as everything began to sink in.

And then the whole scene—just everything—faded away.

10

A minute or so after I was stabbed to death I stood on the shore of an obnoxiously bright lake.

I was still wearing my camo tank top, my emerald-green skirt, and my flip flops. My blood was collecting and then draining out viscid at my toes. There were stab wounds on my abdomen, stomach, forearms, palms, neck, face, and groin. Most of my skin was drenched with blood. I wanted to wash it off and curl up somewhere. I wanted the mouse.

The bright water was right in front of me. It was the only place left to go. It was calm and welcoming.

I tried not to think of Nora, Jennifer, Debbie, Brooke, or my mom.

I wanted to go home.

I didn't know where I was. That happened to me a lot in dreams, I'd float to someplace I couldn't recognize. It always felt uncanny and bewildering. But this was different. I couldn't scare myself awake.

I crouched onto the tightly-packed sand and watched the sun-bright, milk-white water.

And then I saw the mouse.

It broke the surface of the lake, forming small ripples that glided out to me. It sat on the same cushion it died on and peered in my direction. I'm not sure what it thought of me looking all gross. The mouse brightened, and invited me to come into the water.

I wanted to look like my old self again.

I wanted be cleansed.

Plus, there was the mouse again—calling me, *accepting* me.

I went in.

The water felt nice and calming, and I began to wade toward the mouse. Its tail writhed happily and its whiskers moved as if it was eating something. Then I remembered the poison.

I called out to it, "*NO DON'T!*"

It was at the D-CON, a little sprinkling of death. I had to get the mouse to stop eating, to spit the poison out. Then realized I was too late when it stopped moving its tail, and fell onto its side. Its hind legs twitched in the air a moment, and then stopped.

The mouse faded away.

I lost my sense of direction. I felt a new fear that I'd hit a dead end of some new mistake. There was nothing around me but the lake's vast, white featurelessness.

It got colder as I looked down at myself, and saw my wounds bleeding worse than before, forming dark, swirling rivulets around me in the bright water.

I kept swimming, desperate to regain the mouse and try to save it. A shadow moved ahead of me—it was something to lock onto. I rushed toward it, until I hit the stark reality of the far shore.

I emerged from the lake. I was drenched and cold, and my wounds still bled. I looked around.

Everything around me was just as unvarying the lake, a simple white all around me, even more disorienting than the water, because there was no horizon.

The mouse was gone.

11

An hour or so after I was stabbed to death, I still hadn't found my way. There was nothing to latch on to, just that bright haze all around. After wandering for a while, I finally came to a rift. It looked like someone had cut an exit door in a veil of white lace. I couldn't see anything through it but darkness, yet maybe it offered a way out. I went through the opening, and found myself back at the rest stop.

It was still night.

The pizza guy was sulking in the back of a police car. My blood was all over him. I went back into the food court, toward the bathroom. My body had been removed, and the homicide detectives were testing the scene. There was blood everywhere. Someone was muttering about my being trans, that I was probably HIV positive, and that they probably needed hazmat gear. He went on to say there wasn't much mystery to what provoked the attack. I didn't want to stick around and listen to him extrapolate.

I left them and rose into the summer air. The woods were dark, and the roads not so busy at that late hour. I let the winds take me wherever, and I screamed at the stars until dawn.

12

The day after I was stabbed to death, I visited the house I'd lived in with Debbie and Brooke. The mouse couch was still there. I wondered if anyone was home. The kitchen was empty.

I went right up to my room. I still had some weed left, and I wanted to smoke it all at one throw. I knew it wouldn't do anything for me, but I liked the thought anyway. My desk still had a half-full mug of orange tea on it, and I wanted to drink the rest. I looked at the books on my shelf, and I wanted to finish reading them.

I went down the kitchen and tried to think things through.

I looked across into the TV room, at the mouse couch. Nothing there. I groaned.

I didn't find Brooke in her workshop, so I figured I'd just leave.

I went out into the calm summer day, and heard a clamor of voices down the block.

I followed the noise.

Brooke and Debbie were sitting at the bus stop, holding each other. Their contorted faces were huge and open. Debbie was screaming through her sobs.

I watched them for a little while. I couldn't reach out to them and say goodbye or anything, so I shot up into the sky. When I returned to the white, featureless waste, I reached level ground and looked down at myself.

I was still bleeding all over my front. It seemed to be *pulsing* out rhythmically, as with an artificial heartbeat. I dropped to my hands and knees and began to crawl, leaving a trail of slime behind me that reached back forever.

13

A week after I was stabbed to death, my mom buried me.

She was the last person on earth I wanted to claim my body, but she did.

I hadn't made a will, so she dragged her toxic ass-crack into the morgue and instructed them to completely detransition me, starting with cutting my hair short. My breasts had grown a little from about two years of HRT, but she put me in a button-down shirt two sizes too big to conceal that. They acetoned my nail polish off. The tie they clipped onto me was a sober navy blue, and it looked stupid—the suit jacket looked even worse.

This was such an indignity, and she carved my deadname onto the cold, Plexiglas marker even though I had legally corrected my name several months before. She even made the wake open-casket to drive her point home. The media came in droves, gloating over the scandalous marvels of aberrant existence.

My mom didn't cry once. She just looked inconvenienced. She might as well have worn a tracksuit to the ceremony.

I hope I never see her again.

I was curious to see who the Pizza Mania guy was, so I went to his arraignment. His name was Paul Butler. He'd been a registered sex offender for six years and had assaulted four women since his late twenties. Class act.

Someone decided to be awesome, and held a candlelight vigil for me near The Common. A few hundred people showed up, including Nora, Jennifer, Brooke, Debbie, Allison, and even our landlady. They walked about a mile to the state house, and someone I didn't know (she looked famous) gave a speech about the need for stronger hate crime laws and that the so-called "bathroom bills" were just hate-legislature, by my very example alone. I don't think any new laws would have stopped the pizza guy from doing what he did to me, but it was nice to have someone finally speaking up in my favor.

Nora hooked up with Brooke. I watched them holding each other at night. They looked happy. It was good that Nora found a better person than me.

Someone on Fox News suggested that Paul Butler had killed me to prevent me from sexually assaulting a young girl in the ladies' room, therefore my murder was justified.

The clip was re-Tweeted and liked thousands of times.

I attended Paul Butler's trial. I hovered in the back. They tried to play on that "bathroom" and "trans panic" defense, but it didn't fly. He never showed any emotion, even during his sentencing. He was found guilty, and he's in prison for a while. He reads his Bible a lot. Every time I go to check to see if he's feeling sorry for what he did to me, there's just less and less of him. Our fun is over.

14

The month after I was stabbed to death, Jennifer died of a blood clot that traveled to her lungs. She'd rubbed her sprained ankle after falling off a horse and after she began to fade, her roommates rushed her to the hospital the next morning.

She died on the way there.

I felt the shockwave and raced to her side. I saw her hovering near a far ceiling corner in the brightly-lit morgue. I asked her if she was okay and if we could be friends again. She turned to me slowly, then her face scrunched up as if she was trying to see something past a glare. She shrugged and went away. I looked down at her body. She looked peaceful.

Unlike mine, her wake was packed with real people. She was cremated according to her wishes, and she was eulogized under her correct name and pronouns. Her parents were nice to everyone who went up to them. I wanted to say something about how happy she'd made me when she'd first asked me out. I had never thought anyone would like me, and she ended up showing me a world of animals, music, and kindness. She had helped me feel better. The memory of my time with her stood in such stark contrast with how I'd felt before, and how I feel now.

Toward the end, when people were lining up to pass by Jennifer's remains, her white roses, and her photograph, I saw her hovering high up at the back of the chapel. She wore a billowing, white, knee-length dress. Her shoulders looked pretty, and her hair floated like a bed of happy eels. I floundered toward her but my progress was slow, like when you try to run waist-deep in the ocean.

I called to her and she looked up at the rafters, as if she sort of heard me but couldn't pinpoint the direction of my voice. I saw her smile at something else up there, and then she glided forth, eclipsed a sunbeam, then vanished completely.

I never saw Jennifer again.

15

The Christmas after I was stabbed to death, something odd happened.

As I stumbled through the bright, unchanging haze—sobbing and bleeding as usual—I encountered another presence. It was small, and at first I thought I bumped into a mannequin or something. But no, there was someone else there. Alarmed, I shot upright. I couldn't believe I had made physical contact.

But she was there, crouched in a fetal position, covering her ears with her hands. She wore a pretty white dress like the one Jennifer's spirit had on during her wake. Her hair was a little shorter than mine had been when I was murdered. She looked up at me, and then stood about the same height as me. Her eyes looked familiar, but I couldn't quite place her. I said hi. I told her my name and asked hers.

"Hi?" she said. "I—don't think I have a name."

I nodded, sure.

I didn't press her to try to remember it.

She's confused and traumatized—maybe even a fresh death, I thought. *Just try to draw her out. You fucking need her, whoever she is.*

I felt a little embarrassed in her presence too, there was no way for her to *not* notice my horrific appearance. Blood pumped from each of my stab wounds. But I remembered and applied what I'd tried to practice in life—when I was in the presence of another person, I always tried to at least *seem* affable. That was usually impossible when I was alone, because I couldn't stand myself. And now that I found another person in that void, I felt I should try and help *her* not feel alone.

She squinted into the mists about us, and finding nothing to lock onto from her old life, she looked up at me.

"How do we get out of here?" she asked me.

"There's nowhere else to go."

"How can that be?"

"I've been back in the world—it's worse, because there's nothing left to see," I said. "That gets old after a while."

"You can go back?"

"Only as an apparition. I can't touch or feel anything there, and it's too painful to see my friends going on with their lives, having new experiences, as if no one misses me. It wore me down. So, I just stay here now."

She looked around again, insecure and anxious.

I wanted to help her.

"You can sense and feel me?" I asked her.

She brushed my arm and nodded. Again, I felt contact.

I asked her to describe what she saw. She said she saw me in a white dress, billowing hair, serene bearing. No stab wounds.

We could only see our own shattered bodies in death. To others, we looked fine.

"I don't want to stay here," she winced. "I want to go back."

I had no answer to that. I didn't want her to leave me behind. So, I tried to tell her my story and what had happened to me. The high-profile cruelty of my death seemed to appall her.

I hoped my candor would bring out her own story, but she didn't reciprocate.

Still hopeful, I went to my most vulnerable place, and told her about the mouse I saw dying on that summer day.

"Wait," she said, coming closer to me, as if to verify the honesty in my face. "Where did you live?"

I told her about my neighborhood, and when I mentioned Debbie and Brooke, and her eyes widened. She told me they were her housemates too, and that was the house where she'd died.

We looked at each other up and down, and as we recognized ourselves, each in the other, a terrible realization hit us both. When I'd seen the mouse dying, I'd wanted a second chance to help the poor thing so badly I had offered up my own life in exchange for the life of the mouse. And my wish was granted, only not how I'd thought possible.

The result stood before me.

Instead of killing myself, I had to be murdered. No wonder I'd had my meltdown. I couldn't commit suicide, but I needed to die.

I saved the mouse. It didn't succumb to the poison. It went free.

No wonder I hadn't found its body.

The girl and I looked at one another in disbelief and horror. We'd both just met the stark *possibility* of something we'd been so desperate to prevent in life. And still—it was all for the sake of the mouse.

Suddenly, something that sounded like a low-flying jet screamed above us. The ground imploded beneath our feet. A darkness blossomed, and then we were shoved apart by cold blast of rusty-smelling air. We cried out as the distance between us yawned, and the bright haze turned to ash. I never saw my ghost again.

16

It's now been a year since I was stabbed to death.

I can't stop crying and bleeding all over myself.

I didn't want to die. I wanted to *live*. I wanted to be with Nora and have picnics with her on the summer grass. I wanted to ride horses. I wanted to be reunited with my people. I wanted my mom to finally come to her senses, and love me as her daughter. I wanted to find a great place to sit, drink tea, and read for hours. I wanted to help weak and small things. I wanted the mouse.

But now I'm lost in this wasteland of regret. I guess that's just the way things are. And they will be this way forever.

And yet, today I decided to find a way back into the living world, its love and warmth and promise walled off from my being. It's a place where I may never have existed to begin with. I'm still going back.

And even though it's going to hurt a lot, and make me feel even more sad and tired, I'm going to keep looking for the mouse.

There's something I need to ask it.

The Walking Man
Matt Bechtel

Not all ghosts are dead.

There's this guy who walks around my neighborhood. I see him when I'm out running, and I run all the time. I call him "The Walking Man," because that's all he ever does — just walk, slowly down the sidewalk, apparently to nowhere. Although that's being kind of me, because honestly, he doesn't walk well; his left leg is mangled, deformed, and encased in a massive brace, so I should really call him "The Limping Man."

But that seems mean, because his leg is the least of his problems.

The left side of his body is burnt, covered in scars that make his skin look like a half-peeled beet. Particularly his face. It's harder to notice when his hair gets shaggy, but he looks like a Batman villain when he's cleaned up and it's cut short.

But that seems mean, because the burns aren't his worst problem, either.

The Walking Man is … not well. I don't know how to put it more delicately than that. He's not all there. He barks at himself — or, at least, I hope at himself — as he shuffles down the street, his eyes typically locked on his underperforming feet. On the days he's particularly agitated (when I assume he's off his medication), he punctuates his shouts by throwing punches at the breeze. The saddest part is that he can't even clench a fist with his left hand, so he swipes at whatever demons are tormenting him with a pathetic claw.

I've even seen him off the sidewalk a few times, pacing across an empty church parking lot or some random family's back yard. I've almost stopped my run to try to get him help or to alert a homeowner that there was a potentially dangerous person on their property.

There's a home for the mentally handicapped on Hope Street, right at the bus stop two blocks up from the Y and three blocks down from the little mom and pop liquor store. I don't know for sure, but it doesn't take a genius to figure out where The Walking Man lives.

I'll come clean and admit that, no matter how un-PC it is of me, I'm not comfortable around the mentally disabled. I know it's not their fault, and I know they're not bad people, but they just give me the heebie-jeebies. I think it's because I know that there, but for the grace of God, go I. I'm an athlete and strong and healthy and bright, yet the only difference between The Walking Man and me is one genetic imperfection. One chromosome a tiny bit off. That's why whenever I see him, whenever I pass him running in the opposite direction as he's struggling his way up the sidewalk, I look away. I check for foot traffic coming up behind me, gaze across the street, or even follow his lead and keep my head down until I'm clear of him. In other words, I do pretty much anything to avoid acknowledging him.

It usually works, but every so often, it doesn't. With how much I run and how often he's out walking in the same neighborhood, the law of averages dictates that there are times when our gazes catch one another. And it's when we share a fleeting glimpse as I race past that The Walking Man really, truly, scares me.

His eyes are like the un-boarded windows of an abandoned house — dark, reflective, and clinging to the feint memory of who used to live within.

My left leg acts up whenever it rains. It's from an old injury, and it's been that way for so long that it'll literally start to ache the second the sky darkens and I can smell the atmospheric change of an impending shower. Fortunately for me, the bus stop I mentioned (the one right in front of the group home) is a perfect place to pause for a stretch. All the pedestrian foot traffic passes in front, so I'll sneak behind it for a few lunges and hamstring stretches to keep myself loose and my leg from cramping up. It was on one such drizzly day that The Walking Man left the house at the same time that I had stopped. I turned away from him per usual, but as he passed one of the nurses, who was clearly waiting for her ride home, she waved to him.

"Enjoy your walk!" she called with a genuine smile.

The Walking Man meekly raised his good hand in a sad wave as he pulled his body down the street in the other direction.

There was an elderly woman waiting at the bus stop as well. She patted the nurse on her thigh and told her, "You're a saint, working with those poor people!"

The nurse smiled. "I especially have a soft spot for him. Such a tragedy!"

My ears pricked up and I stretched towards the back of the bus stop to eavesdrop.

"How so?" the old woman asked.

"He wasn't born like that," the nurse explained. "Traumatic brain injury. He was out jogging in the rain one day and a drunk hydroplaned and jumped the curb. His leg got caught underneath the car."

"No!" the old woman gasped.

"It took four surgeries to save it. But nothing could save his mind — he got dragged along for a block and a half, his head bouncing the whole way like a basketball!"

"So … so those burns …?"

The nurse nodded. "They're 'road rash.' Pavement scars."

"Dear God!" the old woman exclaimed. "That poor child!"

"You get used to working with the disabled," the nurse explained, "but him? It's just so, so sad. He *lives* for his afternoon walks; says he enjoys them because they remind him of who he used to be. That's why we use them as his reward. When he takes his meds and finishes his P.T. every day, he gets to go out walking."

I couldn't bring myself to listen anymore, so I finished my stretching and shot off in the opposite direction of The Walking Man.

It took me a solid half-mile to realize why I had bolted so suddenly — I was wracked with guilt. Everything I had assumed about The Walking Man had been wrong. He wasn't born like that, with a gimpy leg and an even more gimpy brain. And the burns I'd always figured were the remnants of an uncontrollable act of self-harm were a horrific reminder of the hell through which he'd literally been dragged.

Most of all, I felt guilty because I'd been right — there, but for the grace of God, went I. Not from some freak genetic crapshoot, but from pure, dumb, unfathomable, tragic luck. I can't tell you how many miles I've logged over the years running these very streets; on any given day, that drunk who jumped the curb could've jumped into me.

Which was when I decided to stop being such a piece of shit to The Walking Man. There would be no more looking away, no more avoiding those glances that scared me so much. On that day, I made a solemn vow to myself that I'd wave or smile or nod whenever I saw him. I knew he was capable of reciprocating since I'd seen him wave to the nurse, so once we'd established that level of comfort I'd start saying, "Hello!" as I passed. I wouldn't push him and I'd take it slowly. It's not like I envisioned us becoming friends and going out for coffee, but I was determined to treat him like a person instead of some feral animal. After all, this was his neighborhood, too.

My plans may have been good and pure, but The Walking Man seemed to want no part of them.

It was only a few days later that I found myself barreling towards him as he dragged his way up the street, shouting and gesturing at God-knows-what as he did. He was in front of the little Mexican bar and restaurant that always had really good chips and salsa, but really mediocre everything else. Unabashedly, I focused my eyes on his like lasers and smiled the biggest, most sincere smile I could fashion.

The Walking Man stopped in his tracks and stared straight through me, dumbfounded, as I ran by.

Undaunted, I decided to up the ante the next time I saw him, which again was only a matter of days. Every so often, when I feel like mixing things up and running a few sprints, I'll hit my old high school for a couple of laps around the track (in fact, I'm there often enough that the track team doesn't pay me any mind as I lap their best runners). I was just leaving one afternoon, crossing the lot where they park all the school buses for the night, when I spotted him. He was a block down and shuffling up the other side of the street, so I darted across a crosswalk and bee-lined toward him. He stopped and stared when he saw me approaching. *Good!* I thought. *Progress!* This time I not only smiled, but flared my eyebrows and nodded three times.

Still, no response. The Walking Man gazed through me with a slack jaw, as if it were unbelievable to him that someone would show him a bit of kindness.

So I upped my ante again and changed my normal running route to essentially loop around and around his block. Since I knew he walked every afternoon, I figured I'd have more chances to interact with him the more time I spent close to the group home. I was right, because I caught him two blocks up the very next day at the front steps of the public library (right by the weird street sculpture the city commissioned from a local artist years ago that never made any sense in front of a library). This time I threw it all at him at once — the broad smile, the nods, and the flared eyebrows. I even waved, a subtle two-finger-salute that undeniably conveyed acknowledgment and goodwill.

Again, The Walking Man did nothing. He just stopped and stared at me with what I would swear was incredulity.

About five steps past where he'd planted himself, I looked over my shoulder to see his empty, perplexed stare had followed me up the street. Although I realize now that I was reaching and seeing what I wanted to see, I honestly thought that might have been a positive sign.

Then, the next time I saw him, I almost ran into him.

I don't know why I wasn't thinking more about him that day; I guess I was just zoned out and focused on my run. Still, I was on my new route around his block, and without realizing it I almost steamrolled the poor guy. I had my head down and he had just left for his afternoon walk. We met at the junction point of his front path and the sidewalk like a pair of trains with no conductor working the crossing. Fortunately, I slammed on my foot brakes a half a step before we collided and threw my hands up like airbags. He stopped, startled, and for the first time I was face to face with The Walking Man.

I smiled, nodded, and spoke my first words to him. "Hello!" I said. "Heading out for a walk?"

The Walking Man started screaming.

I stepped back and started apologizing profusely. "It's okay!" I insisted, trying to calm him and to keep myself from freaking out in kind. "It's okay! I'm sorry! I didn't mean to frighten you!"

But he wouldn't stop shouting. Over and over again, unintelligible and violent sounds burst from his mouth as he wildly swung his hands at everything around him except me. Pedestrians across the street stopped and stared, and cars driving by slowed to a crawl.

"Please!" I tried again. "Please, I'm sorry! It's okay! We're both okay! No one got hurt!"

Mercifully, reinforcements arrived when the nurse whom I'd seen at the bus stop charged down the front walk with two other nurses in tow. "Martin!" she called as she approached him. "Martin! What's wrong?"

"I'm … I'm so sorry!" I tried to explain to her, "I almost ran into him, but I stopped! I didn't touch him! I promise, he's not hurt!"

She ignored me and put her hands on The Walking Man's shoulders. At first he tried to wriggle away, but she was insistent (clearly, unlike me, she knew what she was doing and how to handle him when he got like this). "Martin!" she demanded. "Look at me! Look at me!" When he finally did, her voice became soothing. "Tell me what's wrong, Martin."

That was when I heard The Walking Man speak for the first time. "I …" he stammered, with a tongue that sounded four sizes too big for his mouth, "I saw 'im 'gain."

"Saw him?" the nurse asked. "Saw who? Saw who again?"

"I'm sorry," I repeated, "I almost ran into him! I think he's talking about …"

"Me," The Walking Man interrupted me. "I saw me 'gain. Me before."

"Um, hi!" I tried to interject, this time with half a chuckle. "I'm not sure what he thinks he saw, but I'm pretty sure this is all my fault!"

"Martin, we've been over this," the nurse explained in voice that was somehow tired, comforting, and yet stern all at the same time. "You did not see yourself. There's no young version of you running around the neighborhood."

"Excuse me!" I tried to get her attention more forcefully, but to no avail.

The nurse slid her hands down to hold The Walking Man's to keep them from flailing, and another stepped forward and gently rubbed his back and shoulders. Slowly but surely, his rage and fear melted, but he wouldn't stop shaking his head. When he finally looked up again, I caught a twinge of honest pain in his usually vacant, dark eyes.

"Was me," The Walking Man insisted. "Wear ... my old ... Clash tee."

I took two steps back from the group gathered around him and stared down at my chest, right at a faded silkscreen image of the album artwork of *London Calling*. I'd bought this shirt at the first concert I'd ever seen, back when they played The Pavilion across town the summer when I was fifteen.

I didn't know what to do, so I just started running again, sprinting off in the other direction as fast as my legs could churn. That was when I realized that I couldn't remember the last time I *wasn't* out running. I couldn't remember the last time I'd eaten, or slept, or showered, or went to work, or even went home. Hell, I couldn't remember the last time I'd spoken with anyone. I'd just been running, for as long as I could remember.

Which was when I remembered that my name is Martin.

I was right about one thing — not all ghosts are dead. Sometimes, whatever it is that makes us, *us*, gets separated from our bodies by other means. It took getting dragged through the rain for a block and a half by a drunk to knock me out of mine.

But I was very, very wrong about another thing when it came to The Walking Man. There, without the grace of God, I went.

I'll be lying if I tell you I have any clue what's going to happen to me or how long I'll spend running these streets, but I know one thing for certain — I'll avoid The Walking Man's block from now on. There's no need for me to haunt him; he's suffered enough, and he deserves to enjoy his walks in peace.

My Work is Not Yet Completed
Nick Manzolillo

"I do not fear death. I had been dead for billions and billions of years before I was born, and had not suffered the slightest inconvenience from it."- Mark Twain

By the time Samuel Clemens stopped being entirely dead, the world had moved on. He wasn't surprised to find himself back in New York, within the West Village apartment he had inhabited for several years at the dawn of the twentieth century. He was born on the eve of Halley's comet soaring across the night sky and as he predicted throughout his whole life, he died the day after it returned, on his seventy-fourth birthday.

He died a rich man, whose every artistic whim had been met. He died with more friends than names he could ever remember, from celebrities to politicians to all the obscure and brilliant men in between. In his last years, he was told that he would be remembered. That America would remember him.

Samuel Clemens died alone, leaving behind a vast body of work and not a single living relative. He was not surprised that he awoke, a thin specter still clad in the white suit he requested to be buried in. He was not surprised, for there was one puzzle in his life that he never had the chance, nor found the courage, to solve, and it was that of his former apartment building in the West Village, a century old brownstone known only to the locals as *The House of Death.*

As a specter with his feet not quite planted on the floor and his hands incapable of touching the walls and stroking the cool glass of the window panes, Samuel was aware of the bitter irony of the place he haunted. How fitting, to find oneself a spirit in *The House of Death.* If he only could have drawn his fingers across a typewriter, he would have loved to write about it. He could walk through walls with ease, like panels of water, but he couldn't access the roof nor take a step out the front door. The worst irony of leaving something unsolved was that he was now a prisoner to his own curiosity.

Samuel's mother claimed that he was walking by the age of one, yet Samuel's first step after his re-emergence, if it could have even been called a step, lasted several decades. Unstuck in time, his mind swimming in and out of memories of who he was and what he had become, the world around him evolved. He was dimly aware, while peering through the building's many windows in the grips of lunacy, that the city was growing disproportionately, sprouting clumps of steel and brick like hair on a puberty-ridden body. Before he became conscious of his actions, Samuel watched through dulled senses as marvels sprung out through the world around him.

Advances in technology that influenced the lights, buildings and the streets themselves, all rebuilt countless times into vaguely familiar shades of what they once were. The irony, yes, Samuel knew it well. His entire catalogue of published work was based off satire.

Eventually, all rocking ships either sink or still and Samuel found himself in control of his mind and ethereal body. The decades stopped fluttering by him like the thumbed pages of a novel, and he became aware of the individual apartments and tenants around him. Mere moments after the revelation that he was back, that he had completed his transformation into a conscious spirit, he encountered the overwhelming presence of dread that he first encountered in this building as a living man.

The shadows that twitch of their own accord in the corner of a partially lit room, the wandering things just outside one's field of vision, and the chills in the air that draw visible the breath from the tenants living their partially aware lives around him. As a mortal, Samuel had little doubts that there was an evil in *The House of Death*, that there was a reason it was given such a name long before his last breath.

While inhabiting his West Village apartment, Samuel lived each and every day to the fullest. At night, with his dear wife Livy by his side, his alcohol-glazed rest was disturbed by a presence disguised as nightmares. The incidents were random and almost always after he'd been drinking; as if something were peering into his mind, running its bone-thin fingertips over his arms and lapping up some of the essence that made him real, that made him an artist. His work suffered and it was only after his wife became ill and they moved out that he became truly aware something had been wrong. Something had been sharing his and Lilly's bed, the very air they breathed. Years later, he wondered if it had fostered the sickness that killed her.

Despite being anchored in time, Samuel found himself suffering from some inexplicable phenomena that plagued both the dead and the mentally handicapped. One moment he would be wandering the apartment of a journalist and his wife on the third floor, and the next he'd be on the first, nodding his head back and forth by a street side window. Travelling up and down the four-story building's staircase would inexplicably take hours, during which he could only stare at the steps his shoes weren't connecting with, as if hypnotized by their rectangular symmetry. While giving a lecture in South Africa, he learned that certain tribes believed stitching an intricate pattern onto a quilt could fixate spirits and demons and offer protection. This fit in with what he knew of other superstitious architects in the world, from the creators of actual labyrinths to hotel corridors. There was also Sarah Winchester, a madwoman who used her fortune to build a mystery house full of stairs that lead nowhere, backwards rooms and hidden passageways, all in an attempt to confuse the legions of ghosts that allegedly haunted her. Samuel had assumed she was mad, but perhaps she was more intelligent than anybody.

Being dead, Samuel found that he was ridden with apathy. There was a certain restlessness - he could care less about life and death, as well as his purpose for returning to his former apartment building. His wife and daughters along with his parents and siblings, who had all died years before him, were just names and faces once dear to another man. Samuel lingered by the windows, half curious if anyone could see him from the streets below. Occasionally a child being dragged along by his mother would stop and point, only to be hurried along as its parents passed a wary eye over Samuel.

His curiosity would flare over the memory that spirits would oft be seen in windows and doorways, watching the living much like how he would sit in his garden before his death, watching cardinals and humming birds. Samuel's curiosity would fade before it could do him any good, before it could give him that familiar spark of inspiration, of desire and purpose. It wasn't until a child was dead that he began to feel alive again.

Aside from their modest wealth, there was nothing unusual about the building's tenants; accountants, artists, architects, the usual mix of the New York middle and upper class. Samuel passively flickered through their lives, imperceptible and having no impact on the environment around him. Snapping his fingers in front of a man's face registered nothing. Watching a young couple sleep didn't cause them to shiver and nude occupants the building over showed no signs of shame when he spotted them fresh out of a bath. Children, on the other hand, were a different matter entirely.

They couldn't see him, but they knew he was there. There were three children in the building, one a newborn often confined to her crib and the other two, toddlers, barely of speaking age. On the second floor, in the same unremarkable unit Samuel used to live in, a little girl living with her single mother pointed right at Samuel and said "man," which the mother promptly ignored while she was on the telephone, a fascinating device whose wirings had somehow wormed there way through the walls of the building. Considering the building was built in the mid 1800's, it was likely no stranger to such rude re-workings. Samuel paid the little girl no mind as he gravitated toward the window. He received only the briefest memory of his daughter Suzy, before the meningitis swept her away from a forever incomplete chapter of his life.

Despite being a dead thing, night was more uncomfortable for Samuel as a spirit than it had ever been when he was mortal. He was banished to the darkness after the tenants shut off their lights, and not even the distant glow of the streetlights could illuminate the rooms around him. The eye's natural ability to dilate when the lights went out didn't carry over into the afterlife for Samuel. The darkness around him was stronger than it had any right to be, which is why it took him a long while to become aware of the snakelike thing darting in and out of the shadows throughout the bedroom of the crib-bound infant. Samuel had been peering out the window with his arms clasped behind his back when something moved out of the corner of his eye and there was a sudden chill along his spine. Later, he would realize this was the first physical sensation he had felt during his re-emergence. He would also realize that chill was directly associated to the presence of the long shadow, as it made its way toward the child.

Through the faint aura of streetlights, Samuel watched as the shadow spiraled around the crib, disappearing entirely in clumps of pure blackness like an Amazonian beast stalking its prey through the underbrush. The roving shadow – had it dripped over Samuel during his stay here as a living thing? Had this been what had seeped into his dreams, perpetuated his wife's illness? A memory of emotion became reality, a dull spark burned in his chest. He imagined he could feel his heart beating. The reason he had come back, the reason he wasn't with his wife and his children was *there*. In that child's bedroom, within a physical world he could no more influence than an old woman's prayers.

"Be gone!" Samuel shouted, his mind conjuring up an image of a priest screaming at a scaly demon. It was worth a shot. Nothing within the bedroom and all that blackness changed, until a moment later when the door burst inward and the infant's father stumbled in.

Drunk, Samuel could tell from the way he staggered. A light switched on and the man peered over the crib. Samuel made to stand beside him just as the father began screaming and sobbing, shaking the crib and the soundless, still thing within. The shadow was a thief of more than pleasant dreams. It was a coward, snuffing out all that was weaker than it. Samuel faded through the floor then, his mind nearly scrubbed blank by the horror of what he'd just witnessed.

After the child's death, the entire building seemed alive with those roving shadows, hovering over shoulders and cradling ears. The building's twenty-one tenants all went through their various stages of grief, tears staining the floorboards around them as they'd sob and speak to one another in hushed tones before tossing and turning the night away. A few weeks later the doomed, now-childless couple moved out of the building, the father drunk as ever. Samuel, helpless, began to cling to the rekindled memories of his wife and daughters, and how they were stolen from him.

He first fell in love with his wife, Livy, when her brother showed him a portrait of her while they were aboard the USS Quaker City Steamship. It had been mostly a chance encounter, the man had heard of Samuel's celebrity status, read some of his novels, and sought him out. It's funny that Samuel never made a point of getting down the name of the artist who painted that portrait of Livy, who created a longing in his heart through a few expert slashes of paint and oil.

He hardly believed his luck when Livy's brother agreed to introduce them. A few years later, when she told him she was pregnant, oh his luck, where did it go wrong? His daughter Suzy died first, before the illness began to invade Livy and his other daughter, Jane. It took them both longer to die, Samuel having to lie to Livy about Jane's condition. The doctors with their halfwit diagnoses, deeming it necessary that Samuel not spend Livy's last few weeks with her; over concerns that he would "overexcite her". Samuel would slip her notes with the finest, most cheerful writing he could drive himself to produce. He recalled Livy's heart giving out. Jane's final seizure occurring in the tub she then drowned in. The years alone, before he died. Watching Halley's Comet come to mirror his birth, and complete his cycle. He remembers the warmth of the grass meeting his face as he collapsed, the sweet spring scent of an impending bloom. The moment of dying wasn't so bad, given the pounds of grief that had come before it.

Did the shadow hound Samuel because of the deaths that would overshadow all of his achievements? Was it warning him, those nights that he and Livy comforted each other after Suzy's passing? Or was it just sniffing him, admiring that whiff of impending misery? Samuel found himself howling, in a building where no one could hear him, with lungs that would never give out. He tilted his head to the ceiling, rising to the fourth floor and howled and howled as the days turned to night and Samuel could feel again, still dead but numb no more.

Settling down, he began his investigation anew. He had returned to this particular place for a reason. He couldn't face Livy and his daughters without proving to them that he could confront the roving shadow. That he could beat it back, and free them. Wandering from room to room, eyeing the dark spots that lingered in every corner, Samuel thought of his friend, the blossoming young scientist and inventor, Nikola Tesla. The young man was surely older now, unless he died too, but what he had proven to Samuel still rung in his newly awakened mind.   The electricity that the human body produces is awe-inspiring. Once, during a visit to Tesla's lab, Samuel was given a demonstration on how the human body can act as a conductor when holding a wire in one hand and a phosphorescent light bulb in the other. Several photographs taken of Samuel holding the illuminated bulb in the air were the proudest conversational props he had to his name, next to signed letters from the president.

The human body is capable of strange wonders under the vague guise of science, and given Samuel's present state and lack of mention of his current circumstances in the Bible, it was fair for him to assume that science ruled the world with a mightier grip than belief. And so it was with an analytical, scientist's rationale that Samuel began rooting out the darkness that inhabited the West Village building.

He studied each of the building's tenants like lab specimens under a microscope. He mentally checked off an ever-infinite list of quirks and expressions the tenants would make. The things they would say to one another and the faces they would make in private. The way one woman told her husband she loved him in one moment, and then clenched her fists and worked her jaw in frustration as she stepped into the next room. The building was inhabited by several cats and two dogs, all of whom detected Samuel's presence to a lesser extent then the children, twitching their noses and staring at him as he passed, the dogs occasionally letting loose a low throated growl which they'd then shrug off like he were no more than a pesky house fly.

Weeks and months trickled on. Samuel made a special effort to monitor the building's two toddlers, who both ignored him the older they got, only occasionally staring at him or frowning in his direction. Samuel found nothing amiss, no invaders seeping through the shadows. He at times wondered if he'd imagined the incident with the infant's death. Perhaps the only otherworldly mischief lay in the dreams of the living. Then again, Samuel thought, "I am here."

Despite his best efforts, time leapt forward. Tenants came and went, and Samuel continued his observations. During the moments when the tenants were asleep, he would lie in wait, diligent in spotting the shadow's return.

One afternoon he studied a mother and daughter—one of the same little girls who had waved to him as an infant—while they listened to the radio. The mother, Sarah Cleland, adjusted the transmission while her daughter, Jennifer Cleland waited patiently, her hands folded over her dress, her feet swinging back and forth in the chair. The advancements in radio fascinated Samuel, and were the first true wondrous additions to his afterlife. He couldn't physically manipulate a book or turn the pages but the radio, ah, he could listen to music and serial narratives to no end.

The little girl turned and looked at Samuel, springing to her feet and knocking her chair over in the same instant. "It's, it's…" she stuttered as her mother turned around and, to Samuel's surprise, she saw him too.

"Who…" Sarah began, rising to stand between Samuel and her daughter.

"It's Mark Twain, he used to live here!" The little girl shouted. Sarah's face grew pale. She recognized him. Hearing his stage name brought a smile to his lips.

"What are you doing here?" Jennifer asked as Samuel rose a few feet from the ground. The radio played Jazz.

"My work here is not yet completed." Samuel made as if to stroke the mustache he couldn't feel. Both Sarah and Jane jumped back with fright.

"He's gone!" Sarah shouted.

"He was a ghost!" Jennifer said and Samuel felt strange, since he continued to stand before them.

"He did Huckleberry Finn, Mom!" Sarah hushed her as she reached for Samuel, waving her hand through him.

"I know who he was. That man…" Sarah shook her head, peering around the room as if trying to catch him hiding in the corner.

"I told you there were ghosts, like that rotting smell in the hallway. He said his work wasn't done, do you think he's writing another book? Do we have any paper?" Jennifer ran across the room to the desk Sarah liked to open her mail at.

Smell in the hallway? What else has been going on in front of me? Jennifer slapped down pencils and paper and Samuel recalled a time his Suzy, no more than six years of age, asked him to tell her a story that was just for her and that nobody else was allowed to hear.

It involved a talking fish that liked to smoke pipe tobacco and play checkers, and Samuel would do anything to break his promise and tell it to Jennifer; to speak and cause a reaction other than fright. Then again, he should be lucky he was able to make his voice heard at all.

Sarah, a quick thinker, began to mess around with the radio antenna. It made Samuel think of his friend Tesla. If only he could somehow contact the man. There were ways to communicate with the living after all, ways to break down the barrier. It was then that Samuel wished he had warned Sarah and Jennifer. Or least asked them to spread the word about infant-devouring shadows.

There is tragedy in the form of an accident, and then there is malice. Sarah continued to fiddle with the radio while Samuel posed, ready to make his re-emergence, practicing what he would say. Sarah spent an hour with that thing, but they never saw Samuel again.

Time, what effect does it truly have on intention? When Samuel was a boy in Missouri, he thought he'd grow up to be a steamship captain. As a businessman, he nearly lost all of his book earnings with his idea for a typesetting machine, that blasted thing. Given that Samuel had no money to lose or prestigious awards to win in his current state, he wondered where he would draw the line and decide that he failed in his investigation. What would become of him when he did so? If he gave up, would he move on? What would Liv and the girls think of him? Surely they were watching.

A young family moved into the building, a man and a woman and their two daughters, ages six and nine months. For upwards of a year, they were fine, despite Samuel spending so much time roaming their third-floor unit that he forgot details about the other tenants. He even stopped monitoring Sarah and Jennifer, who continued to tell their story of seeing him to everyone in the building, maybe even the city. Hell, Samuel thought, maybe in some way he was the 'Bell of New York' all over again.

Evil is never consistent, he began to conclude. It rests often, for it would be otherwise discovered. Like a criminal pushing his luck, score after score, body after body. Evil is intelligence and if it gets its way, evil is forever. There is solace to be found in this, though. If evil knows to sleep and lay low, then that means there are forces out there who hold the ability to vanquish it. Evil fears death, the true death that brings with it an end to all levels of existence. Samuel smiled to himself upon realizing that there's always a way to kill something. If only he had someone to tell that to. Oh, what is a wordsmith without an audience?

As the young family went untouched, Samuel told stories to tenants while they slept. Notably Jennifer, but others, too, like the politician on the fourth-floor penthouse. A good man, fighting establishments that continuously buy out other members of his ilk. Samuel would have loved to talk with him in life, so he made sure to do so in death.

A lively, old woman, Mrs. Potter, startled Samuel into action by screaming in the stairwell on the first floor. Samuel made the mistake of traveling down the stairwell instead of floating through the floors, and in doing so became stuck in that incessant loop, helpless to hear her screams echo on and on.

"Stay with me, please," a man shouted as Mrs. Potter moaned.

"They were smiling the wrong way…" Samuel heard Mrs. Potter whisper and choke. By the time he was free of the endless maze of stairwells that seemed to go on and on in Samuel's mind, Mrs. Potter was dead and an EMT was loading her onto a stretcher, her body shrouded by a white sheet.

"I think she saw some type of animal," Samuel heard a man who turned out to be her nephew say, before wondering what type of beast that shadow truly was.

Samuel didn't like the television when he first saw it. In fact, he downright hated it. Hated the way it captured people, the way they moved and laughed. Picture and radio recordings were one thing but people? Moving around in that little box? To think that a ghost was disturbing…. What if television recordings made ghosts of everyone? Samuel began to feel silly, as he hovered over his would-be-friend of a politician night after night, watching that make-believe world.

He found the shadow through nothing more than dumb luck. Something wasn't right about the family with the two young children on the third floor. Samuel had no doubts that the infant was in danger, despite its rapid growth. Old ladies and infants, they fit together. Samuel was surprised to find the shadow slithering along the ceiling above the father, as he drank.

The shadow was the father's own personal black cloud and Samuel watched it, in awe, for so long that he didn't realize just how the man was drinking. Staring at the can, tilting it back, placing it back on the table without releasing his grip before launching it back again. Like a machine, drinking without thought, his eyes blank, his lips grim. The eyes weren't entirely blank, Samuel realized. He could see it, a part of the shadow dancing next to each of his pupils.

"Why?" Samuel asked. What manner of devil gained from death? Samuel always imagined hell as being in suffering.

"You don't know what pain is," the father said, finishing his beer and standing up. Was he talking to Samuel?

"I lost my wife, my daughters, years before I passed," Samuel said. There's no worse a person than one that measures you by your tragedies. The father ignored him, retrieved another beer from the fridge, and sat back down. The mother and the children remained in their rooms unaware.

The father, faster than before, finished his beer and then stood, walked right through Samuel and made his way toward his kids' room. Before opening the door, he turned, looked right at Samuel and said, "it gets easier, after a while," and then he strolled into his children's room and slammed the door loud enough to shake the apartment. Samuel made to follow him before a wall of shadow blocked his path.

Rippling and crackling like fire, the wall of black seemed to mock him, chuckling in a never-ending cascade like rainfall. Samuel raised a hand to the wall and the fingers on his left hand began to melt, his skin flaking off to reveal pulpy flesh and bone as he reeled back in horror. "Why?" he shouted again, hoping against half-logic that if one somehow caused evil to question itself, it'd collapse under the weight of its own intent.

Samuel rose from the floor, floating and flying without any sense of pleasure. Screams were coming from within the children's room. It was too easy to imagine what the fists of a two-hundred-and-ten-pound man could do to any adversary of flesh and bone, let alone children. Samuel began to scream, and as he did so, the light bulbs on either side of him flickered before shattering in an eruption of sparks and glass. He wasn't spared a moment to consider this new way of interacting with the world, as he was thrust into the total darkness, at the mercy of the shadow's intentions.

"Carlos what's happening? Carlos?" an unfortunate mother cried her mind-sapped husband's name. The chuckling flames of shadow surrounded Samuel. "What have you done? What have you done?" Samuel heard the mother's screams and realized two things. One, the shadow had been waiting a long time to use a man to do its dirty work. It had been salivating over the kind of horror it could create and it was pleased it now had an audience to its evolution. Two, Samuel was utterly helpless and incapable of saving a single person in the unit. He tried to vanish through the floor, but the shadow wouldn't let him. It had him. It was finally paying attention.

Time for Samuel became a grandfather clock dumped over the side of a steamship and sunk to the muddy bottom of the Mississippi. When he got a hold of himself, the world was reborn. The century had turned again. The television and its miniature companions ruled. People held themselves to a different standard. As Samuel shifted through the floorboards, he wondered where the shadow had taken him. How had it snuffed out valuable moments from his afterlife? He wasn't robbed of much, but something all the same. He found that everyone he had come to know as tenants within the building were dead, or moved out. So much for Sarah and Jennifer and Samuel's own easing into the advancements of the world. The shadow wanted him further out of his element, another confused spirit moaning over indecencies centuries past. No, Samuel wouldn't be taken for a fool.

He deduced the shadow must have a true lair, if not in the hearts and minds of men. If not within the walls themselves. The shadow must have a place to sleep, and rest, because unlike Samuel, the shadow was at home in its house of death. It had everything it needed and maybe, like Samuel, it was bound there. It's one slice of the afterlife to call its own. Maybe, somehow, the shadow had once been like him. It could have been

Samuel's imagination, but his white suit was much more silver and gray than he remembered

On the first floor, he paced the beginning of the stairwell and thought of Mrs. Parker. The front door had changed, wires had been strewn throughout the walls and the building, how much of it was truly the same? Like the ship of Theseus consistently rebuilt until not a plank of wood remained of the original vessel, what was it that kept the building the same? What bound it other than a miserable shadow and a frustrated dead man? Samuel clenched his fists, and found himself sinking.

An age-old question he once pondered as a boy was, what if a ghost sank to the center of the earth? What if it sank and kept right on sinking and ended up in China? Or wherever bouts Missouri was lined up with if you stuck a pencil through a globe. Samuel sunk up to his chest and hoped he'd find out that answer quickly. Try as he did to go through the front door and emerge onto the roof, he never considered what might lie below. The house had no root cellar that he knew of, no underground labyrinth guarded by a minotaur to call its own. Samuel tilted his nose up and gave in. Failure as he was, he was ready to leave the house in the West Village, one way or another.

He found himself in the deep, dripping black of a sewer. It could have been nothing else. He didn't need to see or smell. He could feel it, shivering along the nerves he wasn't supposed to have. This is where it slept, the shadow. This was its true kingdom, it was never a resident of the building at all. An invader, much like Samuel. Like Samuel, slowly learning to influence the world, only, in this case, by snuffing a fresh pair of lungs, tripping an old lady and manipulating the open mind of a drunk. Samuel had talents, too. Much like how one is born with a knack for an art or a calling, in death you have ways of manipulating the world—even if the world has to catch up to you—through lights, radios and wires of all sorts. As Samuel he was forgettable, but as Mr. Twain? He was timeless.

The shadow was weakened, preparing for a long hibernation. He had it cornered. Twain's emotion, when tuned just right, could burst a light bulb. He couldn't touch the shadow, couldn't physically harm it. But the house of death? He couldn't make the shadow bleed, so he'd make it homeless.

Mark Twain rose above the sewers, shaking free the dancing nerves that tried to curl his spine. It was nightfall, and he visited each tenant, whispering into their sleeping heads and changing the pattern of their lives. He waited until morning. One by one, each of the tenants left the building: some for work, some for school or the pleasantries of a day off. Others oddly, with little reasoning as they lumbered to Washington

Square Park, unsure of their intentions. All behaved exactly as Mark Twain intended.

As the sole not-quite-living resident of the building, aside from the shadow, of course, Mark positioned himself within the building's middle, between floors and units, within a nest of wires and electric outlets. Born and perished in the passing blaze of a comet, he had landed here, in a place where reason and logic were shredded into lunacy. Where his words and his whit no longer mattered and he was stripped to nothing more than a good suit only he could admire. Mark Twain reached out and clenched his eyes shut of a world gone strange.

As a boy, he once worked on steamship with his brother. Called away to follow his passions as a journalist, his brother was killed by an exploding boiler on the very steamship they had operated on together. Death laughed at him, from the very beginning of his lifetime. It took his wife and children as compensation and left a rich man with no one to leave his possessions to. Mark Twain only had his words, tossed among the world and also taken from him, taken and twisted by all who may use them. He would have a say in one matter, at the very least, before pulling with every ounce of soul he had left in his pale, spectral form.

TVs exploded. Outlets poured flame and light bulbs shone like miniature supernovas. Mark Twain fed the sparks until all around him melted and oozed, charred and blackened. For a moment, he admired the distinct beauty of such immense flames. Within them, he could feel his heart and how it soared and wept, for all the tenants lost, for the black clouds that would rise above his dear New York and how all of West and Greenwich Village would be a mess of soot and ash for weeks to come.

Mark Twain rode the collapsing floorboards with his feet pointed like daggers, stabbing into the shadow's lair within the sewer. It squealed, too tired to flee as the fire consumed it. "Passion!" he screamed into laughter, for the troubles of the world occasionally needed to be illuminated, dug up and made to answer for all the pain they've caused.

Mark Twain drowned out the shadow's squeals with his own laughter, before the flames parted and he stepped through a door that may have always been there, waiting for him to knock. As always, he left this world like a man who knows how enter, and exit, the stage.

Ghosts In Their Eyes

Trisha J. Wooldridge

1.

She watches. She watches. She watches their eyes.
She watches. She watches. In silence, she cries.
Penance for silence, see the ghosts in their eyes.

Nurse Emma remembers so, so many years
as nurse, secret keeper for Doctor Audaire.
She wishes she forgot so, so, many tears.
It would be easier if she didn't care.
But she still has her own family at risk—
so she still does her job. Keeps secrets, tells lies.
When other families worry themselves sick
'cause they see their loved ones with ghosts in their eyes.

Watching every window; she lurks at each door.
She welcomes each patient with speeches prepared.
Shows the facility, gives families the tour.
Shows each state-of-the-art room—except downstairs.
Modernized Victorian, at the road's end.
Private yet accessible—it's rated as best.
One hundred fifty acres usable land.
Yet *she* knows ghosts wander at Pinehaven Rest.

"Momma, I promise, this is all for the best."
They all say that, you know, she says in her head,
as they walk through the doors of Pinehaven Rest.
They check for quality food, what type of bed,
if there's mentally stimulating programs,
and if the nurses all know how to read 'scripts.

'Cause it's Dad or it's Mom or it's Dearest Grams,
and the last argument ended in tearful fits.

Pinehaven Rest is the old Audaire home.
And the doctor is third generation heir
to the house, to the land, to every stone
of this practice—and all those under his care.
He's followed the footsteps of family pride.
Not one doctorate, he has many degrees.
In psychiatry's realm, he's been published wide;
more hushed is his work in occult psychi'try.

Visitors come—all flowers and cheery glow.
Spirits soon wane within the Asphodel suites.
"Of course, I remember, that thing what...you know?
That time, with those people. Your favorite treats."
"Does she even know me? Who I am? I'm here..."
"He's just a little out of it. Anxiety.
We just gave him some meds. There's nothing to fear."
"What do they stare at? It's like no one can see."

Nurse Emma, she knows what her patients do see.
She's watched enough patients have their ghosts pushed out.
Doctor Audaire said he was searching to free
his patients from mortal fear and soulful doubt.
If a patient could be outside the body
and return, safe and sound, a small taste of death—
why worry, afterlife's promise was shoddy.
Epiphany's price—he steals but a few breaths.

2.

She watches. She watches. She watches their eyes.
She watches. She watches. In silence, she lies.
Penance for silence, see the ghosts in their eyes.

"At the next rest stop, can we *please* have a smoke?"
"I'm trying to quit, Gram," Cass weakly protests.
"Besides, you're on oxygen—you shouldn't smoke!"
"Even criminals condemned get their last cigarette.
"Gram please," Cass begs, "This isn't some sentence—"
"It's for my own good. So you told me. I know."

Sick to her stomach, Cass wonders her penance.
All Gram can think is I am making her go.

The kids shouldn't have to live through extra fear.
Worrying if Gram should forget meds or fall.
Seeing her hide crumpled butts, sneaking Dan's beer.
No kid should make those daily 9-1-1 calls.
Medicine. Money. Care. So many reasons.
Gram would be better off at Pinehaven Rest.
Cass turns off the highway. Necessary treason.
She reaches for her lighter and cigarettes.

"Gram, look, there's even Bingo, like at St. Joe's."
With narrow eyes, Gram asks, "So why all the glass?
I don't play Bingo on display, for a show.
That's what it looks like, a zoo. Take me home, Cass."
"Mrs. Bihari, please, just give us a chance—"
"It's *Ms.* and no. Leave us. Why can't I stay home?"
Cass glares tears at the floor, shifts a nervous dance.
"It's not safe for the kids if you come back home."

"Nonsense!" cries the woman, stopping short to cough.
"Gramma, please. They followed you into the forest
when you left your O2 tank. You all got lost!"
"So you just put me in a warehouse of corpses?
I was fine! So were they! Was an adventure.
The tank would have only just slowed us all down.
And who's this woman acting this show, this tour—"
"Nurse Emma, Gram. Please. Let her show us around?"

Nurses say Teresa, not Terezia.
She tells Cass when she visits. "Such rude manners!"
Cass listens and tutors, "Please, Tay-rey-tzee-ya."
Emma nods, writes phonetics on the planner.
"I don't trust people here. Don't you feel the air?"
"It's dry," Cass agrees, "And too warm, I suppose..."
"Most people her age get chilled, so we take care,"
Nurse Emma explains. "Extra heat. Extra clothes."

"It's to hide all the ghosts," Terezia says.
"What ghosts?" Nurse Emma asks, fooling just Cass.
"Gram, there are no ghosts. Let the dead just stay dead.
You know, your stories got Nick sent home from class?

It's safe here for you, Gram. I promise; I swear."
"Dear child you know not what you speak. And I
dismiss foolish vows. And I don't speak from fear.
But take care if you see there's a ghost in my eye."

3.

She watches. She watches. She watches their eyes.
She watches. She watches. In silence, she sighs.
Penance for silence, see the ghosts in their eyes.

The doctor hadn't known that Nurse Emma was there.
She'd gone downstairs, though she knew it forbidden;
her patient was begging for Doctor Audaire.
To this day, she still keeps what she saw hidden.
Two patients bound to tables, wired, side-by-side.
Soft words from the lips of the Doctor Audaire.
A cup of liquid drunk. A switch thrown. Both died.
Only for a moment. Their spirits in air.

Zagging roads of lightning redirected to hosts.
Both opened their eyes wide. Their eyes weren't their own.
Each looked at each other. And saw each their ghosts.
Trapped inside. Dead alive. Foreign skin, wrong bone.
Throw the switch. Lightning flare. Free spirits once more.
They sought their own bodies—Audaire spoke their names.
Holding them moments more, light pulled from their cores.
Though back to their bodies, neither was the same.

Once loosened from body, spirits are bolder.
What the doctor has stolen, they now must steal.
From a body less sick, one that's less older.
Push out someone's ghost, and from stolen life heal.
And then when their time comes to pass, they do stay.
Holding onto this world, unfamiliar eyes stare
at children, grandchildren, the loved ones who pray
a piece of mom or dad or grandma is there.

And what from this torture gets Doctor Audaire?
A little more life, the power of a god.
Knowledge, secrets, of such so few are aware.
"You look young for your age." Vanity does nod.

If he knows, if he cares, what loosed spirits do—
Nurse Emma can't tell and would never dare ask.
Surrounded by ghosts dead and still living too,
she calms worried fam'lies; fear keeps her on task.

"Nurse Emma, my office. It's time that we talk."
Doctor Audaire turned around, walked down the stairs.
Shaking, quaking, Nurse Emma could hardly walk.
But she followed the doctor down those same stairs.
He motioned for her to sit by two empty
tables. She does, but wonders who lay there last.
"Nurse Emma, look at me. Now, what did you see
when you came looking, down here, not two months past?"

"Doctor Audaire, if asked... I can't really say...
I wouldn't say anything—see anything...
I mean..." She stopped, too scared to even pray.
"You care for your fam'ly. Your pay, your earnings?"
"I...yes." She thought of her sister, nephews and—
"Your father, he's getting well up in his years?
You know he can come here." Audaire took her hand.
Dad will never come here. Emma fought her tears.

4.

She watches. She watches. She watches their eyes.
She watches. She watches. In silence, she cries.
Penance for silence, see the ghosts in their eyes.

"Why's her hair not colored?" asks Cass one visit.
"We pay for the service. It means much to her."
"Last time we tried she attacked the assistant.
With her anxiety, no one can touch her."
"Perhaps I can come out... help and be near her?"
"Are you licensed or trained?" Nurse Emma enquires.
"Well, no, but... I thought that..." Cass says in murmurs.
"It's all right, dear, just trust the people you hired."

"I don't trust them at all," Terezia says.
One lucid moment, one difficult visit.
Cass talks in that moment, sits closer, and says,
"Why don't you trust them, Gram? Tell me, what is it?"

"You know my necklace, the one with the symbol?
Bring it to me, and never let them take it."
Cass thought to protest; the request was simple.
"I'll find it and bring it next time I can make it."

"Did you bring my necklace?" Terezia frets.
"Shit! I knew I forgot... I was running so late.
Sorry, Gram. Next time, I promise, I won't forget."
"If there is a next time..." Her gram turns away.
"Don't be so dramatic—" Cass starts to chastise.
"Don't you dare, Cassandra, I know what's at stake.
You don't believe now, but look into their eyes.
All of them. In this place. Do they look awake?"

"Gram, there's no—" Cass started to speak.
"There *is*, and there *are* ghosts. Right now. Right *here*.
I *see* them, I *feel* them. They prey on the weak.
I tell you, these nurses, they know—and they fear."
"You're speaking in stories; you're making no sense."
Gram said, "I speak more sense then you'll ever know."
Is she lucid? Is this some mental defense?
"If you care, bring my necklace. Till then, just go."

Outside, Cass paces. Twenty feet from the doors.
Was she hurting her Gram? Just making things worse?
She paces and puffs two cigarettes or more.
I remember thinking 'put necklace in purse.'
But Nicky woke late, and Dan went in early.
Jessie nearly forgot her homework, at that.
Full-time job, full-time wife... caretaker? Surely—
she couldn't do it all. Still, sobbing, she sat...

"Honey, don't cry." Nurse Emma comes to the curb.
"You're doing your best, and don't you forget it.
This...seeing our parents like this...it will hurt.
But you've made the best choice. Don't you regret it."
"I wish I could do more. Be here, do something..."
"So does everyone else in this situation.
Remember, you're here now, not doing nothing.
Cherish *now*. Time just worsens her condition."

5.

She watches. She watches. She watches their eyes.
She watches. She watches. In silence, she lies.
Penance for silence, see the ghosts in their eyes.

Terezia sees her, hiding the needle.
Two orderlies come in; she fights and she fails.
Medicine injected. Downstairs. On a table.
Eyes Doctor Audaire, neither flinches nor pales.
She can't move, hardly breathe, while they bind her tight.
The two orderlies leave; *that* one nurse stays.
At least no one promises she'll be all right.

She didn't trust the doctor when they first met.
He asked too many questions; his eyes were dead.
His soul reeked of poison—aura slimy, wet.
While ghosts wandered all round, from him they fled.
And this room, this basement, void of spirits too.
Though her body is drugged, mind medically blurred—
Why she is here, why the ghosts—why this...she knew.
Doctor Audaire tells her without any words.

The lightning is blinding, pain swirling black hole.
Drugs and fear gurgle gasping laughter in screams.
The tearing of essence rips body and soul.
But worse is the light being stolen in streams.
The doctor's eyes glow, light from living ghost.
Into Terezia bores dark empty chasms.
Her ghost eyes see herself, Audaire's captive host.
When the doctor is done, she snaps back in spasms.

On the floor, she's returned, no longer intact.
Now bound to oxygen, body and mind
still don't work the same. A delay to react.
Eyes no longer can tell life from spirit kind.
Still weak, Terezia is pushed out a crack
by another who wears her body like a dress.
She sees her own eyes, and a stranger looks back.
When that spirit leaves, she returns feeling less.

"God, what happened to her?" cries Cass at first sight.
Of course Dan and the kids had come this visit.
"Gram-gram, you okay?" Jessie snuggles beside.

Nicky shakes, looks away, quietly he sits.
"Stay with them," Cass tells Dan, finds the first nurse.
"What the hell happened? Why does she look like that?"
"She lashed out. Paranoid. Was like she was cursed—"
"Bullshit," says Cass. "Is there video of that?"

"There's no video," Nurse Emma says with care
as she arrives. "Last night's storm took power out.
"But you can discuss it with Doctor Audaire."
Cass looks at her family gathered about
their great gram, her gram—her second mother.
Those years Gram protected, and loved—she deserved
to be cared for the same. Loved like no other.
"Yeah. Where's his office?" Something prickles Cass's nerves.

Terezia watches her fam'ly through mist.
Their voices, a moment, come after their words.
Cass asks a question; its meaning she misses.
Just keeping together her own spirit hurts.
Were they ghosts, still alive? Were her own eyes dead?
When she opens her mouth, the wrong words escape.
"Gram-gram...we don't know what you're asking," Jess says.
"Spirits see...come apart... necklace home... I break..."

She sighs, closes her eyes, and tears start to fall.
"Gram-gram are there ghosts? Is that why you're so scared?"
"Nicky, don't ask that," Dan says. His voice is appalled.
"But if that's what hurt her..." She feels unprepared.
She gasps and tries to breathe; nothing has an effect.
Flails. What now? Dan switches her oxygen on.
Her beloved family, she cannot protect.
So helpless, so useless, who has she become?

"What happened to my Gram?" Cass folds her arms.
"What Nurse Emma told you," says Doctor Audaire.
"She had an episode. We stopped further harm."
"And you have proof you acted in her best care?"
"You researched our facility when you chose us.
Do you question your choice? What you chose for her?"
"Should I?" Cass asks. "Tell me about her bruises."
"She attacked her nurse, crying ghostly horror."

Cass leaves Doctor Audaire's office feeling worse—

powerless, helpless—has she made a mistake?
She needed a smoke so she reached in her purse.
No, you're trying to quit. She tried not to shake.
She returned to her Gram, to her family,
but they all looked worried; only Jessie spoke—
prattling hopefully as Gram sat silently.
But her eyes—Gram's eyes looked like those of a ghost.

6.

She watches. She watches. She watches their eyes.
She watches. She watches. In silence, she sighs.
Penance for silence, see the ghosts in their eyes.

Cass checks three extra times. She will not forget.
Gram's request, the necklace. She hopes it will help.
If it makes Gram more calm, helps make her less stressed...
If I visited more, that also would help...
Brushes her hand on the pendant, fingered its
surface and chain. Would it banish her guilt
as it banished the ghosts? What else could it fix?
Cass sits in the car, frozen by all she's felt.

What's wrong? I love Gram. I should want to see her.
Deliberate, Cass breathes and turns off her car.
Stomach twinges ill each step she takes nearer.
It isn't long to arrive; the trip isn't far.
Gram sits in her room; eyes shine empty like glass.
Please, see me Gram. She says, "Hey, Gram. It's me, Cass."
"I know you." Gram reaches a weak hand; Cass grasps.
"I brought this for you." Cass attaches the necklace.

It takes some time—and even more patience.
She hears Cass in the hall, admonishing *her*—
Nurse Emma. "I promise, no one will touch that necklace."
Not ready to speak, she just thinks, *Liar.*
Her trembling hand, now trembling less, tucks inside
her prize, her power, her secreted defense.
Before Cass leaves, Terezia shows her pride.
"I luh-love you, Cass." She smiles; her words make sense.

"I love you, too, Gram." Cass wipes new tears away.

Strength grows, and clarity, fraction by fraction.
Enough for her to ask, "Cass, You...you please stay?"
Terezia needs time, rest before action.
And Nurse Bitch won't come in—won't ruin her plans—
with Cass in the room paying close attention.
Bless her granddaughter, she nods, taking her hands.
To keep Cass while she heals, she asks more questions.

Strangely, Nurse Emma's forgotten the necklace.
Or doesn't know better... Terezia thinks.
What is her alliance? Just what is her place?
As the old woman plans, she doesn't want kinks.
She still sees the ghosts, but they all avoid her.
Confidence moves her; she's reclaimed her power.
Even toting oxygen, using her walker.
She observes what happens every hour.

That devil of a doctor keeps strict schedules.
Terezia watches each resident's state...
When the doctor does take them, steal from their souls,
she notes each recovery, how long it takes.
Before how long is the next soul pulled to feed?
How long before it is Terezia's turn
to be taken for Audaire's abhorrent need?
And what she learns is she hasn't time to burn.

The wise woman knows she has no time to spare.
She wanders all hallways, explores every room.
She spies on the doctor when he's not downstairs.
When he's not, and it's safe, she goes down there too.
With protective measures from her mother's gram,
she studies the tables, the machine, the wires.
Mechanical dark magic, work of the damned...
How hard *would* it be... an electrical fire?

As if they know, as if they too are watching,
ghosts follow Terezia through others' eyes—
Torturing those pushed out and stuck watching
their tortured families staring at empty eyes.
I'll end their suffering. I will fix this all.
She sneaks oxygen tanks from storage downstairs.
Days pass, she waits for Cass to visit or call.
Then it's time to be brought to Doctor Audaire.

She still fights, she still loses, she's drugged and tied.
Brought downstairs and restrained, she maintains her glare.
She does not look where her mischief's work all hides.
Instead, she focuses hate on Doctor Audaire.
Unfazed by her scorn, he sets all his buttons.
He narrows his eyes, fixes them on her neck.
He pulls at the pendant; it won't come undone.
"You must think you're clever with this little trick?"

The old woman bats her eyes innocently.
"Emma," orders Audaire, "Do take care of this."
"You promised." Terezia burns intensity.
The nurse pauses, at least, but does as he bids.
That nurse pockets the necklace, walks out the door.
Flip the switch. Spirit split. Steals life from her soul.
And this time it hurts so much more than before.
Back in her room, she knows she's so much less whole.

7.

She watches. She watches. She watches their eyes.
She watches. She watches. In silence, she cries.
Penance for silence, see the ghosts in their eyes.

The very next day, Cass comes for a visit.
Terezia fights with the ghost who possesses...
too weak to reclaim her own body that sits
staring at nothing, while she floats so useless.
"Gram, can you hear me? It's your granddaughter, Cass."
They were careful enough so as not to leave
obvious injuries, so Cass can't assess
the truth of dark magic; she only can grieve.

"I thought you'd be better..." Cass turns to hide tears.
"And I thought you might let them color your hair..."
Cass smooths away roots of grey—something appears!
A light, a glow, between them. A touch of care.
Terezia smiles. *Dear, there's magic in you yet!*
You may shun the truth of your blood, but it's there.
That moment of love, its own magic begets.
Terezia reclaims herself—ghosts beware.

Like before, it takes time to fully come back.
But Cass's embrace heals the doctor's damage.
Her arm, her hand... she waves, grasping at her neck.
"What's wrong? Can you breath—Your necklace! Those bastards!"
Cass kisses her forehead. "I'll be right back, Gram."
Around her, the ghosts fight to take her once more.
Hurry, Cass, she thinks, bracing for a last stand.
Her granddaughter's voice commands the corridor.

Cass returns victorious, necklace in hand.
Combined magic sutures back body and soul.
Terezia works out the last of her plan.
She coughs and wheezes, spits bile into a bowl.
"Water... please, bring...water...?" she begs her granddaughter.
"Of course, Gram," Cass leaves, purse still on the bed.
She smiles again when Cass returns with water;
she's got the last piece, lighter and cigarette.

Terezia now has more time to review,
recover her strength—she has only one chance.
Cass visits unknowing it's her last "Love you."
For the next day has scheduled a staff conference.
You're not getting younger...why not choose your death?
Ghosts press against her; she's not felt so alive—
even though with each step she struggles for breath.
Down the hall, down the stairs. *It's time.* She arrives.

While taking a walk by the nurses station,
Terezia ambled close enough to view
the calendar notes, meetings and vacations,
a staff conference—her window she now knew.
The old woman stumbles to each hiding place.
She left the ghosts behind, yet their presence weighs...
What if her plan strips them of any last grace?
What of those who were trapped, who unwillingly stay?

She passes and releases each tank's O2 hiss.
When all are open, she takes the doctor's chair.
She thinks, she debates—is there something she's missed?
No. Now finish before you can't breathe the air.
She takes out a pen, she pulls her cigarette,
and she writes her spell out on the wrapping paper.
It's time to end the pain at Pinehaven Rest—

From the stairs Doctor Audaire does appear.

Terezia fumbles, dropping the lighter.
Moving faster than she, the doctor attacks.
He pushes her down. "I know you're a fighter.
I came prepared." He puts a knife to her back.
With a chant, he begins his final dark spell.
Terezia struggles, but cannot break free.
Thud. A violent release. "You're done with this Hell."
"Nurse Emma?" Can she believe what she sees?

That nurse stands over that now-fallen doctor.
O2 tank in her hands, and blood on his face.
She swings again. And again. Once more.
She looks at Terezia. "Let's end this place."
Terezia prepares her last cigarette.
She lights up the butt, takes a drag from her smoke.
Nurse Emma snickers, like she's just won a bet.
"What? You expected this place would just explode?"

"All you medical people told me to quit!
Just one fucking spark and my house would catch fire!"
"Can only you smoke that magic cigarette?"
She passes it with more annoyance than ire.
"Oxygen accelerates, but it doesn't ignite."
Nurse Emma puffs, then shows the butt's now half ash.
"First, you need more of a fire. Now pass me your light...
O2 makes a small flame blaze up in a flash."

Nurse Emma walks over to the doctor's chair.
"What you wrote here—this...spell?—just what will it do?"
Terezia followed, one eye on Audaire.
"'To an appropriate end' once the fire burns through."
Nodding, Emma turns to the doctor's console.
She smacks the lighter until fluid drips out...
onto his seat, soaking through the fabric's holes.
Hands the butt. "Last puff's yours, before it goes out."

Terezia inhales, nods, meets Emma's eyes,
and drops the smoldering butt down.
The chair catches, but the flames don't quickly rise.
A groan sounds; Doctor Audair moves on the ground.
"Fuck," mutters Terezia, turning his way.

Lifting her own tank, she pommels him once more—
then sees the knife he dropped, and pulls it away.
One quick stab. The ghosts in his eyes are no more.

"Is that it? Did you kill him?" Nurse Emma gapes.
"Does that...undo the ghosts? Do we still have to—"
"We do. This place must burn." Terezia states.
"He's dead, yes, but magic's not easy to 'undo.'
It's filled this house, each board, every corner.
To 'undo' this evil, it all has to burn."
Nurse Emma coughs, sobs "...done something sooner...
Wait here. If it must burn, I'll make sure it burns."

Terezia says nothing; it's getting hard to breathe.
Flames engulf the chair, smoke gathers, filling down.
Blood pools from the doctor...one more spell to weave.
She coats her hands in blood, crawls close to the ground.
Between the two tables, she writes one more spell.
Nurse Emma comes downstairs, dragging wet linens.
She looks at Terezia. "What the hell?"
"To harm just evil souls... Magic insurance."

"I hope you're right. I don't really want to die..."
"Oh, we'll still die. But the *good* souls will be free."
"You take confessions?" Nurse Emma sadly sighs.
Terezia pauses. Smoke and fire she sees.
"A quick one, if you must. Or we won't end this."
"I'm older than you... He gave me...what he stole...
"I didn't say no." Emma coughs and confesses.
"My fam'ly died. They never knew what I know."

The flames on the chair have lessened in the smoke.
"Terezia," Nurse Emma says. "I'm sorry."
"Then finish this, now. Before our fire gets cold.
"Help me up to the console... over here, hurry."
Nurse Emma leaves the linens draped up the stairs,
helps Terezia move—so close to the fire!
"Now... I need you to move the chair in there."

Nurse Emma shakes her head. The chair is burning!
"I'll join you shortly, but I must do this first."
Terezia moved dials, flipping and turning.
Nurse Emma grasps the chair; the pain is the worst.

Pushing through pain, pushes the chair on the spell.
Lightning crackles above, a buzz fills the room.
Terezia grabs Emma's hand with a yell.
Her necklace dangles between them. And *boom*.

8.

She watches. She watches. She watches her eyes.
She watches. She watches. In silence, she sighs.
Penance and silence, end the ghosts in their eyes.

Cass sits in her car. The police tape still sways.
In her hand, Gram's necklace—charred, blackened rust.
In front of her smolders the burnt bone remains
of the mansion once known as Pinehaven Rest.
The cul de sac's empty, police and fire gone.
Two days ago, it burned—burned down to the ground.
They collected the remains, little more than bones,
identifying bodies with items they found.

Cass gets out of her car. Twilight falls darkly.
In her hand, Gram's necklace burns like it's on fire.
She moves closer, eyes narrow, trying to see.
I saw something. Something. I'm not crazy, I swear.
The fire and smoke still stain the air that she breathes.
Like an unfiltered cigarette's smoking taste.
She crunches over crisp wood, inside she seethes.
What are you doing here? This is just a waste—

"Cassandra." She stops. What did she just hear?
"Cassandra." Something. Something *is* just there!
"Cassandra." She knows that voice on the air.
"Cassandra." "Gram, I hear you. Tell me where—"

Terezia stands in the very center
of the smoking wreckage, holding someone's hand—
Nurse Emma. Fading and edged with cinders.
Cass freezes and stares. "Gram, I don't understand..."
The two spirits look at each other, at Cass.
Terezia releases the nurse; she rises.
Embers dance inward from her edges consume
till only a spark, like a star, entices
more ghosts to rise from the mansion's burnt ruin.

Breath stops in her throat. Cass clutches at her chest.
The necklace twines hotter around her fingers.
Each spirit lifts, lined in sparks of unrest.
Edges burn inward on spirits who linger.
Up, up, each ghost flies, flickering souls burning,
disappearing among stars starting to shine.
Watching each ghost's leaving, Cass feels a yearning.
Gram's necklace glows in her hands. *This gift is mine.*

She looks to the place where her Gram was standing.
Light shines so bright, she must cover her eyes.
When she can open them, a pyre enchanting
of fiery sparkles twirls up, into the skies.
No more words are spoken. Cass wipes tears and goes.
The truth and the story, the meaning of lies.
Love, guilt, pride, penance, fear—all this she now knows.
She puts on Gram's necklace. Ghosts live in her eyes.

She watches. She watches. She watches her eyes.
She watches. She watches. No longer she cries.
Penance is over, through the ghosts in her eyes.

They Come With The Storm
Dan Foley

The night was filled with the howling wind and thunder of breakers beating against the eroding beach. Ghostly figures rode within the waves. They came with the first winter storm when cold winds from the north signaled the death of summer and the coming season of darkness. They emerged from the waves crashing upon the shore. The sea passed over them, around them, through them. Their groans and shrieks entwined with the wind as it assaulted the land. They were white as the seafoam they emerged from, light as the spray that surrounded them. They wore the fog like a shroud as they approached the village and the warm bodies that awaited their arrival. In the morning much of the sand would be gone, swept away by an angry ocean. But more than sand would be lost this night.

The fog drifted over and around the homes of the town, small cottages mostly made of stone. If any had dared to peer closely into it, they would find specters of the dead, drowned in the sea, staring back at them. But no one did. Instead, they huddled in their homes, shivering behind closed doors and shutters, waiting for the night and the storm to pass.

"Do you think it will be enough?" Manda asked her Da as they huddled in their darkened cottage.

"Of course," her Da replied to reassure her. "It always has been." There was doubt in his response. He had barred the door, shuttered the windows. A fire roared in the fire place barring entry there. Just because it had always been enough in the past didn't mean it always would be.

Outside, the bleating of the sheep tied to the sac-pole fought to be heard through the howling of the storm. Then it was suddenly cut off, leaving only the sound of the ghosts and wind to rule the night. Their offering had been accepted. In the morning, when the storm passed and the dead returned to the sea, they would see how their neighbors had fared.

Manda was out the door when the first ray of sunshine filtered into the kitchen through the thickly leaded glass of the room's single window.

Da and Ma followed on her heels. Soon, others emerged from the protection of their homes. There were no celebrations, however, the terror of the night was too fresh.

The sheep, an old ewe that had been tied to the sac-pole was gone. The rope, which had held it tethered, lay slack on the ground. The loop that had been around its neck was unbroken. The animal had been torn from it in pieces, but not a drop of blood marred the ground. The shades had taken everything. They always did.

Relief, then apprehension, surged through Manda. She had made it safely through the reaping, but what about William? Had he been as fortunate? She breathed a sigh of relief when she saw him coming down the lane toward her. She didn't know what she would do if he was ever taken. Her elation died when she saw the look on his face. Someone had not made it through the night.

"Who?" she asked when he reached her.

"My brother, Sean," he answered, his voice cracking in grief.

The elation she had felt at seeing him safe evaporated. "Oh, William. I'm so sorry. What happened? He had sheep to spare."

"He was tired, and with Jenna gone, he felt he had nothing to live for. He locked his sheep in the barn and left his door open. When the sun came, he was gone."

Manda shivered in his arms. Leaving his door open was as good as suicide. If the legends were true, he was with them now. The next time they came, Sean would be among their number.

"We should leave this island. Go somewhere safe," she told him.

"We can't leave. You know that. We have nowhere to go, and they would never let us," he answered, nodding at the men and women who were staring at them.

Manda looked around at the knot of villagers and knew he was right. They would never be permitted to leave. They were part of the island's future. Already there were whispers that they should be married and that she should be pregnant, heavy with the next generation. Without children, the island would die.

What of it? she thought. *Maybe it should die.* Any children she might have would be doomed to the same fate as all the island folk. The men would fish the angry sea. The women would till the earth and breed. The lucky ones would die on land and be buried in the rocky soil. The rest would drown or be taken by the dead that came with the first winter storm.

William took her hand and stared into her eyes. "Marry me," he said for what seemed like the hundredth time. "Sean's cottage and sheep are mine now. He left a note, leaving them to me. We can be married and raise a family there."

She just shrugged and slipped her hand from his. In another place she would have fallen into his arms and kissed him with abandon. But here, on this island of the doomed, she would not. She would not conceive a child only to feed it to the insatiable appetites of those that came with the storm.

*   *   *

"I saw you with William," her Da said that night at the dinner table. "Has he asked you to marry him yet?"

"Of course he did," her Ma said. "What did you tell him?"

"Nothing," Manda admitted.

Her Ma frowned and her Da shook his head. "You should marry that boy before he finds another. He has a cottage now and can provide for you. If you love him you should take him for your husband. He won't wait forever. Justine has flowered and she has eyes for him. She would take him in an instant."

She knew they were right. She did love him . . . and he wouldn't wait forever. Like all things, even love will die if left unfed. If she wasn't willing to accept his love, Justine, or some other girl would. The next time he asked, she would accept.

But he didn't ask the next day, or the next. Manda was tempted to ask him, but that wasn't the way things were done. She would be patient. But, as the days turned into weeks, William drifted away from her. They spent less time together and she sometimes found him in the presence of Justine. William seemed uninterested in the girl, but she was obviously infatuated with him.

Finally, when enough was enough, she approached him. "You've been a bit distant lately? Is something wrong?"

William shook his head and stared at his hands before answering. "You've made it clear we have no future together. I can't go on that way. I hope we'll always be friends, but I need to be with someone who wants to share their life with me."

Manda was dismayed by his answer. "Oh, William . . . I do want to share my life with you. I was foolish to deny you all the times you asked to marry. Ask me again and my answer will be different."

William glanced around nervously, but didn't answer. Then Manda saw Justine watching them from across the lane. "Fine," Manda told him. "Decide which one of us you want. Just don't take too long. I could change my mind again."

William's mind was made up for him when Justine's belly started to swell.

Manda heard the whispers and went in search of William to demand to know if they were true. When she found him, he was holding Justine's hands in his and she was crying. That was all the answer Manda needed. Heartbroken, she turned and fled without approaching them. What a fool she had been. She had lost the boy she had loved since they were children.

Justine and William were married the next week. Most of the village was there. Manda did not attend the wedding or the reception. Instead, she sat alone on a cliff staring out to sea, shed the last of her tears for him, and then hardened her heart. She vowed she would never love another.

Manda struggled through the pregnancy, watching Justine's belly swell with the life growing inside her, and with each day her resentment and anger grew. Justine had stolen her man and her future because the trollop had been willing to spread her legs while she had not. When the babe was born, and it was a beautiful, healthy girl, Manda lost any good feelings she might have harbored for William. Only hate now filled her heart.

In the days, weeks and months that followed, Manda sank into a deep depression. She longed to leave the island, but none would take her and she could not do it on her own. She would sit on the cliffs overlooking the sea or seclude herself in the cottage to avoid a chance meeting with William or Justine and the babe.

In November, when the sky turned dark and the winds blew with a chill from the north, Manda's mood was as black as her future. Her only relief would be to follow Sean into oblivion.

*   *   *

Manda watched from the bluff as the approaching storm howled on the horizon. She heard voices crying in the wind, hollow laments filled with sorrow and desire from the throats of kindred spirits to her despair. Let William and the rest of the village hide behind stone walls and sacrificial sheep. On this night she would meet the wraiths face to face.

As the fury of the storm grew, so did the screams and moans of the dead. When they burst from the sea, Manda's mind rebelled at the sight. Bodies that had been whole and firm in life were torn and ravaged. Clothes hung off them, torn into rags by the sea and wind. Eyes that had once been blue, or brown, or green, now shown red in the night. Faces that had laughed or smiled in life howled in despair, or screamed in rage.

Manda watched as they made their way from the beach below her to the village filled with life. Her desire to join them vanished in the stark reality of their presence. There was no adventure here, no romantic tragedy, just fear and hate. There was no way she could get to the safety of the cottage where her Da and Ma now sheltered. Her only hope was to hide here on the cliffs and hope they would pass her by.

They had almost passed her by when one specter broke from the hoard and looked directly at the place where she hid cowering in the sea grass. *Stay away!* She thought, but the ghost streamed toward her. Its passage seemed smooth and effortless over the broken ground. When she jumped up to run, it closed the distance between them in an instant. It only took a second for her to recognize him . . . Sean.

His once beautiful face was bloated. His smile was marred by missing teeth, and those that remained were sharp and pointed like a shark. His eyes burned with a fire neither the sea nor the storm could extinguish. Manda opened her mouth to scream, but her voice froze in her throat when the ghost invaded her body.

Her muscles went rigid. The cold was so intense it burned. Worse than that was the attack on her mind. Sean poured all the sorrow, the regrets and the hate that had driven him to open the door of his home to the revenants. He fed her the fear and revulsion he had felt when one of them invaded *his* mind and body. *No,* she tried to scream, but her voice was frozen. *Yes,* he hissed, and took control of her body.

She tried to fight him but it was useless. Her body was no longer her own. He walked her down to the shore, uncaring as she stumbled over sharp outcroppings of stone and shale. By the time they reached the breakers she was cut and bruised, bleeding in a dozen places. He walked her into the ocean. The saltwater that licked at her body eagerly sucked the blood away. Sean drove her onward, past her knees, her waist, her neck. And finally, her head.

Manda tried not to breath in the cold sea, but Sean would not have it. He made her inhale the ocean as if it was a sweet summer breeze. Saltwater filled her throat and lungs. She gagged, but only drew in more. When her heart stopped beating, Manda's battered body was being drawn out to sea by the raging waves. She would be trapped within it until the fish, crabs and worms reduced it to nothing but bone.

∗   ∗   ∗

The next day, William stood on the cliff overlooking the surging sea. Was Manda out there, lost in its depths? No one, not even her Da or Ma had seen her since before the storm. When the storm came, and the people of the island had tied a sheep or goat to their sac-poles and retreated to the safety of their homes, Manda had not been with them. He had loved her their entire lives. He had never stopped loving her, even when she had hardened her heart against him. If he hadn't turned to

Justine in a foolish attempt to make her jealous, they would be together now. But the babe had changed everything. Once he had planted the seed in Justine's belly, all their lives had changed.

"I'm sorry," he said, as he dropped the handful of late blooming flowers he had gathered on his way to the top of the cliff into the sea below. Everyone in the village was looking for her, but he knew they wouldn't find her. She was gone. She had finally fulfilled her dream of leaving the island. Just not the way she had wanted.

During the next year William watched his child grow. A second babe now filled Justine's belly. He thought of Manda less with each passing day. At first, when he went to sea to fish with the rest of the men in the village he feared he would find her ravaged body in the nets as he drew them in. As the months passed and the only things he found in the nets were struggling fish, their mouths opening and closing in a futile effort to breath, Manda receded into the depths of his memory.

Life on the island was too hard to allow time for thoughts of the past. At least until the chill of October and the threat of storms rolling in from the north filled him with dread. Had she joined the lost souls who returned to the island with the first storm of the season? Would he hear her voice entwined with the moans and shrieks of the dead mingled within the howls of the wind?

The storm, when it came, was unexpected. It blew in fast from the north. One minute the sea was calm, and the next white caps rose up to slap at the sides of boats racing for home. William reached the dock just as a flash of lightning tore through the sky. He only had time to tie off a single bow line before the first screams of the dead reached him. He ran for his life, not even daring to look back. When he reached his cottage, Justine had already tied a ewe to the sac-pole and was waiting for him at the door.

"Get inside," she yelled as he reached the yard. William barely heard her over the scream of the pursuing hoard. He was hardly inside when Justine slammed the door closed and threw the bar in place. He was bending over, sucking wind and rubbing the pain in his side when Justine screamed, grabbed the babe and ran for the bedroom where the shuttered windows blocked the view of the world outside. When William looked up to see what had terrified her, he saw Manda's ravaged visage staring at him through the window. It only took him two quick steps to reach it and slam the shutters shut, blocking her from his view.

William went into the bedroom where he sat on the bed with Justine and the babe. Even with the door closed and the wind howling outside they could hear Manda calling to him . . . "*William, William,*" . . . as she circled the house looking for a way in. Justine sobbed and the babe wailed with each haunting cry.

"Go away," he finally screamed when he could bear it no more.

*   *   *

Manda ignored the terrified bleating of the sacrificial ewe tied to the sac-pole. She hungered for more than animal blood. What was it, compared to the life of the man who had scorned her? She would have him or nothing. Time after time she circled the cottage, looking for any crack or crevice which might afford her entry. She was finally forced back to the sea when the storms fury started to wane and the sun threatened to break through the cloud-filled sky. "*William*," she screamed one final time before retreating to the cold embrace of the sea.

Every year, Manda came with the first storm. William waited in the cottage while Justine and the children sheltered with her Da and Ma. He would listen to her call his name as she endlessly circled the cabin. He could not escape the island, but he finally escaped Manda when death claimed him in his eighty-second year and he was buried in the welcoming arms of the island's rocky soil.

Turn Up The Old Victrola
Tom Deady

I never liked yard sales. It felt like buying someone else's trash. What made me stop that day, I'll never know. But I did stop, that's the point of the story.

Let me back up, it started before the yard sale. The real beginning was when my uncle died. Billy was always the "cool uncle" that every kid has. The one that teaches you the shit your parents try to shield from you. The one that swears in front of you when you're too young, and later buys you cigarettes or beers or condoms. Anyway, Uncle Billy was the guy that introduced me to music. I'd go over to his house and we'd sit and listen to everything from the Beatles and the Stones to Miles Davis and John Coltrane. Always on vinyl. Even when the rest of the world moved on to cassettes and eventually compact discs, Uncle Billy played records.

When he passed away last year – sclerosis of the liver, even the coolest uncles can't defy the evils of alcohol – he left me his record collection. Over three hundred albums, some of them over fifty years old with covers so faded you could barely make them out. The problem was, he'd sold his kick-ass stereo equipment to pay his medical bills. *Water, water, everywhere, and not a drop to drink.* Sure, you could get used equipment, but could you get the needles? So, the records stayed in storage for a while.

Then the hipsters brought back vinyl. It was *retro*. Record players hit the market again, what's old became new. The next shoe to drop could be the return of bell bottoms, God help us if that happens. So, I picked up a system and dug Billy's records out of storage and let the nostalgia roll over me.

I'll never really understand why vinyl came back. The quality sucks! It's all scratchy and the records skip. Listening to records when you could have digital quality is like washing clothes by hand in the river when you own a washing machine. It's pretty fucked up when you think about it. So, the collection sat, right next to my overpriced "retro" sound system.

The other thing I learned from Uncle Billy was the joy ride. He'd pick me up and we'd drive along country roads, music cranked (cassettes then) and end up wherever we ended up. That's how I ended up lost on some back road in a town whose sole claim to fame was probably having a Blockbuster video store.

I rounded a hairpin curve and had to slow. Ahead, flashing yellow lights and cones signaled a delay. Probably some redneck ran his confederate-flag-adorned pickup into a tree. I approached, and realized I was mistaken. A tree was down across the road. A *big* tree. The crew was furiously working to clear the block, saws buzzing in the late-morning sun, but it would be a while.

I was about to make a U-turn when I noticed a tattered sign tacked to a tree just ahead: *Yard Sale*. I needed directions anyway, so I eased the car over to the shoulder and got out. The yard was crowded with the usual yard sale detritus; old toys, out-of-style clothes, rusty tools, and knick-knacks that seem to gather in every elderly person's home. I could purchase most of the stuff brand new for less money at any Christmas Tree Shop or Job Lot.

I ambled across the grass, spying an old couple by the weathered cape-style house. I wondered if they were selling everything to move to a condo, maybe in Florida. They appeared to be arguing, then the man brushed by her and into the house. I turned away, and my eyes fell on the Victrola. It was old, much like the one in that RCA ad with the dog. It looked to be in pretty good shape and I thought of the collection of vinyl back at my place.

Unable to find a price tag, I walked towards the old woman. "Hi, I was wondering what you wanted for the old Victrola?"

Her eyes narrowed and she took a step backwards, but didn't answer.

"You know, the old-fashioned record player?" I motioned toward it.

Her eyes widened and her hand reached up to her forehead. I swear she was about to make the sign of the cross. "It's not for sale," she whispered.

I opened my mouth to reply but realized I had nothing to say. The screen door screeched open and the old man reappeared. He looked angry, like he was about to lay into his wife, but he saw me and managed a smile. "What can we do for you, young man?"

"Well, uh, I was asking about the Victrola, but your...she said it wasn't for sale." I realized there was a resemblance between the man and woman and that they might be brother and sister.

"Nonsense," the man said – a bit too loudly and cheerily – "let's take a look."

He walked past me without a look at the woman. I hung back, watching her. She met my gaze with a look of terror, shook her head, and ran into the house. I turned and followed the man back to the Victrola.

"Does it work?"

His head snapped toward me and just for a split-second I saw a look of fear in his eyes. "Sure, it works." His voice was cautious, no more of the chipper old man from a moment ago.

"How much?"

He looked at it, then back at me. "I guess I could let it go for twenty."

I pulled out my wallet and handed him a twenty without thinking about it. He snatched the money and stepped back from the Victrola.

"That's gonna look pretty cool on display. You got one of those man caves to put it in?"

I smiled. "This baby's going in my living room. I've got a killer collection of vinyl."

The old man's face contorted into a look I couldn't identify. "Well, I mean, it works, but, uh, it sounds crappy. Don't go ruining your collection on this old relic."

His eyes were begging, for what, I wasn't sure. I picked the machine up gently and felt something ripple through me, like a weak electric current. I shook my head and turned to thank the man, but he was already moving quickly back toward the house. I placed the Victrola in the trunk and turned my car around, heading somewhere.

*   *   *

The following weekend, my buddy Jason and I were hanging out at my place having a few beers. "Hey Mark, why don't you throw an album on the turntable and we can relive the not-so-glory days of analog sound?"

I remembered the Victrola sitting in the trunk. "I'll do you one better, Jay. Grab me another beer, I'll be right back." I ignored his look of confusion and went to the garage. I popped the trunk and grabbed the ancient machine, again feeling a shock course through me. All the apprehension of the day at the yard sale returned. For a moment, I considered closing the trunk and forgetting the Victrola existed, but I shook the feeling off and carried it inside.

"Whoa, dude, do you have a time machine in your garage?"

I laughed. "No, but twenty bucks at a yard sale is almost as good as a time machine."

Jason helped me set up the Victrola and clean it off. I cranked it up and the turntable spun silently. I grabbed an obscure blues album that

Billy had loved – no way was I hacking up a Springsteen or Eagles album if this thing didn't work right.

"Come on, fire it up," Jason urged.

I slid the disk onto the spindle and moved the needle in place. Just before I released it, I had the distinct feeling that I was setting something in motion that I would not be able to stop. I let go of the tone arm and once again a surge of current ripped through my body, much stronger than the previous times.

A scratchy sound, like a kitten trying to tell you it wants to come inside, emitted from the horn, then the music kicked in. The rhythm guitar started slow, joined by a subtle drum beat. Then the bass and the horns exploded and the gritty voice of Billy's hero, Johnny "Orleans" Johnson began his tale of sorrow.

I stared at the big horn of the Victrola, lost in the music. Jason said something but it didn't register. There was another sound, beneath the music and song, but I couldn't make it out. It was like trying to hear a whisper over the roar of the ocean. I strained to understand the words, all the while staring into the gaping void of the horn. The darkness there was complete, somehow refusing the ambient light of the room to penetrate its mouth. And it did look like a mouth, and it began to move like a mouth, and only then did I finally hear the message.

* * *

I woke to murky splinters of sunlight stabbing the dim room, bright enough to send pulsing pain through my head. My tongue felt too big for my mouth and my heart was beating like I'd just run a race. A fucking hangover. *How is that possible, I only had a couple of beers?* I remembered setting up the Victrola and playing a blues record, then... *Then what?* I had no memory of what happened after putting on Orleans Johnson's record. Everything before that was crystal clear, then nothing.

I stumbled into the kitchen and guzzled some orange juice out of the carton, then stood still while my stomach did flip-flops. When I was sure I was going to keep it down, I noticed the time on the microwave: 11:37. I hadn't slept this late since college. I found my cell on the couch and called Jason. It went straight to voicemail. I noticed the Orleans Johnson was still on the turntable. Resisting a sudden urge to turn the crank and play it again, I put it back in its sleeve and returned it to the collection.

I tried Jason again, this time leaving him a message to call me back. "Shit." I remembered I had a date with my sometimes-girlfriend, sometimes-nemesis, Angie Giordano. We'd been through a rough patch and I finally got her to agree to see me without having to beg. Barely. She was a firecracker; her Italian blood ran hot at times and I seemed to be the spark to heat it. I'd been looking forward to this for a week, and now I felt like shit. I went to the kitchen to make some toast and start trying to shake my hangover.

The day passed in a kind of fuzzy blur, sometimes dragging, other times seeming to fly by. I couldn't sleep. The idea of putting a record, any record, on the turntable was almost a physical thing. I avoided it by going out driving.

I found myself on the backroads, realizing I was looking for the house where I'd bought the Victrola. I tried Jason a few times but it always went straight to voicemail. A little tickle began in my belly and I knew if I didn't get in touch with Jason, it would blossom into fear. I thought about my hangover and how there were only a few empties back home. I didn't find the yard sale house, and went home to get ready for my date with Angie.

I picked her up early in the evening and we went to a steak house for dinner. There was a great Italian place in town, but it would never live up to her mother's cooking. Things started out slow but we fell back into our groove after a while and laughed a lot. We went to the movies, some chick flick that I barely stayed awake for, then back to my place.

As soon as we entered the apartment, she saw the Victrola. "Wow, Mark, where did you get this?" She ran her hands around the lip of the horn. I shivered.

"Picked it up at a yard sale," I said as I fetched us a couple of beers from the fridge.

"Does it work?"

I stopped halfway back to the living room, almost dropping the beers. Sweat broke out on my forehead. *What is wrong with me?* "Yeah, Jason and I had it working last night."

Angie didn't get along with Jason. In fact, she couldn't stand him. It was part of the reason we fought a lot. I knew better than to even mention his name, and by the look on Angie's face, I probably just sent the date into a tailspin.

"Can we play a record?"

I handed her a beer, happy to have avoided the subject of Jason. "Sure, pick something out." I said it casually despite my dry mouth and beating-way-too-fast heart.

She handed me *Stranger in Town*, one of my favorites. Maybe the night was salvageable after all. I set it on the turntable and dropped the tone arm. I wound the crank and let go of the turntable. The hiss of static lasted just a few seconds before the familiar opening of "Hollywood Nights" blasted from the horn.

I took a long draw from my beer, almost coughing it up when Angie's hand slid up my thigh. Her eyes were full of mischief and longing.

I leaned in and kissed her. I wanted nothing more than to get lost in her body...but something was distracting me. The lights in the room dimmed and I got a sudden chill. But that wasn't the problem; it was the whispers. Just like last night, I heard something between the words and music of the song. Or maybe *behind* it.

"What's wrong, Mark?"

I heard Angie speak but her voice was miles away. And so meaningless. All that mattered was the other voice. It spoke softly but it knew. It had all the truths and it promised to share them with me. The voice's name was Julian Black. He had so much to teach me. Angie's voice faded as Julian whispered to me.

*   *   *

Sunday morning was like Groundhog's Day of Saturday. The sun was too bright, my tongue felt like a giant wad of cotton, and my head throbbed to the beat of my heart. "What the fuck." I was on the couch, Angie was gone, and so was my memory of anything that happened after "Hollywood Nights." Saturday, I was annoyed. Sunday, I was scared.

Julian Black. The name exploded in my head. It did nothing to assuage my fear. Fragments of memories, of conversations, teased me from behind a thick blanket of haze. *Did I speak to someone last night?* I fumbled around for my cell and called Angie. Straight to voicemail. Same for Jason. My fear was taking steroids, pumping itself up to terror. I took a ragged deep breath and tried to calm myself down.

My eyes found the Victrola and any sense of calm abandoned me. There was still a record on the turntable. I knew it would be Seger before I got there to see it. Side one. Whatever happened, happened fast. I reached for the disk, but my hand ended up on the crank. I started to turn it, then yanked my hand away.

I ran out to my car and peeled out of the driveway. I knew if I got away from that...thing, Julian couldn't reach me. At least, I hoped so. I drove aimlessly, trying to clear my mind. It was hard with the radio off, but I was too afraid that I'd start to hear him, or *it*. I had to find a way to stop this, whatever *this* was. *Maybe you're going crazy.* Of course, the thought had occurred to me, but I dismissed it, there was too much pointing at something else going on. *Isn't that what all the crazies say?* I shook my head. "No, there's definitely—" I stopped myself, trying to focus on a rational plan.

"I have to find the house, talk to the people I bought the Victrola from." I nodded my head. "Shit." The self-talk had to end. I thought back to last weekend; what was I doing before I stumbled on the yard sale? I had volunteered at the library book sale, then grabbed a bagel and a large coffee, and started driving. The day was warm and sunny, I had the windows down and the music on. "Raven's Point!" I looked around to get my bearings, then headed toward West Drumlin.

There had been a lot of down time at the library book sale. One of the books I flipped through to pass the time was a New England points of interest guide. There was a "hidden gem" section – most of the places weren't that hidden and weren't really gems – but Raven's Point caught my attention. The article said it was the highest point in West Drumlin with "breathtaking views" and "abundant wildlife." What really grabbed me was the waterfall - "just a short hike from the trailhead."

I had been trying to find the trailhead when I ran into the roadblock and stopped at the yard sale. After that, I'd completely forgotten about Raven's Point. Even though I'd been lost, at least I'd be able to put myself in the general area. I had an unusually good memory for roads and knew I could find my way back to the house. Whether I'd get any answers there was another story. The old couple was creepy and seemed scared. *They knew.* They knew about Julian Black and sold me that fucking thing anyway.

My thoughts were clearer the farther away from home I traveled. *You mean the farther away from that thing.* I'd considered just trashing the Victrola, driving somewhere and tossing it off a cliff, but my gut told me it wouldn't work. Whatever was going on, whatever Julian Black was, I didn't think he'd *let* me destroy the Victrola. I surprised myself by thinking logically about something so illogical. It's not that I didn't believe in certain supernatural phenomenon, it's just that I really needed to *see* something to truly believe: I'd seen enough. As soon as I found the house and got whatever I could from the old guy that sold me that haunted piece of shit, I was going to track down Jay and Angie and make sure they were okay. The alternative threatened to cripple me with despair.

I cranked up the oldies station, fuck Julian Black, and watched the landscape fly by. I smiled when I saw the sign for the Raven's Point trailhead. *If I had found the sign that day, I wouldn't be in this mess.* Joe Cocker was singing about friends and I thought of Jay and wondered just how much of a mess I was in. A few minutes later, I passed an old farmhouse that had an old grain silo that was so tilted it defied gravity. I flashed back to that day – *the day I bought the Victrola was now officially that day* – and remembered thinking it looked like the leaning tower of Pisa. *I'm close.*

A few turns later, I knew I was on the right road. I slowed the car and stared at the trees on the right side, knowing there would be a hairpin turn up ahead, then the old cape-style house. I took the turn, my stomach suddenly tight, and slowed the car to a crawl. The break in the trees was just ahead, but when I reached it, something was wrong.

The house was there…but different. What had been a tired but livable old house was now a decrepit ruin. The front yard was a tangled mess of overgrown weeds. The bushes closest to the house threatened to swallow the structure, looming hungrily around it. I pulled into the driveway and switched off the ignition. My stomach felt like someone held it in their fist and was slowly squeezing. I got out of the car and walked along the road, staring into the woods, searching for evidence of the fallen tree that had blocked the road. I reached the spot where I thought it should be and crashed through the undergrowth. It took a few minutes and cost me a few nasty scratches from some thorn bushes, but I found it. I wished I hadn't.

The tree trunk was there, but there was no way the tree had fallen just a week earlier. There was no sign of any damage to the bushes and smaller trees that would have been crushed when the big tree fell. What remained of the stump was worn by time and elements. New shoots of whatever kind of tree it was had sprouted and they were taller than me, their trunks as thick as my wrist. The grip on my stomach tightened and an inescapable feeling of dread attached to me. With a sigh, I turned back and made my way back to the road.

I approached the house slowly, as if it were a dog I wasn't sure was friendly. The closer I got, the more I had the sense I was being watched. There was no breeze. In fact, it felt like the air had been sucked out of the day and I was in a vacuum. There were no cars on the road and none of the usual sounds of insects or birds. The quiet was preternatural. The urge to run to my car was overwhelming, but where would I go? Back to the Victrola?

I stood at the foot of the porch steps looking up at the house. How could it have only been a week ago I stood in this spot talking to an old woman about a record player? I remembered her hand moving like she was going to bless herself and telling me it wasn't for sale. Then the screen door had opened…. I looked at the door now, hanging from one rusty hinge, the screen in tatters. It wasn't possible.

My hands were clenched as I moved toward the porch. The stairs were rotted, I was careful to step on the stringers on my way to the door. I pulled the handle and the remaining hinge gave way with an ugly screech. The door crashed to the porch next to me. I twisted the knob of the interior door and pushed. The door resisted, swollen in place, then exploded inward with a groan. The reek of stale air hit me like a warm fetid blanket and I gagged. The expulsion hinted of something worse than decay, it felt wrong. *Evil.* I hesitated, licking my lips and breathing hard. I wanted to turn and run back to my car but I knew the Victrola and Julian Black waited for me at home.

I stepped inside and was struck by a sense of grief that made tears pool in my eyes. There was no cause for it, it was just there. The sorrow was crippling but I felt compelled to go on. I made my way through the ruins of the house, tears streaming down my face, looking for something. I didn't know what it was, but I knew it was there and I was meant to find it.

Random images flooded my mind, a slideshow of misery. A young woman crying by the side of an empty crib. An old man standing in the rain as a coffin is lowered into the ground. A middle-aged man kneeling by the body of a lifeless child, the boy's bicycle a tangled mess in the grill of the man's car. The visions threatened to break me, to drive me insane with their burden, but I continued deeper into the house.

I reached what must have been the living room. The shag carpet stunk of mold and the wallpaper was peeling off the walls in skin-like strips. But it was the fireplace that drew me. I stood in front of it, trying to ignore the hateful pictures flashing through my head. I reached out and pulled on one of the bricks, then another. On the fifth try, I felt the brick move at my touch. I wiggled it a few times and pulled it out, letting it drop to the floor with a muffled thud. I reached in, knowing this was why I was here. I pulled the thick leather-bound book from its hiding spot, and ran from the house as fast as I could make my trembling legs move.

As soon as I was outside, the visions disappeared. I fell to my knees, the residual sadness finally weighing me down. I cried for all the people, real or not, that had invaded my consciousness while I was in that house. I felt gutted, but eventually the tears dried up and I returned to my car.

I drove in a daze, my eyes constantly moving to the journal. I waffled between thinking it was my way out of the mess I was in, and thinking it was going to seal my fate. It hit me that if I went home, I just might put the book down and play a record. The thought jarred me and I pulled into the first parking lot I saw, ironically it was a boarded-up Strawberries record store. A bad omen, I thought.

I reached for the journal with shaky hands. *It's just a book.* It felt hot in my hands and I told myself it was just from being in the car. *Sure, and the thing at home is just an old record player.* The first entry, in ink so faded it was barely visible, was from June of 1929. It was written by my newly-made acquaintance, Julian Black. He described his life in somewhat mundane terms and I skimmed ahead. In the early 1930s, Black fell ill and his entries became hard to read, not only due to the trembling hand he must have written them with, but because of their content.

Black spoke of his sudden, though given his condition not unexpected, interest in life-after-death and earth-bound spirits. His entries went from the pseudo-scientific to fever-induced madness. My throat tightened when he mentioned the Victrola. He described insane experiments and his mood went from manic when he perceived things going well, to near-suicidal when another of his lunatic ideas failed. His final entry was dated June 21, 1934: "I've done it."

I swallowed hard and licked my lips with a dry tongue. I flipped ahead a few pages and was shocked to see more writing. The dates were in the 1940s. I looked closer, noticing a difference in the writing. *Could he have recovered?* Then I saw the signature. Someone else had continued the journal, not Julian Black.

These entries were signed by Frederick Gainsborough. He picked up the Victrola at an estate auction, and almost immediately began experiencing what he called "fugues." Gainsborough spoke of entire nights that he had no memory of, and the disappearance of friends and family members. I gulped in shallow breaths as I read on. In Gainsborough's last entry, he outlined a plan to seduce a woman he'd had his eye on. His method? A nice bottle of wine and some soft music on the Victrola.

I turned the pages of the journal, sweat dripping from my brow. The names changed over the years, but the story was always the same. The last completed pages of the journal were dated October of 2007. The author was Francine Jacobs. Her entries were filled with the same pattern: amnesia, missing friends, and the damned Victrola. Francine's last entry was different than the others – her husband was going to try to make her sell the thing.

I closed the journal and leaned my head on the steering wheel. I knew if I researched Francine Jacobs, her last address would be the house I just came from. I also knew that she killed her husband then committed suicide on the day I bought the Victrola at their yard sale. What I didn't know was *when* that happened. For me, it was last weekend, but the date in the journal was ten years ago, and the house certainly looked like it had been vacant for a long time.

I flipped back through the journal and found the same gaps in time between each of the previous owners. It didn't explain anything, but it fit a pattern. A crippling sense of resignation overtook me. Twenty bucks was what I sold my life for? My soul? I started the car and headed home.

I arrived forty-five minutes later to find a police car parked in front of my house. A cop was walking toward the cruiser from my front door. I grabbed the journal, feeling its heat, and stepped out of the car. My shirt was soaked with sweat and I felt like the word "guilty" was stamped on my forehead. *But guilty of what?* Images of Jay and Angie flickered in my mind. "Can I help you, Officer?"

He looked up, then back at his notes. "I'm Officer Tobin. Are you Mark Armstrong?"

"Yes, I live here. Is something wrong?" *Of course, something's wrong, two people you know are missing.*

He looked at his notes again. "Do you know a Jason Schmidt?"

I always wondered why cops always added the "a" before the name they were asking about. I smiled, but it didn't feel right. "I've known Jay forever. Is he in trouble?"

The cop stared at me for a long minute before answering. "I was hoping you could tell me."

Fucking Colombo. "Tell you what? If he's in trouble?" The cop stared and I wondered if this tactic ever worked. Did criminals just wilt under a cop's gaze and confess everything? This time my smile was real and the cop frowned at me.

"Mr. Armstrong, when was the last time you saw Jason Schmidt?"

"Last weekend. We hung out here listening to music and having a few beers." The idea of inviting the cop in and putting on a record was hard to resist. "I've been trying to get in touch with him all week. Listen, do you want to come in and tell me what's going on?" I motioned toward the house. *What are you doing?*

"I think that would be best." He stepped back and let me go first.

I entered the house and immediately my eyes locked on the Victrola. Whatever shit I was in, this wasn't going to get me out of it. I put the journal on the coffee table and motioned to the couch. "Have a seat, if you like. Can I get you a drink?"

"No, thank you. I just have a few questions... Hey, does that thing work?"

I felt my lips curl into a smile. "As a matter of fact, it does." Tobin had stepped over to the Victrola and was looking it over. His glance moved to the record collection.

"Would you mind putting something on? My grandparents had one just like this. I never thought I'd see one again, never mind *hear* one."

I pulled out "Agents of Fortune" by Blue Oyster Cult. The opening of "This Ain't The Summer of Love" sounded like shit coming out of the horn, tinny and scratchy. But it wasn't the music I was hearing, it was the whispering *behind* the music. Julian Black had all the answers. *His master's voice.*

Later that night, I sat on the couch and began writing in the journal.

Ghost Maker
Emma J. Gibbon

I am a man who creates ghosts for a living. *Ghost Catcher* is in its fourth season now and I've been there since the beginning as their only cameraman. I'm sure you've seen it on the Paranormal Channel, at least the commercials. Two friends dedicated to unveiling the truth about the supernatural after a shared high school experience. In reality, Jamie and Trent are two pretty faces picked up by the production company to run around in the dark and get excited about "orbs." They're household names now. You can even buy t-shirts with their fake-tan faces on them. I make fun of them, but they're genuine guys. They really believe in this supernatural stuff. They know about the fake stuff we pull, but all the things they say on the talk shows about the show being like a big happy family—they mean that.

Today we're at an old Cape in Connecticut. The owner is typical of who we get writing in: an overweight housewife with a homely face and too bright lipstick. She has good hair, though, and when I look over at Bob, the production manager, his eyes are big and shiny like a puppy. He has a soft spot for women like her.

"Dave," he says to me, "show the young lady the new camera," and I oblige. I can see Bob's round face going red when she smiles at him. He's been lonely since his wife left him last year. He just wants someone to go home to after work. His ex got bored with him and started going to night classes and retreats. Last I heard she was traveling in Egypt with a women's group. I should just get him on a dating site. Poor guy is so lonely.

I think about my wife and what she'll be like at that age. In my head I've already divorced myself from Jackie's future. Divorced myself from her but I don't have the balls to do it in actuality. I won't know her when she gets to be that old. I never saw *us* in the future. When she used to talk about growing old together, I let my thoughts drift away to avoid listening to her and think that one day, I would be sure, stay or leave. But I just keep floating on and am non-committal as ever.

The housewife thinks she's psychic (they all do), but these days the word is 'sensitive.' "I've seen a full-bodied apparition," she says, eyes wide. "A Civil War soldier who walked from here," she points to a threadbare sofa, "to here." With a flourish, she motions to the door and I move the camera. Next we're going to film the attic section. The golden duo isn't here yet; they show up for the night filming.

People think we just film overnight, but what they don't know is that it takes at least a week to film enough that is usable, even with all our trickery. Perhaps *trickery* is too strong a word for it. It doesn't take much to pause a camera in order to make something appear to move on its own: a chair, a bedspread, a Bible if we're going for the demon thing, or use a piece of fishing line to pull the back of someone's sweater. Doors will close on their own with a swift kick, and a disembodied voice can easily rise from the duct system. This is what I spend my life doing.

I'd like to say there is some art to it, but really there isn't. Most of it we don't need to fake: an old furnace will produce the bangs, dust makes great orbs, a creaky floorboard is a godsend, and warm breath in a cold room can make a convincing, eerie mist. I'm sworn to secrecy but everyone knows. As long as we spook the viewers and get the ratings, no-one cares. I think the viewers know, too. Most people aren't that stupid; they just want to be entertained. Occasionally we have the odd thing we can't explain, but we couldn't make a show on it.

I follow Bob's chubby butt up the steps to the attic. Once we're there, the air is stuffy like any other, and I've been in quite a few. Old toys and Christmas decorations spill out of soggy cardboard boxes. My throat starts to clog with dust and insulation fibers. This place is about as paranormal as Chuck E. Cheese.

"We sometimes sense a young presence here…" I miss the rest of what the woman is saying. I can see Bob trying his best not to ogle her breasts. They're substantial, and heave with emotion as we interview her. Bob has frosting on his chin from eating doughnuts at breakfast. The lady is still talking, "That's why we keep these toys up here. My children have outgrown them now. I could give them to Goodwill…" I think of Jackie. There will be no toys in our attic.

*   *   *

It was a month ago and a Saturday, late at night; I was at home in the den flipping through channels. You'd think I'd get sick of TV through work but I find it hard to sleep, too used to staying awake all night filming. Jackie came and stood in the doorway. She was wearing her fluffy white bath robe and her pale yellow hair was floating with static. Behind her was the warm glow from the kitchen light. Her face flickered blue with the screen.

"We need to talk," she said. I felt my stomach plunge with a kind of dread tinged with excitement, like when you're a kid and you know you have to have a tooth pulled. I looked over at her. Her features were indistinct, mushy.

"What's the matter?" I thought she was going to tell me it was over. If she ended it then I wouldn't have to. I turned the TV sound off. It wasn't like I just woke up one day and realized I didn't love her. I just coasted along with everything and at some point realized she loved me more than I loved her. She didn't say it was over, however. She walked over to the couch, sat beside me and took my hand.

"We're having a baby."

I looked at her. She squeezed my hand and I looked into eyes that seemed brown in the dark even though they are blue. They were open wide and I could see a reflection of the TV screen in each iris. She was doing that smile where she shows all her teeth. When I didn't say anything, her smile got smaller. Her face diminished.

"We're having a baby, David. I'm three weeks along." She raised her hand and picked at the dry skin on her lip. I'd seen her do this many times.

"Have you taken a test?"

Her brow furrowed. "Yes, of course. You were away filming and I couldn't wait."

I sat and looked at her and tried to re-arrange my face into something that was appropriate. Her eyes were searching my face and I couldn't quite keep up with them, make it right.

"Aren't you happy?" she said. I almost looked around to see if she was talking to me.

"You have to get rid of it," I said.

She looked at me in silence. It may have been seconds, it may have been minutes, but time seemed to stretch and slow. I noticed an itch behind my knee. When time sped up again she began to sob, dry, heaving gulps that didn't make a sound. She didn't look away or close her eyes. Her gaze didn't move. I sat there with her limp hand in mine and wished I was somewhere else.

*   *   *

We kill the lights in the Cape as the sun goes down. I film Jamie and Trent as they stalk through the kitchen. Trent holds up an EMF reader and shouts out readings while Jamie explains to the audience: "Some people believe electromagnetic fields are evidence of spirits. Ghosts use this energy to manifest. We could be in the presence of the supernatural." More likely it's the refrigerator kicking out rays, but who am I to say? Next Trent pulls out a digital sound recorder to capture EVPs. We'll review them later and see if we can get the white noise to say "Get Out!" but for now we wander into the hallway, asking questions into thin air. I found a talking doll upstairs that's going to go off on its own, and later we'll walk up and down the stairs for the camera's microphone to pick up. Jamie turns and gives me a wholesome grin; I wish someone would tell him that the infra-red doesn't pick up tan.

Off camera, Bob is talking to the housewife, "Of course we believe that this house is haunted. It's not just for the TV. Spirits don't work on a schedule, I'm afraid, but we do. It's just to help it along. I really hope that we do catch some real activity and then we won't need all this." He smiles at her crestfallen face. It occurs to me that I don't even know if Bob believes in the paranormal. I know about his failed marriage, his problems with his weight and the fact that he's borderline diabetic yet I don't know his opinions on the very thing we work together on.

I want to tell him about Jackie but I know he'll be disappointed in me. I can just imagine the look in his eyes when I tell him that my wife is pregnant and I'm making her get rid of the baby.

We move to the living room. Trent and Jamie try to make contact with the ghost of the soldier. We don't mix it up much on this show. There's a formula we stick to. It's a formula that works, though—for the ratings, rather than finding actual ghosts. Jamie asks: "Is there anyone there? Give us a sign. Show us your presence," and nothing happens. They make a big deal on this show about it being dark but what they don't mention is that I'm in the dark, too, and walking backwards; I have the torn up ankles to prove it. What I see is the little square on the viewing screen in front of me as I stumble backwards into the unknown.

We return to the kitchen. We debated having some plates fly around but in the end decided to go for the Civil War angle. It's a popular one in New England. Bob begins to go upstairs with his boots on to do the heavy footsteps. We joke about him being the heaviest and he laughs. I wonder if he ever regrets not having kids. Maybe his wife would have stayed if they had. Once we get the footsteps wrapped up I go into the attic to check the camera.

* * *

After Jackie had finished crying we went to bed. I stared at the ceiling while she lay with her back to me. We didn't talk. What could we say? I stayed awake for a long time, and it wasn't just the usual insomnia. I could tell by her breathing that she wasn't asleep either. She lay very still.

I could hear her gulping and snuffling. I reached out to touch her but stopped before my hand connected with her skin.

Years ago she had said things like, "When we have kids." That had changed to, "if we have kids" and then it had stopped. I assumed the matter had been dropped, that she was thinking along the same lines as me. I thought about the madness of me being a father, of something swimming around in Jackie that we had made. How could I have created that spark of life without some sort of sign? I wondered if the thing was a person yet, if it had a soul. Where does its soul go if we get rid of it? If Jackie doesn't have this kid will I be making a ghost?

The next morning, she wouldn't talk to me, wouldn't look at me but once I'd been away to work and come home again, she thawed. We talked, awkwardly, about nothing important. Later, she showed me the appointment letter. I nodded and told her I'd be away filming.

*   *   *

Despite the mustiness, I like hanging out in attics. Give me an attic rather than the basement any day. The camera is set up fine, so I root around in a few of the boxes, flip through some old magazines, and find a stack of yearbooks where the pictures of bad eighties haircuts are spotted with water damage and mold. Right at the back, I see a lawn chair and wonder if I can balance it across the joists. I walk across the beams and drag it over to where it's not in shot. I figure I have a bit of time to relax before the others get here to film the next section. I turn off the light and settle into the chair. My shoulders are knotted and I've been clenching my jaw so hard I have a headache. I open my mouth a couple of times to ease the pressure.

I'll call Jackie in the morning. She deserves more than that but she has her appointment at the clinic tomorrow. I'll tell her I think she should go ahead with the abortion. Tell her that everything is going to be alright. Tell her we'll get through this, even though I don't believe it myself.

The chair is comfy and the attic is hot. I close my eyes, tilting my head back on the head rest. The tension drops from my shoulders; my arms dangle over the sides of the chair. As I start to drift into sleep, all my body hair stands on end. I sit up and look around. It's dark but I see the outline of boxes in the light filtering from downstairs, where the others are bumping around. It won't be long before they're up here. The air in the attic gets colder and I wonder where I've left my jacket. I rub my arms with the palms of my hands. For once, I am desperate for sleep and settle back into the chair. Not very professional, but it's not the first time someone has fallen asleep on this job.

I half-dream about Jackie, the way she sits on the bed and brushes her hair. How the blonde strands rise up to meet the bristles as she moves to the crown of her head. I fall into the rhythm of it, the rise and fall of her arm, the tilt of her head.

It is then I feel a tiny hand rest on my forehead. It wakes me. I know I'm not asleep. I am not dreaming. It is not a breeze and it is not a spider web. It is a child's hand that is so soft and so small that I want to grab hold of it and squeeze it. I feel the fingertips and the palm and the side of the thumb resting as if checking whether I have a fever. Only two people have ever felt my head like this: my mother when I was very young, and Jackie. I do not move because I don't want to disturb it. I open my eyes wide but even in the dark I can see there is no one there. The hand feels warm and dry. I think of what the woman said about the presence. I don't want it to go. I can feel it breathing on me. Small, feathery breaths, warm and quick. How the hell can it be breathing? I sit there for two or twenty minutes—I lose track—with the hand placed on my forehead. It never moves and the pressure doesn't change. The breathing on my face gets closer and closer. I think about Jackie and her blue eyes that look brown in the dark. I think about how I am making her get an abortion. I think about her blond hair. I tell whatever is there, "Sorry," and the breathing gets really close then. Small, dry lips indent my cheek.

Then the hand is gone. I whisper, "come back," but I know it is no longer there. I wipe the grit of fiberglass from my eyes and squint into the room. When Bob throws open the attic door, appearing in a square of yellow light, I am still in the dark, exploring my forehead with my fingertips and trying to hide from him that I am crying.

Later, Bob will walk away with the housewife's phone number. Turns out she's divorced and lonely too. Jamie and Trent will finish their close-ups and then swan off in their top-of-the-range RV. I will walk down those attic stairs on wobbly legs, call Jackie and tell her to stop. Cancel the appointment. If she wants that baby, then she should have it. No matter what my opinion is. As for me and her? I still don't know. I just know that this particular ghost is not mine to make.

But for now I have to put batteries in this doll. It says "Mama" and the whole attic space is filled with its electronic voice.

The Pick Apart
Paul McMahon

Ashley had come to bury her father. Nothing more. Jimmy knew this, she'd made it abundantly clear, and yet he kept pushing closure on her as he steered the rental car toward her father's home.

"Something drove him to it," Jimmy said. "You said he seemed happy over the past year. I can't believe you don't want answers."

"I didn't drive through three states to solve a mystery," she said.

"Of course not, Ash. No one ever sets out to solve a mystery, but sometimes mysteries fall out of the sky."

"Jimmy—"

"Leaving them unsolved only makes us feel antsy, you know? Like there's something we were supposed to do, but we've forgotten. Don't you want to know why your Dad's friend refused to take over his business? This is a motor head, a *mechanic* we're talking about. This guy should have jumped at a chance to own a junkyard."

"I don't want to talk about it, Jimmy." Ashley resumed looking out the car window. Men were so full of shit. Dad, with his monthly "everything is rays of sunshine" lies, that fat lawyer with his "your Dad *wanted* you to inherit his land" lies, and now Jimmy and his goddamned "mysteries fall out of the sky" lies.

"I'm just saying, is all," Jimmy muttered.

She hadn't wanted him to come. They'd only been dating a few months. Last week he'd bought a toothbrush to keep at her apartment, but she wasn't sure how she felt about that. He'd hovered at her elbow throughout the afternoon's wake, constantly asking if she was "okay," if she "needed anything," if he could "do anything for her."

He had stepped up, though, when the big, unshaven man had leaned much too close to her and introduced himself as Rollo. Dad's friend, she realized. The one who'd refused to accept Dad's business. She and Dad had Skyped monthly, so she knew he and Rollo had been close for a long time, but they'd suffered a falling out over... she wasn't sure what. Dad had used the pronouns "she" and "her," but these days that could refer to a woman or a car. He'd never specified, and Ashley never asked.

149

Rollo had spoken in a hoarse whisper, saying he and her father had been best friends for years. Said he was sorry for her loss, couldn't imagine how he would fill the hole in his life that her father's death had left behind. More lies. Dad hadn't suffered a death; he'd committed suicide. Plus, the last time they'd Skyped, Dad had said he and Rollo hadn't spoken for a month. Of course, Dad had also insisted everything was hunky-dory, but later actions had put the lie to that.

Rollo had asked nonchalantly if she'd gotten a motel room for the night. As if being a school teacher gave her money to throw around. The rental car had been enough. She'd told him she was staying at her father's house. He'd gaped at her. Told her she was a fool if she stayed *there*. That's how he said it, *there*, set off in tone as if he feared the place would hear him. He'd grabbed her arms and begged her to stay somewhere else.

"You don't know," he'd said. "You don't know."

Jimmy had stepped in then, signaling to the men who worked for the funeral home.

"Are you staying *there* as well?" Rollo had asked Jimmy.

"I'm with Ashley, so...."

Three funeral home workers had surrounded Rollo and herded him toward the door. "Neither of you has the sense God gave a duck," he'd yelled.

As soon as they were gone, Jimmy had wrapped her in a hug.

"Is this our left?"

Ashley blinked, surprised to find herself back in the rental car.

"It's... I think it's..." she squinted toward the turn. "Is there a street sign?"

Jimmy slowed. "I don't see one."

"There. In the trees. Esker Road. Left here."

"Left it is."

Jimmy turned and sped up.

"All the way up, on the right," Ashley said.

She focused out the windshield as they drove, determined not to space out again.

Trees hugged the road on both sides. As they progressed, the forest thinned. Half a mile in, the occasional single-story modular homes appeared in cleared-out sections. Ashley wondered what kind of life decisions you had to make to end up in one of those.

"This must be the bridge," Jimmy said. It came into view around a curve.

On his side, the bridge still had its original stone wall, reinforced with steel slats bolted along its length. On Ashley's side, though, most of the stone wall was crumbled into a deep ravine. She'd guess fifty feet, at least. Construction barrels lined the drop, wrapped generously in yellow "caution" tape.

"Jesus," Jimmy said. "Somebody did a number on that." He slowed the car as they neared and came to a stop on the bridge. He pushed himself up and leaned over Ashley to look down into the ravine. She refrained from shoving him back into the driver's seat. He gave a low whistle. "Was that from an Earthquake? How deep to you think it goes?"

Ashley's pulse raced. Dad had dived from here. She couldn't see the bottom, but the sides were lined with rocks. They'd been the last things her father had seen, and now Jimmy wanted to gawk. "I don't know," she said. Her voice was barely a whisper.

"How'd the bridge break in the first place, Ash? Did your father ever talk about it?" Thankfully, he settled back into his seat.

"It was an accident earlier this year," she said, trying to remember the tale. She hadn't paid close attention when Dad told the story, and now he wasn't around to tell it again. "I don't remember. Some couple were on their way home. Had a fight and crashed through. He survived; his girlfriend didn't."

"Ouch."

"He walked back here a few days later. Two and a half miles. Moved the barrels aside and took a header into the ravine."

"Really?" Jimmy said. "And you don't want--"

"No. I don't. Get me to the house. I want to take a nap."

Jimmy sighed. He looked out the windshield for a moment, then sighed again. He slipped the car into gear, but didn't move them off the bridge. "I'm just saying."

"Can we go?"

He still didn't drive. Ashley looked out the windshield. From here forward, a stockade fence ran along the road. Dad had told her his junkyard was completely fenced in, but one section of fence was missing along the ravine, where it ran up into the woods. In that space, she saw rows of cars, each of them stripped to various degrees. Dad's Pick Apart.

Dad owned five acres of land stretching back into the woods. Well, *she* owned them now. It was a smallish plot, as these things went, but situated as it was near the edges of three small towns, it did a fair amount of business. According to Dad, he'd started drawing customers from towns further away. He'd joked that the place was keeping him in cat food.

"Is she supposed to be there?" Jimmy asked.

Ashley focused. She'd started to space out again. Jimmy was staring at the missing section of stockade fence. She didn't see anyone.

"Is *who* supposed to be there?"

"Her. Wait. I thought someone... must have been a shadow." He eased off the bridge and sped up. They travelled in silence for a moment before the stockade fence ended. Jimmy stopped in front of a driveway gated with a section of highway guardrail. Hanging from it was a hand-lettered sign. Dale's PICK APART. "The gate's closed. You have the key?"

Ashley looked at him.

"The key? The lawyer gave you the key."

She remembered the fat man handing her something.

"You put it in your purse."

She opened her purse and looked inside. One small key ring sat on top. Even holding it before her eyes, she couldn't remember seeing it before. Six dirty golden keys on a simple metal ring. "Maybe it's one of these?"

Jimmy took them and got out of the car.

Her attention wandered to the tiny house built on an incline at the edge of the property, not much larger than a trailer. Another modular home. Figured. She'd just been looking down her nose at people who lived in these. Of course, Dad had always referred to it as his "palace," which called up grandiose images in her mind. Another lie.

She heard a scrape. Jimmy dragging the gate aside. She watched him pocket the keys and rub dirt off his hands as he returned to the car. He dropped into the driver's seat, then slipped the car into gear and drove through.

No lights shone inside the little house. She wondered if they'd turned off the electricity. If that was the case, she and Jimmy might end up doing what Rollo wanted and going back into town—

Jimmy stopped the car and got out.

"Where are you going?"

"To close the gate," he muttered.

Ashley heard the annoyance in his voice. She wasn't giving him the responses or attention he wanted; wasn't itching to delve into the mystery of why her father dove into the ravine, especially now that they knew the boy who survived the original accident had returned to do just that. Well, tough shit. She would grieve her own way. If he wanted to fight about it, he was out of luck. She hadn't driven through three states to deal with *him*, either.

The driveway was large enough for six cars to park side-by-side. Jimmy ignored the spaces and pulled alongside the front of the house. "We got here just in time," he said as he killed the engine. "Sun's almost down."

Ashley opened her door and stood.

What Dad had called a "palace" brought only one word to her mind. "Squat." Thankfully, she only had to sleep here one night. After the funeral tomorrow morning, they'd be most of the way back across three states before the sun set again.

"She's in the yard," Jimmy said. He stood beside the car, his door open, staring toward the stockade fence enclosing the Pick Apart. Ashley noted the double swing gate. When opened, cars could be driven in and out. A heavy chain, fed through holes drilled in each door, secured them with a padlock. To the side, out of the way of the gate, stood a storage shed, which she imagined housed the cash register Dad used and a chair or two for the hours he opened the yard.

"She's in there," Jimmy said.

"What are you talking about?"

"She's singing." He walked toward the gate. "I can hear her." He fished the keys out of his pocket as he reached the gate, then went to work on the chain.

"Jimmy," she called. She heard the click of the lock opening. Felt dumbfounded as he started to open the gate. "JIMMY!"

He turned toward her.

"At least give me the keys so I can get our stuff inside," she said.

He lobbed them at her and turned away before they clinked on the ground two yards short of her feet.

An industrial *bong* rang in the stillness. "You didn't close your door," she told him. Jimmy didn't respond. She stepped forward and picked up the keys. "Jimmy?" Exasperated, she walked to the trunk and jabbed the release button under the lip. It popped open with a dull *sprong*. She pulled out her overnight bag and turned.

Jimmy stood in the open gate of the Pick Apart. The setting sun reduced him to a silhouette.

"You're really not going to help me with these bags?"

"She's lost, Ashley. She needs help. Can't you hear her?"

Ashley listened. "All I hear is your 'door open' chime."

He stepped to his right and disappeared completely.

"Unbelievable." Ashley shouldered the strap of her bag and walked around the car to slam Jimmy's door. She watched the entrance to the yard, but Jimmy didn't return. With the light getting dimmer, she made her way to the house. It was almost too dark to see, but she got the screen door open and managed to find the keyhole. The second key opened the door. She found four light switches on the inside wall. The nearest turned on the bulb over the door, easing her fears that the electricity had been shut off. The light illuminated the six-foot by twelve-foot landing outside the door, the single folding chair, and the artificial grass rug. She dragged her foot on it and it scratched like fingernails on a chalkboard. "Palace," indeed.

She leaned into the house and flicked the next switch. Two exposed light bulbs came on over a round dining room table just inside the front door. Above the four-switch panel, she found a stretch of eight more, all in the "off" position. These must turn on lights in the junkyard. Since she had more than enough light to get the bags into the house, she left them off. Jimmy could feel his way around in the dark.

Ashley unshouldered her bag and dropped it on the table. Straight ahead, toward the back of the house, was a stove and sink. The refrigerator stood to the side. Directly to her left, Dad's green leather couch sat in front of an old tube-style TV set. She could make out the indentation in the back cushion where he'd rested his head during his off hours. A hint of his cologne lingered in the air, but it didn't mask the mustiness. Two pictures hung on the wall above the TV. The first, her parents' wedding picture, made her miss Dad so much she crumbled a little inside. Mom had died far too long ago for her image to affect her. The second picture was her graduation photo. Not the formal one, the one snapped right after the event. Ashley had a big smile, a bouquet of yellow roses, and one hand on her graduation cap because the wind had been grabby.

As much as she wanted to explore the rest of the house, she pocketed the keys and decided to get Jimmy's bag. Typical guy, he'd finish whatever he was doing and come right inside, assuming she'd done all the menial labor. He was already acting annoyed with her mood, as if dealing with her father's suicide and being unexpectedly saddled with the junkyard didn't provide reason enough for her foul attitude.

His toothbrush would be going in the trash when she got home.

Ashley turned for the car. Her breath stopped when she saw the face watching her through the screen door.

"You need to get away from here," Rollo said.

Ashley stepped back and bumped the table. Her fear morphed into anger. "Why?"

Rollo looked at her, then shook his head. "You wouldn't believe me if I told you."

"You're probably right. Tell me anyway."

"The girl. Mary Bedigian."

Ashley just blinked at him.

Rollo made a noise like a cat upchucking a hairball. "I told you, you wouldn't believe me." He turned to leave.

"Who is she? I have no idea who you're talking about. Was my Dad seeing someone?"

Rollo turned back to her, incredulous. "Seeing someone? As if." His crooked smile made her wonder if he'd recovered from a stroke or suffered from Bell's Palsy.

"Then who is she? Did she try to sue him or something?"

"She was killed, girl. When her boyfriend's car went over the bridge."

Great. This guy was crazy, and she was alone with him. Only the flimsy screen door kept them apart. It wasn't even locked. Rollo could be inside as soon as he decided to be. Ashley would run to the kitchen and grab a knife if he tried to come through the door.

"She doesn't know she's dead," Rollo said. "She wants someone to bring her home. I told your Dad to stay away from there, but he didn't listen to me."

She sighed. "You were right. I don't believe you."

Rollo grunted, obviously frustrated. "Your Dad and I were playing cards the night it happened." He pointed at the table. "We heard the crash. I ran outside while your Dad called for help. I climbed into the ravine. The boy was banged up, but Mary was dead."

Ashley nodded. "Dad didn't say much about it."

"They dragged the car up into the yard after the accident. That same night. Took down part of the fence and your Dad never replaced it. Then he went and let them leave the car in the Pick Apart overnight. I told him not to, told him it was bad luck, but he didn't listen."

"How long ago was this?"

"Month."

"And they haven't rebuilt the bridge yet?"

Rollo chuffed. "Have you seen this area? This town? The board ain't gonna spend money on that."

"Tell me why you didn't want the business."

Rollo's lips moved, but he hesitated.

"And what did you and my Dad fight about?"

"We never—"

"Stop lying. Dad told me you abandoned him."

Rollo shook his head, his mouth agape in a crooked semblance of innocence and surprise, but he saw the expression on her face and deflated. "I saw her the next night. Mary."

"You saw her." She couldn't believe she was hearing this.

"Standing on the street by the bridge. Looking lost and afraid. I felt like I needed to help her. Then I remembered I'd seen her dead. I ran up here. Told your Dad. He didn't believe me."

"So, you and Dad had a falling out over a *ghost?*"

Rollo shooed a moth fluttering around the outside light, his quick, unexpected movement almost stopped her heart. He put his hand on the handle of the screen door. She readied to run to the kitchen, but his expression grew confused. He looked left, then right, then turned to look over his shoulder.

"There was a boy with you. Where is he?"

Ashley swallowed. "He's around."

Rollo looked at her through the screen door. "He's in the yard?"

She shrugged.

"He saw her, didn't he?"

She shrugged again.

"You've got to go get him." He glanced toward the yard, his hand playing at the base of his throat. Then he looked at her again. "When the police come, I was never here."

He turned and raced off the porch. Ashley stared at the empty screen. A moment later, she stepped up to the door and saw Rollo swinging a leg over the guardrail gate before running up Esker Road, away from the Pick Apart.

Ashley opened the door and looked toward the yard. The house was higher than the stockade fence, but although she could see most of it from here, it was too dark to make out anything but shadows and blackness. She reached toward the panel of eight switches. Each one she flicked turned on another pole light in the yard, revealing car bodies with missing doors and hoods. The last switch turned on the pole in the corner nearest the bridge. It illuminated barely enough for her to see Jimmy, only Jimmy, standing with his back to her.

She looked around for a flashlight. There was no reason for her pulse to be hammering. Ghost stories were bullshit. Lies. She'd heard so many of them from so many men today she was acting silly.

Ashley stepped onto the porch, nearly cried out when the plastic grass crinkled under her feet. She didn't want to walk to the edge of the ravine without a flashlight. She saw the rental car and smiled. She had all the light she could need.

She stepped off the porch and jogged around the storage shed to open double swing doors of the Pick Apart wide. She jogged back to the rental car, shutting the trunk on the way by. The keys hung in the ignition where Jimmy had left them.

It started right up, giving her none of the crap her own car would have. She turned around and drove into the Pick Apart, turning right, toward the road. Dad had arranged the cars in rows with plenty of space between them. This made it easy for him to replace the junkers after they'd been picked clean. She had no idea if the cars were arranged in any kind of order. It didn't look like it. She saw sedans next to Jeeps next to sportsy models.

She turned left at the last row. The pole lights weren't nearly bright enough. It took a moment to find the high beam controls, and when she did, she sighed with relief that Jimmy still stood where she could see him. What the hell was he doing?

She drove up behind him slowly, trying not to let the movement of his huge shadow on the trees beyond freak her out. She stopped the car a few feet behind him and waited for him to react. He didn't. She gritted her teeth, then leaned over and opened the passenger door.

"Get in," she called.

He didn't move.

"Jimmy!" A tiny movement of shadow told her that Jimmy was talking. To who? There was no one else here. "I can't hear you."

He didn't turn. Made no effort to speak louder.

Ashley cursed, then opened her door and stood. The door chime *bonged*, so she stepped aside and closed it.

"Jimmy?"

Jimmy was gone.

Ashley stepped toward the space, her gaze intent on the ravine. Someone had tried to keep the gap in the stockade fence secure by stapling a stretch of chicken wire between the poles, but now it was only attached to one side. The wire mesh dangled into the ravine. The headlights exaggerated her shadow's movements, making her dizzy. Near the edge, she stopped. Looked down. She saw only darkness.

"Jimmy?"

"I'm here, Ash."

His voice rose from the abyss.

"Where are you?" she asked. She felt cold. She leaned forward, peered into the ravine.

"Over here."

Jimmy stood on the street, between the construction barrels and the broken bridge wall. He must have moved while she was getting out of the car.

"Jimmy, come back over here. You're making me nervous."

"No."

She blinked. Hadn't expected that.

"Jimmy, please." He'd made her come all the way down here to fetch him. Wasn't that enough affirmation for him? What more could he expect? "Come back to the house with me."

"She's down there, Ash."

Ashley bit her lip. She'd assumed Jimmy was playing with her, getting her to the lip of the ravine so she would talk about why her father had killed himself. He didn't seem interested in that anymore, though.

"She needs help."

Ashley's shallow breathing echoed in her ears. "You're scaring me, Jimmy."

"She wants someone to bring her home."

Reality seemed to fold as she recognized Rollo's words. She tried to summon anger, but failed. Her voice sounded panicked. "Jimmy, get in the car right now. We'll get through the funeral and be home by tomorrow night."

He looked up at her. "Why?"

"Why what?"

"Why would I want to go home? You're just going to dump me when we get there."

She swallowed. "What are you talking about?"

"I'm only here because you didn't want to be alone for your father's funeral. Once it's over, you're done with me."

"That's not true. You know that's not true."

Jimmy held her gaze for a moment, then looked back into the ravine. "Now who's lying?"

"Jimmy—"

"Bring her home, Ash." He leaned forward, stiff as a falling tree. Ashley couldn't find the breath to scream as gravity took him and the blackness swallowed him. It seemed like forever until he landed.

Ashley stepped back and dropped to the ground. The headlights flooded over her, illuminating the trees and making strange shadows among the leaves. "Jimmy," she said.

She wants someone to bring her home, Rollo had said, and Jimmy had said it, too. Had Mary picked off her father and then Jimmy to bring her here? Is that what was happening here?

Jimmy had said he could hear her singing. Ashley listened for a long time, but all she heard was the thump of someone closing the passenger door.

She stood, but couldn't make herself turn around, sure she'd see a face watching her from the passenger seat.

The Stranding Off Schoodic Point

R.C. Mulhare

October 30th, 1863

The late October sky hung like a pale blue bowl inverted over the ocean waters of the Gulf of Maine. Lavinny Sterne rowed one of the fishing dories of her great uncle Seamus Malone's fishing schooner, the *Sunny Green*, with her partner, Teague Washington sitting in the bow, plying the second set of oars. Seagulls wheeled about, their creaks and caws drowned out by the creak of the oars as they tried to swipe at the bucket of bait in the well of the dory. The sky wouldn't remain clear nor the weather calm for much longer. The fishing crew would hole up for the winter, before the cold wind of November blew in and froze Frenchman Bay, which lay between Schoodic Peninsula and Mount Desert Island. One last catch and the cash from it along with her nest egg from the season would provide for her mother and sisters and brother for the winter. With her father away in the Shenandoah Valley patching up the soldiers fighting Johnny Reb, someone had to stand as the man of the house. Ma could tend to the women and children of Winter Harbor Village, but her needlework wasn't as keen for the kind of injuries the hands experienced.

Thus in the middle of the spring, when Malone needed another hand on one of his dories, Lavinny had offered to take the oars. She'd spent enough time digging clams with her grandmother and on the water with Ma's Pa before the grippe took him from them five years ago. Then, she helped Grandpa's brother when he took charge of his schooner, but not 'til this summer had he let her go to sea with his crew. Ma had objected at first.

"There could be work for you on shore, or digging clams." She'd warned her about someone on the crew having malicious intentions. But Malone had given his word to throw anyone off the boat who so much as looked at Lavinny wrong; including dropping the cad in the middle of George's Bank and leaving him there for the sharks. That did little to quell Ma's concerns, despite Lavinny's decision. Nearly every time they pulled in with a catch, they found Ma walking the quay, watching and waiting, like one of those widows in the old ghost tales, keeping watch for a ship that would never come back.

Lavinny hadn't minded; if anything, it charmed her. Until Ma tried to talk her out of the job yet again. Ma had proposed she find a husband, either in town or by post, to provide for her and make the household a little smaller Lavinny had tossed that notion over the side.

"I ain't having myself shipped overland to Minnesota or the back end of beyond, like a parcel of wool or a box of salt cod, and I ain't going down to Arkham to see if your Ma's people can set me up with some dandy who's never hoisted anything heavier than a pen," she'd said. The one time she'd visited Father's family in Arkham, she'd pitied her laced-up lady-cousins in their unwieldy crinolines. If that's how they did things among the so-called civilized world of the flatlanders, she'd take the rustic ways of Maine. "Besides, it would leave you and the little ones on shortened circumstances."

Teague raised his oars, looking to her, the movement calling her back to the here and now. "This a good spot, Lavinny?" he asked.

"Good a place as any this late in the season," Lavinny said, raising her own oars. Teague took up the bucket of bait, standing and dumping it into the water. Lavinny raised the net from the bottom of the boat, shaking it out and casting it over the ripples, watched it sink. Now came the hardest part of fishing, waiting for the fish to find their way into the net. Lavinny set to work looking over the spare net for worn spots to mend, while Teague dug out a ball of twine against any needlework they had to do.

The lines tethering the net to the boat twitched. Lavinny set aside her work and stood, balancing carefully, reaching for the lines closest to her. Teague dropped his mending to grab the further lines. When they hauled in the net, they found only a handful of haddock and a few halibut, but this late in the season the fish were running deeper and further out to sea. It would have to suffice; hopefully Malone would pay her well. Goodness knows one or two of the crew grumbled that he favored her on account of her pretty face and their kinship, but the old man would growl at them, reminding them her father was away binding the wounds of their sons and brothers at Gettysburg and other blood-soaked battlefields.

"It'll do," Lavinny said, as they sat back in the boat and pulled toward the *Sunny Green*, which stood further up the bay, awaiting the return of her daughter vessels.

They'd passed Schoodic Island on their starboard side, and approached Little Moose Island, turning west toward Big Moose Island before rounding it and sailing to the spot where the *Sunny Green* had dropped anchor off Turtle Island. They passed Finch Island, a tiny island named for a tiny bird, little more than a rock that stood up from the water. They gave the rocks space, in case the current got frisky and drove them against it, and had almost come around it, when a cry rose on the wind, desperate yet weary. Probably Jake Gilhooly, who'd run up on the rocks again, but a fisher in distress was still a brother, no matter how big of a nuisance he made of himself.

"Teague, you hear that?" she asked.

Teague glanced over his shoulder at her. "I hear gulls, if that's what you mean."

"Awfully human-sounding gulls, if you ask me," Lavinny said. "And it's coming from Finch Island. You see a gull atop of it?" No gulls circled the boat. The smell of their catch should have attracted even more but not a one perched on the rock.

Teague looked toward it. "No, you're right." And a hint of pallor showed in his dark face.

"Bring the boat around, let's see who's there." Teague plied his port-side oar, turning the boat, as did Lavinny, bringing the boat closer to the rock.

As they came around, a figure came into their view, a human form in tattered oilskins clinging to the rock, pieces of wood and a broken oar floating on the water around him.

"Hey! Help!" the figure called. Not the voice or face of Jake Gilhooly, but a richer voice and a darker, olive-skinned face. Possibly one of the Portuguese fishermen come down from Nova Scotia or Newfoundland or up from Gloucester.

"Ho there!" Lavinny called. "Hold fast, we're bringing her close." The figure raised his face to her, his eyes dark like her own.

Teague looked to her, his black eyes narrowed and the pallor still showing in his dark face. "Should we get close? The current's awful strong today."

"That could be us someday. I'd want someone to do us the same turn," she said. "Bring her in." They rowed in as close as they dared without ramming or riding up on the rock or scraping it. *One way to remove the barnacles*, she thought with a wry smirk, but she could also rip the bottom out and they'd end up like the man on the rock. As they came alongside him, the man slid into the water, as if he'd hung on so long he'd lost his strength.

Finding the tether line for the dory, she threw it into the water. "Here, catch!" she called. The stranded man grabbed at the line, missed, then took hold. She hauled on the line, drawing the man closer to the boat. Teague braced on the opposite side as she helped the stranded fisherman aboard.

"You out for a catch?" she asked.

The stranded man huddled in the bottom. "I was," he said. Despite the wind on the water, Lavinny pulled off her oilskin jacket, draping it over the man, to keep the water's spray from chilling him any further.

Lavinny reached for one set of the oars. "Teague, let's pull back to the ship." The sooner they got back, the sooner they could warm the man, whoever he was. The cold could take your life, if you weren't careful to get below and into a warm bunk with two people on either side of you, or if you were onshore, in between two cows or two sheep.

The ship's lanterns had just been lit as they pulled up to the *Sunny Green*, Malone waiting on the deck for them. "Declare yer cargo, lassie," Malone said, his rugged face tired after a long day, as two other crewmen took the lines of the dory and winched her aboard.

"Got a few haddock and halibut, but I also have a passenger," she said, and she pulled back the oilskin. Aside from the fish still in the net, the bottom of the boat lay empty.

She looked to Teague. "Did you see him go over the side?"

"No, 'Vinia. Been watchin' the boat since we pulled that guy in," Teague replied, getting out of the dory as quickly as he could.

Malone looked into the bottom of the dory, then to the darkening sky above, then to Lavinny. "Too late in the day for sunstroke. You woolgathering out there?"

"No, sir: we came alongside Big Moose Island and Finch Island, when we found him on Finch. His boat had broke up and he was hanging on. Practically fell in when Teague and I pulled him aboard," she said.

Malone said nothing for a long moment, looking from Lavinny to Teague, then into the boat. "Which island?" Malone asked, his face blanching under his old sailor's tan.

"Finch, off Big Moose, about a mile from here, why?" Lavinny asked.

The boys on deck had hauled the net from the bottom of the dory and started untangling the haddock from it and dropping them into the fish pots, but they slowed their work, glancing at Malone and pretending they hadn't cocked an ear apiece to listen.

Malone crossed himself. "You just saw Constantino Serrano's ghost."

Lavinny leaned in to sniff at Malone's breath. He might take a wee drop of "the craychur" from time to time, but never when he was at work. "That wasn't a ghost. He was flesh and blood. Cold flesh and blood, but I felt his weight pulling on the line I threw him. He tipped my boat as well. Would have ended up in the bay, if Teague hadn't braced hard."

"No one's told you about Constantino Serrano?" Teague asked.

"First time I've heard the name," she said. "Who is he? *Was he*, I suppose, if you're speaking the truth."

"He was a Portuguese sailor who'd put down roots here, about twenty-some odd years ago," Malone said. "Came down from Halifax. Used to fish out of Schoodic with your grandfather's crew, till he was out getting one last catch at the end of the season, right about this time of year, some sixteen, seventeen years back. Never made it back to his ship, but the boys on yer grandfather's crew found the pieces of his dory broke up near the shoals the next morning. Never found him, so it's safe to assume the seas took him.

"But once in a great while, usually this time o' year, when the Irish folk are carving turnip lanterns and before the witch of November casts her spell on the sea, someone finds him on the rocks and brings him in. Either to their ship or to shore. By the time they get him to safety, he vanishes, like he was never in their boat. Haven't seen him myself, met some that did and took him in. Too many for it t' be just a story."

They cleaned the last of their catch, Teague wondering out loud if their encounter on the rocks was a sign of good fortune, "Like Abraham offering dinner to the angels who brought him and Sarah the good news." Then they put sails east and north, heading home to Winter Harbor.

They pulled into the quay with the half moon rising over the hills, and unloaded their catch before Malone settled the account and gave out the last pay of the season. Word must have got out that the ship had docked. As Lavinny walked from the fish warehouse and up the quay, Malone trailing her on the way to his own home, she saw her mother Elnora walking toward the dock, her cloak wrapped about her shoulders and a shawl over her head. Lavinny's sister Letitia was at her side, a lantern in hand. Ma hugged Lavinny close, releasing her to shake Malone's hand. "Thank you, Seamus, for bringing her back to us."

Malone pressed Ma's hand before releasing it. "She'd bring herself back, if it came to that y' gal has more gumption than some o' the lads workin' the ship."

Lavinny tried to cover this by reaching into her coveralls and taking out the pocketbook containing her pay, and an advance on her last catch, to hand to Ma.

"Should keep you an' the gals in ribbons till the spring running," Malone said.

"Unless Maria wants more new books from the post out of Portland," Ma said.

"As long as she hasn't been lurking around where I hid my nest-egg," Lavinny grumbled.

Malone made his farewells and went to see about setting his boat in winter storage. Ma lead Lavinny up the quay and onto the main road of the village. Letitia carried the lantern ahead of them to relieve the darkness picked out by lights in a few windows and a few early turnip lanterns on Maisie Gilhooly's porch steps.

"Lavinia, your face looks as cold as a December sea. What's wrong?" Ma asked.

"Nothing, I had a long day for the last day of the season, and my haul was middling," Lavinny said.

Ma's shawl rustled as she turned to look to Lavinny. "You've never looked that worried after a middling haul before. Tell me, you've always confided in me."

Lavinny looked to Letitia, then slowed down her steps, but kept the light in view. "We found a fisherman stranded on the rocks off the point. Teague and I hauled him on board and we brought him back to the ship, but before we could get him onto the *Sunny Green*, he vanished out the boat."

Now Ma slowed her pace, pausing to look full into Lavinny's face. Then looking to Letitia's light bobbing further up the road, she murmured, "Let's get home before your brother Caleb and the little ones get restless, and Katie wants to call out the bloodhounds to look for us."

They didn't say more about the man on the rocks till they got back to their rooms above Father's dispensary. Once home, while Caleb collected fresh logs for the kitchen range that Katie the kitchen maid clattered about, and when Ma had settled a squabble between Maria and Cora, the younger ones, Ma took Lavinny to her and Father's room, on the pretext of settling the family accounts.

Once Ma had lit the lamp in the room and closed the door, she set her ear to it, as if to make certain no one lurked outside. Then she stepped close to Lavinny, taking both of the girl's rough hands in hers.

"Lavinny, the man you found on the rocks, did he have curly black hair and dark eyes? Was he swarthy and young, perhaps in his early twenties?" Ma asked.

"Yes, he didn't speak much, because the cold had hit him. But he had an accent like some of the Portuguese fishermen we've met in Bar Harbor and Portland," Lavinny said. "Why do you ask?"

Ma hesitated, said nothing for a long moment, looked away to the far corner of the room, then looked back Lavinny. "Lavinia, that was your father." Ma never called Lavinny by her given name unless she spoke in all seriousness.

"My father? My father is John Sterne, the man you married, who went to war when Lincoln called for doctors to treat the Union boys."

"John Sterne gave you his name and raised you, but he wasn't the one who gave you to me."

Lavinny felt the world turn slower under her boot heels. "The lads on the crew said Teague and I found a ghost."

Ma nodded. "I've heard the stories that people tell, of what they've found on the rocks. It's why I worried at your going to sea. But you're more like Constantino than like me. He was stubborn but so brave. He'd started in the merchant marine, till he'd been injured while unloading his ship. Your grandfather took him aboard after his captain cast him off, gave him a home away from home. Once he'd mended, he'd climb to the very top of the masthead like a monkey and hang on like a bird. Drove me dizzy to watch him, but he always came down when he saw it drove me to distraction. He promised one day he'd buy me a pearl ring with his earnings, but I'd tell him to keep dreaming. Until Christmas, when he gave me a ring with a pearl he'd found in an oyster and had a jeweler in Portland set for me. I told him he would have to get a ship of his own, even something as small as a catboat to pay that off. He promised me that he would do that. Bless him if he didn't save his money and buy his own catboat at the beginning of the next season.

I kept my end of the promise and we married at Easter, just before he set sail, tailing my father's ship. By midsummer, I could tell him he was going to have a son or daughter, come the following Easter. He couldn't have been more happy than if someone told him his nets would never again come up empty."

Ma hesitated. Lavinny took the opportunity to ask the question that lurked on the tip of her tongue. "But what happened? How did he end up on the rocks?"

Ma's face gathered as if she might cry, but she did not. "Before the night he vanished, when he set out two days before, I had told him to take care out there, that the skies looked raw. He promised me he'd be home with his last and biggest catch of the season and that I shouldn't worry, in my condition. Call it a premonition, but it came as no shock to me, when your grandfather and Malone came home without no trace of your father but a broken oar and the shards of wood from his boat, including the name plate.

I fainted, and your grandfather ran for John Sterne, the new doctor in town, to come tend me. In the days after that, he came around often to see that I and you were well. Even after you were born, he kept coming around, and his kindness lingered with me so much that when he asked me if he could be a father to you, I told him I was about to ask him the same question.

"In the spring, he was at my side when you came into this world. He might not have given me to you, but he was there from the moment you saw daylight."

Lavinny took a half a step back from Ma. "But why didn't anyone tell me about this sooner? Why did you keep this from me?"

Ma gave her a worried look, but her eyes softened like she understood. "There wasn't any ill will, if that's what has you cross. I had hoped the past could live in the past and stay there, and we all could go forward as a family. And for the greater portion, we have. But sometimes the past doesn't stay there. Sometimes it calls out to you and creates echoes. Maybe that's how ghosts happen, because the past has something to tell you."

Lavinny leaned closer to Ma. "Maybe it wasn't just my decisions that took me to the sea, maybe he was calling to me to assure me that I'd chosen the right course."

Ma reached up to smooth back Lavinny's hair, as she'd done so many times over the years. "I always said you had sea water in your blood."

"And now I know I have it from both streams," she said.

*   *   *

At the end of the following March, when the worst winter storm had passed and the waves had lost their wintry fury, with Father soon to return home from Virginia, Lavinny rowed her dory out from the *Sunny Green* as it rode Frenchman's Bay on the first day of the season. As the dory passed Finch Island, and when she thought Teague couldn't see, she raised her oars and reached inside her oilskin, taking out a handkerchief wound around a bundle of snowdrops and fir twigs she had gathered from the woods behind her family's home. With a word to the heavens to look kindly on her father's shade and a word to the depths that his bones would lie in peace, she cast the nosegay onto the water. It sank, then bobbed back to the surface, riding the ripples.

Teague caught her movement and raising his oars for a moment bowed his head, slow and respectful.

Looking away from the posy floating on the water, Lavinny leaned into the oars. "Come on, Teague, let's see if the first halibut of the season are running."

As they pulled away, she thought she heard a second set of oars creaking in another pair of oarlocks, but when she glanced about, she saw no other boats besides the rest of her crew, too far away to sound that close.

Triumph of the Spirit
GD Dearborn

1.

She stands in the doorway, my angel of death.

I am laying on my death bed. My angel is weeping.

My angel... my daughter.

"Daddy? I'm here."

With great effort, I move my chest. In. Out. In.

Get a good lungful.

Ow! It hurts to breathe.

I summon her with a wave. She comes close. The mask, positive pressure, O2. I claw it off. Her face ignites in shock.

"No, Daddy! You need to breathe!"

"Hush! I need... to say something to you. Can't... with mask on. Don't..."

Fast beeping. O2 sat 85. Here comes the nurse.

"Doctor, you need to keep that mask on!"

I try to remove it, but practiced hands force the mask back on my face. She cinches the straps tighter than before. Involuntarily, I gasp in more oxygen. Just breathing is excruciating.

"Doctor, are you in pain?"

My head feebly nods before I can stop it.

I can't have morphine now, it will arrest my breathing. I think my diaphragm has torn.

"Okay, I have standing orders from Dr. Hayata. This will take the pain away."

No! Stupid bitch! Quack bastard! You need to image me, stat!

The drug works rapidly. I am wrapped in a cocoon of black cotton. The room goes dark.

The last thing I ever see is my precious angel sobbing, sobbing because her heart is breaking, because she knows that this is the end.

\#

I am swaddled in darkness.

I hear muffled voices. My angel is screaming. The nurse is shouting. "Code Blue!"

Rapid beeping. An alarm screeches.

"Start chest compressions!"

And then the voices stop.

2.

Am I dead? I can still remember...

I remember the car. I loved that car. Triumph Spitfire '77 convertible, British Racing Green. I bought it on a whim on eBay with some of the net profit after I sold the big house and bought the condo in Florida; after Gracie left me, after she died.

My angel came down to visit after the auction. She grieved her mother, of course, but it was okay. They hadn't seen eye to eye on anything in years. She was Daddy's girl. She wanted me to stay in the Granite State, said I would miss the snow. Well, fuck that Yankee bullshit. Florida is pleasantly warm when it should be, and the condo has AC and a pool for the rest of the year. It's not like I'd never go back, I told her. But of course, I never did.

Gracie's cancer used up a chunk of the nest egg, but I still was doing okay with my IRA. I could afford a small indulgence. The guy I bought it from let it go for just a few thou, but it needed work, and his brother just happened to own the only import parts shop in the city. *Convenient.*

I didn't care. I didn't care that I couldn't afford anything better, nor that I paid three times what the car cost me to restore her. I didn't care that I had become a walking cliché. Stereotypes happen for a reason, after all. It kept my mind off things and gave me an excuse to not make friends with the neighbors. And the timing was just about perfect.

My angel finished the last of her executrix duties a few days after I finished sprucing up the Triumph. She and the kiddo flew down a week after that. I promised them we could go to Disney and all those other attractions, but to be honest, my heart wasn't in it. With the car done, I had nothing left to do except drive it, and when I drove, I thought of Gracie. And thinking of Gracie hurt.

I'd drive for hours with no one but the voice of the GPS for company, going nowhere and getting there fast. Some days I'd leave at dawn and get home at dusk, and I couldn't remember anything I saw that day. I couldn't remember what I had for lunch, or anything about whatever greasy spoon I ate it in. All my memories were of Gracie.

When Angel & Kiddo showed up on my door stoop, there wasn't a thing to eat in the house. She dumped her bags in the spare bedroom and asked me for my keys. I balked, offered to spring for delivery, but she insisted. So Kiddo and I watched Cartoon Network for a while and waited for her to come home. It seemed like ages before I heard my key turn in the door.

As soon as I looked at her, I knew that I was screwed. The apple doesn't fall far from the tree, and before she handed back my key ring, she opened it up and took two keys off.

"I got a spare made, Dad. You don't mind?"

She snapped the two loose keys onto her own ring. That girl loved convertibles, all right.

"Dad, could you help me get the groceries in? You're a pal!"

I don't know why she even bothered to make a spare set of keys. I never got to drive my car again.

#
black
no sound no light no sense of being
just nothing
just peace

.

#
I… exist!
Excruciating pain!
Agony!
Light.
Where am I?
Lying on my back. Looking up at a cheap chandelier.
How did I get here?
Sounds. People, talking. Low tones. Whispers. Crying… who is crying?
Angel?
A rush of colors and suddenly I can see through her eyes.
I am looking at myself.
I am in a casket.
I look like shit.
What the hell? I thought I made myself clear! After we saw what those bastards did to her mom, I specifically told that girl I wanted to be cremated. "No embalming. No makeup. No coffin, no wake, no funeral. If you want, you can say a few words before you spread my ashes. Then go get drunk on my dime with your friends."
This is bullshit!

She's talking to people. Sometimes they hug her. She is numb. Like a robot she says, "Thank you," over and over again.

She's leaving. She's with her boyfriend. Not the a-hole, the new one. She's going back to his place.

Oh, hell! Like a father needs to see this...

\#

nothing
nothing is okay

.

\#

Pain. Light. Sun.
Too bright! Hurts.
I am back in Florida. I am lying back in my chaise lounge. I've got a G&T in one hand and a good cigar in the other. I can hear myself thinking....
Life is good.
She's sitting in the chair next to me, big straw hat, sunglasses, black one-piece cut low in the back. I can hear *her* thoughts, too. She doesn't like to show her stretch marks, but she still turns heads. She reminds me so much of Gracie, it hurts. Her memories are like a movie. So are mine.
Am I watching this movie or am I acting in it? Can it be both?
We watch Kiddo playing in the pool with the neighbor's kids. The older one is nearly seventeen and not unattractive herself. I feel ashamed for noticing. Gracie always said that men are pigs. Tomorrow the girl is going to sit for Kiddo while his mom and I drive across the state.
This morning my daughter told me the final figures on Gracie's estate, including the auction. I'm a bit more flush than I thought.
Maybe I can afford a boat after all!
There is a nice one I saw online, 35-footer, berthed in Tampa. My plan was drive out there, take a look at her, eat a pressed Cuban with bacon, buy some more of these fine cigars, and be back home before *Agents of Shield* comes on. Kiddo and I don't have a lot to talk about yet, but superheroes and baseball are enough for now.
I probably won't get that boat anyway. Kiddo needs a better school.
"Dad, no! Mark's school is fine. And after that, the public high school will be fine, too. He doesn't need to go to Phillips."
"Honey, you know I had always hoped to do better for you. Let me do this for him. He's bright enough."
"Well, how about my old Catholic school? I liked it okay. Some of my teachers are still there."
"*That's* your idea? Let me tell you why it sucks."
She sighs, rolls her eyes. I ignore it.

"First of all, you are a liar. You bitched and moaned every day you were in that place. Second, you only went there because your mother thought it was the right thing to do, so you would be a good Catholic. A devout churchgoer, your mom. But I happen to know you've never stepped inside a church since the day we dropped you off at college."

She winces.

"Oh, honey, no, I'm sorry!"

Idiot. I forgot about the funeral mass.

"It's all right, Dad. I'm all right. But I *was* thinking that maybe it would be okay if Mark started going to church. He needs something to believe in…"

It's my turn to wince. She *knows* how I feel about this. Particularly after what Gracie went through. The years she spent, suffering, dying by inches. Right up until the end, she had faith. Faith in her god. Faith in her man. She was wrong on both accounts. A doctor's wife is not exempt from the ravages of an incurable disease. Medicine failed her. All the prayers from her church friends didn't do any better. The final score was God 0, Medicine 0, game called after eleven excruciating innings.

I never was a believer. My parents were nominally Methodist; we almost never went to church. I became an agnostic when I went off to college, and then an atheist after my first cadaver dissection in med school. People are just meat.

The point was moot once I met Gracie. She was a staunch Catholic from a line of staunch Catholics. Her mother almost became a nun. So long as I promised to let Gracie raise our kids as Catholics, we could get married in the Church. She wouldn't marry me anywhere else. I was never evangelical about my atheism anyway.

The parochial schools that my wife sent our daughter to tried to fill Angela's head with nonsense, but I figured time was on my side. I didn't have a long wait. She hung up her faith along with her Catholic school uniform on graduation day.

I can't believe that she now wants to subject her own child to what she had been through. It would be less ridiculous if she was telling me she and the boy donned capes and masks and fought crime by moonlight. This is seriously pissing me off.

"Dad, don't you have any hope that you'll see Mom again? That it could at least be a possibility? She hoped for your salvation, said prayers for you, right up until the end."

"Dammit! Shut up, honey, won't you? Just shut the hell up! I can't believe what I'm hearing coming out of your mouth. *You* are the one she used to pray for. Sure, I was happy when you gave up that pie-in-the-sky nonsense. I've always told you to think critically and believe in the truth of your own experience. But I also taught you about tact and respect for people's feelings. When you quit the Church, you didn't have to rub your mom's nose in it so… viciously! She was a good woman, why did you have to antagonize her?"

Tears roll down my angel's cheeks.

Aw shit, I stepped in it again. Who's the mean one now, asshole?

"Dad, maybe I was being a bitch. But maybe I was also wrong. I wish I hadn't said those mean things to her. And if she was right about heaven, maybe it's not too late to tell her so. I've been praying, Dad. Just like the nuns taught me to. And it makes me feel better. Death is not the end, Daddy. It is just the beginning."

I take a sip of my G&T. Then I knock it back until it is just rocks. I puff on my cigar for the long count.

"Sweetie. I love you and Mark, and I loved your mother. But dead is dead. There is no afterlife. This is all we've got. In my career, I signed over two thousand death certificates. I know what 'dead' means. I never once saw anything that made me believe in a soul that persists after death. When I am gone, I'm gone. So, mourn your mom. Grieve her. But then let her go. Live your own life. Be there for your son. Let the dead be dead…"

And then, instantaneously, it's not noon anymore. It is dusk. It's as if I've woken suddenly from a dream, into another dream. My angel is standing by the pool, alone, but it is cool out. Chilly. She's not in her bathing suit. She's wearing a dress and a light sweater. This can't be August. It feels like November. The pool chairs have been stacked neatly in their racks. The surface of the pool is scattered with dead leaves. They mustn't be cleaning it every day.

My angel is crying.

"Dad. Daddy? Can you hear me? I hope you were wrong, you sour old bastard. I hope you are with Mom now. Because you were a good man, Daddy. You deserve to be with her, in Heaven."

But I'm not in Heaven. I'm here with you. You keep calling me back. And that pain you're feeling, some of it is mine.

She walks on the white-pebbled path back to the condo. Her condo, now.

She turns off the television. The boy has fallen asleep with the TV on, again. He's too big to carry anymore. She marches him to his bed without waking him. It's like she's a master puppeteer making a marionette sleepwalk.

He looks an inch taller.

They grow so fast!

Then she sits on the couch and clicks the remote. Imaginary people live only seconds as the channels flick by. She pours herself a drink, and then another one. And another. Until at last darkness claims her, and she falls asleep on the couch herself.

> #
> *void nothingness oblivion*
> *i do not think therefore i am not*
> *i am not*
> *an endless, waveless ocean of black*
> *peace*
>
> .
>
> #

I see my picture on the mantelpiece. It's dusty. It makes her cry. She picks up the picture.

It hurts *to be here... Stop it! Let me go!*

The picture slips from her fingers. It falls on the hearthstones. *Crash!* Broken glass goes everywhere.

> #
> *black*
>
>
> .
>
>
> #

Oh. *This* again. I am in the Triumph. She's in the driver's seat, not saying much. She's trying to hold on to her grudge from yesterday, but we always make up. We will be laughing together before we get to Tampa.

She's Daddy's Girl. She knows that I was teasing this morning when I called her "showoff bitch," as she raced me to the car and leapt into the driver's seat without opening the door. I can't do that anymore. I'm not out of shape, but sixty is sixty. Can't do everything I could do when I was twenty, but I am not dead, not yet...

No, I am. But not when she remembers me.

In fact, maybe I retired too early. I should go back into medical practice. I could get a second condo, in New Hampshire. I'd take a locum tenens job in Orlando every winter, see snowbird patients. Then I could migrate back north with the snowbirds in the spring and work at my old job for the summer. Everyone wants to take three weeks off when it's warm, but we can't get coverage for that. They can't. Well, I could cover everyone's vacations for them.

I will tell her my plans while we are eating Cubans in Tampa today. She will be pleased, I know. And I can watch the boy play in Little League. Maybe take him to

Fenway to see the Sox sometimes. Movies, too. There is a Marvel movie every summer, I think. Those are his favorite.

She has cramps. It's her time of the month.

No wonder she was so moody yesterday. She's driving awfully damn fast...

And then it happens. Again. Like it always does. The Truck.

She's impatient. Traffic is too slow for her. She always drives faster when she's mad at me.

We are on a blue highway. Single lane in both directions. She's tailgating a mother with an SUV full of kids. The yellow line is solid as we go around the bend. She honks and tries to pass. The Triumph handles well, she's confident. There is a truck ahead! *A lumber truck? What is a lumber truck doing in Florida?* She tries to merge back in right, but there are two cars ahead of the SUV. The truck jams on its brakes. Something's coming at us, a wooden pole, not large, but stout. Like a javelin, arcing through the air, coming down straight at me. Just before she cuts sharply into the space between the two cars, the shaft pierces my chest...

And suddenly I am at her house, in New Hampshire. The Triumph is on the back of a truck. She's had it trucked all the way up here.

Why didn't she drive it herself? Because she couldn't, that's why. She couldn't because Mark's in school. No, that's not the reason. He is in school, but it's a boarding school. She couldn't drive it because it would hurt her too much. But she couldn't get rid of the Triumph either. She knows I loved that car. It is the last place she ever saw me.

She pays the man, the truck leaves. She's alone, with her memories. Alone with me.

The pain is excruciating! Is it her pain? Is it my pain? I don't want to be here!

The phone in the house rings. It's not Mark, he'd call her cell. It breaks her reverie, she goes in to answer it.

#
black
off in the distance...
 a light?
 no, just a color
  shapeless
  and noise
  twittering
  coming closer
#

She's handing Kiddo my old stethoscope. "Here it is. You tell your girlfriend to take good care of this."

"Thanks, Mom. She will. And she's not my girlfriend."

They are standing in Mark's room. Faded posters—Iron Man, Batman—and a Sox pennant adorn the walls. My old desk is in the corner. They must have saved it from the big house. There is some sort of electrical apparatus on it, a circuit board, wires, a lantern battery. Weird science from the five & dime. No, those don't exist anymore. Dollar store?

A miniature football field painted on a green sheet of Formica is also on the desk, next to the gizmo. A small steel ball rests on the fifty-yard line.

"So, explain this thing to me." Her tone of voice is a mixture of awe and pride.

"Okay. It's not that big a deal. You know that a current only flows in a complete circuit, right? You have to close the switch or the current won't flow, the light bulb will be dark. But make the connection and the light bulb lights up."

His mom nods her head. She got good grades in school, until she had to drop out. But that must be fifteen years ago now.

"When the current flows it makes a magnetic field in those two iron rods in each goal at the ends of the gridiron. The ball is attracted to whichever electromagnet is stronger." He points to the circuit board. "The sensors on our fingers measure galvanic skin response and feed the data to the microcontroller, which adjusts the strength of the electromagnets based on the relative GSRs. It's similar to a lie detector. Instead of recording the response on paper, it moves the ball, but it's really the same thing. The more relaxed you are, the stronger your magnet is, and the brighter your light is. The player that moves the ball into their goal wins."

"So how I feel is what moves the ball?"

"Well, yeah. Kind of. Living things generate electromagnetic fields. They can be seen with Kirlian photography. Your emotional response changes the colors of your E-M field."

Colors?

"Oh, yeah. I know what you mean. Like auras, right? I had a friend when I was about your age that was into that stuff. She said she could see people's auras. She could tell if good things or bad were going to happen to a person. Negative energy brings bad luck, she said."

"Yeah mom, but this is *real* science…"

"Well it's *really* impressive. I am sure you will win the science fair. I hope your friend-who's-a-girl gets a ribbon too. I wish your Grampa was still here, he would have let her round with him at the hospital."

"Yeah. You miss him a lot still, don't you?" She nods.

Yeah. She does. Whenever she does, here I am. It's excruciating. I don't belong here.

"Anyway, I don't think I will win. Billy Cronin's display is about quantum entanglement. 'Spooky action at a distance.' My only hope is that his project is all on poster board. Too bad for him, they don't make quantum mechanics science kits for kids."

"OK, I confess. I'm an idiot. What is "spooky action at distance?""

"Oh, that's what Einstein called entanglement. Sub-atomic particles that have become entangled together still influence each other, even if separated by great distances of space. Or space-time, I think. Don't worry about it. I don't totally get it myself. Billy's wicked smart, but I don't think he *really* gets it either. Quantum physicists are still puzzling it out."

He grins.

"Actually, I might win the blue ribbon after all. I've heard Billy's presentation, and it's good, but a physicist from the U is one of the judges. If she asks a pointed question, Billy will have to bullshit his way through it. I understand my project completely."

Kiddo has a good grin.

The doorbell rings. "Hey, I bet that's Tom. You better go now, Mom. Have fun!"

I fade away.

\#

Mark is a man now. He's wearing a cap and gown. He's standing with his mom. She feels so proud. She should, she's done all right. She brushes the hair from Mark's face, a wedding ring on her hand. My angel!

"You are so handsome. You look just like your granddad."

Mark smiles.

She's right, I see the resemblance. He's got my smile.

"You wish he was here now, don't you, Mom?"

"Yeah, kiddo, I do. But I think he is. I still think of him, but not so often anymore."

She beams at a guy—her husband— holding a toddler by the hand. She squeezes his other hand. Somehow that softens my pain. It still hurts to be here, but not as much as before.

"Family picture?" the guy says.

I know this face. He was her boyfriend. Not the asshole, the nice one. He's got a beard now.

"Honey, how is your headache? Is it rough today?" he whispers to her alone

"I'm fine, Tom. Let's not worry about that. This is Mark's special day. We'll tell him tomorrow. Just take the picture."

"Selfie!" says Mark to his girlfriend. They cuddle together, Mark's arm stretched out in front of him with his phone in his hand.

Where is *that asshole anyway? Too drunk to see your kid graduate?*

"Now a proper one with the whole family," Tom says.

"Beth, would you ask your dad to take a picture of us?" He hands Mark's girlfriend a camera.

Angel picks up her baby girl. The five of them stand next to each other. Mark and his girl are holding hands. She, too, is wearing a ring.

"Cheese!"

\#

black
but not quiet
i hear something
birds? pipes?
always getting louder
something in the nothing
here with me
moving…
\#

The kids have come home for Christmas. They have a baby of their own. Angel's teenager grabs the baby from Mark's hands.

"Gimme! Come to Auntie! Who's Auntie's little angel? You are!"

My angel is on the couch, drinking a Gin & Tonic. Why does she drink G&T's in the winter?

Oh.

My picture is not on the mantel. It's in a new frame, hanging up next to other family pictures on the wall. From the couch, she can see it clearly. She raises her glass to it, the hint of a smile dotting her face.

My pain is soft. Like cotton.

And suddenly I feel younger. I have a full head of hair. That smell… I am in the big house. My angel is only three. I am picking her up so she can hang her stocking. She's so excited!

And then suddenly I feel old and tired again. Back at her house.

"Tom! The kids are here! Bring down the presents!"

\#

i am not alone
it is attracted to me
or am i moving towards it?
no point of reference
cacophony
colors
i am not nothing anymore

i am fear

#

I am with her once more. The pain of existence feels better than fear.

Mark is sitting behind the wheel of the Triumph. It needs a wash. There is a big orange sticker on the rear fender; black block letters: *ICV*. A New Hampshire state seal, a number, and a date are printed on the sticker.

Mark's hair has thinned out.

Just like mine did when I was his age.

His mother is scolding him. She's got a touch of gray. She's wearing glasses. She won't admit it to the boy, but she's feeling worse. The treatments.

"I ought to have my head examined, letting you take that car from me."

"Geez, Mom. You hardly drive it anymore. But it's still in pretty good shape. Once I get it retro-fitted for electric, it'll be back on the road every day again. We've been over this. You said it was time to let it go."

"Yeah, I know. You are right. And it's better than just scrapping it. But it won't be the same. EVs don't purr the way an ICV does. It's like cutting the balls off a tomcat."

"Well, do you want me to take it over to the shop now or not? We had a deal. You can renege on me if you want, but the ICV sticker expires at midnight. It will cost you an arm and a leg for a new one. And there aren't even many places to buy gasoline anymore. Seems like a lot of bother to take a joy ride every fourth Sunday."

She sighs.

"Okay, son. You've out argued me. Your granddad would say, 'What goes around, comes around.' Just take it."

She's let go of me.

The pain is gone.

I feel nothing at all.

After all these years, my Angel has finally found what I could never give her.

Peace.

I slip back into oblivion.

I don't want to go...

3.

colors
acrid smell
a roaring whisper

madness
oblivion gone sour
i don't want to be here anymore...

#

"I'm sorry Angela. The scan doesn't look good. I'm afraid it's inoperable."

#

the other
i can sense its need
it's very close now
it's almost here
it's hungry
i must get away from it
i need to escape!

angel! think of me! for the love of christ, please think about your daddy again...
!

4.

Dad?
I wake up. Smell of antiseptic. Bright. Sunny. Flowers. Tom. My hospital room.
A good day. I'll see Mom and Dad soon.
Pain.
Where is my Mark?
My son stands in the doorway, my angel of death...

#
all is dark
?
cigar...
where's my dad? i think he was just here. i can smell him.
another smell... acrid...
there was something else here with him... something... wrong.
dad!
daddy?

Ghost on a Swing by Judi Calhoun

The Road to Gallway
Rob Smales

"Excuse me?"

Isabel looked up from the book in her lap. She'd been vaguely aware they'd stopped for gas, even momentarily registering the old-fashioned ding of the alarm bell hose alerting the attendant he had a customer, but she'd been far too deep in the world of Magnus Bane to take real notice of anything other than that the car had stopped. Now Dad stood at the pump, and from the tone of the *Excuse me?* Isabel worried that she'd not heard Mom the first time . . . but no, Mom was looking through her open window toward the next pump island.

There was a huge old car over there, a real blue boat. On the far side of it stood the station attendant, all gray coveralls and graying hair, and tall—tall enough that he was able to lean over the big car and squeegee the full expanse of the wide windshield with a single sweep of his long arm.

"I said," he replied laconically, wiping the squeegee's edge with a rag before leaning over to give the glass another swipe, "I'd mind the speed limit in the stretch between here and Gallway, if I were you."

"Okay, uh . . . thanks." Mom said, but Isabel could tell she didn't know what to make of this warning.

Dad stood too close to the car for Isabel to see his face, but she clearly heard his voice through Mom's open window. "What's between here and Gallway? There a speed trap or something?"

For a time there was nothing but the whir of Dad's pump, the numbers—not digital numbers, Isabel saw, or a screen, but actual, physical digits mounted on scrolling wheels, something she thought looked old, but kind of cool in a steampunky way—rolled up and up, slowly filling the Camry's tank. Isabel looked down at *The Bane Chronicles* again. She'd begun "The Midnight Heir," and Magnus was just facing a boy with a gun . . . but a speed trap? Seriously?

The attendant finished with the windshield, then bent low to give a brief finger wave to the white-haired woman behind the wheel. "You drive safe now, Doris." He plunked the squeegee in and out of its bucket of cleaner as the big car coughed to life and lumbered away from the pump, then strode over and offered Mom a smile as he slapped the sponge side of the squeegee on the Camry's windshield and began washing road dust off the glass in long, slow strokes. The left breast of his shirt, Isabel saw when he leaned over the car, was embroidered with his name: *Paul*.

"Speed trap? No, sir, not so far as I know—though I might not put it past some of our local boys in blue to sit out there watching cars go by from time to time. But between here and there's a few turny bits and a whole lot of straightaway, and just the kind of road where people like to open her up some." He flipped the squeegee blade-side-down and began slicking the dirty water away. "That, and you have Massachusetts plates."

"What," said Mom, "that whole Masshole thing?"

"Oh, no ma'am. That's not what I was saying at all."

Finished with the windshield, Paul moved to the back of the vehicle, ducking his head to throw a wink and a "Good evening, miss," in to Isabel before starting the sponge across the rear window.

"Folks from around your way *do* have a bit of a reputation behind the wheel," he said to Mom. "But this road's a place where us locals tend to step a little heavy on the gas, too. No, I just wouldn't want you runnin' afoul of Old Charlie, and he seems to have a special place in his heart for cars with out-of-state plates."

Mom and Dad exchanged a glance through the windshield, questioning whether they should even ask, but Isabel had no doubts. She stuck a bookmark between the pages as she scooted to that side of the backseat and buzzed the window open. "Who's Old Charlie?"

Paul took a step back so he could see her without bending, wiping the squeegee's blade again. "Well, now, Charlie's kind of a local legend we have, but there's plenty who've claimed to've seen him. Mostly out-of-state folks, like yourselves. Charlie's a ghost, you see. There was some drag racing going on for a while, and Charlie, well . . . well, a little lady like you don't need to know all the nasty details. Let's just say Charlie died, and now he haunts the stretch between here and Gallway, and he don't take kindly to speeders on his turf. Takes it as a kind of challenge, if I had to guess. People tell stories—mostly out-of-staters, like I said—of seeing a big set of headlights coming up behind 'em—it's hard to miss them big Crown Vic lights, lots of people mistake him for a state trooper on patrol at first—and the next thing they know, there's Old Charlie, trying to get 'em off the road."

The pump stopped and Dad racked the fill nozzle. "Well, thanks for the warning," said Mom, "but we're on our way to Hilton Head to visit friends, and we've already been on the road for almost ten hours. It's been a long day, and all we really want to do is find somewhere we can get some food and sleep, so we can get back on the road in the morning."

"You have a good night," said Dad, opening the car door. As he slipped behind the wheel, Paul stooped and offered them a finger wave, just as he had Doris. "Y'all drive safe now—you're about a half hour from Gallway, if you stick to the posted. And little lady? You might pass the time keeping an eye out for Old Charlie." He offered her another wink as Dad started the car, and then they were rolling out from beneath the station's bright lights and onto the dark road, following the Camry's headlights toward dinner and a bed, thirty minutes away.

*   *   *

"Can you believe that guy?" said Mom.

"It's just a story," Dad said. "I don't think he meant anything by it."

"But he was telling it to Isa, like he was trying to scare her or something. And 'keep an eye out for Old Charlie'?"

"Oh, I think the old guy was just playing it up. You know, being local color." Dad's eyes appeared in the rearview mirror. "What do you think, Isabel?"

"I think the speed limit's forty-five, Dad," she said, watching a sign slip through the outer edge of the headlights. Dad's eyes dipped as he checked his speed.

"You see?" said Mom.

"I'm *doing* forty-five," Dad said, eyes meeting Isabel's in the mirror again. "Honey, you know that was just a story, right? That there's no such thing as ghosts?"

"Oh, I know. But what was that you said about speed traps?"

Dad snorted a short laugh. "You see?" he said to Mom. "Just local color."

Well, I half know they're not real, Isabel admitted to herself. *Mostly. Sort of? Anyway, it would be cool if we saw a ghost car. Scary, but cool.* Her book remained closed as she did what Tall Paul had suggested and kept an eye out for any sign of big, bright headlights. She snuck glances between Mom and Dad as they talked, watching the speedometer climb from 45 through 50, and maybe just a little more than 55. *Speeding,* she thought. *With out-of-state plates . . .*

Isabel remained vigilant. Five minutes passed. Then seven. Nine? There was just too much nothing going on. The book opened.

The page brightened and darkened.

Isabel glanced at the travel light she'd clipped to the back of the book. Usually when the batteries started to wear out the bulb just slowly dimmed, it didn't pulse or anything. Why had it—

Everything around her brightened and darkened. *What the—?*

She looked out the rear window—still pretty clean, thanks to Tall Paul—and caught a glimpse of headlights in the distance disappearing behind a bend in the road. "Dad? There's someone behind us."

"I saw him, hon. But he's way back there. Nothing to worry about."

Isabel kept an eye out the rear window just the same. It wasn't like there was anything to see: there weren't any streetlights along this road, so aside from their own taillights splashing redly off the tarmac and trees, there was nothing behind them but blackness. It was a little like they were driving through deep space, except there weren't any sta—

Headlights came into view far behind them, though not as far as they had been. It was difficult to tell, really, with the complete lack of visible landmarks, but when she'd caught the glimpse earlier it had looked like just one bright light in the night; now it was close enough that she could make out two, side by side. Two brilliant pinholes in the night . . . and they *were* drawing closer.

"Uh, Dad? I think they're gaining."

"Yeah," he said, sounding thoughtful. "I see that."

Mom looked back. "I guess that guy at the gas station was right about people around here opening it up along this road."

Isabel peered at the speedometer: still just over 55. She glanced back at the headlights; they were bigger now, and visibly farther apart: the car was still gaining. *Okay*, she thought, feeling the thump of her forgotten book sliding to the floor at her feet, *that whole* ghost car *thing? A little more scary than cool.* "You don't think it's—"

"It was just a story," said Mom, though that Isabel hadn't even needed to complete the question told her it had been on Mom's mind, too. Another speed limit sign flashed through their headlights—Isabel hadn't been looking for them for a while—this one reading 55.

"Well, that kind of explains it," Dad said, and Isabel felt the car accelerate.

"What are you doing?" said Mom.

"This must be one of the straightaways that guy mentioned. The limit here's fifty-five, and if the locals tend to step on the gas a little, then I really *am* driving like a pokey tourist. I'm not going to go crazy, but we're what, twenty minutes from Gallway? I can pick it up and try not to annoy anyone. Besides, the quicker we get there, the quicker we eat, right?"

"If you say so," said Mom.

"I'm not all that hungry," said Isabel, then thought, *I'm being silly. Dad's right: there's no such thing as ghosts.*

Right?

The speedometer settled on 60 for a minute, but the car behind still gained. The needle crept higher, hovering just shy of 65. The headlights drew closer. Isabel could make out their shape: bright rectangles set to either side of a wide grill.

"Oh, no." Mom was hunkered down a little, staring into her side-view mirror. "Is that a cop?" A chill ran down Isabel's spine as in her mind's ear she heard slow, deep words: *lots of people mistake him for a statie on patrol at first.* "It's just a story," Mom said again, but Isabel couldn't tell who she was trying to convince: her daughter or herself.

The car was near them now, as close as regular highway traffic, and though the headlights were startlingly bright and high—shining right over the Camry's trunk—Isabel could see straight back through the windshield. What she saw made her feel a little far away, like the time the dentist had used laughing gas on her. "It's not a cop."

"I can't see through those lights." Dad angrily flipped the rearview mirror to night mode as the car drew even closer, tailgating them. "Who is it, can you see? Some jackass kids?"

"I can't tell," said Mom.

"It's not kids," said Isabel, and speaking the words still felt odd, like hollow sounds from a hollow girl. "It's an old man."

Even as she said it the car's driver glared at her, hair floating wild about his head, a match for his thick eyebrows. She thought it may have all been white, at least as pale as his skin, but everything was tinted a weird green in the glow from his dashboard lights—everything but his eyes, sunk so deep in their sockets the light didn't touch them, black pits of shadow in his bright, bony face. Isabel met his gaze for a moment—or, what passed for his gaze—then looked up front in time to catch Mom and Dad exchanging a glance.

"Okay, look," said Mom. "This is just too weird. Slow down and let him pass."

"I don't know if I can." Dad looked from the rearview to his side mirror and back, trying to get a better look at the big car. "He's so close, I think if I touch the brakes he'll be in the backseat with Isa."

Isabel tried to remember what Tall Paul had said, to recall *everything* he had said about—"It's Old Charlie." She expected Mom to say *It's just a story.* Wanted her to say it. Needed to hear the *words.*

"It'll be fine," Mom said. "Everything'll be fine." She tapped Dad's shoulder, patting him lightly. "Erik, slow down."

"I'll try."

The car shifted slightly as Dad took his foot off the gas, but he hadn't actually stepped on the brake before a loud brassy horn blasted the hollow feeling right out of Isabel's chest and jammed fear in its place. Her scream was short, but piercing.

"Jesus!" The Camry leapt forward as Dad stomped on the gas again.

The last thing Tall Paul had said about Old Charlie popped into Isabel's head, and that chill that had been climbing about on her spine moved into her stomach: *the next thing they know, there's Old Charlie, trying to get 'em off the road.*

"Slow down," Mom shouted. "Slow down, let him pass!"

"I *can't* slo—whoa!"

Isabel fell hard against the door as tires squealed and the Camry slewed into a turn.

"Hang on!" Dad swung the wheel the other way, tires shrieking louder as Isabel was thrown away from the door, her lap belt the only thing keeping her from rolling across the seat. The straightaway had ended and they'd entered one of Tall Paul's *turny bits* at speed. *The Bane Chronicles* rolled over the low center hump, bouncing to the other side of the car as Isabel struggled to sit upright. The characters in her books faced danger all the time, and it always seemed more exciting than scary, but it was very different in the real world: in the real world, it was just terrifying. Trees blurred through the headlights and the horn came again as Dad let up on the gas. "What is he, crazy?" Dad said, fighting the wheel through another turn. "He's right on me!"

"He's trying to get us off the road," Isabel shouted. Mom looked back at her but didn't argue this time.

"It's straightening out ahead," said Dad, and Mom reached to pat his shoulder again.

"Let him pass!"

Now that she wasn't being thrown about the backseat, Isabel craned her neck to look back at Old Charlie. He'd followed them out of the turn so close she couldn't see the bottom half of his headlights, and through the lessened glare he looked even more hunched and angry, brows drawn down over the pits of his eyes in a sharp, bushy V. He jerked the wheel to his left and the boxy car followed suit, and with a terrific roar of thrashing pistons he pulled alongside them. The horrible head turned, pinning Isabel with its black-shadow eyes. *Here it comes*, she thought. *He's going to ram into us and put us off the road, like Tall Paul said!*

The bigger car drew even . . . but then kept going, accelerating like a bullet in the barrel of a gun, flying ahead, speed already bleeding from the Camry as Dad lifted his foot from the gas once more.

"Jesus," Dad said. "He's got to be doing a hundred!"

"That was him," said Isabel. "Old Charlie." No one in the front seat replied, just watched the tail lights dwindle in the distance. Seconds later, nothing but far-off red dots in the night by then, the lights flared bright for an instant and disappeared, the fast-moving car apparently entering another turn. Mom finally twisted in her seat.

"Now, hon." Mom was trying to sound flat and reasonable, Isabel could tell, and she was *almost* succeeding. "You know that was just some old man, and there's no such thing as . . . oh, what now?"

She stared past her daughter, through the rear window. Isabel craned around to see, though she was already aware of the car brightening around her. Her heart jumped when she saw more lights coming out of the night—but it was *lots* of lights this time: a police cruiser had exited the turn behind them, red and blue strobes flashing.

Dad hit the brakes and directional, easing the car over to let the speeding police vehicle pass with a "Yeah, go get him!" He followed it with an "Oh, you have to be *kidding* me!" when the cruiser slowed and drew up behind them, indicating they should pull over. "This is crazy," he said, tires crunching in grit as he parked on the shoulder. "What about that old guy? He was going *way* faster than—"

"Just calm down," said Mom. "Maybe we can explain—"

"I *am* calm!" Dad caught himself, took a breath, and repeated in a quieter tone. "I am calm. But this is really—"

They all jumped at the rap on his window. He rolled the glass down with an over-bright "Good evening, Officer."

"It's Deputy, sir. License and registration, please."

"Deputy, sorry, if I could just explain—"

"License and registration, please," the man repeated, shining his flashlight into the car, illuminating Dad, then Mom, then Isabel, before returning to her father. "We can just get that out of the way, if you don't mind, sir. Then we can get to your explanation."

Isabel studied the sheriff's deputy while he waited: not quite so tall as Tall Paul—though maybe a few years older—he still reminded her of the gangly gas station attendant. It may have been that he spoke in the same slow drawl. He certainly wasn't as friendly or talkative as the pump jockey, offering only a curt "Thank you, sir," when he accepted the paperwork and took everything back to his own car.

"I *asked* about speed traps," said Dad. "You remember? I said—"

"We remember," soothed Mom. "We were there. But are you going to tell me we *weren't* speeding?"

"Well, okay, yes, but—"

"We have to ask why he pulled us over instead of that old man, that's what we have to do."

"Old Charlie," Isabel piped up.

"Sweetheart." Mom looked back at Isabel with serious eyes. "We both told you, there's no such thing as—"

"Do you happen to know the speed limit along here, sir?" The deputy was back at Dad's window, holding out the paperwork, the star on his breast winking in his cruiser's flashing lights.

"Fifty-five?" Dad said, passing the license and registration along to Mom. "I know I was speeding, but—"

"Along the straightaways, yes sir, but it slows down for the turns. It's forty-five back there in that windy bit you just come out of, but do you know what I clocked you at coming through there?"

"I don't know. Maybe sixty? But—"

"Sixty-*seven*! Sixty-seven miles per hour on a twisty stretch of road like that is about the least safe thing you can do, especially with your young daughter in the car."

"But, Deputy—" Mom leaned over to read the nameplate on the man's breast. ". . . Campton? What about the other car? The one that *passed* us coming out of that turn? And driving much *faster*?"

Deputy Campton's eyes were blank. "What other car?"

"What other car?" Dad sounded incredulous. "The one riding so close he was practically in my trunk, running his high beams and leaning on the horn? *That* other car?"

Campton stared at Dad levelly for a moment, then: "Am I going to have to make you take a field sobriety test, sir?"

Mom made an angry sound, but Isabel was already powering her own window down. "There really was another car, Mr. Campton, and it was right behind us. I could see the driver, and it was an old man and he looked *so* angry, and I couldn't ever see his eyes, and his horn scared me . . . and then he drove by *so* fast . . ." She realized she was babbling, and her words ran out of steam. ". . . and it was Old Charlie," she finished. "You know. The ghost."

The deputy looked from Isabel to her father, and took his time answering. "Look," he said, finally. "I don't know what y'all thought you saw, okay? But what *I* saw—and I was *looking*, mind—was one car come barrel-assing—excuse me, little missy—through some dangerous turns at more than twenty miles over the speed limit. *More than twenty.* Then, when I pull them over, it turns out not to be joyriding kids but a married couple with their child in the car. I didn't see any old angry man, and I sure as hell—pardon me—didn't see any ghost car."

He looked in at Isabel. "Whoever told you about 'Old Charlie,' or a ghost car or somesuch, they were just tellin' campfire stories. Pulling your leg. There ain't no such thing as ghosts, little missy. Especially not on my stretch of road. I wouldn't allow it."

He turned to Dad. "That being said, sir, maybe you think you saw something, or maybe you're just pulling *my* leg. Doesn't matter. What you do once you *get* to Gallway is your business, but *until* you get there it's mine. *Slow down.*" He tore the top ticket off his pad and thrust it into Dad's hand. Then he grinned. "You have a nice night, now." He straightened, gave a double rap on the Camry's roof, and walked back to his cruiser.

Inside the Camry, Dad was quietly exploding.

"Two hundred and twenty bucks? Really? Two hundred and twenty bucks! This is—" He crumpled half the ticket in his fist and raised his hand, preparing to fling the offending paper to the car floor, then took a deep breath and smoothed the ticket on his thigh. "We can fight it later," he said, folding and slipping it into his shirt pocket.

Mom said, quietly, "He didn't see the other car?"

"He *saw* the other car. We were just easier to catch."

"He didn't *sound* like he saw the other car."

"*I* saw the car *and* the old man," said Isabel. "And I don't think he had any eyes. I think he was—"

"Old Charlie," Mom said with her.

"Look," said Dad. "You heard Deputy Champion—"

"Campton," corrected Mom.

"—Campton, fine, whatever. You heard him. He says there's no such thing as ghosts, and he's out here all the time. If there *were* anything to see, he'd have seen it, don't you think?"

"I guess," said Isabel.

"It was just an old man who probably speeds through here all the time, so he knows the road." He turned to Mom. "And if he *is* through here all the time, then Deputy Kramden—"

"Campton."

"—probably recognized the car and would rather give some strangers a ticket than run down one of his good ol' boys. Hell, he could have been Campton's father for all we know."

Mom nodded, but Isabel didn't think she looked convinced. Dad pulled the Camry back on the road and they drove away from Deputy Campton's cruiser. Isabel didn't say anything for the ten minutes it took to round the bend and find Gallway ahead, electric lights glowing in the dark, but Isabel stared out the rear window, watching for headlights; she saw only the night the entire time.

*   *   *

"Shouldn't we just go straight to the hotel?" said Mom.

"It's been a weird night," answered Dad. "And there are people here, and I think we're all hungry." The car slid into an open parking spot near the door of the diner, and Dad ratcheted the gearshift into park. "I just want a little dose of normal before we turn in. Sound like a plan?"

"I want a chicken basket," said Isabel.

"Okay, then," said Mom, levering her door open.

Inside, the half-full diner was brightly lit, with lots of chrome accents and leather banquets set up in a fifties theme—or maybe the place was really that old, and all this was original. Either way, though, Isabel still wanted her chicken basket, the smell of the place had her thinking about dessert; she couldn't identify it, but there seemed to be cinnamon in the air, and brown sugar, and something else just as awesome. There were pies on display beneath the glass counter by the register, and she suspected one or more of them might be the culprit.

"Three?" said the uniformed waitress, her pink dress and white apron fitting right in with the decor of the place, though a delicate nose stud and the tribal tattoo encircling her upper arm spoke of more modern times. "Would you like a booth, or are you sitting at the counter tonight?"

"Booth," said Mom, and with a nod the waitress scooped up some menus and headed across the floor. Mom started after her and Isabel followed, eyes still on the pies she suspected of full-blown wonderfulness.

"Watch where you're going, Isa," Dad said behind her. Reluctantly, Isabel turned from the glass counter, seeking Mom's back—and recoiled with a gasp, thumping against Dad's chest. "What is it, hon? Are you okay?"

"It's him!"

She couldn't look away from the man sitting on one of the counter stools, and if she'd had any doubts before, they evaporated when he turned her way and frowned, watery blue eyes so deep set they were almost hidden even in the bright fluorescent lighting. She pointed. "It's him! It's Old Charlie!"

"I didn't touch her," the man said loudly, raising both palms in a *hands-off* gesture, though they'd been on the counter and nowhere near Isabel. "I don't know what she's on about, but I didn't touch her."

"Honey?" Dad took her shoulders and spun her away from the man with the raised hands. "What are you—"

"That's *him*," Isabel insisted. "*Old Charlie*. I was looking right at him, Dad, and even when he passed us he was looking back at me, and"—she pointed again—"that's *him*!"

"Is there a problem?" said a new voice. Isabel half-turned to see a pair of uniformed sheriff's deputies rising from their stools at the far end of the counter.

"I'll say there's a problem," Mom said from behind them, having left the waitress standing in confusion by an empty booth. "We just got here, and on the way in from Eaton someone harassed us and tried to run us off the road. Almost killed us trying to get by."

The deputies had turned to Mom as she spoke, but the old man, hands resting on the counter again, just stared straight ahead, as if he had no idea he was the topic of discussion. "Hey, Went?" said the cop closest to him. "I didn't see you come in, but you haven't gotten through a whole lot of that burger yet. And you live up outside of Eaton, don't you?"

The old man made no move or reply, just stared even harder. Isabel followed his gaze to something she hadn't seen before, a serious break in the theme: a good-sized flat screen high-definition TV behind the counter, right across from where Went sat. The sound was off so as not to disturb the patrons, but the closed-captioning was on, words flashing across the bottom of a screen showing a football game in progress. The deputy stepped closer, laying a hand on a bony shoulder. "Hey, Wentworth? I'm talking to you."

The old man's head snapped around. "Huh? Look, I done told you: I don't know her, didn't touch her. Dunno what she's on about, but the game is on. Lemme watch, I got . . . I'm a fan, all right?"

"*You* probably have money on the game," said the second cop, looking at his watch. "And kickoff was just five minutes ago. You barely made it."

"I don't know what you're talking about."

"Went?" said the first deputy, hand still on the old man's shoulder. "Did you almost run these nice people off the road?"

"Well, they were going too *slow!*" the old man bellowed, even now trying to keep at least one eye on the game. "My TV's busted, and I was trying to make kickoff. I got—I mean this is worth—look, I'm a fan!"

The deputy's eyes shifted to Dad and Isabel. "Sir, would you like to file a complaint against this old buzzard here? I'll gladly take your statement, if that's what you want."

"You bet I want," said Dad. "And I'd like to get the ticket I got cleared up, too! Old Went here was all high beams and honking horn, but your Deputy Campton claimed he never even saw him and gave *me* a ticket! That's ridiculous, and I—"

"You saw Campton?" the deputy interrupted.

"Yes! He pulled me over and gave—"

"Looks like we got us another one," the man said over his shoulder, and the second deputy nodded.

"Another one?" Dad said, just as Mom asked "Another what?"

"Another, uh,"—the second deputy searched for a word—"*sighting,* I guess you'd say. You saw Deputy Campton?"

"Yes we saw him," said Dad, pointing at Went. "And I told him about this guy. Can't you radio him or something? He'll back my—"

"Can't do that, sir," said the first deputy, the older of the two. "Old Charlie Campton died pursuing a couple of drag racers almost eleven years ago."

"*Old Charlie,*" Isabel whispered, while behind her, Dad sounded a bit strangled.

"What are you talking about? Campton pulled us over. Talked to all of us. Even gave me a ticket, for Christ's sake!"

Dad reached into his shirt pocket to fetch the half-crumpled piece of paper to wave at the deputies. He poked, prodded, and patted, moving

from shirt to pants, checking every pocket twice.
The ticket was nowhere to be found.

The Thin Place
Morgan Sylvia

Analea was nothing but shadows and mist, the first time I saw her.

I was in the garden tending my roses, my black and white husky, Lela, dozing at my feet. My husband, Jacob, was at sea, so I was home alone. I'd just finished watering the flowers, and the rich, earthy smell of plants hung heavy in the late summer air. In the fading golden daylight, the blood-red roses looked so vivid that they almost glowed. Through the towering pines in the back yard, I could see the rocky cliffs of our coastline, and the blue-silver-gold waters of the harbor. Lobster boats and windjammers dotted the waves, a peaceful and familiar sight.

Someone called my name and I looked up, startled. Though we lived near town, our house stood on a wooded, isolated road. With the exception of old Mr. Harrett, who never missed his daily stroll, few people walked past.

I didn't see anything at first. But as I turned, I smelled smoke, which immediately made me uneasy. It had been dry, that summer. Too dry. Wildfires blazed across lower Maine, and the weather reports were filled with warnings and fire restrictions.

Fire terrified me. Just the smell of it, the sound of crackling flames, made me nervous. Not long after my wedding, a massive wildfire had ravaged the island, razing everything in its path. Everyone had to evacuate, and fast. Local fishermen took dozens by boat, while bulldozers worked frantically to clear the main road so vehicles could get through. Jacob was at sea, so I drove our new Chevy through the inferno, joining the caravan of cars fleeing the flames. My best friend, Marie, sat beside me, her face pale and frightened in the flickering orange light as we sped through a blizzard of sparks, the night sky above us lit with a hellish glow. Flames licked the side of the road, transforming the ancient forest into a hellscape.

The smell of smoke brought it all back. I could almost see the flames approaching. Uneasy, I looked around.

That's when I saw her.

A pale thing stood in the trees at the edge of the yard, on the border between shadow and sunlight. She wore a white dress, and her hair fell long and loose. I could not see her face. I thought at first that she was real; a lost tourist, perhaps, exploring the wrong trail.

Then I realized I could see through her.

The ghost did not move or speak, but just looked at me. The world went silent around us: the familiar sounds of seagulls and the waves crashing against the shore seemed distant, muted.

A moment later, she was gone. I would have doubted that I ever saw her, but Lela looked in that direction and tensed, growling. I grabbed her collar just before she lunged, and spent what seemed an eternity hauling her back inside.

Jacob and I had always suspected that we weren't alone in the house. Strange, though trivial, incidents had plagued us since we'd moved in. Doors opened themselves. Things disappeared, only to turn up in strange places. We would find rooms we never used rearranged. Once, we discovered the attic window open, though neither of us had been up there in weeks. We'd heard things, too: sobbing coming from the cellar, children laughing outside, footsteps running through the kitchen. The dirt basement was the worst: its spiderweb-draped beams and dank earthy smell always made me nervous. Even Lela refused to set foot—or paw— in it. The previous owners had left a big wardrobe down there, an elaborate, antique mahogany piece with mirrors on the inside of both doors. I often found it open, though the latch was sturdy. That wardrobe always gave me the creeps.

Grandma sensed it when she visited us, the summer before she died. As I was showing her the house, she had paused at the cellar door and looked down the stairs, frowning.

"What is it, Grandma?" I asked, frowning. "You look pale."

"Just a vision," she said, putting her hand to her forehead. I took her arm and gently guided her to a chair. Her voice was weak and shaky, as was she. "This is a thin place, child."

A thin place, according to Grandma, was a spot where the veil between worlds was thin.

"There are many types of thin places," she told me. "Doors, windows, mirrors, lakes, caves. Even a cupboard or a closet can be thin. There are thin times, as well. Like Samhain, when the doors between worlds open. And ghosts aren't the only things that can come through."

"What do you mean?"

"These northern woods are full of phantasms," she said. "Ghosts and werewolves and all sorts of beings. And fetches, spirit doubles that come to take the dead. Some say that such things don't exist. But mark my words, child, the old myths are true. I myself saw one of the ghost ships that sail these waves, *The Aria*, a phantom spirit at her bow."

I believed her. How could I not? We'd all grown up hearing about *The Aria*. Our tiny harbor had its fair share of ghost stories. Haunted inns, farms, caves, and forests: we had it all. That wasn't even counting the numerous tales of ghost ships and sea spirits. Stories of the restless dead hovered around the campfires of August and the fireplace flames of December alike. One legend held that the gates of hell were nearby, at Salisbury Cove. Marie and I had both seen the ghost of Ledgelawn Inn. And then there was Witches Hollow, a cranberry field just down the road. According to legend, the witch, Sarah Browne, had caused the deaths of two children, and haunted the place to this day.

Marie and I had grown up playing at Witches Hollow. For a time, we were fascinated by the supernatural. We read tarot cards and told ghost stories, and had slumber-party séances. Her mother had inherited an old, beautiful, intricately carved spirit board, and we spent many a night summoning spirits, until at last we grew frightened and locked the board in a chest in her cellar. We never stopped going to the cranberry field, but after that, we spent our time there drinking blueberry wine, reading magazines, and gossiping.

The harbor buoy bell rang, tolling the familiar, specific note of our harbor. Shivering, I went back inside. Our old farmhouse was plain and tiny compared to the millionaires' castles that dotted the coastline, but it was clean and cozy. The wooden floors and furniture gleamed against the white walls, and the colorful rugs and pillows and whimsical art gave it a bright, welcoming air.

The world around me appeared unchanged. The waves still beat against the shore, the seals kept sunning themselves on the rocks, and the sea wind carried the haunting cries of gulls and the scent of pine and saltwater. But something wasn't right.

I listened to the news, hoping the sound of human voices would soothe me. But the topics—forest fires, the Paris Treaty, rising tensions with Russia, UFOs, and the Doomsday Clock—were hardly reassuring. I settled in to watch *The Wizard of Oz*, Lela sprawled out at my feet.

That night, I suffered a horrible night terror. Shadowy figures clustered around me, calling my name, dragging truth and secrets from my soul. The air around them shimmered, as though I were underwater. One of them wore Marie's face and Marie's voice, but I knew it wasn't her. I sensed something nearby, something dark, but I couldn't run or even move.

I woke at midnight, sweaty and frightened, in a tangle of sheets. Lela was pacing back and forth, restless. Unable to fall asleep again, I went to get a glass of water. Glancing up, I looked through the kitchen window.

The dead thing stood at the edge of the rose garden, clearly visible in the moonlight filtering through the pines. She looked washed out, a black and white character in a color movie. An ethereal, opalescent glow emanated from her pallid skin.

Her whisper cut through the night air like a knife. "The sea takes what is hers," she said. "And then quietly kisses your feet."

My blood ran cold. Jacob had said those very words to me once. We'd been at the shore, near Thunder Hole. I remembered him throwing a shell into the waves as he spoke, and then turning to smile at me. He'd been trying to soothe me, knowing I was worried about him sailing off. I enjoyed the ocean's beauty, but I also understood its power: I'd almost drowned as a child, and had never forgotten the feel of the cold dark waters closing in over my head.

The ghost faded into nothingness. I backed into the shadows of the house.

The next morning, I stood on my porch for hours, staring at my dying garden.

*   *   *

The next few days passed without incident. I hoped at first that the ghost had gone back to where she'd come from, but as time went by I began to feel that something wasn't right. I often sensed that I was being watched. I would see movement out of the corner of my eye, or notice things I hadn't touched misplaced. I went about my usual tasks, but the heaviness in the air became a constant burden.

Every day, my garden faded a bit more.

Every night, the apparition drew closer.

Then, when the moon rose full, I found the phantasm in the kitchen, pale and faceless. Her greyish flesh didn't look solid, or even real; it reminded me of television snow. Her eyes were black, pupil-less holes, watching me. I wanted to tell her to move on, that she was not welcome. But the words stuck in my throat.

The cellar door swung open silently. Analea turned and walked down the stairs, into the darkness below the house.

As soon as she was out of sight, I heard her voice in my ear. Her breath tickled my cheek. "They never called me by my real name."

I spun around. There was no one there.

Then the power went out, leaving the house pitch black.

*   *   *

In the light of day, I almost convinced myself that I'd been dreaming, but the lack of electricity was harder to dismiss. I tried calling the power company, but the phone was dead. After discovering that the car wouldn't start, I walked into town.

Summer was over. The crisp air smelled of coffee and burning leaves, the trees had changed, and the trappings of autumn were everywhere. This did nothing to lift my spirits. I hated fall. The blaze of color that transformed the island was, to me, a living memory of that terrible fire. I also dreaded what was coming, the long cold months of darkness, the feeling of being trapped in isolation by snow and ice.

The wind coming in off the sea was cold that day, the waves choppy and capped with churning froth. Most of the businesses had already closed for winter, leaving the storefronts boarded up and lifeless. Even the harbor seemed deserted: only a few weather-beaten lobster boats dared the rough waters. I wound through half-empty streets, passing gruff, bearded lobstermen and a few leaf peepers. When I finally reached the power company, the office was closed. I'd forgotten it was a weekend.

When I turned to make my way back through town, I found myself standing outside the fortune teller's shop. *Madame Cara*, the sign said. *Clairvoyant. 2-for-1 Specials*.

I had always dismissed the lady as a charlatan. Grandma insisted that her séances were nothing but parlor tricks, that she could no more talk to the dead than she could call the president. But I had no one else to turn to.

I entered the shop. She looked up, startled to see me. This was to be expected. With winter closing in, her business was slow.

"You're troubled," she said, by way of greeting.

"There's a ghost in my house," I said.

She looked at me thoughtfully, and then closed her mascara-laden eyes and did some mumbo-jumbo with her hands, her heavy rings flashing in the light.

A moment later, her eyes snapped open. "Analea," she said. "A victim of the fire."

That explained why I always smelled smoke when she was near. "What does she want?"

She shrugged. "Sometimes the dead linger. Sometimes they are bound here. Sometimes they need help moving on. And some are trapped, bound to a certain place or object."

"Why?"

Madame Cara laughed, a chuckle that turned into a cough. "There's as many answers to that as there are ghost stories."

I wanted to roll my eyes at the drama in her voice, the theatrics Grandma had warned me about. But I couldn't dismiss what she'd said. "There's something else. Dark figures come into my room at night. They stand around my bed, and force me to answer questions."

Her eyes narrowed. "Mirrors and spirit boards," she said, "are nothing to toy with."

"I haven't fooled with any of that in years," I said. "But I live in a thin place."

She frowned, disapproval clear on her face, and then lit some incense. The air filled with sweet, thick smoke. I began to feel lightheaded. "What do I do?"

Madame Cara made some signs over me. I felt nothing, save a vague annoyance and a mild headache.

After a few moments, she shook her head. "I cannot help you."

I stared at her. "What? Why?"

"The dead don't move on until they are ready," she told me. "And besides, you think I'm a fraud." She waved me out, her hand flapping like a bejeweled fish. "Go home. Get some rest."

Angry, I turned and walked out, setting the bells on her door jangling as I left.

A group of girls passed me on the street, laughing and chattering, their conversation hanging the salty air like a cloud. One of them looked back as they went by. Something about her reminded me of Marie, and a lump rose in my throat.

I paused once more on the way back, this time at the edge of the cranberry field. The crimson berries stood out against a colorless, drab bog.

Some said the fire had started there. Marie and I had been there that day, eating berries and drinking hot apple cider from the orchard down the road. Her fiancé was out of town, so she was spending the night.

She'd just bought a bright red lipstick. We both tried it on. "It looks better on you," I told her. "It makes me look like I've eaten too many of these berries."

"That's the point." Marie laughed and put her cigarette down, rubbing her heel against it. "When does Jacob come home?"

"Not for several months. I'll have to finish the redecorating myself, before he returns. There's just so much to do." I looked at her, smiling. "I may need your help, if I'm going to finish it before the baby comes."

Her face lit up, and she hugged me. "Elizabeth, that's wonderful! I'm so happy for you!"

We stayed a few minutes longer, laughing and talking, and then ran home. It was very windy that day. Gusts caught at our dresses and whipped our hair around, and sent fallen leaves fluttering down the road.

Looking up, I saw a crow fighting the wind. It gave up, and perched on a fencepost.

I'd always wondered, afterwards, if that cigarette was really out.

Looking at the cranberry bog, I could almost hear our laughter. A fog was rolling in from offshore, cloaking the land in cold mist. I huddled into my coat, and hurried home.

When I reached the house, I found every single light on, even the cellar light. The radio was blaring at full blast, and Lela was barking frantically. I had to take several deep breaths before I found the resolve to go inside.

The radio and lights turned off as soon as I stepped through the door.

Horror rose through me as I looked around. The paint, which had been fresh and white just hours before, was dirty and chipped. Several floorboards had rotted out, and the sink was covered in rust stains. The windows were grimy and cracked. One of the kitchen floor tiles was displaced, and an ugly yellow water stain marred the ceiling. My windowsill herbs were dried and shriveled, though they had looked green and healthy when I'd left that morning. Only the pictures on the wall seemed unchanged. But when I reached out to touch my favorite—Jacob at the dock, standing before his father's lobster boat—it crumbled to dust.

That night, the dark figures again gathered around my bed, calling my name.

The next day, desperate, I returned to the fortune teller. But the business was boarded up, closed for the winter. Like the birds and tourists, she had gone south to warmer lands to escape winter's frozen bite.

The haunting continued, as did the drought.

*   *   *

Over the next few weeks, the house began to show more signs of wear. The lawn and garden shriveled, leaving my prized roses nothing but dried, withered husks. I often felt weak and dizzy, as though I, too, were fading. Lela ran away, disappearing into the mists one moonless night. I spent days wandering the woods looking for her, but to no avail.

One day, not long after that, I had to go down into the cellar to bring up some winter things. I made quick work of sorting through the trunks and boxes for my warmer clothes.

I wasn't fast enough.

When I started up the stairs, Analea was standing at the door, looking down at me. Startled, I stumbled backwards, losing my balance. My stomach gave sickening lurch as I fell through the air. I tumbled down the steps, and fell through a cloud of spiderwebs before hitting the dirt floor.

The blow stunned me. I closed my eyes and wiped the spiderwebs away, telling myself it wasn't real, that she would be gone soon.

She wasn't.

When I looked up, she was coming down the steps towards me. Her feet never touched the stairs. I could not make out her face, but I again smelled the acrid tang of smoke.

My heart thudded in my chest. "Go away," I shouted. "This is my house!"

The ghost regarded me for a moment. She opened her mouth, which hinged back to an impossible angle, like the jaws of a snake, and screamed my rage back at me. As she did so, her flesh—or the semblance of her flesh—turned dark. The light fled her, as though she had banished it. Instead of emanating a pale glow, the ghost now appeared blackened and shriveled. Thin trails of vapor seeped from her skin. Tendrils of that foul smoke curled around me, invading my mouth and nose.

The world faded to black.

When I woke, my head was pounding, and I felt weak, disoriented. The wardrobe lay on its side, the door on the bottom fallen open. When I looked up at the open cellar door, the light from upstairs hurt my eyes, and made my head throb. As much as I hated the cellar, I almost wanted to stay there, in the cool darkness. But one glimpse of that wardrobe was all I needed.

Going up the stairs was an almost impossible chore. When I reached the top of the stairs, the light was so blinding I had to shield my eyes.

I made my way into the back bedroom and rested there in familiar shadows, fading in and out of consciousness.

*   *   *

I woke after dark on Samhain, to the sound of breaking glass. Rising, I found my wedding picture on the floor, the glass shattered. I stepped on one of the shards and cut my foot, but though I left bloody footprints on the rotted floorboards, I felt no pain.

The smell of smoke hung heavy in the cold autumn air.

I stepped onto the decaying porch in my nightgown, looking at the peeling paint, the decaying steps, the dirty windows. All that remained of my prized gardens were a few dead, withered bushes. Nightshade climbed up the side of the house: the poisonous vine was the only thing still thriving. Most of the leaves had fallen by then. The trees looked bare and skeletal, like bony fingers reaching into the night sky.

The woods seemed unnaturally still and silent. I heard no gulls, no wind. Even the sea was a rare, flat calm.

In the distance, I heard a familiar bark. I froze. "Lela?" I called.

I strained my ears to listen. The distant trailing sound of children's voices carried through the air. Far below, the waves crashed against the rocks.

And then I heard Lela again. I ran into the yard, looking around. But the dog was nowhere to be seen. I looked and saw a girl in a white dress and a boy in shorts running through the trees. They moved out of my sight, flitting into the woods, and were soon swallowed in thick shadow. Moments later, old Mr. Harrett trudged past, looking, as always, neither left nor right. I thought of calling to him, but he was rather senile, and would have been of little help.

I sensed it before I saw it.

On the trail that led to the shore, a shape was taking form in the darkness.

Analea.

She no longer looked pale, or ethereal, but flesh and blood. She moved towards me, her eyes fixed on my face, her stride quick and purposeful. Terror rose through me, an icy hand clenching my heart. I raced back towards the house. As I grabbed the doorknob, a searing pain shot up my arm. I snatched my hand back, shouting. Looking down, I could already see burn marks forming on my palm.

I glanced back. Analea was halfway across the yard. Behind her, a thick black fog was rolling in, draping the forest in shadow.

"We didn't mean to start the fire!" I shouted.

She kept coming.

I gritted my teeth, and, using my skirt as a buffer, opened the door. Once inside, I locked it behind me and backed away from the door, moving further into the room.

Shadows and spiderwebs clustered in gloomy corners. As I stood there, the darkness in the room grew thicker. A black, pitch-like substance began to drip from the walls and ceiling, oozing across the floor. Dark spores of mold covered the cabinets. Vines grew across the dusty windows, blocking out the pallid moonlight. The swirling grey-black mists thickened, enveloping the house in fog. I heard a creaking sound from the cellar that I knew was the wardrobe door opening.

And then I heard something behind me.

I turned slowly. Analea stood there, so close I could feel the chill she emanated. As she moved closer, I felt a sense of the void, an endless black emptiness, a darkness that could swallow suns. Fear paralyzed me, leaving me unable to run or scream.

She reached out her hand, beckoning me, and I saw the scar on her wrist.

Somewhere in my soul, I felt a sickening realization take hold. I glanced down at my own wrist, upon which lay an identical scar, which I'd gotten courtesy of a rusty nail in an old barn. Stunned, I looked at the pale dead thing standing before me. That was when I finally saw her face, and recognized her features as my own.

The world fell away from me then. Or perhaps, I fell away from the world.

The house decayed around me in a matter of seconds. The walls and ceilings blackened, and the windows cracked and shattered. Beams collapsed, and chunks of wood and plaster fell to the floor, raising huge clouds of dust. Then, with a massive rumble that shook the ground, it all blackened and crumbled to ash.

I looked into the face of the dead thing, and saw truth flickering like flames in her dark eyes. Visions and memories rose through my thoughts, shapes taking form in the gloomy mists of my mind. The past came rushing back, and I felt the fires reaching for me once more.

We had joined the desperate stream of cars fleeing the fire. But our attempts to escape the inferno had been blocked at every turn. Desperate, we drove back to the house. Marie wanted to take the trail down to the shore, saying that we could get into the water if worst came to worst. But I was afraid of the cliffs and the pounding waves, terrified that I would fall and hurt the baby, or that the crashing surf would dash me against the rocks. I wasn't thinking straight. I'd just learned about Jacob's ship going down, and the shock was still raw and fresh. As the flames drew nearer, I'd told Marie to go on without me. As she ran down the trail, I saw the eerie orange glow in the sky, the dance of flames reflected on the water, the wall of fire approaching. A huge fireball shot out over the ocean as I watched. I'd grabbed Lela and gone down into the cellar, certain that the fire would pass over us.

It hadn't.

I coughed and tried in vain to fight off the flames, but the inferno refused to let me go. Lela and I climbed into the wardrobe as a last resort. Then everything melted into a searing crimson blur.

Analea died gasping, staring at her own reflection in the mirror as her lungs filled with smoke.

Afterwards, I rose in a swirl of vapor, and stood on my porch, which was a smoldering mass of charred beams, looking out at the smoking, burnt forest before me. The ancient evergreen forest I had grown up in had been transformed into an eerie, desolate wasteland. As far as I could see, there was nothing but ash and embers and the blackened bones of scorched trees. Only my chimney still stood, a bony finger wrapped in acrid smoke.

A pale glow shone in the distance. I looked, but I didn't see Jacob among the line of souls trudging towards it. I knew he wasn't there. I could feel it. And so I fled in the other direction, sinking into the cool depths of the earth, into coal and ash and dirt. As the blackened ground closed in around me, I summoned a final, cindery tear, and then shut my eyes and let death's brighter dreams envelop me.

My death certificate bore the name the orphanage had given me, which neither I nor my adoptive parents had ever used.

Analea.

The town forgot me. The forest and the waves forgot me. Only my fetch remembered. I slept, dreaming in eternal nothingness with the dead and the unborn, until Marie's granddaughter found that old spirit board and called my name, awakening me.

Memory made me whole, if not free. The mists lifted, leaving the sky clear. The stars seemed almost close enough to touch, and I noticed strange hues of color in the night sky. I looked around at what had once been my yard. Wilderness had reclaimed the land. The ruins of the house and garden were draped in thorns and bramble and winterberry bushes. Only a few charred timbers and a foundation gave any indication that a house had ever stood there at all.

I felt Analea beside me.

"I know who you are now," I said. "I know what you are. I saw you the day of the fire. I was splashing water on my face, and I saw your reflection in the mirror, beside mine. And then later, as we were driving away from the fire, I saw you in the rear-view mirror, sitting in the back seat. But I was so distraught over the news about Jacob's ship, I thought I was hallucinating. I had forgotten these things. But I remember now."

The voice of the fetch was like the sound of dead branches shivering in the wind. "You've been dreaming long enough. It's time to go."

Looking up, I saw a paling in the sky. The air shimmered, and an opal, swirling mass took shape. The vortex sank through the sky, drawing closer, until it was right before me. On the other side, I saw the familiar scene of Marie's parlor, and looked at the girls gathered around the spirit board.

Marie's granddaughter called through the vortex. The sound of her voice cut through the darkness, seeming to come from the sky. *Are you there? Give us a sign.*

Reaching forward, I put my hand through the veil.

The fetch watched quietly, its black, pupil-less eyes filled with warning.

I withdrew my hand.

Something caught my eye. I looked up and noticed the two children I had seen earlier standing at the edge of the yard, holding hands. Mr. Harrett walked past again, his eyes fixed on the ground before him.

In the distance, I saw the glow of fire against the sky.

The fetch did not react to any of this. "Come," it said, in a voice of smoke and dried bones. "You've been waiting here since 1947. It's time to move on."

The sound of the harbor bell rang out through the darkness. It wasn't the familiar peal I'd heard all my life, but the tone of another harbor, a darker, funereal note that sounded off-key, discordant. I looked down at the mirror-calm water, and saw an old schooner pass into the mists, a spectral woman standing at her bow. The world shimmered and blackened around the edges of my vision, a fading dream.

The fetch held out its hand.

I looked back one last time. A single white rose grew amidst the winterberries, in the wild tangle of brush that had overtaken the lot. In the ruins, something bright shone with a pale, ethereal glow, reflecting the moonlight.

I frowned, seeing it. "The wardrobe mirror . . ."

The fetch followed my gaze. "The world is full of thin places," it said.

Lela appeared on the trail, tail wagging. She barked once.

Still I hesitated.

"The flames cannot touch you where you are going," the fetch told me. "Come. Jacob is waiting."

I took her hand and let her guide me down to the sea.

Tripping the Ghost
Barry Lee Dejasu

Mark looked up from the spread of papers on the desk before him when he heard a vehicle pull up outside. He glanced at the clock: six-thirty on the dot, exactly as Constance had promised.

"Chad," he called into the next room, "she's here." He got up from the desk and moved to the front door, and found a grey minivan idling in their driveway, and was even more surprised to see a bald man climb out of the driver's seat. The late September sun had almost completely set, but the man was wearing sunglasses.

What is up *with these people?* Mark thought. "Can I help you?" he called to the man.

Instead of a response, the man went around to the back of the van.

Footsteps approached Mark from behind. "Where's Constance?" Chad said.

"Dunno," Mark muttered.

"*Who* is *that?*" Chad asked, moving closer.

Mark turned and shaped a word with his lips, but couldn't bring himself to speak as a sick, cold feeling wriggled through his chest.

Maybe Constance hadn't felt the need to be present for the drop-off. Although logical, this thought brought only a fleeting sense of comfort—because what if this man *wasn't* an associate of hers at all?

Chewing on his lower lip, Mark stepped back inside and reached up to a secret shelf they'd installed above the nearby curtains, and removed a .38 revolver.

"Ah, fuck," Chad said, turning and walking further into the room behind them. Mark knew he was probably going for the shotgun hidden beneath the desk.

Holding the revolver down against the back of his thigh, Mark slowly headed back outside.

There was a thump from behind the van, and something big and dark moved into view from behind its open rear doors. Tensing, Mark lifted the gun—then lowered it as he saw the man step into view, clutching something big and dark above his right shoulder.

"Did Constance send you?" Mark asked him, but the man didn't reply. If he nodded, it was hard to tell, as his head and torso were crooked under the case's weight. As he approached, he showed no signs of strain or even discomfort, nor even made any sounds of labored breathing; Mark could only hear the soft thumps and crunches of the man's feet on the dead grass and leaves. He stopped directly in front of Mark, then waited.

"Oh, uh—" Mark unconvincingly tried to tuck the gun behind his leg; but if the man had seen it, he didn't seem bothered. "Just follow me," Mark said, turning to find Chad waiting in the doorway, one arm out of view, no doubt holding the shotgun. Mark shook his head and started walking around the house, and he heard the man follow him.

The backyard was a pool of shadows crowded by a tight ring of trees. The property was never something that Mark or Chad had invested much time or money in; even during the day it was dark and foreboding, choked with weeds and shrubs and the occasional yard pest. The lack of care had been a big price cut on the property, along with the realtor's allegation that the house itself was haunted; it had been the perfect place for Mark and Chad to set up their business.

Mark nodded to the sloped cellar doors. "Right over here." He glanced sheepishly at the man, but couldn't make out much more than his shape in the dark, crookedly crowned by the case. Praying he didn't accidentally shoot his foot off, Mark twisted and shoved the revolver into his pocket. He reached for the short, heavy chain that had been threaded through the handles on the cellar doors and undid the combination lock, then pulled the chain out with a noisy jangle. As he did, a hairline of pale light appeared between the doors and around their edges, and muffled thumps rose from within. The left door thumped, then popped open, swinging up with a rusty squeal. Chad appeared, silhouetted by the lights from the basement. He looked to the man and frowned, then back at Mark, who offered a slight shrug in response, then pulled the other door open, and the man stepped forward and carefully descended the concrete stairs.

Mark let out a heavy breath, looked around, then followed him down.

Chad was directing the man to a long, empty table; he wordlessly moved beside it, and at Chad's order, crouched beside it and half-slid, half-shrugged the case onto its surface. Under the fluorescent bulbs set along the middle of the ceiling, Mark could see that the case was made of dark wood, its surface a mottled blend of sheens and worn, water- and dirt-stained blemishes. He instantly recognized the blackened metal handles on its sides and its arched upper surface, although its size was curiously small.

It was a child's coffin.

"Uh..." Mark said, and beside him, the man straightened and turned to him. "This— This is it? This is from Constance?" Mark expected silence in response, and that was exactly what he got.

Mark's hand moved alongside the gun as he watched the man reached inside his jacket pocket, but he relaxed when a thick envelope appeared. The man silently held it out, and Mark gingerly took it from him. "Thanks." It was all he could think to say.

The man didn't nod, didn't smile; he simply turned and walked back to the stairway.

Mark and Chad exchanged another look, then followed him up the stairs, back along the house and stopped as the man returned to the minivan. They watched him climb inside and reverse down their driveway. Then he was gone.

*　　*　　*

"Wanna tell me what the actual fuck *that* was?" Chad said.

Mark shook his head, puffing his cheeks out as he looked down at the coffin. "I know as much as you do."

"How much is in there?" Chad said, and Mark realized that he was still clutching the envelope in his hand. "That *is* money in there, right?"

Mark was briefly nauseous as he lifted the metal fasteners on the top of the envelope and pulled it open, then sighed with a slight chuckle as he saw the sandwiched lines of greenish-grey inside. "*Whoo*, yeah it is." He frowned, lifted the envelope closer, and saw a folded white sheet inside, as well.

"How much?" Chad repeated.

"Hold on," Mark said, pulling the paper out and unfolding it. Chad snatched the envelope from his hand, and Mark glared at him, then began to read the typed letter.

"*Ho*, lee, shit," Chad said, leafing through the wad of bills he'd removed from the envelope. "There's gotta be..." He began counting, but Mark didn't look up, wasn't even listening, as he read the letter.

Hello, boys.

As promised, here is your resource commandée. I do think you'll find it rather perfectly meets the requirements of your methods, (Mark, hadn't you said something about "quality and quantity?"), and I think that it shall more than adequately provide the desired effects. But of course, please don't hesitate to reach me if there are any problems with it—I would be happy to provide a different resource for your fascinating production.

Sincerely,
Constance

Mark didn't move, didn't even lower the letter; instead, his eyes darted up over its edge to glance at the coffin on the table.

"Did you hear—?" Chad fell silent as he looked at Mark. "What?"

"I'm...not sure if I like the sound of this."

"Why?"

Mark handed him the letter and waited while he read it. When he was done, he was frowning, too, and they both turned to the coffin.

"So what's *in* there?" Chad asked.

"Well, we're about to find out." Mark approached a cabinet on the wall nearby and started pulling down gloves, face masks, and tools. He and Chad geared up, then set to work opening the coffin. It was unmarked, but it looked a bit like one that they'd unearthed several months before from a Westport, Rhode Island house which had dated back to the 1870's; so if this was even remotely similar, it would be easy enough to open.

As Mark tapped a chisel and hammer along the dirt-lined seam of the coffin's lid, Chad wheeled over a large, re-purposed aquarium tank on a small cart.

A series of ticks and creaks came from the coffin as Mark loosened the lid, and then planting his fingers into its edge, he gave it a cursory tug. Its hinges worked with a squealing groan. Even through his mask, he thought he could smell the unsealed air that wafted out. As Chad came over, Mark pulled the lid up—then dropped it back in place with a hollow thud.

"Oh, what in the Christly *fuck?*" Chad cried, backing up, and Mark found himself doing the same.

"The fuck *was* that?" Mark whispered

"That— That—"

"That's *not* a fucking dead kid!"

"That's not a fucking *person!*"

Mark's jaw was stretching wide beneath his mask, which threatened to slip down off the bridge of his nose as he shook his head. "So— What? Did Constance pull a fast one on us or something?"

"A *ten grand* fast one?"

Mark's eyes widened. "Seriously?"

"*Yes,*" Chad spat, then pointed at the coffin. "But *that...* I mean, who the hell would want to trip the ghost on *that?*"

"Okay, okay. Hold on." Mark turned away, taking a deep breath and almost pressing his hand to his head before remembering where it had just been. "So...whatever that is, *that's* what she wants us to work with. Assuming it *does* work, and the spores *do* take... Well, who the hell would want…?" He shook his head, feeling an itch in his shoulder erupt into a full-body shiver.

"Got me, man. I mean, —"

"*No!*" Mark shook his head. "Seriously?"

Chad shrugged. "You want to make the other five or what?"

Mark looked back at the coffin, then sighed heavily. "Alright, alright. Let's give it a shot. Worse comes to worst—"

…I would be happy to provide a different resource…

Mark suppressed another shiver.

Chad stepped forward and tugged the lid up and threw it against the wall, and Mark slowly moved over and gave the thing in the coffin a good, long look.

To say that time and the elements had been kind to the body was a bit of an understatement; but then, perhaps they had taken pity upon the deformed entity inside the coffin—pity, or fearful avoidance. The jumble of too-too-many twisted limbs reminded Mark of gnarled tree roots and overgrown vines, yet were punctuated with angled joints—unmistakably *limbs.* The shrunken skin was a pale brownish-grey, almost *moist*-looking. Each limb ended in uneven appendages; some were fully-formed fingers, and others were little more than a cluster of lumps. Between what may or may not have been a couple of legs, a dark, shrunken mass offered no suggestion of a sex. And the head…

Mark looked away, knowing full well that that twisted, forever-silenced scream would never leave his mind in even the most restful slumbers. He turned to Chad, but all they could do was stare at each other.

No amount of waiting could prepare them for what they had to do next. They moved the tank beside the table and reached inside the coffin. Mark wriggled his fingers beneath a few of the more heavily-layered groups of limbs, and Chad its tiny shoulders. Chad counted to three, and they gingerly pulled it up and out.

The body was surprisingly light, no more than fifty pounds; it took all of Mark's resolve to avoid gagging as he felt the squishy give of thing's impossibly-spongy flesh in his gloved hands. They carefully maneuvered the body above the rim of the coffin and over the tank, and began lowering it in—

"*FUCK!*" Chad shrieked, dropping his end of the body. Cursing, Mark followed suit, and it fell into the tank, landing with a sickening cacophony of thumps.

"What the *fuck* was that?" Mark snapped.

"It fucking moved!"

"*What?*"

"I *swear* to God, man, the fucking thing moved a couple of its arms!"

"That was probably *me holding it*, jerk!"

"*I fucking saw it*, man!"

Mark's jaw worked, but he looked down at the thing in the tank. "Whatever," he said weakly. "Let's— just get it sealed and ready."

And then get some fucking questions ready for Mrs. Constance.

*   *   *

After they sealed the tank, they brought it over to the stairwell and began hoisting the cart up on sheets of plywood. Once it was upstairs, Mark slammed the basement door shut. They'd not bothered to do anything with the coffin; it was their unspoken agreement to leave *that* for the next day.

Wheeling the coffin into the converted living room of the old house, Mark couldn't help but appreciate—even find comfort in—all the other tanks that they passed. So much routine, so much normalcy, so much *sanity*, lay in each tank. They were moving through the central aisle of what they called the Garden.

Mark and Chad turned the corner and moved to the empty row of tables on the far wall. They stopped at the far end, then stooped to grab either end of the tank, grateful to have a quarter of an inch of acrylic between them and the thing inside as they moved it onto a table.

While Chad went to fetch an extension cord, Mark turned to the refrigerator—then stopped and looked quickly back at the tank.

It didn't move, he told himself, staring a snarl of tangled limbs for a long, breathless moment. *Not then, and not now.*

Ignoring a chill, Mark stepped to the other side of the room and opened the refrigerator. Inside, bottles of water crowded the top shelf, and beneath, rows of small, foil-sealed containers filled the remaining shelves beneath. He took an open bottle and one of the containers back to the tank, then removed a small cork that crowned a hollow pin in the middle of a socket on the top of the tank.

Chad returned then, carrying an extension cord. Plugging it in, Mark reached for a switch on the top of the tank cover, and bright lights flicked on. Ignoring what they illuminated, he turned on the vents, then uncapped the water and poured some into a small tube. Upending the foil-topped container, he pushed it onto the pin, hearing it puncture the foil as he screwed the container's mouth into the socket.

"Let there be...*something*," Chad muttered. Mark waited to make sure that the aeration process began, and when a fine, faint fog of greenish-grey began to puff into the tank, they walked away.

In the nearest row of tanks, the most recent acquisition had finally begun to take. It had been a bit of an older specimen, and had taken nearly a week to grow, but yesterday, the incomplete stack of shins, femurs, and vertebra had finally sprouted a grey coating. Earlier that morning, a few buttons had begun to form. Chad had been especially curious as to what results it would yield; the bones had once belonged to a man whose house still sometimes smelled of the fire that had killed him over twenty years before.

The specimens in the next row were much farther along; skulls, shins, pelvises, and rib cages had begun to lose their familiar shapes under blankets of young fruiting bodies. The newest ones were still weeks away from cultivation, but judging from their sheer numbers, they would make for a good harvest.

The ones in the last row were at their most advanced stages of necrosynthetic myceliation, the bones literally falling apart under the mere weight of the fruiting bodies that sprouted thick and moist above them. Two of the tanks were nearly empty, the cultivated mushrooms leaving only anonymous piles of wrinkled, shrunken, crumbling remains of old bones.

Mark had been planning to check on a few crops that he'd gathered earlier, but after everything that they'd dealt with tonight, all his energy was spent. He and Chad locked up, muttered superficial wishes of good nights that both knew they'd not be getting, and got in their cars and went home.

*   *   *

Chad couldn't help but grin as he stared into the tank. "Look at you," he said.

The strange body had proved to be unique in more ways than one; only three days after they'd prepared it, a grey mold began to form a blanket that mercifully obscured the revolting shapes beneath. The very next day, buttons had sprouted. And now, not even a full week later, the fruiting bodies were growing perfectly.

Chad scribbled some notes in his notebook. If this was any indication of how bountiful this new specimen was going to be...

He licked his lips and looked back in the tank.

Most of the fruiting bodies were still young and small, but a few larger ones were sprouting up from the middle of the cadaver, their caps nearly at full width. It was far too soon to pick them, Chad knew—but then again, it was also far too soon for them to even be *growing*, and yet here they were.

He pulled his phone out of his pocket and then put it back. Mark was over in Providence, picking up a fresh batch of spores from his supplier—something that always got Mark really tense and distracted; not that Chad could blame him, because the supplier was an absolute creep. *So, why stress him out even more?* Chad thought, smirking and setting his notebook and pen down beside the tank.

He fetched a pair of gloves and a small knife from the supply cabinets, then carefully removed the lid of the tank and set it aside. Reaching in with his free hand, he grabbed the largest cap and gingerly tugged it. It was, of course, still firmly rooted in the body, and so he brought the knife in and began to slowly cut around its base, the spongy matter between fungus and flesh splitting moistly around the blade. He gave the mushroom another tug—and frowned when it still refused to separate. "*C'mon…,*" Chad said softly, pulling with a little more force, and it finally obliged.

He lifted the mushroom out and held it up in the light, but as he examined it, his grin withered into a frown.

Green liquid, so dark it was nearly black, glittered on the base of the mushroom, swelling into a bead which then dripped down onto his jeans. Cursing, Chad held the mushroom away from himself, glanced into the tank—then gasped.

The spot that he'd cut the mushroom from was now a glistening pool of that same dark liquid.

Groaning in disgust, Chad set the mushroom down on the table and forcefully shoved the lid of the tank back in place. He tore his gloves off and tossed them aside, cursing again as he realized he still had to pick up the mushroom.

He grabbed his pen and notebook, jotted down a few quick lines, then gingerly carried the mushroom into the kitchen. While he fired up the oven, he cut off a few slices and threw them into onto a pan, which he then shoved into the oven.

When their distinctly acrid odor hit his nostrils, he took them out, grabbed a bag of half-stale bread and removed a slice, then placed the cooling, dried mushroom slices onto it. He took some more notes, then dumped the soft, tan coins onto the bread, folded it over, and gingerly took a bite.

"*Eurrrmph,*" he groaned, forcing himself to chew and swallow the rancid-tasting sandwich. He poured himself some water from the sink and started to down it when he heard a soft thump. He lowered the glass and listened.

It didn't repeat.

Chad suppressed a shiver, remembering their first weeks in the house. They'd seen no specters nor heard any wails or clanking chains, but there *had* seemed to be some kind of draft bringing cool air into rooms during those long, hot, summer days. Of course, all that had come to an end when they'd found the overgrown grave in the backyard, but—

There, again. It hadn't been from the front door, nor the back; it was hard to tell *where* it came from.

He doubted that it was an effect of the mushrooms; the trip hadn't started yet.

Chad found himself thinking of the strange body again, of how its arms had *twitched* as he and Mark had lifted it out of its coffin. He'd known what he'd seen that night, what he'd *felt*…

…and yet now, he could only hope that that *thing* wasn't causing the sounds he was hearing now.

He went back to the Garden and straight to the tank, his breath held.

The body was still there.

It hadn't moved.

It was exactly as he'd left it earlier.

Letting out his breath, he shook his head, then gasped. Little black spots had begun to appear in his vision.

Grinning, he ran back into the kitchen, fetched his notebook and pen, and went down into the basement where a chair and a lamp stood in a corner for exactly this purpose. Flipping open his notebook to a blank page, he poised his pen over the paper. As the black spots began to multiply and swell, crowding his vision, he thought he heard that thumping sound again, much louder now; but then the black spots coalesced, and he could only stare straight into the opening window of darkness, and smile.

*   *   *

Mark tapped his finger harder and faster on his phone, lowered it from his ear and hung up. Chad wasn't picking up; Mark knew the majority of their conversation would have to wait until he got back, but he still had a lot to get off his chest, and the sooner he could vent, the better.

He had gotten rather alarming news back in Providence. Apparently, recent construction work posed a threat to the unique conditions under which the source mushrooms grew in their secluded crop; his supplier had hinted that there was a good chance that his rates were going to go up—considerably.

Mark had considered telling Constance; perhaps she could talk to his supplier and make a more affordable trade—and then immediately dismissed the thought. If that bizarre body she'd commissioned them with was any indication of her idea of business, then this was the *last* he wanted to deal with her.

Crossing into Massachusetts, he turned off the highway and proceeded down several long, winding roads. Pulling into their driveway, he parked behind Chad's car and hauled out the tub of freshly-picked mushrooms and went inside.

"Yo," he called out, wrinkling his nose at the immediately familiar, acrid, burnt-smelling odor on the air.

He walked into the kitchen to find, as expected, a half-sliced mushroom lying on the counter beside an empty pan. "Shit," he cursed, his patience evaporating as he raised his voice. "Chad?"

He moved into the Garden and straight to the tank on the far side of the room, then gasped.

The fine greyish mold ringed the bottom of the tank, pockmarked by a few half-formed buttons; but the middle of the tank was an expanse of stained, moist glass in the rough size and shape of the bizarre body that no longer occupied it.

Mark's wide eyes wandered to the top of the tank, and he frowned when he saw the lid appeared to be very much in place. Around the tank, he saw only a pair of discarded latex gloves and a filthy knife; but otherwise, the table and the floor were bare and clean.

"*Chad!*" he hollered and, looking around, he saw the basement door was ajar.

Mark descended the stairs, ready to yell at him, to ask him what the hell he'd been thinking, to demand where he'd moved the body. All of those thoughts vanished, however, when the burnt smell was replaced with a thicker, more coppery, one.

And then he saw the red puddle spreading across the floor: blood. *So* much blood, everywhere.

In the middle of it was something small, dark, and rectangular. Chad's journal.

Mark's jaw worked uselessly, trying and failing to form words that he already knew nobody else would be able to hear.

He was so transfixed by the reddened floor that he somehow didn't notice the figure slumped on the chair until now. His eyes took it in and widened when they found Chad's—as much as was left of them in the ruined red mess spread upon the chair—and then he finally found his voice.

*   *   *

Mark stood in the front doorway and stared at his twin reflections in the huge, round, black lenses of Constance's sunglasses. As with the first time he'd met her, they'd stayed on, even now that the sun had long ago set. She was dressed in a neat, grey business outfit, her skirt and jacket clean and well-kept, jewelry glittering at the base of her neck and her wrists.

After reaching her over a private messaging network, Mark had received a call from Constance's private number. Her surprise had quickly shifted from pleased to curious as he'd demanded that she come see him at once.

He'd spent the long wait for her arrival debating exactly what he was going to tell her. More than once, he'd suspected her of somehow being behind what had happened; yet he knew that this was unlikely. There were a million other ways she could have stolen the body without having to harm a hair on Chad's or his heads.

After an hour that had felt like eternity, Constance arrived. As soon as she came close to the door, Mark told her that Chad was dead, and that the body she'd sent them was missing.

He waited for her to scowl, to yell, to coolly threaten him. Instead, she cocked her head, eyebrows disappearing behind her black shades. "Please show me."

Mark turned and led her inside, listening to the clicks and snaps of her high heels on the tiles and floorboards behind him. He took her through the Garden, not stopping to show her the empty tank—not yet—and brought her straight downstairs to what was left of his friend.

"Oh, *my*," Constance said, and Mark was surprised to watch her walk toward the couch, stopping and crouching down directly before the uneven ring of red gobs and puddles.

Mark couldn't look at the chair again; he turned away, cringing as he noticed the puddle of puke he'd left upon discovering the massacre.

"This *is* quite bad," Constance continued, and when Mark looked, he saw her hand moving beside her face, fingers lifting away from her shades. She stood slowly, one heel tapping on the concrete as she straightened and turned to look back at Mark. "You don't have any clue as to what happened?"

"None."

"Any kind of indoor security cameras?"

Mark shook his head, looking away, glassy-eyed.

He could hear Constance murmuring something about tunnels, and turned to find her glancing around at the basement floor. After a moment, she slowly looked back to the pulpy, red flower spread out on the chair.

Mark felt a chill in the back of his neck even before Constance turned back to him, and he started shaking his head.

Constance continued to stare at the bloody chair. "Perhaps—"

"*No*," Mark growled.

"—*he* could show us," she said, her thin lips curling into a smile.

*   *   *

Constance continued to speak to Mark as if he'd chimed in, as if he'd shown any sign of interest; but all he could do was stare at the nearest area of unbloodied floor and listen. When Constance was done talking, Mark silently began walking for the stairs, and she followed.

Up in the Garden, he showed her the empty tank. She muttered something that sounded like *fascinating*, and Mark turned to find her staring at it. "It... It came from a former monastery in Barbados," she said. "Locals said it—"

"No more," Mark said quietly. When Constance turned to him, he shook his head slowly. "No more. We're done."

He waited for an inevitable retort, some kind of menacingly aloof promise that he couldn't back out of their deal; but much to his surprise, she simply said, "I understand."

Mark looked into her unreadable lenses for a long moment before turning away.

"I...do know certain folks who are very good at cleaning things up," she said. "In more ways than one."

Mark said nothing.

Constance sighed heavily, then said, "I'm very sorry about your friend."

Mark's lips tightened.

After a long moment, Constance turned and made her way back into the office.

When Mark heard the car start up, he forced himself back into the basement.

He spent the rest of the night throwing six years of raised beers, bad movies, girlfriend stories, and a steady business partnership into several black garbage bags, which he then buried in the woods behind the house.

* * *

Over the next several days, Chad's phone buzzed and chimed with increasing frequency. At first, Mark ignored it; but as more and more texts, calls, e-mails, and other messages came through, he finally replied to them, stating (as Chad) that the number and address had changed, and that he'd let them know the new information soon. He didn't know how long he'd be able to keep this up, however; he expected a visit from the authorities before long.

Mark also began cleaning off Chad's notebook as best he could, but soon resigned himself to the fact that it was forever stained with red smears and splatters. It didn't contain much that he hadn't already seen— mainly notes on different bodies and the locations haunted by their spirits, the growth and quality of their mushrooms, and descriptions of the ghost-trips.

But then there had been Chad's last entry.

"*Darkness, a huge, black sky,*" he'd written. "*No stars, but there's a moon, far too big/ too close. So much dead land around me, grey rock stretching to every horizon. No wind, yet there's a weird, echoing sort of hollowness.*

"*Something is standing there in the middle of it all, staring up at the moon. It's got a head like a skull, bony and angular—and it's looking at me, staring at me with those empty, dark sockets.*

"*Its jaw parts in a scream that nobody can hear, because there's nobody, nothing else, absolutely nobody.*

"*No—I'm screaming, screaming and screaming again and again, but nobody can hear me.*

"*It's the great silence, the ultim—*"

On more than one occasion, Mark found himself wishing that he'd not cut Constance off as she'd begun to describe to him where the coffin and its damned contents had come from.

He also frequently thought back on what she'd suggested.

And then, one early October night, after waking from a vivid terror of his friend standing beside his bed, screaming, Mark headed back into the woods with a shovel.

*   *   *

Mark set his jaw as he stared down at the cooling, amber slices of mushroom. "Sorry, buddy," he said, not for the first time.

He and Chad had often made sick jokes about this, but most of them revolved around the image of them as a couple of crotchety old men. They'd never *really* considered this, even as a remote possibility.

With the same, numb, automatic mind that had guided him on the night he'd cleaned up Chad's eviscerated body—the same one that had controlled his hands while digging the grave, and again when he was digging it back up, and when he placed the decomposing remains into one of the tanks—Mark scooped up the slices in his hand and shoved them into his mouth. He didn't bother to grab a slice of bread, nothing in the world could cover the flavor of what he was eating.

Mark sat down at the kitchen table and crossed his arms, ignoring the disgust that threatened to gag him. He waited for the black spots to open into the final sights of his dead friend. He coughed once, twice, opened his eyes—

—Chad was in the basement.

He shook his head. "Holy shit." Now that had been a crazy trip.

He looked back over his notes, making sure he'd jotted down everything—

That strange thumping sound again.

He began to rise from the chair, but his head spun and his stomach lurched. Dropping back down, he let out a shaky breath.

The thump came again, and with it, a high, keening cry.

Chad looked around, frowning; the sound seemed to come from everywhere and nowhere, all at once; above, below, inside, out—what the hell was it? He pressed his thumb and forefinger against his eyes, rubbing out some of the lingering headache from the trip, and when he opened them, he saw the body from upstairs hovering directly before him.

It was still covered in mold and mushrooms, but its many arms and legs had spread, were twisting and swaying, because something was holding it.

Chad looked up and gasped, and then he understood, understood everything, as he saw its full shape, all its many arms—fully-formed, as they should be, not the short, stubby hybrid appendages of the poor, failed offspring that had somehow been cruelly wrested from a despairing mother and into the horror of light that was this world.

He looked down at his notebook as the mother's arms reached for him—

—and Mark began to scream.

we're all haunted here
doungai gam

I don't remember much about those first few hours after I died.

What I do recall was that first moment of awareness when I saw myself lying face down on my bed. I walked over and reached out to touch my physical self. My hand passed through my right shoulder and as it did I felt a tingling sensation throughout my *new* self. That was when I knew.

It took a little longer for the others to realize I was gone. My mom was the one who found me the next day. She came into my room under the assumption that I was asleep after a late night of playing online games with friends from school. It didn't seem to strike her as odd that I was sprawled across my bed, one leg dangling off the side. Any touch of the hangover she might have had from the night before dissipated when she went to shake me awake and the truth wrapped around her with its cold grip.

The strength of her grief could have moved mountains.

My dad came running when he heard my mom. It was bad enough to see Mom breaking down, but to watch my dad, too... I had to leave the room.

I walked the hallway of the only home I had ever known. My mom's cries followed me down the stairs into the living room. Even when I went outside I heard her wailing as if she were next to me. It wasn't long before sirens came screaming down the road and emergency vehicles parked in the driveway. I stayed out on the front porch. I know that probably sounds weird but it seemed like the right thing to do.

Within the hour my sister strolled around the corner of Field and Hoadley. She had spent the night at her friend Julie's house. She stopped when she saw the ambulance, then gripped her backpack and ran for the house, her face a mess of emotions.

"Gwen." I reached out to touch her as she ran by me. I missed her entirely but got a half-hearted swipe at her backpack.

I stood at the doorway and listened.

"What's going on?" my sister said.

My mom was sobbing, clutching my dad as if he too would disappear without notice. Two police officers stood guard at the bottom of the stairs. Their faces lacked emotion but I could see the discomfort in the younger officer's eyes.

Dad patted my mom's arm and she let go of him unwillingly. He stumbled forward, still trying to remain the stoic.

"Your brother…he's gone."

The howl that emerged from my sister crushed me. Her backpack dropped to the floor as she leaned on the nearby recliner. My dad went to her and put his hand on her shoulder, an awkward gesture of support. She hugged him, sobbing and mumbling something into his chest.

"What did you say?"

She pulled away and looked up at him. Mascara and eyeliner stained her cheeks and my dad's t-shirt.

"What happened?" She spoke so quietly I could barely hear her.

He pulled her towards the couch so they could talk. In that moment, my mom let out another wail as she tried to get past the cops standing guard.

"I want to see my son! Let me see him!"

"Ma'am, you're not allowed upstairs." The older cop was gentle but firm with both his words and his grip on my mom.

Gwen pushed my dad towards my mom before sitting down. She stared off into space, her jaw slack. Tears, mascara, and snot ran down her face. She didn't seem to notice or care.

Dad brought my mom to the couch and urged her to sit with Gwen. Mom rocked back and forth, unable to stop crying. My sister took her hand and held tight, still with that shell-shocked look on her own face.

Before too long, a detective showed up. He talked briefly with my folks before going up to my room to investigate. Gwen managed to pull herself together enough to ask the officers if they wanted anything to drink. They both declined. Behind her, I heard my parents giving each other a rare declaration of love.

It hurt so much to stay here and watch, but I was unable to leave. I was tethered to this house, to these beings I had fought, lived, laughed and cried with. I turned away from the scene inside and looked around the immediate neighborhood. Not everyone was home. I saw old Mrs. Wilkins across the street staring at our house through her bay window. She was the neighborhood grump, the one who kept the baseballs that were accidentally hit into her yard. She also had the meanest ankle-biting dogs I ever met.

I glared back at her, knowing she couldn't see me. After a moment, her face went pale and she ran away from her window, leaving the curtains wide open.

Did she see me?

Rattled, I stepped further into the yard and looked around. A few houses down, the Zimmerman twins were sitting on their front porch smoking with their friends. Cars carrying faces both familiar and strange drove by, all of them victims of tunnel vision. A girl wearing headphones walked by, dragged along by her German shepherd. She didn't give the emergency vehicles a second glance.

Around us, life continued on.

Inside, the detective questioned my family. Did I have any health issues? Were they aware of the bong in my closet? Did they know about the nippers hidden at the bottom of my trash can? How well did they know my friends? The inquisition seemed to be never ending.

The detective thanked my family for their cooperation and was gone shortly thereafter. The officers asked my dad to bring Mom into another room as they were going to be taking my body away. She hadn't been doing much more than crying and repeating to herself the events of the day. When she overheard this she stood up, insisting she see her son one last time. It took my dad, sister, and one of the officers to hold her back and keep her in the kitchen. When they wheeled me by, I turned away.

After the police left, Gwen came outside to make the phone calls that no one ever wanted to make. I watched her while she spoke with several different cousins and texted someone—probably her friend, Julie. My suspicions were proven right: Julie's beat up Civic came roaring around the corner as Gwen finished her call with our cousin Linda. My sister had been showing an impressive amount of poise and restraint while on the phone, but she started bawling before Julie got out of the car.

She ran over and reached for my sister, but it was too late and Gwen collapsed on the sidewalk. Julie sat beside her and they embraced. After a couple of minutes Gwen pulled away and rested her head on her friend's lap. Julie stroked her hair and whispered words I couldn't hear. In time, my sister's loud sobs reduced to tiny whimpers. By the time they stood up to go in the house, dusk had shrouded the neighborhood. In happier times they were a pair to behold—Julie the tiny spitfire alongside my tall awkward sister, full of laughter and many inside jokes that went back to their kindergarten days. How I badly wanted to grab them for a group hug as they walked by me.

I followed them into the house. My parents sat inches apart from each other on the couch; the only contact between them was Dad's hand covering my mom's. Mom didn't appear to be with it; her hazel eyes lacked any sign of clarity. She greeted Julie as if she were a stranger. My dad wasn't much better.

The four of them sat without speaking for a long time. Their silence, punctuated by the occasional outburst of sorrow, wove a detailed tapestry of love and hurt that hung heavy over the room and our souls. Perhaps it was because I was no longer connected with my physical being, but the weight became too much to bear and I had to leave.

I went up to my room. Even in darkness I could see everything as if the overhead light was on. My cell phone rested on the desk next to my laptop—no doubt both had been broken into with the expectation of finding... I'm not sure what they would have been looking for. I didn't use email for much, and my social media posts were limited to rants about video games or comic book movies. My cell was used primarily for texting stupid memes to my buddies.

It would have been nice if the detective had left my items in a bit more orderly fashion. The blankets were strewn all over the bed. There were a couple of used tissues on the floor next to the wastebasket that I know weren't there the night before. The bottom dresser drawer was pulled open halfway with one of my Captain America shirts hanging out.

I sat on my bed and looked around. In twenty years I had managed to accumulate more stuff than someone twice my age. One bookshelf contained stacks of D&D manuals and comic books; another was filled with paraphernalia and action figures. A mild sense of embarrassment came over me—this room looked like it was occupied by a twelve year old, not someone who was almost old enough to drink. I'm not sure why all of a sudden it bothered me so much.

Outside, the night strengthened its presence. Julie made her exit with usual flair, backing out of our driveway and nearly hitting a group of guys passing by. One of the Zimmerman twins yelled, "Oh, goddamnit!" as Julie slammed on the brakes just in time. I laughed, knowing there would be a new set of skid marks in the driveway. The realization that I couldn't ever tease her about it hit me hard and I grew solemn.

I heard my sister crying as she went to her room. Her wailing escalated when she closed the door behind her. I waited until it subsided before I dared to check on her. At first when I saw her I did a double take—the person on the bed was my kid sister, but she appeared as a toddler screaming and clutching her broken ankle. That time she fell down the front steps chasing after her mean big brother who threatened to throw her beat-up teddy bear in the trash. I closed my eyes, reeling from the wave of emotion. When I opened them, she had reverted back to a seventeen-year-old clutching her body pillow for dear life and sobbing all over it.

I sat cautiously at the edge of the bed and touched her left ankle, the one she had broken as a kid. Guilt and sorrow surged through me—I could have been a better big brother.

What I wasn't expecting to happen was the sudden burst of comfort that washed some of the guilt away. I looked at Gwen and saw that the tears had stopped. In slumber, she seemed to have found a bit of peace. I moved to the other end of the bed and sat by her, stroking her hair. For the most part, she slept through the night. There was the occasional whimper and plenty of tossing and turning. I wanted to check on my parents, but they had each other.

When the sun came up, Gwen stayed in bed and stared at the ceiling. Outside, the birds sang their morning songs. Kids waited for school buses and adults began their commutes—routines I had done and routines I would never do.

"I miss you, Andrew." Her voice, tiny and broken, slashed through me. I wished she could hear me say how much I missed her already.

The alarm clock went off. Gwen had it set to the local pop station rather than an angry buzz. A bright happy song blared through the air, something about our futures being unwritten. Speak for yourself, I thought bitterly. I was all done. Gwen jabbed at the alarm until it went silent, then she rolled over and stared at the wall.

"He'll never hear the birds again."

I had no way of telling her that I could indeed still hear the birds singing, so I stroked her hair instead. She sighed and within moments her breathing had gone quiet and steady.

I got up and went to check on my parents. They weren't in their room, or mine. I went downstairs and found them on the sofa. My dad's head was tilted backwards as he snored at the ceiling. My mom looked like she hadn't slept at all. Her eyelids were swollen and she drew ragged breaths through her parted lips.

I went and knelt down, resting my hands on their knees. I wanted to tell them how sorry I was for everything: for causing Gwen's broken ankle; for taking Dad's car for a quick ride with my friends (and rear-ending a truck) before I got my license; for stealing money from my mom so I could score weed. I wasn't the worst kid but I wanted to be better. I'd never have the chance to prove it to them now.

Whereas the connection I had made last night with my sister seemed to have helped her, it was the opposite with my parents. My mom's eyes went wide as if she had seen me materialize in front of her. She started bawling all over again, which in turn had my dad waking in a panic. I stood up and averted my eyes as I backed away. Dad whispered words of comfort to my mom and held her tight.

When I looked back at them I had another of those moments like I had with Gwen last night: my parents were still holding each other, but they were now over a decade younger in appearance. Dad had more hair and less belly. Mom was trimmer in the waistline and still crying in my dad's arms. A necklace was entwined in her fingers, a gold chain given to her from her mother who'd passed away when I was eight.

I glanced away. By the time I turned back they had returned to their current form and Gwen appeared at the bottom of the stairs. My parents moved enough so that she could sit between them. She grabbed their hands and they leaned on one another, tears and sorrows mingling.

How I wanted to join them. Oh, how I wish we were whole again, united and ready to take on anything.

*　　*　　*

The next few days were rough. Both my parents took the week off from work, and Gwen stayed home from school. My mom was prescribed sleeping pills because she hadn't slept in over thirty-six hours. So many people came around during all hours of the day, staying late into the night—relatives, classmates, friends and coworkers of my parents. Many came bearing gifts of food, simply because they didn't know what else to do. Mom got on a first-name basis with the Korean lady from the flower shop downtown, who stopped by daily with bouquets sent by relatives who couldn't make it out to see us.

My final arrangements were made. After deliberations over a couple of days my parents decided on a memorial service with a viewing. After that I would be cremated and they would bring my ashes home. Gwen had asked about getting a tiny urn of her own. My mom and sister were getting necklaces that would contain some of my ashes. My parents seemed satisfied with their final decision, but Gwen wasn't dealing so well.

"I don't want to burn him," I heard her say to Julie more than once up until the day of the service. I felt a little weird about the idea too, but I came to accept it. The physical self no longer functioned, so what was the point in throwing the body into the ground? Julie had tried to explain it in her usual blunt manner, but Gwen tuned her out.

My memorial service fell on the first day of spring. The winter had been a mild one; the daffodils and crocuses were already beginning their annual rebirth. The day was warm and my dad's forehead was already beaded with sweat before they arrived at the funeral home. My family took their spots along the wall. I stood by my casket because I had no idea where I should go.

I became emotional at all the people who took the time to show up to pay final respects. There were so many relatives, former teachers and classmates, and even a couple of ex-girlfriends. I couldn't help but smile at how many friends showed up in t-shirts with depictions of comic book characters. I missed most of the service; I was too engrossed in staring at everyone. The back wall was packed with people and there was overflow into another room. My sister got up and spoke briefly; I'll never know how she had the strength to speak in front of a packed room and not break down once.

Afterwards, many stopped by the casket one last time. As my friends filed by to say goodbye, leave little gifts, a strange thing started happening: I saw their future. It wasn't always pretty. My buddy Mike would be dead within the year. My pal Tommy, who had been through his *own* tragedy a couple of years back, would remain haunted by his ghosts for the rest of his years. My first girlfriend, Stacey, had much tragedy ahead of her, but she would persevere.

In the end, the last to leave were my parents and sister.

Dad had written me a letter and stuffed it awkwardly into the pocket of my jacket. I saw depression in his future and I wanted so badly for him to open up to someone, learn how to express himself so he could find some peace.

Mom touched the rosary beads in my hands and cried. I had worried about her drinking before, and it was going to become a more serious problem as the years went on.

Gwen asked for a moment alone. She put a Spider Man stuffed toy in the casket and tried to slip a note of her own between my folded hands. It wouldn't go and she eventually stuck it halfway inside my jacket.

"I miss you, Andrew." Big shiny tears rolled down her cheeks. "I can't believe you're making me do this alone. You're supposed to be the one who helps me with Mom and Dad when they get older. Why did you leave me?" She continued to cry, no longer able to speak.

I went to her and put my arms around her. I saw her future: it was full of happiness and heartbreak. There would be many an adventure, and much pain and depression. But her life would be a long and fulfilling one. Knowing that brought me comfort.

I released my hold on her and stepped back. The living claim they're the ones haunted by ghosts, but those of us already dead are every bit as haunted by the ones we left behind.

Murmur

Jeremy Flagg

Even the mute scream.

Tabitha remembered this as she cupped the stretched cheeks of the remnant, a ghost nearing its end. The ghost's jaw remained trapped in an expression of perpetual terror. Blue flickering lights moved between the tortured's mouth to the tips of her thumbs. Leaning in, she licked the bottom lip of the remnant, coaxing tiny sparks onto her own tongue. With an established connection, Tabitha experienced the remnant's memories of death.

*   *   *

The thin lance sank into the space between her eye and her nose. With one tap, then two, the small mallet drove the piece of metal into her tear duct. Limbs remained frozen in place as she begged her muscles to respond. The man in white turned the skewer forty-five degrees counter clockwise. Straps tightened across her chest as her body convulsed, her spine threatening to fold in two.

The doctor turned the device to and fro while nurses scrambled to hold her body in the operating chair. Narcotics swelled through her veins stealing her free will. Another seizure subsided, presenting an opportunity for the neuromancer to remove the instrument. The thin piece of metal slid from her tear duct, dark red dripping onto the end of her nose. His breath washed across her skin as he leaned, inspecting the success of his operation.

The doctor pulled down the mask covering his mouth, the strings pulling at his ears, forcing them to fold outward. The instrument slid along an outstretched tongue, blood coating his lips. Eyes shut, he held his breath while he savored the woman's essence. When he opened his eyes, bright yellow slits replaced his iris while the veins on his neck engorged, leaving him appearing more devil than human.

The man's mouth danced between pursed lips and shiny white teeth as he spoke. Silence. A leather binding fell away from her forehead, letting her slouch to one side. Clear fluid flowed from the hole in her tear duct, mixing with the blood until it dripped from her face.

The scene rebooted. The man secured the strap again...

*   *   *

Tabitha staggered backward, her hands shaking from the remnant's memory of dying. Her fingers twitched, similar to when she used to spend too much time behind a keyboard. Ensuring the memories hadn't been real, she touched the space near the bridge of her nose, inspecting for holes.

In front of her, the remnant, a woman kneeled with hands resting on her thighs and head lowered as she stared to the floor. Tabitha inspected her own hands, the blue light pulsing vividly, radiating outward to a vibrant white. Tabitha wrapped her finger around fading blue light dancing on the woman's skin. With the only magical ability left to her, she severed the ties between the tortured woman and the afterlife.

Strings of blue light snapped like delicate strands of thread, growing dim as they fell away. The woman made no protests, trapped in a continual loop of frightening memories. The edges of the woman's skin turned black, chipping and flaking like peeling paint leaving gaping holes. Tabitha fought the urge to avert her eyes from the ghost's second death. Cracked and crumbling, nothing remained. Like every decoding before, the remnant dissolved into nothing, a husk of the deceased, erased for eternity.

Like every time before, the ghost, remnant, or whatever you called the dead in the afterlife, vanished into nothing. The echo of a person deconstructed forever, released from reliving the torment that brought them to this place. Tabitha silently prayed, that when all she could recall was how she died in the mortal realm, somebody could do the same for her.

In the desolate operating room, from behind an overturned stretcher, a set of eyes fixated on Tabitha. Faint blue tendrils of smoke rose off the boy, similar to the other dead children who found themselves trapped inside the asylum. With his memories still intact, the child had yet to turn into one of the tortured remnants.

Tabitha got to her feet, straightening her back. Both of her hands shimmered a vibrant blue, light pulsing softly from her fingertips. The color reminded her of when she awoke on the floor of the hospital auditorium, before her essence started to slip away. For a brief moment, she expected her lungs to require air again. A gasp would break the perpetual silence, a deafening hiss crossing her dry lips in a world where the volume dial remained on zero.

The intensity of the young ghost's eyes sent a shiver along her skin. The boy must be six, only a few years older than her daughter. Hiding in the room, the child had witnessed her reach into a remnant and deconstruct the last of its light. For all the boy knew, she was a ghost killer. He continued cowering as she walked from the operating room. When a heart attack robbed Tabitha of her life, her daughter's eyes had held the same look as they exchanged tearful goodbyes.

Revitalized, her skin lost a bit of the numbness. Stiff paint chips moved under her slender digits as she dragged the tips of her fingers along the wall. The sensation seemed distant, as if she were recalling it from a far-removed memory. Several pieces fell to the ground as she attempted to recount how many ghosts she had deconstructed. Two? A dozen? A hundred? They blurred together.

Tabitha walked through the hallways, glancing into each of the empty operating rooms, looking for more remnants. In life, she had been called many things, but only one title mattered in the afterlife. Witch. Behind her ear should have been a subdermal node, technology granting her access to the internet and her coven. Apparently technology didn't transfer to the afterlife. No longer able to rely on implants or her spell-casting sisters, Tabitha was left with limited innate abilities.

Unlike other young girls, puberty brought many unsuspecting changes. The trauma of her first period had been dwarfed by her ability to see life's source code. Tiny strands of light wove themselves between every object in one beautiful and disorienting web. With effort, she found a talent to manipulate the programming language of the universe. She had been called many things, a freak, a life hacker, even a witch; ultimately, she was one of a few gifted humans. The ghosts came later.

A dim blue figure stood near a filthy window in a recovery room. Tabitha recognized the pigtails on the ghost, a young woman who wandered the halls until recently. Now, with almost no light remaining, she banged her head against the glass, reliving her death. The woman's head turned, eyes clenched shut and mouth gaping as she screamed in silence. The remnant hurled herself to the floor, crawling along the ground until she vanished into the shadows.

Tabitha made note of the room number, promising to come back the next night and deconstruct the woman. For a moment she considered pulling the door shut, expending the energy to grant the woman privacy. Fear of not being able to open it tomorrow forced her hand back at her side. Hanging her head, staring at the warped floorboards covered in mold, she continued further into the asylum, hoping she may find another former witch.

The sun vanished behind the tree line outside the hospital. What little warmth penetrated the dirty windows evaporated. The pitch black of night settled in, pulling at shadows until they stretched across the hall. In an hour, she would be immersed in a world of cerulean. The darkest blues would appear like an abyss, only broken by the lost figures moving through the hospital in a daze.

Adjacent to a nurse's station, wisps of blue light spiraled upward from the floor, coiling together until it resembled a figure. Had this been before her death, she'd have been able to see the universe create a window between worlds, implanting new code before her. As the light solidified, a man had his arms across his face, bracing for impact. A crash victim, one of many who entered the hospital, killed before they had time to make peace with their demise.

She found herself headed toward the auditorium housed in the center of the complex. Once she had been initiated into her coven, it became rare to see the dead. Instead, ghosts desperate to communicate left messages on her computer, cryptic pleas reading, "I'm sorry," or "Farewell." It had never crossed her mind while alive, the dead spoke through the computer because the realm of ghosts stood void of sound.

Crash.

The sound stormed through the hospital, shaking the walls and threatening to drive Tabitha to her knees. Hands covered her ears, trying to protect her eardrums from bursting. As she fell to one knee, she opened her mouth in an attempt to scream, but her vocal chords refused to produce the shriek her body demanded.

Amongst the blue figures, several stared, heads cocked to the side, unaffected by what caused her to topple. Somewhere in the distance, an ear-piercing squeal pricked at her skin like needles. Had she a heartbeat, it'd be racing. Had she a pulse, she would feel the blood pumping. Had she any senses beyond her sight and faint sense of touch, they would react to the terror she felt. In a silent abandoned hospital, surrounded by rot and disuse, the dead only feared the moment when memories vanished and she sought them out.

Forcing herself to her feet, she followed the sound to its source. She weaved her way through opened cage doors and an area where the roof had collapsed. Darting between wards, from quarantine, to trauma, to biohazard, she found herself approaching the front entrance. It took a moment before she realized the scream originated from the last thing she expected.

The living.

* * *

"You know we're not supposed to be in this part of the city, right?" asked a girl with bright pink hair. Each word sounded lyrical, as if at any moment she may burst into song. Tabitha ignored the volume, instead focusing on the faces of the girls. The duo almost looked awkward without glowing blue skin.

"Rena," said the red headed girl with a backpack slung over her shoulder, "it'll be fine, guards are busy patrolling the north side of the city."

The nervous one hung her head, making the sign of the cross on her chest. "Those poor passengers. Do you think the bullet train will run again?"

"Forget that, what about the food? People are going to starve if we can't get supplies from Chicago."

Tabitha noted that Rena's eyes were sunken, her face almost skeletal. The other girl was similar, each of them appearing underfed. The witch leaned forward, captivated by the green of the redhead's eyes. Despite the emaciation, the girl still had an alluring quality about her.

The redhead stood apart from her friend, the alpha of this friendship. The pink-haired girl – Rena – wore loose fitting t-shirts and ripped jeans. She appeared even thinner in the billowing shirt. The redhead however, wearing black gloves, a spiked collar and decorated with a lip, nose and eyebrow ring seemed like she belonged here.

Rena twisted a metal tube in her hand. Light spilled into the lobby, flickering several times. The room returned to its near pitch-black state.

"Ugh, Abigail, it did it again." said Rena, "This is a *you* thing."

The world never grew perfectly dark for Tabitha. Even in the bowels of the hospital, she found herself able to detect her surroundings. She never questioned if it was a trait of the afterlife or of being a witch. For a moment, the room rippled like a pebble dropped in a pond. It had been forever since she experienced a person manipulating the tiny threads that made up reality.

"Fiat lux," breathed Abigail as she held her palm upright in the air.

Due to the perpetual blue monotone of the afterlife, Tabitha basked in the warmth of the lines wrapping around the young girl's arm. Pushing up through her skin, the light ran down her limb like veins until it collected in her hand. The yellow grew brighter until the shadows found themselves outmatched.

A fledgling witch.

Blowing calmly into her hand, the brilliant orb rose into the air, hovering a foot above her head. Tabitha waited for the friend to gasp, or even shriek at the magic, but she barely paid attention to Abigail, instead inspecting the broken surroundings of the hospital. Tabitha recalled in her youth hiding these gifts. Later in life they placed her on the fringes of the lower class. The new world, consumed with famine, plague, even demons, needed magic, but magic never bought her acceptance or respect.

"You sure you want to do this?" Rena's voice held an edge of worry, not entirely sold on being in an abandoned hospital on the bad side of town at night. Tabitha wondered what could have brought them here? What could possibly be so dire these two would journey through this purgatory?

"You don't have to do this." Rena offered a way out if needed. "Seriously, couldn't we do this in your bedroom? Why the hell--"

"Tonight ends the waxing moon. My magic is stronger. Besides, this is where everybody used to go when they were sick. There must be thousands of ghosts roaming these halls, one of them must know her."

By the way Rena slumped her shoulders, it was obvious she didn't like the answer. Abigail continued through double doors and into the hallway leading to the meat of the building. The other followed close behind while the small glowing orb hovered just out of arm's reach above them.

Ghosts wandered the halls. The people froze as the two girls passed. None of the dead took notice of the duo, instead turning their gaze upward, captivated by the shimmering light. Tabitha realized that while the girls were invisible to the ghosts of mundanes, whatever magic Abigail conjured existed in both worlds. With no voice to ask, the elder witch was left with more questions than answers.

"This place is amazing," Abigail said.

"Of course you'd find it amazing," Rena remarked.

"You don't? I mean, before the war, it must have been filled with people. What do you think happened?"

"They died," Rena chimed in.

"But what about the nurses and doctors?"

"Them too," Rena added. "The plague didn't care if they were patients or doctors. It consumed them all."

Tabitha remembered the war as she touched the scar stretching bicep to forearm that once held her bioware. Magic, real magic had started to flow again. Mankind expected it to be a time of wonderment but it came with an infection. Demons. Creatures emerged from the bowels of the biggest cities, devouring, infecting, turning. Tabitha thanked the deities she made it to the afterlife never seeing one of those dog-faced soul suckers.

Abigail pushed at the swinging door to the auditorium. The door creaked open, freezing in place, unwilling to swing shut again. Rena paused, hesitant to enter the space. While she eyed the path, a dozen ghosts closed in, crowding her in the doorway. The teenager didn't react to the dead passing by, brushing against her skin. The girl started in a light trot to catch up to her friend, appearing as if she was swept away by the growing number of ghosts.

Inside the auditorium the two took in the massive room. With furniture hurled against walls and windows with rock sized holes, the space felt abused and depressing. With all paths leading back to this central part of the hospital, it housed the majority of the dead. Where doctors and nurses once met to learn life saving techniques, their failed patients now collected, waiting for whatever came next.

Abigail moved near the center of the room, the orb casting a warm glow in an attempt to push away persistent shadows. The young witch rummaged through her backpack, handing Rena a small rectangular box.

"You have neural gel pads?" asked Rena.

"My foster dad works for the defense station."

"Are you allowed to have these? Are we going to get in trouble?"

Abigail gave Rena a sideways glance. "We're fine."

Tabitha moved closer to the orb. Ghosts backed away from her, ensuring she didn't touch them. A tall man reached up, trying to grasp the spot of brightness, curious about the spectacle. A small circle of ghosts hovered about the pair, a woman leaning over Rena, their bodies almost melded together. Concerned, Tabitha stepped near the girls, causing ghosts to withdraw.

Rena opened the box and freed a silver object. Rena stuck it to her temple without hesitating. When Abigail sat on the floor crossing her legs, the other followed suit.

Tabitha couldn't figure out how the sticky metal pads played into the unfolding scene. Abigail powered up her laptop and pulled a cord from the side while exposing the underside of her forearm. Housed in her arm, three inches above her wrist was a small ethernet port. As Abigail pressed the end of the cord into her forearm, Tabitha listened for the familiar click.

"Valerie, open neural network." Tabitha's own computer had been named Athena, the Greek goddess of wisdom. Every hacker had a story behind the name of their machine, she wondered what significance it held for the fledgling.

The screen on the laptop flashed to life. "The neural safety features are enabled. I can't hear your thoughts. We're not doing a simulation construct, so imagine you're playing a game at home."

"Sure, just like a game." Rena rolled her eyes. "Remind me why I'm *here* again."

"Cause you're the best girlfriend ever."

"I'm starting to reconsider."

Abigail folded the screen backward on the laptop until it was a flat pad and slid the device in between the two of them. Tabitha couldn't figure out how the laptop played into this ritual. In cyberspace, hackers utilized their gifts to parse code at an alarming rate. When a witch reached maturity, magic became nothing more than complex code to hack. However, it was rare for the two worlds to interact like this.

"Valerie, execute Ouija script." Rena gasped as the screen flared bright white.

"Your sight will take a second to sync with the program." Abigail reassured Rena.

Abigail reached behind her ear. Tapping her skin three times, her eyes grew distant, as if she were caught in a memory. Tabitha touched the spot behind her ear, painfully aware of her missing microprocessor.

"Whoa, look at that."

Rena leaned in, focusing on the projection from the pad. Tabitha forced her way past a gentleman crowding the device, sending him to the ground. A rectangle hung in the air, but unlike the Ouija board she played with as a kid, this one remained blank. Tabitha realized the script running on the computer wasn't a clever naming convention, but an actual Ouija board. Like the orb, the ghosts in the room noticed the board as well. Staring at the ghost killer, they hovered, fearful to approach.

"I don't know what to do," Rena said.

"The computer is reading your thoughts so you can manipulate the projection."

"Why don't you need the neural gel?"

"I have a hard line," Abigail said pointing to the cord. "Neural gel doesn't transfer data fast enough for it to reach into the afterlife."

Tabitha couldn't tell if Rena's worried expression was from the technology being explained to her, or because they were trying to talk to ghosts. In all her years of practicing magic, she had never used a Ouija board, an item banned by her coven's high priestess. Seeing ghosts in the middle of the night had been terrifying enough, talking to them would have been worse. Tabitha wondered if Abigail would be able to see the dead once the spell begun.

A woman with scorched patches of skin running along her arm, reached around Rena, grasping at the board. Another ghost snatched the woman, trying to get his hand to the board first. Ghosts grew agitated, emboldened as they pushed past Tabitha, stretching and pushing, to get at the projection. If the girls could see the mass of ghosts writhing as they attempted to best their neighbor, they'd be terrified of the hoard.

A white triangle blinked into existence, resting in the center of the board. Tabitha tried to keep the young witch in her line of sight, but as ghosts surged forward their fear of the ghost killer was replaced with need. They crawled over one another, desperate to reach the middle.

Bodies twisted and contorted, falling around the teenagers like they were nothing more than discarded pieces of furniture.

"Ready?" asked Abigail as a child with a mangled face tried hopping over her.

"I am," Rena replied.

"Sub specie aeternitatis."

Words of power, Latin phrases used by witches to focus their abilities. Unlike the dozen languages she mastered as a programmer, this one carried with it an air of prestige. It took the elder witch a moment to translate.

Under the sight of eternity.

The young witch yelped. Standing and backing away until the cord pulled at her forearm, she frantically looked about the ground. Tabitha recognized the expression on Abigail's face, a mixture of horror and intrigue. The girl saw the ghosts clawing at one another to maintain their place next to the board.

"Are you okay?" asked Rena.

"Yeah, I'm fine, the spell worked."

"How do you know?"

"I see them, all of them."

"Why can't I?"

"Magic," Abigail replied as if that answered everything.

"Your mom?"

"Spirits we welcome you," Abigail said in a squeaky whisper. "Can you hear us?"

"What are they saying?" asked Rena.

"Nothing, I mean, they're too busy trying to get to the board."

"Maybe they need it to speak with us?"

The undead attempting to claim the board reached nearly four dozen, each more frantic than the last. Both girls extended their hands as if they were resting their finger tips on the pointer. As her fingers touched the digital pointer, Rena's eyes widened, a scream escaping her lips.

Abigail's girlfriend found herself trapped on all sides by the ghosts. Rena steadied herself, eyeing the silent carnage being wreaked by the dead. She locked eyes with Tabitha, focusing on the single ghost not attempting to reach the board.

"They're everywhere." Rena said matter-of-factly, and yelped again when she removed her hands. "They're gone."

"They're trying to get to the Ouija board. The spell only works when your hand is on the pointer." Abigail reminded her. Rena took a deep breath, holding it for a moment and exhaling as she placed her hand into the air again.

"Who are you?" asked Abigail.

A young woman rested her hand on the mirage of the pointer. The moment her hand hovered over the projection, the remaining ghosts stopped fighting. Almost complacently, they collected themselves and backed away. Tabitha found herself blocked by a line of ghosts, still managing to see the specter pushing the digital pointer about on the board.

"Megan Faverau," the computer spoke.

Rena didn't hesitate. "Where are you?"

"Somewhere dark."

"We are looking for my mother," Abigail called out into the auditorium.

Tabitha stopped paying attention to the two girls, instead transfixed by a young ghost leaning against a wall in the auditorium. Unlike the others, the boy had no interest in being near the board. No more than ten, he backed himself against the wall, his hands firmly planted against the torn sound-proofing.

"Are they trapped here?" asked Rena. "I mean, can they leave? Are they always there?"

"I don't know," Abigail answered honestly.

A crash sounded outside, like the crack of lightning. Another and another followed. Abigail tapped the spot behind her ear, disconnecting from the computer. They searched for the source, but in the dark, only Tabitha could see the crows crashing into the glass, one after another, dying on impact. Several of the large birds struck their wings against the exterior, determined to break into the auditorium.

As if her heart still beat, the witch grabbed her chest, unsure of what was happening. Abigail clutched her chest in a similar fashion. Decades wiser than the fledgling witch, Tabitha understood something in the source code had changed drastically.

The boy.

The wall behind the young ghost had turned black. Creeping through the plaster like veins, a disease spreading itself until reaching the ceiling. Along the vibrant blue of the boy's face, black lines carved into his skin like tattoos. For however long she had resided in the afterlife, she had never seen a ghost become a remnant like this.

"Something's wrong," Abigail said.

"What?"

"I don't know, something feels off."

Rena gasped, loud enough that Abigail met the girl's eyes. Tabitha turned her attention from the dying child. The ghosts did nothing to stop her as she pulled at them, shoving her way into the center of the circle. The pointer slid about the board.

"Hello." Even the voice of the computer sounded strained.

"Who moved it?" asked Rena trying to identify the ghost.

The woman who had manipulated the pointer before had sunken into the crowd. None of the blue ghosts reached out to touch the pointer. The desperate need Tabitha witnessed earlier had subsided. Now, they stared, fixated by the Ouija board, waiting for the pointer to move of its own accord.

"Abigail," said the computer without the aid of any ghost.

"Mom?"

Whispers. Tabitha watched as Rena took Abigail's hand and squeezed it gently. Both remained silent, waiting for the computer to speak. The hushed speaking grew louder, filling the room almost to the volume she experienced when the girls first arrived. Thousands of tiny voices whispered far too quickly for her to make out their hissing. With hands clasped over her ears, the elder witch tried to concentrate on the board.

"Is that you?" asked Abigail.

"The wall, Abigail."

Abigail turned to face the side of the auditorium and the ghosts parted for her, clearing a path to the boy. Tabitha dashed through the crowd, knocking the dead aside and stepped in front of the young witch. The exertion forced the blue to intensify, making her skin pulsate with energy. Holding her hand out to stop the teen, she shook her head, unsure of what trickery was at hand.

"Mom?"

"We are Murmur," said the computer.

Before Tabitha had a chance to process the cryptic words, a crack ripped through the room, loud enough that even the girls screamed. Cracked in half, the boy's body peeled away, talons reaching outward, tearing away the child's blue skin. As the body split, the disease behind the boy withdrew, pouring into the child's back. Once it vanished, a leg stepped out, then an arm and shoulder. Tabitha recognized the creature the moment it freed itself from the boy's chest cavity. The elongated limbs attached to a torso with exposed ribs was only half as terrifying as the dog-like head resting on its shoulders.

"What's that thing?"

"It's a demon." Abigail's words hung in the air.

"Murmur," the computer's voice repeated the single word on a loop.

Tabitha watched in horror as the giant dog-headed beast seized the closest ghost, tearing at its neck, vaporizing the poor soul. The remaining ghosts fled. The newest of them moved quickly, turning bright blue as they pushed past the oldest ghosts. The demon grabbed a middle-aged man, snapping its gnarly jaws onto his head, tearing until the ghost blinked out of existence.

The witch didn't have time to divine if the demon only existed in the ghostly realm. Her hands surged a bright blue as she ignored the million whispering voices and pushed past the carnage. The demon latched onto her waist, picking her up, its canine maw stretching to snap at her shoulder. Thrusting her hands into the demon's chest, sinking into the black goo, she jerked at the threads of code making the beast and started deconstructing.

Tabitha slipped into the demon's memory, eons before she was born. She found herself consumed by the sensation of wind whipping past her face. A naked man's limp body soared through open sky, speeding downward. Bound tightly to his forearm, a small wooden shield with stretched leather bore the sigil for protection. The ground rushed to cradle his falling body. At his side, wings flailed, trying to slow his descent. A wave of dust spit into the air as he lodged into the dry riverbed.

Tears pooled in his eyes until they spilled over, running down the sides of his head. The warrior's fall caused the bedrock to crack, lines stretching outward from his body in a pattern like giant veins. The man arched his body, forcing himself to sit upright, spitting blood onto his bare chest. Attached to his back mangled wings pulled themselves free from the riverbed. Though he may have once appeared angelic, now, all that remained was a broken man.

He sobbed as his wings twitched, useless. A shadow stepped between him and the sun, casting him into darkness. Hands from the shadow grabbed at the wings and wrenched, tearing them from the man's flesh with a wet sucking sound. His cries kicked up another storm of dust in every direction.

Wrapping its hands around his neck, the shadow lifted the man into the air. Radiating from the unknown figure's fingers, strands of black goo worked their way under the wingless man's skin, spreading until it reached his face. Thin lines of black pushed through his veins, pushing them to the surface until they looked like war paint.

The shadow leaned into the fallen angel's face, close enough for him to make out serpent like eyes. As the black liquid robbed the man's skin of color the shadow hissed, "We are now Murmur." The bones in the angel's jaw cracked, separating, elongating until it resembled a wild dog.

"Levi cum praesidio!"

Tabitha fell backward, black goo clinging to her hands. A burst of light slammed into the demon, sending it reeling. The beast was like every demon before it, an infection determined to spread. Another blast of light erupted in the room, striking the demon in the torso. Unlike the first, this hardly made the demon flinch.

Tabitha turned, motioning the girls to flee. Rena pulled at Abigail's arm, screaming for her to run. The demon dashed past her, sprinting toward the Ouija board. Abigail shouted one last time.

"Valerie, terminate--"

The orb above Abigail exploded in a flash of light, forcing Tabitha to cover her eyes. As the room returned to its dismal state, Abigail remained standing, blinking at the empty spot on the wall. Rena fished her flashlight from her pocket, smacking it until it projected a steady beam.

"We're getting out of here right now."

Abigail. The memories were fuzzy, as if they were just out of reach. The infant's eyes staring at her from the hallway leading into their kitchen. The pink shirt with a unicorn drawn on it always amused her. More time had passed than she imagined. More than a decade, but she took solace in the strong young witch her daughter had become.

"My mom said you were going to be trouble," Rena chided.

Without the board luring them in, ghosts moved away from the auditorium, acting as if the demon had never existed. Tabitha approached her daughter, wishing she had a chance to say goodbye to her one remaining legacy.

The blue of her arms dimmed, an indication she would need to find a remnant before the night ended. She placed her hand on the girl's chest, directly over her heart. The girl's eyes remained unfocused, staring off into space as Rena tugged at her arm. The young witch rested her hand on top of Tabitha's ghostly fingers.

Abigail's eyes focused on Tabitha. A smile spread across her daughter's lips, tears falling from the corners of her eyes. A rush of tiny whispers filled the room until they reached a dull roar. Abigail's voice deepened. "We too, are Murmur, momma," she whispered. Tabitha staggered backward, catching a glimpse at her own hands still covered in the goo. Thin black lines pumped in her veins just beneath the skin.

Pulped

James A. Moore

The first victim had been hit so hard in the face his lips were torn off, leaving a bloody grin in their place. Three bodies, each of them beaten to death. When I say beaten, I mean hammered until bones were broken and the faces were completely unrecognizable. Me and my partner, Dominick Galliano, were the lucky bastards that caught the case.

Fifty years ago The Benson was a decent little pub that catered to the growing Irish population in the area. It also took care of the working stiffs coming back from the factories along Washington Street. These days it was a dive that only the worst sort of people frequented. The wood of the walls was rotting in a few places, the floors were just as bad, and stained with enough spilled drinks to guarantee sticky shoes. It had lost a lot of its charm over the decades. Seeing a beating, a rape or a drug bust take place in the vicinity was common enough, but you didn't have to worry too often about murders. Most of the clientele was too wasted on heroin to actually get into fights.

So seeing the corpses and the condition of the bar was a bit more unsettling than I'd expected. Dom squatted next to the closest corpse, his face scrunched up in an expression of disgust and horror. Whoever had hit the deceased had actually shattered his face. It was the wrong shape and parts were dangling free that shouldn't have been.

"I'm going with either brass knuckles or a meat tenderizing hammer." Dom did not touch, but he looked carefully and took pictures with his phone.

"Seriously?" I could see the mess, but not all of the details. The bar was too dark and the forensics team wasn't around just yet.

"There are marks on the bone, scraped the meat and the bone away in one punch."

I let out a whistle without really thinking about it. The force involved was heavy, like a golden gloves contender. When you added in the brass, it was a hard beat down. I was figuring a crime of passion, only it was done to three men and all of them were the sort that specialized in delivering the beatings rather than taking them.

There were still three people in the place that were alive, aside from Dom and me. Two of them were sleeping off their latest high, so wasted they couldn't even move, though it was possible they were actually awake. The last one was the manager of The Benson, a creep named Jeff Lemon, who kept avoiding arrest because no one could ever find him with any drugs in the place. Druggies? Absolutely. Narcotics? Only on the people he served and never on the premises and never on the bartender.

Dom kept looking at the bodies, careful not to touch. While he was busy with that, I walked over to talk to Lemon. The man shook his head and said, "I didn't see anything."

"Yeah, because that's gonna play out here."

Dom called out, "First victim looks to be Dan Chaney." I looked over and he pointed to the massive ring on the corpse's middle finger. It was a genuine imitation gold nugget that had dented more than one forehead over the years. Chaney wouldn't be caught dead without it. He was still wearing it, proving my point.

I looked back at Lemon. "We playing this game?" We'd gone to school together. We'd never been friends. Jeff Lemon hung out with the druggies even then and I was a jock. I'd probably thumped his head against the wall a dozen times back in the day and I could tell by the look he was giving me that he remembered every time we'd caught each other the wrong way.

"I didn't see anything."

"Don't be stupid." I'm not above using intimidation to close a case. I loomed over Lemon and stared hard into his eyes. That was normally enough to get him talking.

Not this time. He stood his ground, which was not at all like the Lemon I'd known for twenty-odd years.

There was a reason for that, of course, but it took me a while to realize what it was.

When we were done at the scene and the forensics guys were going over the whole place, the two of us headed for the office. By that point, Lemon had been released and allowed to go home. He'd have the next few days off, because I intended to keep the crime scene barricaded for as long as possible. He inconvenienced me and I returned the favor. The two sleeping beauties had been incarcerated, and Dom was yawning so much I expected his face to crack.

It was during the drive that I realized Lemon wasn't growing a backbone. He was still scared. Whatever he'd seen, whoever had done the murders, scared him a lot more than I did and he didn't think I could protect him.

*   *   *

Nice surprise. Jeff Lemon actually had security footage in his piece of shit bar. There were four cameras, all of them with VHS connections instead of digital, but it was still a lucky break. My old pal didn't much want to give the tapes without a search warrant, but I convinced him. I wound up getting a warrant, because I like doing the paperwork, but I made sure Jeff remembered to be afraid of me. My grandfather and my father both worked this job. Being a cop runs deep in my family. I learned the loopholes from them. Sometimes you need to make sure the perpetrators you run across stay honest with you.

Dom looked over the tapes. He was always better with that sort of thing. He liked staring at blurry images. Meanwhile, I followed up with our two junkies, both of whom actually *did* sleep through the murders, and I talked to the M.E. about the murders. The woman I talked to was strictly business, and young enough to be my daughter. Hannah Lindsey was round, had black wire hair that she managed to beat into submission with a lot of hair gel and normally was as cheerful as a pissed off badger. Not that she was ever rude, really, but she could have taken lessons on smiling.

"All three of the victims were hit at least twenty times apiece, and look to have been beaten with brass knuckles or a similar weapon. If they were knuckles, they were custom jobs. The markings aren't familiar with any of the brands we have on file, and we have *everything* on file."

Those words were innocent enough, but I felt a cold dread sneak up my back and nest in my stomach.

"Custom? What sort of markings?"

Hannah showed me a photo from her digital files. It was a close-up on one of the markings. The indentations drove deep, as I had been warned, but the flesh was torn so looking for the exact shape of the knuckle tips was challenging. I ran my finger just across the surface of her iPad screen and asked, "Is that a skull?"

"Yes. But look here." Hannah moved to the next picture in line, her dark brown eyes half hidden behind her thick lenses. Still, I could see the slight shimmer of excitement. This was something out of the routine and when you get down to it, after a while we all want to see something new. The next photo was another extreme close-up of a wound. This time the design was different, a crescent moon shape that had been hammered into brutalized flesh. Before I could say anything she threw up another image, this one more obscure. It took me a second to see the shape of a cat arching its back and hissing.

The chill came back again. Only this time it was different; there was a layer of excitement, too.

"Let me guess. Last one is a Jack O' lantern?"

Hannah pinned me with her gaze. "How did you know?"

"Back in the day, there was a pulp character that had special markings on brass knuckles. He was one of those guys like Doc Savage, or The Shadow. There was a radio show, printed stories. There were even a few movies, but almost no one has copies."

"Really? What was he called?" She actually sounded interested, which was amusing. Most of the women I mentioned this stuff to had their eyes glaze over in thirty seconds or less.

"Doctor Samuel Hanes, also known as The Black Wraith." Nostalgia tugged at me. Unlike most everyone I knew I'd seen the old movies. I'd read all of the books. When I was growing up The Black Wraith was my hero as surely as Batman was.

"Never heard of him."

"Like I said, not as popular as some of the others." I shrugged. "They all had their gimmicks, right? The Shadow could see into the hearts of men. Doc Savage was basically the earthbound version of Superman. He was from Earth but had been raised and trained to be as close to superhuman as he could be. The Spider pretended to be a criminal and wore a ring that left spider-shaped marks on his victims' faces. The Black Wraith was supposed to have been shot dead but came back on Halloween night to offer up justice from beyond the grave. Had special guns that were oversized and in one story used a Tommy gun. Then the movies came along and the brass knuckles got added. They'd have close ups of his fists in their black gloves, each knuckle with a different Halloween thing on it."

"How do you even know about that?"

I smiled at her. "I watched them all growing up. They were kind of awesome."

Turned out Hannah was a fan of the old pulps, so I wrote down some of the few websites that had pictures of the old costume for the Black Wraith and she was good enough to email me the pictures and file information on the dead men.

Me? I kept playing it out in my head, imagining the Black Wraith going on a rampage. One of the things I always loved about the old stories was that they were lurid. They gave graphic descriptions of the way the Wraith hit people and the sort of damage he did. In the stories he really *was* a ghost, but he had a body. They always made that clear. He was dead, but when the sun came up he could hide in plain sight and he did that by becoming Doctor Sam Hanes. Sam Hanes. Samhain. Halloween. Get it? A silly and very likely tongue in cheek comment from the creator of the Black Wraith.

I read an interview where he talked about the creation of the character and how he'd almost called him the Halloween Man or Doctor

Halloween. I never did find out why he changed his mind, but the motif stayed. In the early stories he wore a homemade skull mask. Later he wore a black mask and the brass knuckles. He always wore a tattered cape and a fedora. He originally used smoke bombs to make his getaways and to fight the bad guys, but later he summoned a heavy fog and fought against people who could barely see their own faces through the haze.

In the serials it was always dry ice.

When I got back to the department I showed the pictures to Dom and watched carefully for his reaction. At first he frowned, and his brow got tight. "This a joke, Billy?"

"Not even a little."

"You tell anyone else about it?"

"I mentioned the movies, but no. No one else knows."

Dom nodded and lowered his chin to his chest as he examined the pictures again. I looked at him as he did it. He studied the scene and I studied him. Dark, curly hair, dark eyes, a chiseled jaw line. One of the first things I ever said to him was he looked like Bruce Wayne. He laughed it off. He had a perfect laugh and perfect teeth. He looked like a Hollywood leading man. He still does.

Turns out it runs in the family. Back in the day, as he told me one night over drinks, his great-grandfather had worked in Hollywood. Bit parts in about a dozen movies, normally where he played the best friend or competition of the leading man, but for a short time, he'd made a better name for himself playing a pulp age hero.

For the length of time it took to make four serials and three actual movies, his great-grandfather, the pulp writer that had created the Black Wraith, also played him on the silver screen. There was no budget for the stuff and Anthony Galliano, also known as the pulp writer Walter Slade, took on the name Blake Hadley and became an actor. He made decent enough money. He made the same sort of scratch for his stories.

Dom never talked much about what happened, but there was some sort of Hollywood scandal and before the dust had settled he'd retired to Massachusetts and a different life entirely. Low-level politics, mostly.

Dom loved the fact that his family had a celebrity but, whatever the scandal was, it was bad enough that he didn't talk about it and he almost never spoke about his great-grandfather.

There was a time he thought about going to Hollywood himself, but it never happened.

He turned his eyes toward me and studied me. I mean studied me like I was a perp. He looked worried. Genuinely worried and I couldn't understand why.

"What's up, Dom?"

"I need you to come with me, partner, and I need to show you something." He didn't really ask, but he rose from his desk seat and started for the exit we always used.

I followed him and frowned.

"Dom, seriously, what is going on?"

"I need to show you. I need a witness, okay?"

A witness? I just nodded.

"Did you see anything on the tapes, Dom?" I spoke as we walked from the building.

"I'll show them to you. What we got is nothing. I mean, I can see the guys getting beaten, but there isn't a person doing it to them."

"Come again?"

"No one is in the images, Bill. No one. Just some weird distortions."

Three miles down the road from the station was the house where Dom had lived his entire life. His parents owned it before him (and they would have had it still if they hadn't decided to move to Florida and hang around Disneyworld) and before them his grandparents and before them his great-grandparents. Four generations in the same place. It was a damned nice house; I'd have stayed, too. Dom's place was an old Victorian with lots of gingerbread, a widow's walk, and half an acre of land. He inherited the house but I knew he was paying someone to keep the place looking good for him. Dom is a certified slob.

Not much had changed since the first time I'd been there. That was right after Dom told me about his great-grandfather's books and movies and showed me the collection he had.

The films were in decent shape. Parts of the old celluloid had buckled and crumbled but Dom managed to get all of the stuff put onto DVDs and later onto Blu-Rays and he'd settled us in the room set aside with a dozen theater seats where we'd watched the first of the serials.

We went right to the same room again, but instead of smiling as he entered, Dom frowned, his face set in a brooding expression I seldom saw on him. It added years.

"We gonna watch a movie, Dom?"

"You seen 'em all already."

"Yeah, that's why I'm puzzled."

"I ever tell you what my great-granddad did with all of the props from the movies?"

"Nope. I just figured they were in the same place as all the movies."

Aside from what Dom had, most of the old copies of the Black Wraith films had been destroyed a long time ago. Some had fallen apart, some just vanished, others burned up in a studio fire back in the forties. These were the personal copies of the family, handed down from generation to generation and basically ignored until Dom took enough of an interest to save them.

"So, there are films here. The rest of Black Wraith stuff? It's here, too."

"What? Like the old costumes and such?"

"Exactly."

I nodded. He was worried someone had maybe used the props from the movies, or had stolen them. It took only a couple of minutes to move a few boxes out of the way and reach the old wardrobe that held everything. Was it anything remarkable? Not really. There was a gray suit, pinstriped, a pair of shoes, three capes, each tattered and torn. Two fedoras. Two ties, jet-black. A pair of cloth gloves that looked a bit threadbare, a cloth mask, and a second cloth mask that had been padded and sewn. It was not completely black, was, in fact, a dark gray, but had been highlighted in black, which gave more of an impression of a skull. All of it was well worn and, even in a wardrobe, had managed to gather a bit of dust.

I took all of it in with the eyes of a child instead of a detective. I was supposed to be scrutinizing the stuff and I suppose I was, because I knew it hadn't been moved in a long time. While my inner child was freaking out over a little history from my past, Dom reached into the case and opened a small drawer.

"These were from the movies. Only used for close ups, of course. I think it was my great-grandfather's cousin that made them. They are one of a kind, best of my knowledge." He shrugged. "I always kind of figured I'd get 'em set up in a museum some day or at least make a few bucks off of a collector."

I looked at them carefully, the brass knuckles. They were massive things, the better to show up in the filmed close-ups. Unwieldy and I guessed at least four or five pounds each. That may not sound like much, but that made them much heavier than the real thing. I didn't touch them at first. I went for the gloves in my coat pocket. Dom didn't even think about touching and I knew why: if there were fingerprints to be found he wanted to make sure they weren't his.

I studied them closely before I touched. There was a thin layer of dust. Like with everything else in the wardrobe.

When I finally picked them up I was impressed all over again with their weight. Like I said, they were larger and unbalanced. They'd never been meant to be used. The boring on the metal, where the fingers slipped in, was smooth and well worn. But the designs on the knuckles themselves? I couldn't see the faintest hint of wear. I doubt they'd ever hit so much as a pillow with any force.

"No way, Dom."

"What?"

"No way these were used. I think we need to take them down for a proper examination, but I don't think there's a chance in hell these were ever employed on anything. The metal here? It's too thin and delicate. It would have been marred by hitting someone in the face hard enough to break bone."

Some of the tension flowed out of Dom in that moment. Listen, I knew where it counted that Dom wasn't the type. I'd never once seen him lose his temper and while I knew he could fight well enough, I don't think he's got what it takes to beat three men to death.

Ten minutes later we were on our way to the M.E. offices with the brass knuckles from the old shows. We stopped by the offices before that, so I could look over the video footage.

What I saw was not much. Three men getting torn apart in a fistfight with nothing but an occasional dark smudge. I looked hard at that footage and saw two things. First, the floor was spotty in the images. The ceramic tiles that were inlaid faded a bit here and there. They disappeared like there was something blocking them. Like maybe dry ice.   That was a creepy enough thought, but all three men were seeing something that we could not. I watched four more times and focused on the occasional smudges. They looked a lot like shadows. The sort of shadows that might fall from clothing. Say, a hat and a cape. That is to say, I could almost make out the shadow at the bottom of a hat and the bottom of a cloak or a cape, but there was nothing else there, like bad green screen effects from a show done in a different era, before CGI could hide away the things you weren't supposed to see.

I didn't know what to make of it. I also didn't tell Dom what it looked like to me, because I didn't want to say it first.

After wasting our time with footage that ultimately showed very little by way of a possible culprit, we were on our way to finish drop off of possible evidence.

According to the coroner's reports, the next vicious murder was occurring around the same time.

*   *   *

Seriously, what goes through people's minds? We looked at the single victim this time and I was appalled. That doesn't happen very often.

Edward MacDougal was a big man. I mean, physically he was very nearly a giant. Almost seven feet in height and in excellent physical shape. He wasn't one of the towering and ridiculously thin types you see who suffer from a glandular problem. He came from a family of big people. His sister, Nelly, was six and a half feet tall. I know, because I'd arrested her a few times for beating the shit out of her husband. I wouldn't have busted her, because I knew he liked to use his fists, too, but she gave me no choice when she threw the drunken bastard through a window and went after him.

Violence was a thing with the family and Eddie had long since made the best of that. He worked in protections and usually just held out a hand and got the money. No one wanted him pulling them in half and most people assumed he could.

One of the only things I ever liked about Eddie is he never resisted arrest. Trust me, I thanked the Almighty for that fact on a few occasions.

Like the others he had been beaten so severely that I genuinely couldn't have recognized his face, not even with his carrot orange hair. I would have recognized the rings on his fingers though, and his height and weight helped a lot. The fact that he'd tattooed his own name across both of his biceps also helped. Even in October, when the air was bitter, Eddie walked around in a too tight t-shirt and didn't bother with a coat.

I don't think a jackhammer could have ruined his face more completely.

His body was a wreck. I mean that. The bastard had been beaten so badly that I even felt bad for him and considering our history I wouldn't have thought that possible. Big as he had been in life, he'd been whittled down.

Dom looked at the corpse for a long time. I guess we both did, but his scrutiny of the crime scene was more intense than usual – as I already said, he was the one who liked to study crime scenes.

"No part of his face is intact." He gestured me over so I could look with him. Without touching anything, he pointed to the markings on the ruin and where the flesh had been torn away, where the imprints of knuckles like the ones we had in an evidence bag could be seen clearly. "He got hit harder than I thought a person could punch."

"He got nailed to the fucking wall, Dom." There were a couple of uniforms standing nearby and I knew them both. They were good at their jobs but I could see both of them had been busy looking because, seriously, they were a bit green around the edges and looked ready to toss their last meals as soon as they could.

We waited for the M.E. and said nothing. They'd collect the body and be on the way and then we would be on ours. Until then, we both thought long and hard about the kind of force needed to break that many bones with a fist, whether or not brass was involved. The human skull is strong. It has to be. Its bone can withstand a lot of force. Not as much as some of the leg bones, but still, you have to work at it to break that much. I'd seen freshly ground meat that looked more intact and right then I never wanted to see hamburger again. It struck too close to home.

When it was all over, and the scene secured, we went on our way. I didn't leave the evidence with the guys who picked up the corpse. Until they said otherwise the old movie props and the crime had nothing to do with each other, and I didn't want to taint the scene or their perceptions. Also, Dom would have shit himself. The idea of pointing out the possible connection wouldn't sit well with my partner.

"How did your great-granddad die, Dom?"

His brow got all knotted up in thought. "I don't know, but I guess maybe I should look into that."

"Your folks never said?"

"I never asked 'em, Billy. Never crossed my mind, but something is going on here and I need to know what."

While he talked, I Googled. Took me all of three minutes to find out that Anthony Galliano, AKA Walter Slade, AKA Blake Hadley vanished and was presumed dead a long time ago. No body was ever found, no proof of a death, and they waited the mandatory seven years to make sure it wasn't just a case of the man walking off for a pack of cigarettes and finding another family. Believe me, stranger things happen every day. There was evidence of foul play. That was as far as the article said. I told Dom what I'd found and he told me that his ancestor had died here in town and was buried in the cemetery on Mill Street. Local made things easier. We'd have to dig a bit but the police report, if one existed, would be local, at least.

More paperwork. Have I ever mentioned how much of the job is paperwork? I'd bitch more about it, but the next clue we were looking for would revolve around, you guessed it, paperwork.

It didn't take a lot of work to find out the truth of the matter.

Anthony Galliano had, in fact, vanished. His body was never found, but the very night that he disappeared, the cops answered a complaint at The Benson and discovered serious signs of a disturbance. The pub had been trashed and it looked like there must have been a serious fight somewhere along the way. Broken furniture, shattered beer mugs and of course, a copious amount of blood all over the floor and the bar.

No surprise, no one claimed to know what had happened. There would have been no mention of anything at all, but a couple of off duty cops had stopped by to grab a brew after work and came across the evidence.

The place where three men had been beaten to death was also the last place Dom's celebrity great-grandfather had ever been seen alive. The difference was fifty years in time, but I got a chill just the same, and I felt it where it counts: there was a genuine connection.

I told Dom and he nodded. "My old man talked about that a few times. Said The Benson used to be a classy place. Hasn't been for a long time, though. I guess maybe signs of a murder going down could do that to a pub's reputation."

I snorted at that. I've been to plenty of locations where a body count didn't change a thing. But that isn't always the case, is it? We're talking about a neighborhood pub, and sometimes people don't like to go back to places where the atmosphere has soured. I know a lot of places like Benson's that survived fifty years in neighborhoods that changed a dozen times, falling into ruin and then being "gentrified," etc, and they always managed to stay popular. Benson's? Not so much.

"Well, maybe it's haunted." I meant it as a joke, honest.

The look I got from Dom said he didn't much think it was funny. Next thing I knew we were on our way back to the pub.

Dom kept looking around, his eyes studying everything in the place. The old wainscoting, the hardwood paneling, all had long since passed their glory days. The old marble tile floor that had seen better days half a century ago. I could see the previous grandeur hidden in the decay. It made me sad some days, but right then as I looked at the taped outlines of bodies on the bloodied floor, it made me nervous.

The day was fading and night was creeping in. Dom didn't say what he was looking for, but he took his time scrutinizing the place. I did some looking myself, wondering if his great-grandfather, a man who had been my idol when I was a kid, could have really been murdered here.

"What connects them, Dom? We have four bodies, but what do they have in common?"

Dom looked up at me and shook his head. The expression on his face was mildly scolding. "You ever study this neighborhood? Every one of those guys has a family history in this area as long as mine. Longer, four or more generations back, Billy. Every last one."

That thought gave me a wicked case of the creeps.

"You need to find out more if you can, Dom. From your dad."

"I know that." He cast a hard look my way. The shadows in the Benson hid half of his face, but I could see his eyes well enough. He looked angry and scared and more stressed than I'd ever seen him.

I thought of his great-grandfather on those old serials, and how much they looked alike. Like I said before, Hollywood looks.

I spoke before I could stop myself, because there was only one reason we were here and even though neither of us had said it, we both knew it. "Okay, so if somebody is going after the guys who maybe did in your great-grandfather, why? What could they gain at this point? I doubt any of the people who were alive when it happened are still alive now, or even if they are, they're ancient, like celebrating their late nineties. So what's the point?"

"I've been trying to figure out any possible angle myself, and I can't. I don't know what the hell is going on, except someone is beating some serious creeps to death."

Neither of us said it but that part wasn't such a bad thing. We'd had plenty of discussions about it in the past, when one or another of the punks who ran in the wrong crowds met a bad ending.

My partner pulled out his flashlight and started looking. He moved chairs, checked around the edges of the walls, and even lifted an old carpet that had probably been sitting there since dinosaurs roamed the earth.

"What are you looking for, Dom?"

"Seeing if there are signs that a body was ever buried here."

"What? Seriously?"

That was maybe a mistake. The look Dom threw me was not kind or forgiving. "What do you want me to do? Go look at pictures in the Cold Case files? I saw the images you brought up on your phone. They're probably the same ones."

"How would you even hope to find anything now, Dom?" I shrugged. "Fifty years is a long time."

"Gotta at least look, Billy. Come on, what would you do?"

"Same thing, I guess. But I think you'd get more from your dad if he remembers any of the old stories. He knew the man right? The guy was his granddad."

Dom nodded and said nothing, he agreed, maybe, but he had to do this his way first. I could respect that.

The sun finished setting. Aside from his flashlight the place was nearly dark. There were lights outside, but neither of us had thought to turn on the interior lights. Hell, I wouldn't even know where to look.

Instead of being useless, I went back toward the kitchen and started looking for a light switch.

That meant I got to see the Black Wraith first.

There was a doorway that was nothing remarkable. It was locked and painted a faded white. So when the Black Wraith came through it I could see every detail.

He looked like he had in the old serials, only more so. The suit was a gray pinstripe, the jacket open enough to let me see the shoulder holsters for two very large pistols. The shoes were glossy and looked like they belonged to a different era. The hat was a wide-brimmed fedora, and the cloak over the shoulders of the suit looked like someone had torn a funeral shroud off a rotting corpse and decided to make a fashion statement with it. The gloves were jet black and so was the mask.

How can I describe it? It was a skull. There were features to that mask. It had sharp, crisp angles and I could see the teeth, each and every

252

one of them, done up in black. There was a cavern where the nose should have been, just like you see on a skull, and there were eye sockets and a bony ridge above. I've looked at enough pictures of skulls. This was just that, a skull. Only if I'm honest it looked like someone had covered it in felt, or carefully glued a thin layer of cloth to the thing, so that the bones were carefully hidden under a fine, thin fabric.

All of that worked fine until I got to the eyes. I didn't see them. I sensed them. They looked my way and held my gaze, and much as I wish I could tell you I did the manly thing and drew my weapon to secure an enemy, I froze, horrified and fascinated.

I had no doubt in my mind what I was looking at. I was staring at a ghost. Not just the Black Wraith, but a genuine specter. Those teeth grinned at me. Those eyes studied me and judged me and I think they maybe found me less than ideal.

The figure was as tall as me, maybe a little taller. He moved with purpose, he didn't walk, he strode as he turned away from me and headed for the door.

"Wait. Come back, I have to ask you questions." I could barely make my throat work. It was too dry and my words just sort of fell away like so much ash.

I shook a little. Not going to lie, I was scared. Seriously scared but I shook it off and followed the Black Wraith as he moved toward the front of the place and toward Dom.

"Dom! Dom! Look out!" My voice was a croak, but it was loud enough.

The swinging door that separated the kitchen from the serving area slammed open as the Black Wraith walked away from me. I followed and shoved the door back before it could hit me in the face.

Even as I walked, I felt the chill in the air and saw the vapor pouring from the walls, from the ground, filling the area with a dense fog.

I also saw Dom looking at the same shape I was following. His eyes nearly popped out of his head. His mouth opened in a wide gape and I suspect I had a similar look on my face.

The Black Wraith walked past him, and as he walked, I saw his gloved hands reaching into his coat and pulling out a massive pair of brass knuckles, well tarnished and stained with blood.

Each knuckle had a different shape on it. They were so coated with dried gore that I couldn't make out the designs.

Dom was smarter than me. He stayed put. I tried moving for the figure heading toward the front doors of Benson's. I had questions. A lot of them, and I wanted answers.

My hand touched the right shoulder of that figure and I pulled him back toward me as my fingers clenched around fabric.

That fabric felt like it covered only bones. The shoulder felt too thin for the way it filled out the jacket under the shroud. Cold sucked the warmth from my hand as the Black Wraith stopped moving and turned his head toward me.

The fog was growing thicker, and even from a few feet away the shape of the pulp hero I had adored as a kid started getting lost. Hell, I could barely even see my own hand.

It was Dom who spoke. "Billy. Don't. Don't do it."

I knew what he meant. Don't be this stupid. Don't start something with a dead man who was already a hard killer. Don't touch a fucking ghost. Don't interfere. Don't get your damned fool self killed. All of that and more.

I got wise and listened.

The Black Wraith, a ghost that could not possibly exist, a ghost of a fictional character, nodded curtly and then moved forward and I removed my hand from his shoulder. The front door did not open. Instead the dark shape moved through the door. As it stepped outside I saw the fog rising from the ground, obscuring the feet and legs of the shape that walked through wood and glass like it wasn't there.

The mist-shrouded shape turned toward the left and looked through the windows at me and at Dom alike. I felt the eyes looking at us.

It took about four seconds for the form to get lost in the fog.

I stared after it for a lot longer. I'm not sure how long, but before I looked away the fog had lifted and the street was dark again, except for a few lights that seemed more faded than before.

We didn't speak.

We'd been partners long enough that without a single word spoken, I looked at the questions in Dom's eyes and knew he wanted answers as badly as I did.

I showed him where the Black Wraith had come from and he followed, opened the door. It was locked. That didn't stop him. Cat burglars couldn't have used lock picks as easily as he did.

He went down the stairs into the cellar. It was maybe ten minutes before he found the spot where the ancient concrete of the floor was misshapen.

That night there was one more death. A third generation mobster named Tommy Robbins got pounded so hard his scalp was left on the wall where he'd been attacked. The killer came into Robbins' apartment, ignored the man's wife and children, and ruined Robbins with a dozen punches to his head. Each and every one of those punches shattered bone and pushed flesh around until there was nothing left but strings of meat to hide the ruination.

The widow Robbins explained to us that she'd seen the man who killed her husband and had tried to stop him. She even took a swing with a cast iron skillet that would have easily knocked Muhammad Ali into a coma. I blame adrenaline for her even being able to lift the damn thing.

The pan never touched the assailant, but her swing left a dent in the wall where it landed.

She said it went right through him, and I quote, "Like he was a fucking ghost."

Two days later, after some digging around with a pick axe and a jackhammer, a collection of bones was found under the cement in the basement of Benson's Pub.

The miracles of modern science. The DNA linked the bones to Dom's family. It may not be positive identification, but it was enough for Dom and the local newscasters. Even made the national news for a day or two, because whether or not he was a big celebrity, Anthony Galliano was once a star in Hollywood. That put paid to a footnote in at least a dozen books of faded celebrities who'd vanished over the decades.

In a perfect world I'd say that the murders had ended and Dom was making a fortune based on the old movies his family still owned. Some of that is true. Dom made a deal and is getting a nice income from the residuals on his great-grandfather's films. We both got a nice pat on the back for solving a cold case and finding a body. Looking into the old files, yes, the people the Black Wraith beat to death were all related to other people who had been seen at Benson's the night the blood was seen all over the floorboards.

The problem is, there were a lot of people in and out of Benson's that night. Most of them might have been innocent bystanders, near as we can tell, but how can we know? Five people were ruined by the Black Wraith. Literally beaten until their faces were nothing but bone and pulp.

That was before we found the body.

Since then three more have been killed in similar fashion. One of those names was on the cold case list of people seen at Benson's Pub, but the other two seem to have no affiliation.

Who can say how many people might have been there the night Anthony Galliano was murdered? Who can say why he was killed?

We're still looking into the situation. We're still investigating.

Want to know something else?

We've both been looking into possible ways of getting rid of a ghost.

So far none of them have worked.

But we're still trying.

I'm stubborn, but Dom is patient.

He's always been a better detective than me. He keeps his cool when I lose mine.

He's classy that way. Him and his Hollywood looks.

Sometimes though, I have to wonder if he's trying as hard as I am.

I mean, at the end of the day, someone killed a member of his family, and Dom and his have always been keen on family.

About the Cover Artist

Mikio Murakami is a Japanese-Canadian graphic designer. He specializes in cover art, T-shirts, logos and drinking bad coffee. His design company SILENT Q DESIGN was founded in Montreal in 2006. Melding together the use of both realistic templates and surreal imagery, SILENT Q DESIGN's artistry proves, at first glance, that a professional for art is still alive, and that no musician, magazine, or venue should suffer from the same bland designs that have been re-hashed over and over. The evolution of artwork ranges both locally and internationally. SILENT Q DESIGN has commissioned work for Montreal and surrounding area bands such as Synastry, Endast and The Agonist. Likewise, SILENT Q DESIGN also boasts work for international musician Bob Katsionis (Toshiba-EMI / Lion Music / Century Media) as well as Montreal Radio station 90.3 FM's *Sounds of Steel* music program. Their works go beyond fantasy landscapes and surreal imagery, offering their customers personalised service. SILENT Q DESIGN prides itself on being a multi-faceted entity that can serve even the contemporary business world.

About the Interior Artists

Artist, graphic designer, cartoonist, and fiction author -- **Kali Moulton** is a dreamer of possibilities and "what ifs" who loves exploring art in all of its forms. She's on a mission to open minds through art and writing that twist perspectives. At home in New Hampshire, she spends her weekends cosplaying as a Ghostbuster and practicing magic with her husband and daughter. To see more of Kali Moulton's work, or to pop in for a quick hello, you can find her online at Operation-Art.com or on Facebook & Instagram.

Ogmios is an artist, story-teller and is the publisher for OTB Comics and Games. Art by Ogmios can be seen on many book covers and interior illustrations for publishers and independent authors. He currently illustrates for Loxley, Inc. (a new game company by the original Dungeons & Dragons/TSR staff) as well as working with smaller publishers while developing OTB Comics and Games. Ogmios likes to use pencil, ink and digital paint when illustrating and is focused on

Horror, Fantasy, Sci-Fi and Myth. See more at www.ArtByOgmios.com and www.OTBcomics.com.

Judi Calhoun lives with ferocious black bears and wild wolves that howl at the moon every night in the Great North Woods of New Hampshire. She is both an artist and an author. Her artwork can be found on more than a few e-zine magazine covers, and well over two-dozen articles. Judi's short stories have appeared in many fiction anthologies such as: *Love Free Or Die, NH Pulp Fiction; Snowbound and Zombies, Tales of The Supernatural A John Greenleaf Whittier Inspired life work; Murder Ink, New England Newsroom Crimes; Canopic Jars: Tales of Mummies & Mummification; Bugs Anthology, Tales that Slither, Creep and Crawl;* Green Gecko's *The Passion of Cat* anthology. Her work is featured in many genres such as Horror, Sci-fi and Fantasy, and literary short story publications. Judi is currently looking for an agent and publisher for her new novel, *Dragon Girl*. Artwork can be viewed a http://judiartist2.wix.com/judisartwork

About the Authors

Peter N. Dudar is a United States Postal Worker from Lisbon Falls, Maine. His debut novel, *A Requiem For Dead Flies* was a finalist for the Bram Stoker Award, and his novella *Where Spiders Fear To Spin* was the 2015 winner of the Solstice Award for best long fiction. Dudar is a proud member of the New England Horror Writers, and his story in this anthology marks his fourth inclusion in the NEHW publication series. Ghost stories, by the way, are his favorite thing to read.

Bracken MacLeod has worked as a martial arts teacher, a university philosophy instructor, for a children's non-profit, and as a trial attorney. His short fiction has appeared in several magazines and anthologies including LampLight, ThugLit, and Splatterpunk and has been collected in 13 VIEWS OF THE SUICIDE WOODS by ChiZine Publications, which the New York Times Book Review called, "Superb." He is the author of the novels, MOUNTAIN HOME, STRANDED, and COME TO DUST. He lives outside of Boston with his wife and son, where he is at work on his next novel.

Currently in her second-term as Poet Laureate of New Bedford, Massachusetts, **Patricia Gomes** is the creator of the Octologue, an 8-line syllabic form of poetry. The former editor of Adagio Verse Quarterly, she has been published in numerous literary journals and anthologies. A 2008 Pushcart Prize nominee, Gomes is the author of four chapbooks. Performing her work extensively throughout the New England area, she also conducts workshops for adults, students, and children. Ms. Gomes is the co-founder of the GNB Writers Block as well a member of the SciFi Poetry Association, New England Horror Writers, the Massachusetts Poetry Society, and the Bartleby Scrivener Poetry Group.

KH Vaughan lives in New England with his wife and children. He holds a doctorate in clinical psychology and teaches at local colleges. As a writer, he creates dark fiction and is a frequent panelist a conventions in the area.

Curtis M. Lawson is a writer of unapologetically weird, dark fiction and comics. His work includes *It's a Bad, Bad, Bad, Bad World*, *The Devoured*, and *Black Pantheons: Collected Tales of Gnostic Dread*. Curtis is a member of the Horror Writer's Association, and the organizer of the *Wyra* live horror reading series. He lives in Salem, MA with his wife and their son. When he is not writing, Curtis enjoys tabletop RPGs, under-ground music, playing guitar, and the ocean.

Dan Szczesny is a long-time author and journalist living in Manchester, N.H. He's written travel memoirs, short story collections, poetry books and the occasional ghost story. His book, *The Nepal Chronicles*, won the 2016 State Library Award for Outstanding Work of Non-Fiction. His short story, "White Like Marble," was a finalist in the 2017 Hemingway Foundation Short Shorts Contest. Dan's latest project is *The White Mountain*, a social and cultural history of New Hampshire's Mount Washington, available in spring 2018. More on Dan's books at www.danszczesny.com

Paul R. McNamee is a lifelong resident of Massachusetts He has had short stories published in small press anthologies. His blog is http://paulmcnamee.blogspot.com and he can be found on Twitter @pmcnamee67.

Larissa Glasser is a librarian, genre writer, trans woman from Boston. Her fiction has appeared in The Healing Monsters Volume One and Procyon Press Science Fiction Anthology (2016), along with Tragedy Queens: Stories Inspired by Lana Del Rey and Sylvia Plath (2017). She is a Member at Large of Broad Universe, and an associate member of The Horror Writers Association. She's on Twitter @larissaeglasser and blogs at https://larissaglasser.com

Matt Bechtel was born just south of Detroit, Michigan (cursing him a Lions fan), into a mostly-Irish family of dreamers and writers as opposed to the pharmaceutical or construction giants that share his surname. As such, he has spent most of his years making questionable life decisions and enjoying the results. Mentored by their late-founder Bob Booth, he serves on both the Executive Committee of the Northeastern Writers' Convention (a.k.a. Camp Necon) and as a partner in the Necon E-Books digital publishing company. The author of *Monochromes and Other Stories*, his writing tends towards dark humor / satire and has been compared to Ray Bradbury and Cormac McCarthy. He currently lives in Providence, Rhode Island, and can be found online at www.matt-bechtel.com.

Nick Manzolillo is a homesick Rhode Islander currently living as a bearded Manhattanite wizard in New York City. His writing has appeared in over thirty publications including *Wicked Witches*, the previous anthology, as well as *Grievous Angel, Thuglit, Red Room Magazine*, and the *Tales To Terrify* podcast. He has an MFA in Creative and Professional Writing from Western Connecticut State University. By day he works as a content specialist for TopBuzz, a news app.

Trisha J. Wooldridge writes grown-up horror short stories and weird poetry for anthologies and magazines—some even winning awards! Under her business, A Novel Friend (www.anovelfriend.com), she's edited over fifty novels; written over a hundred articles on food, drink, entertainment, horses, music, and writing for over a dozen different publications; designed and written three online college classes; copy edited the MMORPG *Dungeons & Dragons Stormreach*; edited two geeky anthologies; and has become the events coordinator and consignment manager for Annie's Book Stop of Worcester. Because she is masochistic when it comes to time management, she created the child-friendly persona of **T.J. Wooldridge** and published three scary children's novels, as well as a poem in The Jimmy Fun charity anthology *Now I Lay Me Down To Sleep*. Her recent publications also include two novellas "Tea with Mr. Fuzzypants" and "Mirror of Hearts," and stories and poetry in besides *Dark Luminous Wings*, you can find her most recent work in the 2017 anthologies *Gothic Fantasy Supernatural Horror, Dark Luminous Wings*, and the collector's book of the Blackstone Valley Artists Association 2017 Art and Poetry Showcase.

Dan Foley is an ex-plumber, ex-Navy Nuke, Ex-Senior Reactor Operator and ex-nuclear operations instructor. He is the author of four novels, two novellas, and one collection of short stories. He has lived on the east coast, the west coast, and places in between. Dan attributes his dark sense of humor on growing up in New Jersey and then serving on nuclear submarines. He currently lives in Connecticut. You can reach Dan at www.deathscompanion.com, or on Facebook at www.facebook.com/dan.foley.31

*"**Tom Deady** is a true storyteller, and I can offer no higher words of praise."*
-Richard Chizmar

Tom Deady is the author of HAVEN, winner of the 2016 Bram Stoker Award for Superior Achievement in a First Novel. His second novel, Eternal Darkness, was released in 2017. Tom's next publication, a novella, is scheduled for a Halloween release. He has a Masters Degree in English and Creative Writing. Tom is a lifelong resident of Massachusetts, where he is hard at work on his next novel.

Emma J. Gibbon is originally from Yorkshire in the U.K. and now lives in Topsham, Maine. She is a writer and librarian. She lives with her husband, Steve, and three exceptional animals: Odin, Mothra and M. Bison (also known as Grim).

Paul McMahon finally has an office and is writing like crazy, which is ironic because writing keeps him from losing his mind. His work has most recently appeared in the NEHW anthologies WICKED TALES and WICKED WITCHES, as well as the superhero anthology CAPED and the werewolf anthology FLESH LIKE SMOKE. He contributes two monthly movie review columns on Cinema Knife Fight, where he is known as The Distracted Critic. He is hard at work on a novel and a themed collection of stories tentatively titled BOWER'S CLOUD.

Born in Lowell, Massachusetts, **R.C. Mulhare** grew up in one of the surrounding towns. Her interest in the dark and mysterious started at a young age, when her mother read the faery tales of the Brothers Grimm and quoted the poetry of Edgar Allan Poe to her, while her Irish storyteller father infused her with a fondness for strange characters and quirky situations. When she isn't writing, she moonlights in grocery retail, and given the cross-section of people you see in grocery stores, this gives her a lot of ideas for characters in her stories. An emerging author, her work previously appeared in Atlantean Publishing's "Beyond the Wall of Death: Lovecraft @ 125", "A Terrible Thing", and Awen 96, Macabre Maine's "Lovecraft ME", and FunDead Publication's "Shadows in Salem", "O Horrid Night", "Entombed in Verse", and "One Night in Salem", with four more stories slated for release later in 2017. She shares her home with her family, two small parrots, at least a thousand books and an unknown number of eldritch things that rattle in the walls when she's writing late in the night. She's happy to have visitors online at https://www.facebook.com/rcmulhare

GD Dearborn doesn't own an automobile, but it would be British Racing Green if he did. His previous work has appeared in *Northern Frights: An Anthology by the Horror Writers of Maine* and *Wicked Witches: An Anthology of the New England Horror Writers*. He lives and writes in Portland, Maine.

Rob Smales is the author of *Echoes of Darkness*, which garnered both a five-star Cemetery Dance Online review and a 2016 Pushcart nomination. He's had over two dozen short stories published, and his story "Photo Finish" was also nominated for a Pushcart Prize and won the Preditors & Editors' Readers Choice Award for Best Horror Short Story of 2012. His story "A Night at the Show" received an honorable mention on Ellen Datlow's list of the Best Horror of 2014. Most recently he had two short stories, "A Bee" and "Tracks in the Snow," appeared in the anthology *Insanity Tales III: Seasons of Shadow* (2017, The Storyside Press).

Morgan Sylvia is a writer, a metalhead, a coffee addict, a beer snob, an Aquarius, and a work in progress. A former obituarist, she lives in Maine and is now working as a full-time freelance writer. Her work has appeared in several anthologies, including *Wicked Witches, Twice Upon An Apocalypse*, and *Northern Frights*. In 2014, she released an apocalyptic horror poetry collection, *Whispers From The Apocalypse*. Her debut horror novel, *Abode*, was released from Bloodshot Books in 2017. You can find her on Facebook, Amazon, Pinterest, Wordpress or Twitter.

Barry Lee Dejasu lives with his wife in his native city of Providence, Rhode Island. He is a staff writer for the movie website Cinema Knife Fight, a member of New England Horror Writers, and a reviewer with *New York Journal of Books*. He is also a former contributing editor for **Shock Totem** Magazine and a staff writer for **Modern Fix** Magazine. He has had short fiction published in *Shock Totem, Anthology, Year Three: Distant Dying Ember* (2014, Four Horsemen, LLC), *Wicked Witches* (2016, NEHW Press), and the *NecronomiCon Providence 2017 Memento Book*.

doungjai gam's short fiction has appeared in *LampLight magazine, Distant Dying Ember, Now I Lay Me Down To Sleep*, and the Necon E-Books *Best of Flash Fiction Anthology* series. Born in Thailand, she's spent most of her life in New England (outside of a brief stint in New Jersey, which doesn't get talked about). She currently resides in southern Connecticut with author

Ed Kurtz and her little black cat Oona and is at work on her first collection, *glass slipper dreams, shattered.*

Jeremy Flagg is the author of the *Children of Nostradamus* dystopian science fiction series and *Suburban Zombie High* young adult humor/horror series. Taking his love of pop culture and comic books, he focuses on fast paced, action packed novels with complex characters and contemporary themes.

James A. Moore is the author of over forty novels, including the critically acclaimed *Fireworks, Under The Overtree, Blood Red, Blood Harvest, the Serenity Falls trilogy* (featuring his recurring anti-hero, Jonathan Crowley) *Cherry Hill, Alien: Sea of Sorrows* and the *Seven Forges* series of novels. He has twice been nominated for the Bram Stoker Award and spent three years as an officer in the Horror Writers Association, first as Secretary and later as Vice President. Never one to stay in one genre for too long, James has recently written epic fantasy novels in the series SEVEN FORGES (*Seven Forges, The Blasted Lands, City of Wonders* and *The Silent Army*), and the third of his urban fantasy-crime novels in the *Griffin & Price* Series co-authored with Charles R. Rutledge, *A Hell Within* was released last October. He is working on a new series called *The Tides Of War.* The first book *The Last Sacrifice,* came out last year and the sequel, *Fallen Gods,* in January in 2018.

About the Editors

Scott T. Goudsward: By day Scott is a slave to the cubicle world, by night to the voices in his head. He writes primarily horror but has branched out to sci-fi and fantasy. Scott is one of the coordinators of the New England Horror Writers and a member of two local writing groups. His short fiction has most recently appeared in *Return of the Old Ones, Atomic Age Cthulhu, Snowbound with Zombies* and the forthcoming *Arkham Detective Agency.* His latest novel *Fountain of the Dead* is out from Post Mortem Press, as is the new, co-edited non-fiction book *Horror Guide to Northern New England.* Anthology projects include the new book *Wicked Witches* from the New England Horror Writers and *Twice Upon An Apocalypse* released 2017 from Crystal Lake Publishing. Scott is currently working on a YA novel and looking homes for new anthology possibilities.

David Price lives in Maine with his two children, fiancée and three cats. He is the author of the fantasy novel *Lightbringers,* editor of several anthologies, and has worked in the hardwood floor industry for more than thirty years. He is an active member of the New England Horror Writers, the Science Fiction and Fantasy Writers of America, the Horror Writers Association, and the Horror Writers of Maine.

Daniel G. Keohane is the Bram Stoker-nominated author of *Solomon's Grave*, *Margaret's Ark* and *Plague of Darkness*. Writing as G. Daniel Gunn he's released the horror novel *Destroyer of Worlds* and novella *Nightmare in Greasepaint* (with L.L. Soares). His short fiction has been published in a variety of magazines and anthologies over the years, including *Cemetery Dance*, *Borderlands 6*, *Shroud Magazine*, *Apex Digest*, *Now I lay Me Down To Sleep*, *Madhouse*, *Coach's Midnight Diner* and more. You can visit Dan and keep up-to-date with prior and future work at www.dankeohane.com

The New England Horror Writers (NEHW) provides peer support and networking for authors of horror and dark fantasy in the New England Area. NEHW is primarily a writer's organization, focusing on authors of horror and dark fiction in all mediums (novels, short stories, screenplays, poetry, etc) in the New England area. We are also open to professional editors, artists & illustrators, agents and publishers of horror and dark fiction. NEHW activities include book signings, readings, panel discussions at conventions, and social gatherings. With members ranging from Maine to Connecticut, NEHW events take place in varying locations in an effort to provide support for our members throughout New England. Find us on facebook or at www.newenglandhorror.org.

83235873R00164

Made in the USA
Columbia, SC
23 December 2017